It would have been fine if he had not closed the door like that, Cormac thought later. On such little things could rest the difference between life and death. When an enormous brightness lit the horizon, someone heavy on the trigger exerted just that extra bit of pressure. Even then, things might have continued okay, for one shot slammed into Gant's thigh and two others into the lander's hull.

"Cease fire!" the leader of these men shouted and, when it seemed his men obeyed, he began to move towards Gant. But then the sound of the titanic explosion caught up with its flash, and all the men opened up with their weapons in response.

Cormac staggered back, feeling the missile impacts on his body armour and seeing one bullet become deformed against the chainglass visor that had shot up from his neck ring in time. He flung his arm out to retain balance, and that was enough for Shuriken. The throwing star screamed from its holster, arced around and, with two loud cracks, knocked automatic weapons spinning through the air, bent or chopped halfway through. Then Gant, holes punched through his syntheflesh covering but otherwise unharmed, shot forwards and tore the weapon from another man's grip. By then Shuriken had disarmed the final two men. One of them sat on the ground, swearing in disbelief, clutching his wrist and gaping at a hand now lacking three fingers.

Jack, what the fuck was that? Jack? Jack?

Cormac glanced down at the leader of this trigger-happy bunch. The man was on his knees, clutching at his chest, blood soaking through the front of his uniform.

"Gant," Cormac nodded back towards the lander, "get him inside."

PRAISE FOR *BRASS MAN*

"A satisfyingly baroque plot and strong action sequences ... This violent, fast-moving novel is lots of fun."—*Publishers Weekly*

"A fun, action-filled, high-velocity futuristic adventure that I believe will only get better as the series continues."—*Fantasy Book Critic*

"Fizzing with intelligent ideas and occasionally streaked with black humor. Appalling, mind-boggling, fascinating—and irresistible."—*Kirkus Reviews*

"A complex weaving of a large cast of characters and scientific and philosophical thinking, a tale blending both hard science and fantasy into a satisfying gestalt ... a very good sequel from Neal Asher."—*Curled Up With A Good Book*

PRAISE FOR NEAL ASHER

"Asher is a modern master of sci-fi." —*Starburst* magazine

"Neal Asher's books are like an adrenaline shot targeted directly for the brain." —*New York Times* bestselling author John Scalzi

"With mind-blowing complexity, characters, and combat, Asher's work continues to combine the best of advanced cybertech and military SF." —*Publishers Weekly*, starred review

"A wide-screen special-effects extravaganza, a space opera featuring gods and monsters ... Doc Smith and Olaf Stapledon in a blender, turned up to eleven, with the contents splattering across the ceiling." —Russell Letson, *Locus*

"Asher rocks with XXX adrenaline while delivering a vivid future." —David Brin, *New York Times*-bestselling author of *Kiln People*

BRASS
MAN

BRASS MAN

THE THIRD AGENT CORMAC NOVEL

NEAL ASHER

NIGHT SHADE BOOKS
NEW YORK

Visit our website at www.nightshadebooks.com.

10 9 8 7 6 5 4 3 2 1

Library of Congress Cataloging-in-Publication Data is available on file.

ISBN: 978-1-59780-980-1

Cover artwork by Steve Stone
Cover design by Neil Lang/Pan Macmillan

Printed in Canada

For my parents, Bill and Hazel Asher.
You started all this, obviously.

ACKNOWLEDGEMENTS

Thanks to those readers who told me, on reading *Gridlinked*, "I really liked Mr. Crane!" and from whom this book got its inception—first and foremost of those being Caroline, who still hasn't told me to get a proper job. My thanks also to Keith Starkey for his excellent observations and John Jarrold for his, and as ever to Peter Lavery for that pencil, my growing palate for good red wine, and the trenchant fluffy-bunny editorial mark. No books get to the shelves without the hard work of many others: Steve Rawlings, Rebecca Saunders, Dusty Miller, Emma Giacon, Liz Cowen, Gillian Redfearn and many others. And that mine are arriving on shelves in other countries and in other languages is thanks to: Michelle Taylor, Jon Mitchell, Chantal Noel and Vivienne Nelson. I could now thank those who are selling my books elsewhere—Stefan Bauer, Moshe Feder, David Hartwell, to name but a few—but this is beginning to read like an Oscar speech so I'll shut up now.

PROLOGUE

As this new face of the asteroid turned into view, Salvor swore when he realized the titanium and platinum readings he was picking up were not from some large deposit in the object itself, but from the wreckage strewn on its surface. However, upping the magnification of the image on his main screen dispelled his disappointment. There was something intact down there, something that looked like the head of a giant thistle made out of golden metal. Perhaps he wasn't wasting his time here after all.

"Vulture, match to rotation," he said. "Get me geostat on that thing."

Boosters thrummed inside the small craft, and the image of the metallic object revolved and centred on the screen. The thrumming then continued as the little ship maintained position.

"What is it?" he asked.

Immediately skeletal line images of various objects began to overlay the one already on the screen, flickering on one after another, faster and faster until they became a blur.

"Not a complete ship," replied Vulture. The little survey ship's AI voice was female and silkily sexy. Salvor had based it on a recording of his second wife's voice, just as he'd based the AI's personality template on her as well. This was all before that wife had developed the demeanour of a harpy, and a voice to match.

"No shit? And there was me thinking the rest of that wreckage and the metal vapour all around here had nothing at all to do with it."

"No need to be sarcastic. I was going to add that it is a piece of a ship, and that it is quite obvious which ship, if just a little thought is applied: a piece of the *Occam Razor*."

"Now who's being sarcastic?"

Salvor called up a subscreen in the bottom of the ship's main one, and on that he studied scan results. "Case-hardened ceramal. Are schematics of the *Razor* available?"

"No. Polity AIs are a little bit funny about distributing that sort of information about their battleships. I can't understand why."

The Polity, that ever-growing sphere of human-inhabited worlds, was, on the whole, governed by the Earth Central AI, through the sector AIs, then planetary governors or runcible AIs. Humans came in quite low in the hierarchy, and not much military information was shared with them. Salvor supposed this was because humans were not to be trusted. He ignored Vulture's snipe, and said, "I'm surprised any of it survived, and I'm surprised those Polity investigators haven't found this already—they seem keen to retrieve every fragment. Let's go down and take a look."

"That might not be advisable. The cover story is that the ship's AI went rogue, and that's why it attacked *Elysium*. But there are other stories about some nasty organic tech being involved. Why not report this to the Polity and collect the reward?"

"Nice idea, but the thinking man has to wonder why such rewards are offered. Nothing's for free, you know. You can guarantee their profit margin is even greater. Take us down."

As the *Vulture* descended, the screen kept the image of the metallic object centred. Approaching the surface of the asteroid, to one side of the object, the *Vulture*—a ship that resembled a black maggot ten metres long—spat out anchor spears trailing lines. Brief flashes lighting the screen told Salvor that the bolt charges had blown the anchor spears into the rock and, as the little craft pulled itself down, he stood and propelled himself back from the cockpit.

"I wonder why it's remained on the surface—there's not enough gravity to counter the centrifugal force here," he said, as he took his helmet from its locker, clicked it onto the neck ring of the suit he wore, and activated his suit's system.

"If it hit while hot, then it's likely it fused to the rock below"—Vulture was speaking inside Salvor's helmet—"or some part of it might be snagged into the ground. But there's also the possibility that it was fixed to this asteroid somehow."

That gave Salvor pause. "You mean there might be someone alive inside it?"

"That, or some remaining AI or computerized system."

"Well, it's been a year since the *Occam Razor* was fried, so any surviving humans would be dead or in cold sleep by now."

Salvor pushed himself through the cramped cabin to the airlock, the inner door of which Vulture was already opening. He crammed himself into this even more cramped space, while the inner door closed and the lock cycled. Eventually the outer door opened and he stuck his feet out into the clarity of vacuum. As he stepped down, the suit opened a display in the bottom right-hand corner of his visor to tell him it had turned on the gecko function of his boot soles, and to ask if he would like to change this. The suit, being semi-AI, had already scanned his surroundings and was anticipating his needs. He ignored the screen and after a moment it flicked off. As soon as his feet touched the scoured stone of the asteroid his boot soles bonded, and he began walking across to the titanic piece of wreckage as if across a floor smeared with tar.

"It's noticeable that the stalk section has been detached rather than broken away," Vulture told him over com.

Salvor scanned down the hundred-metre "stalk." He saw that it was square in section and about ten metres across, and all down its length were interface points for fibre optics, gas ducts and fluid pipes. Mating plugs were still engaged in some of these—their pipes, ducts and optics sheared away and trailing into vacuum. Also, along its surfaces, were many other linkages and devices: long racks of gear teeth, hydraulic rams, grav-plates, generators and heavy-load step motors. It was evident that this object was something the *Occam Razor* could move about inside itself. The far end of the stalk was sealed and attached to some huge hydraulic engine, its mating sockets open to vacuum.

"Many Polity battleships possess the utility to rearrange their internal structure for optimum efficiency. Evidently this is part of that movable structure," Vulture told him.

"Really?" Salvor replied drily.

The main part of the object was spherical and about fifty metres in diameter, the profusion of sensor arrays at its far end giving it the appearance of a flowering thistle head. Upon reaching it, Salvor inspected underneath and saw that it had indeed fused to the asteroid, and that this melting process had produced runnels of black rock possessing a disconcertingly organic appearance. But he'd seen weird shit like that often enough before while surveying asteroids. It didn't mean anything.

Eventually, standing where the sensor arrays speared overhead in a metallic forest, he spotted something that looked like an escape hatch. It was partially open, and water ice frosted the shadowy ground below. This immediately told Salvor that it was unlikely anyone was alive inside, because had that ice been the result of only water vapour in an airlock, it would have been gone long before now. This asteroid had been in close orbit of the sun only a few months before, and the temperatures here would have been enough to melt lead. Obviously, atmosphere had been leaking from inside this thing ever since it impacted here, and was still doing so. He ducked under and caught hold of the edge of the hatch. Briefly, it resisted him, then the servos of his suit kicked in and it swung open—its silent shriek transmitted as a vibration through his glove. He moved into an airlock, his suit obligingly turning on his helmet lights, and saw, as he had suspected, that the inner door was open. Hauling himself through this he scanned around inside.

"What is this?"

"Nasty organic tech." Vulture was now—he saw by the display in the bottom corner of his visor—interfaced with his suit and seeing all he was seeing.

"Looks dead to me."

"Even so, decontamination procedures will be advisable when you return."

"I know what this is," said Salvor, observing the control chairs tangled in woody tentacular growth, the massed circuitry underneath the tilted glass floor and the other systems set in the surrounding walls, also pierced by that growth. "It's the bridge pod."

"Yes, I agree. I also advise you to get out of there now—you don't know what you are dealing with."

"Wait a minute. Do you know how much Dreyden would pay for this—or one of the Separatist groups? There'll be a fortune in high-tech systems here, let alone whatever all this other weird shit is."

Salvor now noticed the desiccated corpse lying against the back wall, pinned there by growths that had sprouted from the wall. His attention slid back to the captain's chair and he saw that it was empty. So probably some sort of biotech attack: the ship taken over and made to attack *Elysium*, while the captain himself lay dead back there.

"Nothing I can do about all this right now," he said. "I'll take recordings and put them out on the net—see who makes the biggest offer for its location."

He turned to go, then hesitated when something shifted beside him. A wave of shadow revolved around something, and revealed it. A man stood there: a naked man with hideous burns on the side of his face and down one side of his body, burns deep enough to expose the bone around one empty eye socket, the blackened teeth in his jaws, and burnt ribs in his chest. That same strange growth occupying the bridge pod also occupied this man's body, only in him it was moving like maggots in a corpse. It also cupped the unburnt side of his face and writhed chitinously under his skin. On the opposite side of his head a crystal matrix aug glimmered greenish light, and from it crystal rods speared down into seared flesh around his collarbone.

"Oh fuck," was all Salvor managed before the man's left hand snapped out and caught him by the throat, and the right hand pressed against his suit's visor.

"Salvor! Salv—" Vulture's cries cut off.

The suit's systems went crazy telling him of suit breaches, subversion programs, changes in air mix . . . Salvor fought against the grip crushing his larynx, but it was like fighting a docking clamp. The suit's systems died: all the miniature displays it had flung up along the bottom of his visor going out at once. Then his visor was melting and dark woody tendrils were squirming towards his eyes.

He didn't scream, could not find the breath.

—retroact 1—

Just outside Bangladesh, bright tropical sunshine bathed the lawns surrounding Cybercorp HQ, and the volume of chatter from the crowd was increasing in direct proportion to the amount of chilled champagne consumed. Many members of the press, bored with waiting for the appearance of the new Golem Twenty-five, were finding diversion by feeding canapés to the resident chipmunks. Someone had brought an elephant kitted out in its red and gold regalia. It stood to one side swinging its trunk at the swarming holocams, its Golem mahout looking embarrassed. No one knew why the creature was there; few of them gave a damn.

Sitting on the plinth of a statue of Ganesh, Solenz Garrick of Earthnet used a tissue to wipe raven shit from his businesswear and, with something approaching hatred, eyed the black birds roosting in the nearby date palm. Glancing towards the conglomeration of geodesic domes nestled around the base of the kilometre-tall Corp tower, he shook his head and said something filthy. The launches of the earlier Golem series had certainly been media events, but now, at number Twenty-five, they were becoming passé, and it told Solenz something of his boss's regard for him that he had been sent to attend this event. He now turned and looked up at his own holocam.

"The numbering of Golem is, on the whole, a superfluous distinction now," he announced. Then he stood up, eyed the smear on his shoulder, before turning sideways to the cam.

"The differences between each series are now only small improvements, usually negated when Golem of the earlier series are upgraded by their owners—or, if free, by themselves. Underneath all the hype it can be seen that the prototype Twenty-five only possesses slightly more efficient servomotors and a rather longer-lasting power supply than its predecessor."

"I think that crow said all that needs to be said about your narrative, Solenz." As he swayed up to stand beside Solenz, Barone of *India News* grinned unpleasantly. The man then drained his glass and tossed it on the ground, where a chipmunk came to inspect it, sniffed haughtily, then went on after more canapés.

"It was a raven, actually," said Solenz, uncomfortably aware that he was still live on Earthnet, if only on one of the lower channels.

"Ah, here they come," said Barone.

Out of the arched entranceway to the nearest dome issued Corp execs dressed up like a shower of peacocks. In the centre of this group, towering over them all, walked the new Golem.

"They always build the prototype big for effect—to make up for the lack of any real technical advances," said Solenz sniffily.

"Oh, get with the program, man," said Barone. "It's all about primary ownership, and how big my *cojones* are 'cause I can afford a Golem from the newest series."

Even though he was still live, Solenz turned to Barone and said, "Why don't you just fuck off over there somewhere."

"Oooh, touchy." But Barone moved away.

Like dogs running in to sniff something unmentionable, the press then moved in. Solenz shouldered and elbowed his way to the front of the crowd. The Corp representative—dressed in businesswear superior to his own, Solenz noted—held up his hands and waited for silence, flicking his fingers at the holocams moving in for a closer view of big lanky Golem standing behind him. Solenz prepared himself to be bored, and tried to think of incisive questions to ask once the speechifying was over.

"It has long been the aim of this corporation to bring you only the best, only the forefront of cyber technology," the man said, smilingly superior.

"Well, waggle my dick with a flag on it," someone muttered, and someone else succumbed to a fit of the giggles.

The rep frowned then went on, "To that end I have great pleasure in presenting to the Polity—"

Briefly: a nightmare glimpse of a disc of fire exploding from a holocam and cutting the speaker in half, before the shock wave lifted Solenz up off his feet and deposited him on his back. Almost instinctively he tried to connect through his aug, but felt all the aug channels collapsing as he selected each. He glanced up and saw holocams dropping out of the air.

Fuck. Planar load . . . electronic warfare . . .

People were yelling—and dispersing in panic. It reminded Solenz of his earlier years reporting wars and terrorist attacks on the Line worlds. He saw Barone staggering along with both arms cut away at the elbow. One of the Corp women, who had waltzed out in some diaphanous rainbow creation, was now on her knees, naked and screaming.

Yes! News!

Despite all external links for his aug being out, Solenz started it recording through his own senses—everything he saw, heard, smelt and tasted. There was grit in his mouth, and the acrid chemical smell of explosives in the air. Then some sort of smoke bomb went off with a dull whoomph. Solenz dragged himself to his feet and staggered through the sudden, choking pall towards where the Golem had stood. All around lay human detritus. He stepped in something soft he was loath to look down and identify, but as he slid on that viscous mess, he glimpsed the Golem flat on its back nearby.

Either information virus or EM pulse.

As he moved towards it, a shadow drew across him, and from that—on a chain wrapped with hydraulic hoses and optic cables—dropped a spiderish claw. He watched it grope along the ground, close around the Golem's chest, then haul it up and away. Solenz glanced around, hardly believing his luck in being the only one to see this. He was going to leap up in the ratings. This would be on Channel One!

Just then, an invisible claw closed on *his* chest, and paralysis swept out from it. The nerve agent contained in the smoke killed him before he hit the ground.

One year later, on Channel One, Solenz announced, "By the time the fug cleared and Earth Central Security was paying attention, the gravcar had disappeared into the Indian megaplex. As you may remember, Jovian Separatists claimed responsibility for the attack. I'm happy to report, now Earth Central Security has raised the media blackout on subsequent events, that they later found these killers during an undercover penetration of their organization. The murderers were caught and mind-wiped, their bodies then being used to take cerebral downloads selected from that vast store of minds uploaded from those individuals who avail themselves of the new memplant technology."

Solenz winked at the camera.

"The rumour that some of the killers' bodies now contain the minds of some of those they murdered in the attack cannot be substantiated." Solenz grinned—he liked the grin his new face possessed.

"The prototype Golem Twenty-five was never recovered," he added.

—retroact ends—

1

The lethal results for a human of directly interfacing with an AI have been known since the apotheosis of that being who was, briefly, both Iversus Skaidon and the Craystein Computer. This joining killed Skaidon and sent the Craystein far to the other side of weird, where even other AIs find its communications somewhat . . . gnomic. But what is this "direct interfacing"—surely we do this through our augs and gridlinks? Not so. These two methods of connection, along with planetary servers and so forth, act as buffers between the human and the AI minds. This is necessary because though, in most cases, the human mind is something that an AI could run as a brief sub-program, in some cases it has something that is beyond our silicon saints. Call that something imagination, vision, psychosis . . . it is something that is rooted in our primeval psyche and was never anything to do with the pellucid logic with which we created AI. Direct interfacing gives the AI this human madness, and in turn the human acquires the vast processing power of AI. The resultant composite being transcends all its contemporaries. Briefly, huge synergy is achieved, then the human dies—his mind burnt out like a wristcom connected to a tokomac. Note: In recent years there has been much speculation about the possibility of interface filters and biotech support systems. This is all fog, and my opinion is that if it really could be done then someone, somewhere, would be doing it.

—From *How It Is by Gordon*

Standing on the black glass floor of a virtual viewing chamber aboard the *Jack Ketch*, Cormac took in the scene projected from a holocam a kilometre out from the hull. The ominously named Theta-class attack ship bore the shape of a cuttlefish bone, but with outriggers on either side holding torpedo-shaped weapons nacelles. It was the dark red of old blood, and smooth as polished stone. A more modern product of the Polity, its controlling AI, named Jack, took no orders from any human captain. Cormac wondered if it could withstand Jain technology subversion any better than had the *Occam Razor* and its interfaced captain, Tomalon. In such a ship as this, there was no facility for AI burn—for killing its AI—it having been built after the time of extreme paranoia about AIs taking over . . . when they had.

To one side of the *Jack Ketch* he observed other Polity ships surrounding, like flies around a healing wound, the reconstructed area of *Elysium*. Dreyden, the ruler of this Out-Polity community, had fought against allowing them to render assistance, and threatened them with the smelting mirrors of *Elysium* just as he had used those same mirrors against the attacking *Occam Razor*. But the damage to the community had been more than it could sustain and, without help, his little empire here would have fallen apart anyway, but with a greater resultant loss of life. Now, after one year of quarantine, all assistance had been rendered, and Dreyden was just a businessman in yet another community subsumed by the Polity.

Eight hundred and twenty-three thousand, one hundred and nine . . .

That was the figure at the last count, though by now it would have risen by a few souls as people continued to die in the hospital ship, or took the easier route of memcording to escape bodies made irreparable by isotope poisoning.

My choice.

It had been the risk of this, balanced against the slaughter of millions on Masada. There had been a chance that no one would have died here. But they did. His call.

Cadmean victory . . .

Cormac wondered about the name of this ship he had boarded, now that quarantine was over. Perhaps Jack Ketch the hangman was here for him. He now turned his attention to one whom Earth Central Security was allowing to escape the noose.

The trispherical *Lyric II* was only just visible, by the white light of its fusion drive, as it moved away from *Elysium*. It was unusual for Polity AIs to make such value judgements on the actions of individuals, and normally they applied the law harshly and without favour. John Stanton had been a mercenary killer, in the past working for the Separatist Arian Pelter, and perhaps deserved to die, as had Pelter. Cormac winced at the memories: Pelter's brass killing-machine, Mr. Crane, coming for him; the Golem Cento and Aiden bringing Crane down; and his own subsequent pursuit of Pelter, and killing of the man. Even so, the Earth Central AI had decided, that for what Stanton had since done and risked, no one would be looking when he and his wife Jarvellis returned to their ship and headed away. Cormac observed white fusion flames blink out inside a distortion that seemed to pull at his eyeballs, and knew that the ship had now entered underspace and was gone. He envied John Stanton such freedom—from prosecution, and from responsibility.

"A satisfactory conclusion," said a breathy voice beside his ear.

"Cut visual feed," said Cormac and, as the external image blinked out to reveal the glass-walled projection chamber he stood in, he turned to the ancient Japanese man standing beside him. "This must be a new definition of 'satisfactory' of which I have been unaware. Would you like to elaborate?"

Horace Blegg kept his expression bland as he replied, "Masada and this place are under the control of the Polity, and Skellor now so much interstellar ash."

"And here, and at Masada, nearly a million dead," Cormac added.

"Such loss of life is unfortunate, but base your calculation on lives saved, not lives destroyed. Had you and John Stanton not led Skellor here to be incinerated, he would have killed every human being in the Masadan system, and for him that would have been just the start."

Cormac smiled tiredly. "I'm not an infant; I made that calculation at the time. But you forget, I've been in *Elysium* for a year and seen what happened."

"My assessment still stands. What is there for you to regret?"

"My original assessment of Skellor, I would say."

"You did not know he had gained possession of Jain technology."

"But when I did know, I assumed that, like any Separatist upon encountering Earth Central Security, he would go scuttling for cover. I didn't register how quickly he disappeared after our first encounter, and I didn't make the connection between that disappearance and his work with chameleonware."

"Hindsight can be brilliantly incisive, and never misses the banana skins of existence. Do you want to be punished?"

"No . . . what I want is to go back to Masada and find out who is alive and who is dead. I want to retrieve my Shuriken, and see what Mika has to say about the dracomen there—and find out what the EC decision on them is. But, most of all, I want to know how the fuck you got on board this ship. There was no one here last time I looked, and nothing has docked since then."

"You well know I don't answer such questions." Earth Central's leading and most mysterious agent liked to remain inscrutable.

"You did it on the *Occam Razor*, and I at first thought you a projection. I touched you and you remained solid, though something happened to you when the *Occam* went into U-space. But then, is my memory of events true—because you've screwed with my mind before."

"Your memories are true."

Cormac nodded contemplatively. "I think I know what you are, Blegg. I think I've finally figured it out. You're an avatar of the Earth Central AI—the human face, or interface, which transfers its orders to its agents. Sometimes you're a projection, sometimes Golem." He looked directly at Blegg. "All that bullshit about Hiroshima is precisely that: bullshit."

Blegg grinned. "If only things were so simple. You are perhaps eighty years old in personal time, Ian Cormac, but with a mind possessing the plasticity of youth and a brain constantly replacing its dying nerve cells, and your apprehension of the world is at the foot of an exponential curve. Immortality is possible for all of humankind now, and many humans will discover what it means to keep on learning and keep on understanding, though many more will simply stagnate. I myself am many centuries ahead of the race as a whole."

"Which still doesn't explain how you manage to keep popping up like the Cheshire cat."

"Abilities can be acquired, given the time. This is something you will come to understand, as you are one of those who will definitely not stagnate."

"What abilities had you already acquired that enabled you to survive the blast from an ancient fission weapon at Hiroshima? You were supposedly a child then."

"Maybe I didn't survive it."

Cormac could now feel something, the edge of something he strove to understand, and he knew that Blegg was slipping away from him. With some sense he had never known before, he reached out for the man and found himself groping after shadows.

Quite calmly he said, "You're an avatar, Blegg—I know it."

I am the future . . .

The projection room now contained only Cormac. He sighed and shook his head. One day he would know precisely everything there was to know about Blegg, but that day was not yet close. With cold precision, he compartmentalized speculation. Now Earth Central Security—ECS—had work for him. There was always such work.

When are we heading into U-space? he asked the Jack Ketch AI.

"There is a hold on all transport at present, but when we are ready to go I will inform you," the AI replied.

It was only as he was leaving the projection chamber that Cormac realized he had just used his gridlink—hardware inside his skull that had enabled him a near-direct interface with AI—to communicate, which was impossible. It had been deactivated long ago.

—retroact 2—

Glittering leviathans bearing limbs capable of crushing boulders, and others capable of stacking grains of sand, reared in high pillars of gearbox-grinding movement, hung from the ceiling like mechanical multi-limbed bats, or squatted on the vast plain of the factory floor. All seemed chaotic lethal movement—a whole machine rather than distinct engines—where it seemed a human would be minced and scoured away in seconds. The sight would, Pendle thought, have driven Henry Ford screaming from the premises, especially had he seen the silver skeletons that were the product of this labour. But it was all utterly efficient: a three-dimensional assembly line designed by AI so that no movement was wasted, no process interrupted, no energy squandered . . . Unhuman, and becoming more so.

On the whole, Pendle thought, the execs that were the human face of the corporation were at best glorified sales-men, but mostly shareholders creaming the working credit on their options—the closest a large proportion of Earth's population got to real work. Pendle, however, considered his erstwhile position as creative design consultant in the prognostic body-form section, to be essential. True, Golem contractual rights were now such that imposition of body form was no longer allowed. Directly after uploading to crystal, and before installation in an anthrop chassis, they were now given the choice of form, which meant a loss of over 30 per cent of loaded crystal to AI applications other than to Golem. However, though less than the profit gained per capita for Golem indenture, Cybercorp was still able to reclaim construction costs and a reasonable profit set by Earth Central Economic Control. But then Pendle felt the distinction between the corporation and Earth Central itself was at best only one of nomenclature. Both were part of the same silicon meritocracy—a ruling elite that humans only managed to join by ceasing to be entirely human. Buphal was a prime example.

"Apensat has got the chassis prepped for installation, we can go down there now," Buphal said.

Pendle studied the man. From the left, all you saw were Asiatic features in profile: a beaked nose, brown eyes, and dark eyebrows below plaited hair artfully dotted with grey. He wore monomer coolveralls with ribbed high collar and wrist-sleeves terminating in interface rings for 'factor gloves and helmet. The material of this garment was silvery and contained squares of mem-fab displaying what at first looked like the view from some craft flying through a strange city. Buphal had told him this was in fact an ophthalmoscope view of some ancient valved electronics he had studied during his youth. But it was when you saw the other side of the old man's head that you realized just what he was.

Affixed to the side of his skull, behind his ear, was a grey metal disc. From the edges of this, at one o'clock and seven, bus bars curved round and penetrated his skull. At six o'clock, tubes running down to a plug in the side of his neck piped blood as a coolant. In the centre of the disc, like some trophy on its mounting, was an aug the size and shape of a cockleshell but seemingly fashioned of quartz. In Buphal's right eye, instead of an eyeball and sclera, a glittering square tube penetrated deep into his skull. Pendle knew when Buphal was doing any heavy thinking—the man would start to sweat even though gusts of frigid air would be escaping his coolveralls, for Buphal's aug was semi-AI crystal matrix, buffered from direct interface by band-controlled optic and aural links. People like him were called haimans: a compound of AI and human. The man was as close to attaining AI/human synergy as was possible without burning out the human element like a faulty fuse.

Buphal leading, they made their way along the viewing gallery to the antique spiral stair leading down to what Cybercorp engineers still called the shop floor. This stair, Pendle recollected, Cybercorp had purchased at great expense from Sigural, the Sri Lankan AI that ran the runcible on Sigiria. Apparently these ancient iron staircases, originally brought to that island from the London Underground some-time premillennial, had no longer been considered safe to convey the five million visitors the rock received every year, even if most of them did come in by runcible.

They walked straight into the lethal blur of machinery and, of course, it flinched away from them, creating a space ten metres in diameter around them, until they reached the second stair taking them down to their destination. Here, on a smaller floor, technicians pursued specialist projects whilst, behind a glass wall alongside them, silver skeletons with ribbed chests open like butterflies marched neatly towards a perpetually cycling clean-lock and to the glare beyond where sentience awaited them. In this room it was sometimes difficult to distinguish specialist project from technician. Even pure humans like Pendle were visually identical to Golem who had donned syntheflesh. Sometimes there were humans so in love with the machine it was difficult so see any humanity left in them. Apensat was a silvery thing with the geisha stoop and glittery limbs of a surgical robot. But he also had normal arms and a face in there under the cowling. He looked like a man a huge polished-chrome beetle was gradually subsuming.

With a fluid hand gesture, mirrored by gleaming spidery limbs, Apensat indicated a Golem skeleton standing nearby, its chest open just like the others processing beyond it.

"This is him?" Pendle could see that it must be. The thing was two and a half metres tall, its ceramal bones bearing that slight bluish tint of the newer alloy/ceramofibre composite. Everything about it was heavier, more robust, impressive.

"No," said Buphal, "that's an anthrop chassis. *That's* him."

Pendle looked to where Buphal was pointing at a lozenge of memory crystal sitting in an AI support column on a nearby bench. He walked over, pulled up a swivel chair and sat down, reached out and tapped the base of the column to get the mind's attention. To one side of the column a projec-tion monocle rose off the bench. Below it, the air flickered, and the standard iconic head appeared: metallic—even the eyes, teeth and tongue.

"Unit G25 alpha, I'm going to load some syntheflesh/skin schematics as, with the larger size you chose for yourself, the order must go via Specialist Ordering." Pendle glanced round and saw that both Buphal and Apensat had their attention focused on the Golem chassis. Of course it was all complete rubbish; Pendle's job had been non-existent for three days now since, being described as redundant for a long time, that description had now been made official. However, he felt that though his job was finished, his crusade had only just begun. Out of the top pocket of his Corp overalls he removed a piece of memcrystal the size of a fingernail and inserted it into the slot at the base of the column. Immediately it began to load. The projected head multiplied to infinity as if positioned between facing mirrors. Pendle snatched the monocle out of the air, killing the image. He then retrieved the memcrystal, dropped it between his feet, and ground it into white powder.

"Standard spec," he said, getting to his feet. "They'll be able to handle it in synthetics."

Even though finally ejected from the Cybercorp plant a number of days later, Pendle did manage to turn up at the launch of the Golem Twenty-five, where he waited expectantly. But what happened was most unexpected. The nanoscopic dose of neurotoxin that finally killed him, just after the Golem was stolen, was not the main reason he coughed and gasped so much. That was laughter—Pendle had always been a sucker for irony.

—retroact ends—

Mika knew the doctor mycelium was a small fragment of the Jain technology Skellor had controlled and, like some primitive stumbling across a ground car, she had walked away with a wheel but had no idea about the workings of bearings, electric motors and hydrogen fuel cells. The fragment of nanotechnology resulting in the mycelium inside the Outlinker, Apis Coolant, had been a stored sample she used only because the alternative was to watch the boy die as his fragile body fought a losing battle against the gravity here on Masada. Why she then grew a similar mycelium inside herself was less clear. "For research purposes," was her answer to any who asked—not because it enabled her to live in an asphyxiating atmosphere surrounding her, or because it enabled her to quickly recover from severe injury, and not because her physical strength was now twice normal. But there was a downside . . . as always.

The changes the doctor mycelia were undergoing she was unable to fathom. They were growing thicker and more complex—becoming something more than she required. Perhaps this dangerous experiment was keeping the Polity ships and personnel in orbit, and the quarantine in place. Thus far, their only contact had been via straightforward radio transmission—no signal deep enough to take any kind of computer viral attack from Jain tech on the surface—and ECS stratojets dropping medical supplies, food and equipment. They had every reason to be wary of Jain technology. Using it, Skellor subverted the AI dreadnought *Occam Razor* and left a system in chaos: cylinder worlds containing brain-burnt populations, the wreckage of spacecraft and satellites, and tens of thousands dead. But that was not all the Polity might fear down here.

Standing on the shell of a huge tricone revealed at the top of a mound of debris flung up by the impact of the Dragon sphere that had fallen here, Mika gazed out across the plain of mud now covering some of that creature's remains. Coming towards her, moving birdlike on the mat of rhizomes that had quickly spread across the bared surface, came the rest of Dragon: dracomen—Dragon's children—formed from the body of that dying alien entity.

They ran towards her with seeming urgency, but then they ran everywhere like that. There were twenty of them in this party, and Mika noticed that two were small but with lanky legs. *Children*, for these new dracomen were able to breed. This in itself should be enough to frighten the rulers of the

Polity: dracomen first being biological machines made by Dragon to serve that entity's own obscure purposes.

Dragon, when originally discovered on the planet Aster Colora, had consisted of four conjoined spheres each a kilometre across. After delivering an obscure warning to the human race, it apparently destroyed itself. Only later had they learnt how it had fled, breaking into four distinct spheres as it went. And later still they learnt it was an organic probe sent by an alien race, and had malfunctioned. Ian Cormac destroyed one sphere in punishment for the human catastrophe it later caused, on a planet called Samarkand, while trying to evade its alien Makers. Another had both destroyed and transformed itself here. Two remained: their purposes still obscure, possibly dangerous, and their abilities unplumbed.

As the party drew closer, Mika jumped down from the tricone, recognizing only Scar, one of the original dracomen, by his weapons harness and . . . his scar. He slowed to a walk to mount the slope up towards her. Beyond him, she noticed that four of his fellows were carrying the body of a grazer slung from two poles. This creature, with its multitude of limbs and many-eyed head, looked the offspring of a kangaroo and a lobster. It was one she did not recognize, but dracomen were bringing in all sorts of new species to feed their growing population.

"Polity?" said Scar, as he reached her.

"The last I heard, the quarantine has been lifted at *Elysium*, but still remains in force here. It seems unlikely to be lifted any time soon."

"Danger?" asked Scar.

"No. The most likely decision will be to declare this world below the technological threshold for membership, and leave you all to make your own way," said Mika, assuming that Polity personnel such as herself would be lifted from the surface, if only for the purposes of study.

"Not below any threshold," said Scar, as his companions lugged the dead grazer past.

Mika eyed the prey, her hand straying to her console. She wanted to get samples before it went through a few hundred reptilian digestive tracts—such an urge was almost instinctive for the Life-coven woman. Turning to look where the group was heading, she thought that perhaps Scar was right. Maybe no one down here possessed spacecraft, but there was complex technology aplenty around them.

After the rebellion here against the governing Theocracy, the humans were rebuilding their agricultural base, but now somewhat differently. They produced plascrete to cast into raft fields, in which to grow new crops, or even into crop rafts for the ocean. Also, in the caverns under the mountains, they were building factories to meet the demands of a population suddenly free of the Theocracy yoke. They had established a financial system based on the Polity's, in which they expected shortly to be included. Aerofans, the main form of transport on this boggy world, were a must-have item for many people who had yet to see anything of their world beyond those same caverns or the cities. The factories were continuously turning out breather gear to replace the parasitic life-shortening scoles—products of biotechnology previously inflicted on agricultural workers to enable them to labour outside. People were doing things—building something. Other people, distinguished by scaled hides, bird legs and sharp teeth, were building as well.

The dracomen encampment looked like a mass of huge flattened puffballs spread throughout the flute grasses. These dwellings, Mika knew, the dracomen wove from flute grass itself, bonded and stiffened by a resin in their saliva. Upon testing a sample of this substance, she discovered it to be similar to a tough ceramoplastic normally used in the construction of space habitats. When she finally managed to question Scar about this material, he simply pointed out that this was not commonly a product of dracoman saliva; they produced it just for this purpose. The dracomen, generally, did not need factories—they themselves were factories. The most dramatic example of this was the weapon they used for hunting. Their organic rifle used a muscular spasm of its body to spit poisonous darts that actually grew inside it. The rifle also had to be fed, and Mika had seen this weapon hatched from dracomen eggs. They made other complex items similarly: gestated inside themselves, laid as eggs, then hatched out. Dracomen therefore did not need to develop a biotechnology—they *were* a biotechnology.

Returning to the encampment, Mika saw Thorn and Gant coming out towards her. It was Gant, the uploaded soldier, who mostly communicated with the Polity ships above, via a transceiver built into his tough Golem body.

She had seen neither of these two for a month now—they had been working for Lellan on some project to plant radio beacons in hooders—one of the planet's lethal native predators—to give advance warning of where the creatures were, so people could quickly get out of their way. Gant she had spoken to by radio only a few days previously, when he had told her about the quarantine ending at *Elysium*. Thorn, she noted, wore breather gear and wondered why—for, with the mycelium operating inside him, he did not need such cumbersome equipment.

"We need to talk," said Thorn abruptly, as soon as he and Gant got close. "That includes you," he added to Scar, as the dracoman moved to follow his compatriots.

Scar halted, bared his teeth, then gestured for them to follow him. He led the way between the bulbous walls of dracoman buildings, on pathways of the same woven composite, which rested on top of the rhizome mat. Eventually he brought them to his home: a flattened sphere ten metres across, with a simple circular door set half a metre off the ground. The door opened when he pushed against it—its hinges composed of a dry muscle that was contracted by an electric charge. The door, Mika knew, would not have opened for anyone else, other dracomen included.

Just inside, a small antechamber provided low footbaths and various utensils—fashioned from local materials—for the purpose of preventing mud getting any further inside his residence. With meticulous care, Scar cleaned his clawed feet, then waited until Mika, Thorn and Gant had removed their footwear before he opened the inner door.

Light permeated the structure from outside, complemented by bioluminescent strips inlaid in a grid across the ceiling and down the curving walls. Glass panels inset in the level floor gave glimpses of sealed terrariums and aquariums in which all sorts of curious creatures swam, hopped, slithered or just sat motionless. Mika knew about the creatures—some wild and some manufactured—but had yet to fathom how the dracomen made the flat sheets of chainglass.

Scar dropped himself onto one of the woven saddlelike arrangements that served dracomen as chairs. Mika and Gant sat on an oval couch that Mika thought might be used for sleeping on, though she had never seen a dracoman sleep. Thorn, meanwhile, paced the transparent floor.

"What is it?" Mika finally managed to force a question.

After detaching the compressed-paper mask covering his mouth and nose, Thorn gave her a penetrating look. "Apis—his mycelium isn't working properly any more. You need to come."

Mika chewed that one over, then groped to phrase another question. "How . . . what is the evidence?"

"Eldene found him collapsed out by the spaceport. He'd fainted, and the doctor who tended him diagnosed oxygen starvation. He now has to use breather gear." He gestured to the pack on his own back. "It hasn't happened to me, but I'm taking no chances." He glanced at Gant. "I don't yet have any memplant to save me."

Mika nodded. Gant had died on Samarkand. What stood before them now was a memcording of the soldier, running in a Golem chassis. A debate was still running about whether such were genuinely alive.

"Will you come?" Thorn asked.

"Yes," she said, looking pointedly at Scar. She then winced and ventured a further question: "Is there something else?"

"Oh yeah," Gant said, rounding on the dracoman. "EC's decision on Scar and his kind. It seems that no blame for Dragon's actions will be attached to you and your people. You are free to do what you want, though I suspect that there will be pressure on you to join the Polity."

Mika felt a brief surge of joy at that—the EC decision had been hanging over them like a guillotine ever since the ships had arrived—but Thorn's news tempered her happiness. What was happening with the mycelia? She had no idea how she might go about removing the alien technology, and acutely aware that it might change sufficiently to kill them or, perhaps worse, *change* them.

From where he lay, underneath the wasp-eyed scanning head of the diagnosticer he had cobbled together to try to find out why his gridlink had spontaneously operated, Cormac gazed across the room. Above the counter cluttered with the pieces of dismembered autodoc, a screen flickered on, showing the belt of asteroids lit from one side by the glare of the sun. A small trisection transport appeared in one corner of the screen and, turning slowly, screwed its way across the view on three fusion flames. It was halfway to the belt itself when a black hawkish ship hurtled in behind it. The screen polarized over the glare that followed and, when it returned to full clarity, an asteroid in the belt ahead of the fleeing ship had disappeared.

"A shot across the bows," Cormac guessed, as he watched the ship turn and head rapidly back towards *Elysium*. "Why are you showing me this, Jack?"

"That was a real-time image," the AI replied.

Cormac frowned, not liking what this implied. "Why not just grab him?"

"No contact allowed with the barrier ships."

Cormac sighed and laid his head back. "And the weapon used? I don't think I saw anything like that before."

"Combined CTD and gravity-imploder missile," the AI replied.

"I see—the imploder to prevent the smallest fragment of debris being blasted away, so that the CTD burns everything down to an atomic level, if not below that."

"Correct."

"Right, so now you'll tell me why ECS is chasing ships back to *Elysium*."

"Total quarantine of the *Elysium* system has just been reinstated. The *Elysium* AI has shut down the runcible. Debris has been detected on an asteroid, previously discounted because out of the range of blast scatter from the *Occam Razor*, and moving in an elliptical orbit that took it outside of the search area. Polity capital ships are returning to surround the system."

"You'll be rejoining them?" Cormac asked, sitting up and pushing away the scanning head.

"EC has reapplied previous restrictions: no one who had any physical contact with Jain technology or any of its products is going anywhere. Because I have you aboard, I myself am now not one of the guards but the guarded."

"And this comes direct from Earth Central itself?"

"It does."

"Tell me, has senility long been an AI problem?"

"Amusing, but missing the point," said Jack. "EC knows it is impossible to suppress such a technological juggernaut, but this is a case of attempting to slow it down a little so we can move some people out of the way. Your associate Mika is, as you have told us, already obtaining substantial benefits from Jain tech, and no doubt scraps of it will be picked up all around this area. But consider what would happen if someone were to find, for example, one of those creatures Skellor used to attack you on Masada, and handed it over to some well-organized Separatist enclave."

"Yeah, okay, I've heard this spiel before. But we're talking about one stray asteroid that we missed. I've been okayed as clean, as has most of *Elysium*."

"The order is not open to question—total interdiction."

Cormac remembered what that meant.

He nodded and swung his legs from the surgical bench, noting as he did so the readout on the diagnosticer's screen, informing him that his gridlink was still offline and impossible to use unless reinstated by a high-level AI. But speculation about that he put to the back of his mind—something was happening at last, and he had been bored out of his skull during that latter half of the quarantine period.

"This asteroid, is it going to be obliterated like that one you just showed me, or do we take a look?"

"We take a look."

"We . . . as in you and me?"

"Yes."

Cormac couldn't help grinning as he felt the vibration of the *Jack Ketch*'s fusion drives igniting. Heading for the door to this long-unused surgical facility, he lost his footing outside as he stepped into a corridor in which the gravplates were not operating.

"Sorry about that," said Jack, slowly powering the plates back up so that Cormac settled back down to the floor.

"See, you're as excited about this as me."

Now, with the gravity stabilized, Cormac noticed how the corridor had changed. When he had come aboard this ship, the cabins and corridors were new and skeletal, the *Jack Ketch* not often having had to provide for human passengers. Now his boots came down on pale blue carpet decorated with a nicely repeating pattern of nooses. The spill from spotlights, mounted in ornate brackets, lit the corridor, though their main targets were portraits spaced along walls bearing the uneven look of old plaster.

"Very nice," said Cormac.

"Glad you like it," replied the AI.

"To make us poor humans feel more comfortable?"

"Of course."

Cormac studied one of the portraits, vaguely identifying it as of some very early premillennial cosmonaut, then he broke into a trot towards his destination. The corridor terminated against a dropshaft slanting up at forty-five degrees, and glaringly of the present time. Locating the touch-plate set in an ormolu moulding beside the slanting entrance, Cormac input coordinates, then reached out a hand to check that the gravity field was operating before he stepped inside the shaft. The irised field wafted him in a direction that was now up, and he soon stepped out into what was called the bridge of the ship, though the vessel was not controlled from there. Jack was pilot, navigator and captain, and controlled the ship from wherever his AI mind was located deep inside it.

This chamber occupied the upper level of the ship's nose. The ceiling, curving down to meet the floor ahead of Cormac, was not visible, for a VR projector created the illusion that there was no ceiling at all and that he was walking out onto a platform open to vacuum. This platform, it seemed, possessed a low stone wall to prevent the unwary from stepping off the edge into the abyss. There were no instruments for humans to use, nor any need for them, though Jack could easily project a virtual console here. In the centre of this was what Cormac now mentally referred to as the drawing room.

Below a free-floating crystal chandelier, which might have been merely a projection or the real thing, club chairs, a drinks cabinet, coffee table and other items of premillennial comfort were arranged on a large rug, at the corners of which incongruously stood Victorian cast-iron street lamps giving off a soft gaslight. These were all items from Jack's collection, replicas all, but almost to the molecular level. Now, Cormac saw that off to one side the AI had added something else.

"Is that for my comfort as well?" asked Cormac.

The wooden framework towered against the stars, no doubt perfect in every detail, mechanically sound, its trapdoor oiled.

"It is here because I find it aesthetically pleasing," Jack told him.

Cormac turned to the localized sound of the AI's voice.

Seated in one of the club chairs, the hangman looked like a bank manager or a stockbroker from sometime before the twenty-first century. His antique suit was pinstriped and tight on his thin body, his face white and skull-like. The brim of the bowler hat he never removed was pulled low on his forehead, shading his eyes, so that when the light caught the lenses of his spectacles, they glittered in shadow like something insectile. His overfull briefcase, no doubt containing execution orders and probably a coiled rope, stood beside his chair. Cormac suspected he wore sock suspenders and Y-fronts—for every detail of the hangman was meticulous—just like the mind this ancient automaton represented.

"Your idea of aesthetics is a little worrying," Cormac observed. "I take it that this is not just any old gallows."

"No," said Jack, "it's the Nuremberg one."

Cormac fell silent as he allowed himself to absorb that. Using as an avatar an automaton from an age two centuries ago, rather than a holographic projection, was another strange facet of this AI. But he preferred that to Jack's attraction to devices of execution. Stepping onto the drawing room rug Cormac decided this was a subject best dropped, and instead asked, "How long will it take us to get to this asteroid?"

"It will be ten minutes." With a clinking ticking of gears and levers, Jack stood, turning to face Cormac. "This is a matter of some urgency, so I'm going to drop into U-space."

Cormac strolled across the rug, then out across the black glass floor leading towards the nose of the *Jack Ketch*. Here he gazed over the ersatz stone wall into vacuum. From below and to his right, the sun heated his face as if he had just peeked over a wall beyond which a bonfire burned. Its glare filtered, he was able to look directly at it, and there observed, flung up from its vast infernal plains, an arching lariat of fire that could have swallowed worlds. Curving up from his left, then ahead and up high, before being attenuated to nothing by distance, the asteroid belt seemed an artefact, having been shepherded into neat rings by the larger chunks remaining from whatever cataclysm had shattered the planets of this system. Then the VR feed blanked to infinite grey depth, and Cormac felt that shift into the ineffable as the ship dropped into underspace. He realized he was seeing a representation less real than the one before. No human could experience underspace unshielded.

"Do you look directly into U-space?" he asked Jack.

"Yes, I do." The reply was close at his shoulder, though the hangman automaton still occupied the drawing room behind.

"And you retain your sanity?" Cormac shot a glance at the gallows.

"Yes. AI has never been limited by the four-dimensional view of the universe. It is only by being able to see and comprehend more that we can operate runcibles and ships like this."

"But you are physically confined to that universe and subject to its constraints?"

"For the present."

Cormac let that one go. No way was he going to get into a metaphysical discussion with an AI—he'd done that before and, rather than gaining enlightenment, ended up with a headache.

After a few minutes, the grey flickered away as the ship surfaced in realspace. The sun was not noticeably smaller, but the asteroid belt was now a wall of rocks beside them. The *Jack Ketch* eased itself into this wall, tilting and dipping, the drone of its fusion motors changing constantly as it negotiated its way through. Above, below and to the sides, Cormac observed mountain ranges swinging past as fast as fan blades, and saw flares of incandescent gas where proximity lasers hit smaller rocks.

"This asteroid is actually within the belt then?" he asked.

"Its erratic orbit will take it out in fifteen hours, if it is not obliterated meantime. I have it on visual now."

A square red frame seemingly flickered into existence far ahead of the ship, singling out just one more undistinguished lump of rock.

"You have to wonder if it is a coincidentally erratic orbit," suggested Cormac.

"Almost certainly not."

"Will you be able to moor?"

"No, the longest mooring time in any location on the surface here is eight minutes before some passing object would hit me. I am now taking out of storage a tele-factor unit to send down to investigate."

"I want to go with it," Cormac said.

"That is inadvisable. If there is active Jain technology down there, it might kill or sequester you. The telefactor can find out all we need to know, and it's dispensable."

"Everything's dispensable, and I'm tired of sitting on my hands. Presumably I've retained my authority as an ECS agent?"

"You have, Ian Cormac—I merely advise against you placing yourself in unnecessary danger."

"Noted, but I'm still going down."

"Very well. You can ride down to the surface with the telefactor. I suggest you go and suit up now."

The dropshaft shifted while he was in transit, and took Cormac directly to the telefactor launch area. There was no gravity in the wedge-shaped bay and, while he was pulling himself towards the storage area by an airlock designed for humans, he observed the further wall of the bay revolve aside to reveal the unit itself.

Golem androids were often employed by ECS simply because they were more able to utilize equipment originally designed for humans. But even they were now being replaced in some arenas. Cormac had already seen specialized drones, first in *Elysium* then on Masada. This unit was similar in appearance: a squat cylinder floating vertical to the floor. However, unlike those war drones, this object possessed various arms and probes folded close to its body and a complex array of scanning equipment on its underside. It also possessed no mind of its own, being a telefactor of the *Jack Ketch* AI.

In storage, Cormac found a standard combat space-suit. It was armoured, possessed greater facility for sealing breaches, and had clinging to its belt an autodoc capable of scuttling to any point on the suit's exterior, sealing itself to that point, and cutting its way inside to repair the contained body—if it could. Cormac removed that item and left it in the store—the idea of Jain tech subverting such a doc not holding much appeal for him. In the gloves, belt and flat-visor helmet were interfaces for various weapons. Cormac merely attached his thin-gun to the belt, then commenced the always frustrating task of donning a suit in zero gravity.

By the time he was ready, the unit had drifted over by him, bobbing up and down as if impatient to be on its way. A readout in his suit's visor told him the air was being drained from the bay, then doors, shaped to conform to the edge of the ship, drew back—above and below—onto vacuum.

"Ready," said Cormac.

A ceramal claw snapped out and closed on his belt, and the telefactor unceremoniously dragged him out. Jetting two scalpels of flame, it flung them both towards the revolving stone behemoth. Finally landing, and walking on stick-boots behind the drifting unit, Cormac swore upon coming in sight of the bridge pod of the *Occam Razor*. His subsequent language when he spotted the explosive bolts embedded in stone—sure sign that a ship had recently landed—even evinced some surprise from Jack.

A gust of wind rattled the skeletal branches of the chequer trees and shook free some of their few remaining square leaves, which drifted down like stripped-off skin in the bloody moonlight. The not-rabbits fled into the undergrowth as a still and oppressive heaviness weighed the air. Seemingly from nowhere, the revenant stepped into view: the walking desiccated corpse of a man who had been burnt to death. Walking woodenly out from between the chequered trunks and down the rock-scattered slope to the red mirror of the lake, this zombie creaked and crunched with each step, dry or charred skin and the remains of clothing flaking away from him. In his legs, dry fibrous muscle was visible, fraying and splintering as it was worked by other fibrous tendrils wound through it. Reaching the gritty shore, this creature knelt and dipped its hands into the peaty water, and from those hands fibrous tendrils sprouted and grew, expanding as they absorbed water, diving finally into the fertile mud of the lake bottom. Then the revenant began to change.

In gradual stages, he transformed from a desiccated corpse into something newer, fresher. Skin, burnt black, became grey and slimy, and slewed away from red surfaces glistening with plasma and dotted with blood. Around deeper burns, lumps of seared fat and muscle dropped away to expose similar surfaces. Exposed bone stretched and writhed, flaking away ash to expose gleaming white, which was then marred—and given a metallic hue—by a creeping grid, before being covered by a writhe of veins across its surface.

The revenant tilted his head one way, and the woody structure supporting one side of it turned soft and wet, and began to sink into exposed raw flesh. He then tilted his head the other way, and the crystal of his AI aug, still glittering with green light, was flooded with hair-like tendrils, and deformed itself against his head. Sucking back into itself the rods that connected down into his chest, the aug sank away into his skull, to become skinned over with bone and a sudden growth of veins, then muscles opening like summer flowers. The only sign that remained of it was a glint of green deep in the empty eye socket, but even this blinked out as, starting as a shiny black bead extruded into position, an eyeball expanded to fill the cavity.

Skin formed first as a layer of clear slime, which grew opaque, began to knit, thickened and toughened, and conformed itself to the growing structures underneath. Briefly, it covered completely the new-grown eyeball, then split into lids that sprouted lashes. Brown hair then issued from the bare scalp, while the skull underneath still shifted and deformed, as if the head itself were having difficulties returning to its customary shape with all the extras it now contained. But eventually this settled down too. Now the man removed his hands from the water—no sign of those tendrils he had earlier extruded—and watched his fingernails grow. Eventually he stood, naked in the red moonlight, and looked around. On the horizon, he located the yellow-orange glow of city light—and began to walk towards it.

2

The modern surgical robot is an incredibly sophisticated machine. I am informed that this device wields laser scalpels and cauteries, cell welders and bone welders, ultrasound tumour killers and bone saws, micro tome shears, clamps of every shape and size, nerve shunts and blood filters . . . the list goes on and on and, depending on the surgery intended whole different arrays of instruments can be employed. Suffice to say that such a device can divide a body up into its component organs, keeping those organs alive separately, then put that same body back together again. The modern robot can also be telefactored to human or AI, can be raised to consciousness itself, as many now are in the more sophisticated centres of the Human Polity, or can run the programs necessary for just about any surgical procedure. This is all most admirable, and those, such as me, whose professions can be physically dangerous, should be grateful. I am grateful, but I have to wonder who was responsible for making this thing look like the offspring of a chrome samurai and giant woodlouse. Was it the AIs again? Does this menacing appearance impel us to think twice about putting ourselves in the way of injury—to make hospital seem less attractive to us?
—From How It Is *by Gordon*

The telefactor unit, its scanning equipment extended and working frenetically—dishes spinning, holocorders and gas samplers operating, lasers strobing the area as they measured and were bounced off surfaces to gain spectral information—floated up to a ceiling seemingly interlaced with tree roots. Also surveying the interior of the bridge pod, Cormac remembered how, when he had been aboard the *Occam Razor*, the ship would shift its internal structure. This pod was moved around inside, and even extruded from, the hull. He had known then that the pod could be ejected. Obviously, while the *Elysium* mirrors had focused on the ship itself, this was what had happened, for the heat damage here was not so severe. Some quite combustible items had survived it.

He observed a desiccated corpse resting upright against the back wall, and walked over to inspect it. The ripped interfaces poxing this corpse's skin and the creamy glint of opaque nictitating membranes in the sunken eye sockets confirmed that he had found Tomalon, the captain of the *Occam Razor* before Skellor had taken over. Returning to the command chair, which the woody growth in the rest of this pod had also swamped, he saw where someone had *fitted*—as a human-shaped component in some huge organic machine. Then, observing the other chairs here, he realized that they too had once been occupied by people somehow linked to the same woody growth, though it seemed evident to Cormac that those occupants had not left here in the same way as Skellor, for the upholstery was burnt away and much of the metal of the chairs melted.

"So this is all Jain biotech," he murmured, tempted to reach out and touch, but not prepared to increase his present danger with such unnecessary gratification.

"It is," replied Jack over com. "Initial analysis indicates that from this point Skellor extended nanofilaments along the fibre optics, in order to take control of the ship. These he then, by necessity, had to expand—and you see the result."

"Necessity? Why was it necessary for this stuff to be larger than the fibre optics?"

"Because it is not simply for conveying information. It is capable of movement, transporting materials, and base construction and reconstruction at an atomic level from any point of contact. It also possesses a high-level computing facility, in all areas. It was probably this that Skellor used to build those flying calloraptors that attacked you on Masada."

"I hear everything you say, but most importantly I heard 'is capable of movement'—present tense."

"At the moment its level of function is at that of a plant, since here its energy sources are limited. It is also hierarchical so perhaps requires a dominant controlling mind."

Cormac glanced at the main control chair, and wondered if anyone might volunteer for that position beyond Skellor. He looked up as the telefactor drifted down at an angle from the ceiling towards the tangled wall. He noted, as it settled, that one of its arms was folding out to present an optic interface.

"Is that a good idea?" he asked.

"Probably not, but we'll learn nothing more here by passive observation. Perhaps you would now like to depart the area?"

"No—just get on with it."

The telefactor settled just off the floor, its arm telescoping towards the wall, through a gap between the thick roots of the Jain material, to a shadowed optic plug. The moment the interface connected, the unit jerked as if a large invisible hand had slapped it. Light flickered all around the bridge, at the ends of broken optics, and Cormac was not sure if it was an illusion caused by this that made the surrounding structure seem to move. Then the lights died.

"What the hell happened?" Cormac asked.

"There was an attempt to insert an information virus into my telefactor. The attack withdrew the moment the CTD—which this unit contains—activated. It would seem that either this Jain structure itself wants to survive, or that somewhere here there is still a controlling mind . . . I am now receiving communication . . ."

Cormac felt a flush of cold as the suit's internal air circulation increased to dry the sweat breaking out all over his body. Of course the *Jack Ketch* AI had taken out insurance, he had known that, but he was uncomfortably aware that his insistence on being here at the scene had abruptly put him on the brink of obliteration. Jack could make that decision in a nanosecond.

"There *is* an entity here. I am unable to determine whether it is a physical one in some hidden location, or a stored mentality within the structure itself."

"Can you transfer to me what it's saying?"

"There are words, but they do not relate to the communication, which is in binary code similar to that used in the thought processes of AI."

"Give me the words."

Like a cold breath in his ear, a woman's voice said to him, "*The light, Skellor. The light.*" Then the voice cycled repeatedly, until Jack shut it off.

"And the essence of the communication?" Cormac asked, aware that something was niggling at his memory—some familiarity about that voice.

"It is asking for direct current of a defined wattage. This, I gather, is what it was seeking from my telefactor."

"How much?"

"Eight point three watts made available to the power outlet below the optic plug. I estimate that this could stimulate growth in the structure, but that the risk would be no more than it is at present. The entity is thoroughly aware of my precautions."

"Then give it what it wants and let's see what we get."

Cormac returned his attention to the unit as another arm swung out, holding a simple bayonet power plug uncoiling two power cables from the body of the unit itself. Another arm reached out, and the spidery eight-fingered hand it terminated in closed on the Jain structure and pulled. The woody substance shattered—frangible as charcoal—exposing the power socket. The unit now abruptly stabbed the plug into place. Lights again lit in broken optics all around the interior of the pod. Over com, Cormac heard a whispery hissing, as of a zephyr in woodland, then the tinkling of a rill bubbling down some rocky course—but this second sound became that of fading laughter.

"What is that?"

Jack did not reply, and Cormac wondered just how many seconds remained before the AI detonated the CTD. Then there was movement over by the row of command chairs, specifically where the Jain structure seemed to have gone crazy, spiralling up from the deck like fig vines that have strangled a tree, and blackened towards its interior by fire.

Illusion . . . those optics?

But no, the ghost stepped out into view like a tree sprite departing her home. She was naked, nymphean, and as she moved Cormac could see the skeleton inside her translucent form—moving out of consonance, as if always a little behind. Perhaps it was because of this that he did not instantly recognize her.

"Jack, speak to me."

"My apologies. I was fascinated by the way all the broken optics in there are being utilized to create this holographic image. I have also just received a message from the new Warden of *Elysium*."

Cormac's suit blower was operating noisily. "What message?"

"Obviously, after seeing those anchor points in the rock of the asteroid, it was essential to determine what ship was their source. We have contacted all but one of the ships working the belt asteroids. That one should have returned some time ago, but has been out of contact. It's a survey ship called the *Vulture*."

"That figures," said Cormac, his main attention focused on the spectre in the bridge pod. He went on, "So, Aphran, what's Skellor up to now?"

The breathy voice coming over com replied, "Hunting dragons."

His breathing ragged and his body feeling as if someone had worked him over with a baseball bat, Apis studied the woman he had come to love and wondered at the change that bonding process had wrought in him. Standing with her arms folded and her back against the counter running around the inner wall of this surgical facility, Eldene was by no means a female that an Outlinker should find attractive. The huge improvement in nutrition for her, as for all the pond workers of Masada since their emancipation, had softened the lines of hard muscle built by constant toil, filled out her hips and breasts, and blunted the sharpness of her features, though she still carried little in the way of fat. However, to Outlinker perception, she was grotesquely over-muscled. That perception meant little to him now, as if his own adaptation to living on the planet's surface had changed him psychologically as well as physically. Even amid the pain and debilitating fatigue, looking at Eldene—at those wonderful green eyes framed by her crop of black hair, that fulsome figure and her strong, tricky hands—Apis wanted to make love to her. One more, and possibly last, time. He turned away.

For some time he had sensed the stunted, imperfect growth inside him. That the mycelium was killing him he was certain, and now perhaps he would know how and why. As she returned from her analysis of the data gathered by the probes piercing him like needles stabbed into a grub, Mika looked grim.

"What's it doing, then?" he asked, his gaze wandering from her *How am I going to tell him this* expression to the robot poised over him, like a chrome cobra head but with an underside of complex insectile manipulators and surgical tools. Not for the first time he felt a shudder at the resemblance this device bore to the hooder he and Eldene had seen devour the First Commander of the Theocracy—only a hooder's cutlery served instead the purpose of dissecting its food to be sure the predator did not ingest any poison. That there had been none existing in Dorth had not dissuaded it from this meticulous and lengthy task.

Studying her laptop, Mika replied, "It's forming nodes inside you, but I don't know why—possibly because what it's making is as incomplete as it is itself. In doing this it uses more of the available resources, and so has shut down some of its other functions."

Apis shook his head. "Like enabling me to survive outside."

"Yes, like that . . . It's moved from mutualism to parasitism."

"Like something alive, then," said Apis, knowing such comments unnerved Mika.

She gave him an unreadable look but did not reply.

"What about the pain?" Apis asked.

"That comes from where the growing nodes are trapping your nerves."

Now Eldene, who throughout the investigative procedure had remained silent, spoke up. "What are you going to do about it?"

The expression on the Life-coven woman's face was now readable: embarrassment and pity. She returned her attention to the screen of her laptop.

"You now possess sufficient physical growth to sustain you in this gravity, and that will not go away. I can attempt to save you by surgery."

"What do you mean, 'attempt'?" Eldene asked, her voice rising.

Before Mika could reply to that, Apis said, "It's a mycelium—that would be like trying to remove cobwebs from jelly."

"Not quite, since its filaments are tough and not so easy to snap, which should make them easier to remove. Previously I would have considered such an operation impossible, as the mycelium grew evenly throughout your body. But now it's drawn its main mass into your torso, with trunks extending into your limbs and head. I estimate that I could remove over ninety per cent of it."

"You still haven't explained what you mean by 'attempt,'" Eldene insisted.

Mika turned to her. "The mycelium will work to close any cuts I make. It will actually *fight* the surgery. It will also fight against having itself removed—attempting all the time to return to its . . . home. And even should I manage to remove the main mass, remaining filaments—those reaching into his extremities—might die and cause massive blood poisoning as they break down. Or they might stay alive and grow into a new, complete mycelium. They might even stay alive and become something else."

"What alternatives are there?" Eldene asked.

Mika did not reply, and Eldene bowed her head, knowing the unspoken answer. Apis felt a sudden surge of self-pity, and the need to get out of there, to live whatever time he might have left as fully as possible, but he stamped down on it hard. At least, should he die under the knife, he might provide Mika with enough information to save those others who faced the same prospect: Mika herself and Thorn—but foremost to him, Eldene.

"Can you start now?" he asked.

Mika nodded.

Apis turned to Eldene. "I'd rather you left now."

She looked hurt, but he doubted she would relish the prospect of seeing him open like a gutted fish on this table any more than he relished the prospect of being that way. Mika then tapped out something on her console, and Apis felt a cold spreading through him from where the probes penetrated his flesh. As his consciousness faded, he saw Eldene turning to go. The surgical robot bowed like a geisha, and opened out its glittering tableware.

The man halted and studied their surroundings, and Marlen found himself slavishly tracking the man's gaze.

The chequer trees had shed their square leaves, which now lay like badly applied gilding over the mossy ground, or else caught in layered clumps on spiky sedges. Fallen from the adapted oaks, the blue acorns that punctuated these surfaces like discarded half-sucked sweets were being nibbled at by creatures like birth-defect rabbits, hopping and bouncing as if ever on the point of coming apart. Marlen noted the old damage to the trees, and the occasional lumps of metal protruding from the ground. There had been a battle here between agents of ECS, accompanied by Viridian soldiers, and the Separatist Arian Pelter—this had been one of the first bits of information the man had ripped from Marlen's mind. Glancing at his accomplice in their recent disastrous robbery attempt, Marlen saw that Inther was drooling. What the man had done to them both through their biotech augs must have damaged Inther's brain. Marlen returned his attention to their captor.

He appeared perfectly ordinary: stocky, brown-haired and dressed in a cheap environment suit—not noticeable. But closer inspection revealed that he sank deeper into the soft ground than he should, and that his gaze held a silvery shimmer as if lizard-scales were moving in the sclera of his eyes. What was he, then? Both Marlen and Inther were big men, and boosted too, yet he had tossed them about as if they massed no more than origami sculptures before . . . doing what he did.

The man turned on a scanner. Marlen glimpsed on its screen a translucent image of the ground, in which were buried stones, wood, jags of metal and more macabre objects.

The man pointed to a sunken area. "Dig there," he ordered. Marlen and Inther could only obey—the biotech augs behind their ears were grey, as if seared, and something was poised inside their skulls like a reel of fishhooks.

The two men took up their spades and picks, and immediately set to work. Marlen concentrated on the task in hand—was unable to concentrate on much else. He didn't slack; didn't stop to rest until his muscles were burning from lactic overload, and then he didn't rest for long. He and Inther were a metre down into the soft ground when Marlen's spade sheared up a layer of decaying fabric, exposing rib bones and an intricate line of vertebrae. Marlen noted that long-tailed slugs, the undertakers of Viridian, had eaten away all the flesh and skin, and that a nest of them was balled up in the skeleton's ribcage. They were skinned over with hardened slime while they made the slow transformation to the next stage of their life cycle: a hard-shelled chrysalis that burrowed to the surface to protrude like a tubeworm, its end opening to release the flying adult form of the creature. He poked at this ball with the edge of his spade, fracturing the coating to reveal slithing movement.

"I want the skull," said their captor.

Inther dug at one end of the spine, and Marlen at the other. Marlen hit the pelvis, then turned as Inther unearthed the skull, took hold of it in his big hand and twisted it away from some remaining tendon, before passing it up out of the hole.

"Okay, now dig over there, where I've marked out." As he scrambled from the hole and over to another sunken area— marked out by four twigs shoved into the ground—Marlen glanced at the skull. Its previous owner had obviously been into cerebral augmentation in a big way. Behind where the ear would have been, a grey bean-shaped military aug was still attached by its bone anchors. Extending from this, a square-sectioned pipe lay alongside the temple curving round to enter the left eye socket—some sort of optic link. It was also obvious how this individual had died since, perfectly positioned in the centre of the forehead, was a neat hole ringed by blackened bone—someone had shot this person through the head with a pulse-gun.

"Oh Arian," the man said, "Mr. Crane was so wasted on you."

—retroact 3—

The acrid smell of molten and seared plastic filled the room as Semper welded up the final seals of the covering. Syntheskin was not an option, as firstly it was difficult to obtain, and secondly it was quite thick; layering Mr. Crane with it would only make him bulkier and therefore even more noticeable. Stanton thought the whole humanizing process laughable. The Golem was over two metres tall, possessed huge skull-crushing hands and didn't really move like a person—there was an odd, jerky, sometimes birdlike tendency to his every gesture which somehow hinted at a frightening instability. Now, with his skin-tone plastic covering, Stanton thought he looked even worse. It was like making a crocodile walk upright and wear a suit—some horror from a child's fairy tale.

"Okay," said Semper, "you can put your clothes back on."

Crane, who until then had been standing motionless while Semper worked, abruptly looked down at himself. Negligently he reached down, pinched at the skin over his chest, and tore a piece away.

"Leave that!" Semper reached out and slapped the Golem's hand as if berating a naughty child. The next moment the Golem held him suspended off the floor by his neck.

"Put him down!" Angelina Pelter yelled. "Put. Him. Down!"

She rose from where she had been sitting on one of the packing cases stacked along a wall of the warehouse and, discarding her laptop, rushed over. Mr. Crane's hand snapped open and Semper collapsed to the ground, hacking and gagging. Stanton looked down at his pulse-gun, then returned it to his shoulder holster. There had been no real purpose in him drawing the weapon and, upon studying the file he had taken from Stalek's computer, he discovered that even the sticky mine he had earlier placed on Crane would have no more effect than to briefly knock the Golem off its feet. Really, if they lost control of Crane and he decided to kill them, their only option was to run just as fast as they could, and hope the wrecked AI inside that brass body would soon find some other distraction.

Recovering somewhat, Semper dragged himself away from Crane before standing up. The Golem, as if nothing noteworthy had occurred, turned to the folding chair on which its clothing had been draped, picked up his hat and placed it carefully on his head. After standing utterly still for a second, he then took up the ragged trousers and put them on. Another pause, then the long coat. Watching him then don the big lace-up boots was almost comical. *Almost.*

Semper, who had now moved to stand beside Stanton, said, "Sooner or later, that fucking thing is going to kill one of us."

"You are so right—it certainly is," said a voice from behind them.

Semper whirled, groping for his weapon. Stanton didn't bother—he'd already heard Arian Pelter walking up the aisle, between crates containing dark-otter bone.

"Alston," said Stanton. "On his island." He turned. Alston was also part of the criminal organization supporting the Separatist cause. He was a part Arian Pelter wanted rid of. Stanton studied his boss.

Arian Pelter, Stanton felt, was just as pretty as his sister with his violet eyes, long blond hair and perfectly symmetrical features. Today he was dressed in an expensive white suit and a shirt that perfectly matched the shade of his eyes. He also wore a matching set of platinum New Tiffany jewellery: a single teardrop earring on the opposite side of his head to a matching aug, bracelets on each wrist, and rings on the fore- and mid-fingers of each hand. However, despite this foppish appearance, he was just as ugly on the inside as his sister, and just as dangerous. Stanton was certain it was Alston's contempt for the Pelter vanity, rather than the man's skimming cash from the otter-bone trade, that had made Arian decide he had become a liability. Unfortunately, out on his island, Alston was well protected.

"Dear sister," Arian acknowledged, as Angelina walked over, "so this is our new acquisition." He walked forwards, Semper and Stanton parting before him, then following as he headed over to inspect Mr. Crane. He paced one circuit of the Golem, then turned to Angelina. "Have you tried him with weapons?"

"Not yet. We've only just put on his skin," she replied.

Arian turned to Semper. "Your weapon."

Semper was reluctant, but he handed over his pulse-gun. Arian took it and held it out to Mr. Crane. "Now . . ." He looked around, then pointed to two crates standing one on top of the other on the further side of the warehouse. "Mr. Crane, I want you to take this weapon and destroy the top one of those two crates." He held out the gun.

The weapon looked silly, toylike, in Crane's big hand. With a darting motion, he dipped his head to inspect it. He then turned to face the crates, holding the weapon out to one side as if not sure quite what to do with it. There came a crunching sound and the brief flash of a laminar battery discharging. Pieces of Semper's gun fell about the Golem's feet as he abruptly lurched into motion. With long strides he ate up the ground between himself and the crates. Reaching them, he picked up the top one and just closed his hands on it, smashing the compressed-paper boards and the golden bones inside. Another abrupt movement scattered the debris all about him. He turned and strode back, stopping before Pelter to await further instructions.

Tapping his beringed forefinger against his aug, Arian said, "Well, he followed the instructions precisely, but not quite in the expected manner."

About then, Stanton started to feel it was time for him to collect the money owed to him and depart. He did not want to be around when Mr. Crane took literally one of Arian's psycho "Kill them all" orders. If the Separatists here on Cheyne III wanted to play catch with greased axes, he'd leave them to their game.

—retroact ends—

As he drove his spade into the ground, Marlen kept half an eye on what the man was doing, but he was not entirely certain of what happened next. The skull broke like egg shell in the man's hands. Then, retrieving something small and black from inside it, he discarded the bony remnants as he turned away. When he walked back over to watch his two slaves work, Marlen saw that he now held nothing, and could not shake the impression that the man had put the black object in his mouth and swallowed it.

3

The difference between hotsuits and coldsuits has been a source of sometimes lethal confusion. Does a hotsuit keep you hot, or prevent you from getting hot; and is a coldsuit refrigerated? The rule of thumb I apply is to just remember that the suit's internal temperature remains constant, so the "hot" or "cold" applies to the temperature outside it. Attempts were made to get everyone using "envirosuit" with given temperature ranges, e.g. envirosuit 150–250K (Kelvin). This would have been much better because many suits do not function outside certain ranges and can even be damaged if exposed to temperatures outside them. People have frequently purchased inappropriate coldsuits for cold environments. The envirosuit example quoted, having been raised above 250K, will not then insulate below 200K. Equally, a hotsuit capable of keeping a human alive in temperatures above the melting point of steel will be destroyed by ordinary room temperature (which begs the question of how a human gets in and out of such a suit, but I won't go there just yet). Of course, nothing so logical as the envirosuit nomenclature caught on: human language, go figure.

—From How It Is *by Gordon*

The flare momentarily blacked out the virtual view from the bridge of the *Jack Ketch*. When that view returned, a stray rock half the size of the ship itself had disappeared.

"I didn't know you had imploder missiles aboard as well," Cormac commented, after placing his brandy glass down on the pedestal table beside his club chair.

"No, you didn't," said Jack unhelpfully.

The automaton sat in its usual chair a few paces away, thin-fingered hands flat on his thighs, immobile.

"What other weaponry do you possess?"

"Probably more than you can think of."

"APWs? Lasers?"

"Yes and yes, though I'll add that the former is just one variety of particle beam out of the twelve I possess; and that of the latter I possess the facility to lase light across the spectrum. I also possess masers and tasers, carousels containing missiles that can be tailored to specific purposes, from carrying surveying instrumentation to gigatonne CTDs."

Cormac smiled to himself. Once you got a warship started on the subject of its armament, there was no stopping it. *I am what I am*, he thought.

"Though the imploder missiles are a recent addition, they are not the most powerful weapons I carry. The larger CTDs obviously have a greater yield, but are messy and inelegant. I do carry singularity generators energized by the power surge of a fission warhead. Of course these must not be used unless in dire need—because of the one in two hundred million chance of thus generating a permanent black hole."

As Jack went on to enumerate the various purposes to which he could tailor his missiles, Cormac gazed out at the scenery.

The giant research vessel *Jerusalem* was poised outside the asteroid field—too large to enter it without sustaining damage. Cormac had never really taken notice of the industry in the Polity directed towards acquiring and researching Jain artefacts, but now, seeing the *Jerusalem*, he gained some intimation of its extent, for this was the giant ship's sum purpose. It was a sphere five kilometres in diameter, with a thick band around its equator containing everything from legions of robotic probes up to U-space tugs and grabships, like the one presently departing it. The sphere itself contained whole communities of research scientists, AI and human, all working under the aegis of Jerusalem itself—a sector-class AI some regarded as a demigod—and much of the work carried out inside its colossal structure was classified. Its AI, rather than being based around a crystal matrix, used etched-atom processors, which meant that those regarding it as a demigod might not be so far wrong, and furthermore it possessed the power of intercession, in *any* situation, second only to Earth Central itself.

Entering the asteroid belt, the grabship had closed its claw over one mountain of stone protruding from the asteroid and was now beginning to drag the mass out. Calling up the required views, Cormac observed a vast hold of the research vessel opening like a Titan's mouth. With the asteroid on board, the ship was then to travel to Masada, whereupon those thousands of researchers inside it would begin their work. Not until they had wrung every last scrap of knowledge from the bridge pod, and then the Masadan system, and not until they rendered safe every Jain artefact, would that ship return to Polity space. The *Jack Ketch* hung over the location of the bridge pod, guarding against any further stray lumps of rock. Cormac hoped this would not be a lengthy task.

"Jack," he interrupted, just as the AI was telling him about slow-burn CTDs that could melt their way down to a planet's core. "How much longer until she's uploaded?"

"I am not actually uploading *her*, but a copy. I cannot give a precise period because the process is dependent on what I have to filter. This is not something we can hurry—I for one have no wish to end up going the way of Occam."

That might sound like a philosophy, but in fact referred to the fact of the *Occam Razor*'s AI suiciding rather than allow Skellor to control it.

"Rough estimate, then."

"Three hours."

Cormac rubbed at his cheek and yawned. "Then I'm for bed. The moment she's ready I want you to jump back to *Elysium*."

"You have always had EC's authority," Jack noted.

"You disapprove?"

"Not of the carte blanche agents such as yourself have always possessed, but of allowing someone aboard me who contains active Jain technology inside them."

"Aphran—or Thorn and Mika?"

"All of them."

"You surprise me."

"How would you feel about being the observer locked in a room with, for example, someone with a genetically proactive plague?"

"I guess I wouldn't be so happy."

"Me neither. I may be AI, but I do have feelings, you know."

Cormac grinned—he was beginning to like this AI. "Well, Aphran has told us Skellor hunts dragons. I want Asselis Mika with me because she's the nearest thing we have to an expert in both dragon and Jain technology. Perhaps she might be able to give us some lead on where those two remaining Dragon spheres went. And I want Thorn simply because he deserves to be here."

"As you will."

After eight hours flat out on his bed, Cormac returned to a bridge lit by the gloaming of underspace, and with two additions: a guillotine over to one side, to balance the gallows, and the illusory form of Aphran—the Separatist leader who had once employed Skellor and who had been killed by him. There was no time to interrogate the spectre, though, because within minutes the U-space grey was displaced by a close view of *Elysium*. Such questioning would have to wait for the next journey in the *Jack Ketch*, when it began its pursuit.

The nerve shunt in his neck and the paralytic she had injected through the probes should have prevented the Outlinker from feeling anything, or even moving, but he was writhing, fighting against the clamps that secured him to the table so that they creaked alarmingly, and his face was clenched in agony. It had to be the mycelium—it was bypassing the shunt, and maybe even his nervous system, so as to control his body directly. Mika hoped that in this process it had not restored his consciousness. But as she directed the four grasping claws once again into his torso—into a ribcage opened out like the wings of a macabre butterfly and the clamped-open gut cavity—he opened his eyes and glared at her. There seemed no other option but to do it quickly now, and never mind how brutal she must now be. The claws closed on the writhing mass clinging to his spine, and through the telefactor gloves she wore she initiated the secondary incisions. With brutal efficiency, the autodoc cut through muscle and bone from the lower end of the main incision down each of his thighs, sealing veins, capillaries and arteries as it went.

Usually operations conducted by a surgical robot were bloodless, but with something this major, bleeding was inevitable. Sucking heads hissed over exposed flesh, taking away blood, which rather than cleaning and re-injecting she was replacing with an artificial substitute. It seemed the safest course—his blood was probably loaded with Jain nanomachines. Now she directed incisions across the shoulders and down both his biceps, and also up into his neck. Into all of these secondary incisions she directed wide-focus laser scalpels rather than chainglass ones, as she had found that the mycelium healed straight mechanical cuts made into itself almost immediately. In his thigh she saw the clumped filaments shrivelling away and, despite the vacuum nozzle behind each of the laser scalpels, she smelt burning flesh.

"Now, you bastard!" she said, flicking the sweat on her forehead to one side and sending the instruction to the robot to retract its four claws. Servomotors whined and, with a wet tearing sound, the trunk of Jain filaments, wound around the plum-sized dark nodules it had been growing, began to come up. In his biceps, she saw the severed clumps pulling in towards his torso and disappearing at the end of the incision. Those in his thighs tore up with the main mass. This mycelium, a fibrous blue-grey mass, something like a tree branch, tore up and away, but no tree branch writhed like a hooked ragworm to escape. Following its program, the surgical robot swung aside, bowed and deposited the thing in a chainglass vessel reserved for this purpose, slamming the lid closed on it as a door is closed on a hornet ejected from a house. It then swung back to Apis. Mika checked her readouts. All the life-support equipment was working at its maximum. She could keep Apis alive like this for many hours; but then she would need those hours to put him back together. Tiredly she went to work, cell and bone welders humming and hissing busily. When she finished, he would be complete and physically unscarred, but the remains of the Jain mycelium might still kill him, and if he remembered any of this, he might not be entirely sane.

Two metres down they hit gold, or rather brass.

The head was like something cracked from a brass statue of Apollo, only lines of division and of mechanical linkage showing that this head bore features that had once moved. Marlen reached down, attempting to pick the head up with one hand, but it was too heavy. He put his spade aside and grasped the object in both hands, holding it up to their captor, who took it in one hand, as if it weighed nothing, and inspected it. With a shudder, Marlen glimpsed movement in the grasping hand like something black writhing underneath the skin.

"Case-hardened ceramal covered with a layer of zinc and copper alloy containing the superconductor net," the man said, then turned to the two diggers. "Keep digging. I want it all—every last piece." After a pause, he redirected his attention to the head, and Marlen, turning once again to take up his spade, briefly glimpsed two brass eyelids clicking open to reveal obsidian eyes.

"What a pretty machine you are, Mr. Crane. Aphran was so in awe of you."

Placing the head on the ground, its gaze directed up at the sky, the man took his hand away and the eyes closed.

Soon Marlen and Inther uncovered a heavy ripped-open torso with one leg attached whose weight required both of them to haul it out of the excavation. Then came the other leg, and an arm. Continuing to dig, Marlen and Inther unearthed smaller components and fragments of memory crystal. The man was now getting impatient. Checking his scanner, he paced the entire area, then finally returned to them, obviously angry.

"There's an arm missing," he snarled.

The two diggers gazed up at him dumbly. Then Marlen stooped, picked up another of the lumps of memory crystal, and placed it at the rim of the hole. The man now turned his attention to this, and abruptly smiled. "Find *all* of that." He turned and headed over to the laid-out pieces of android. Still digging, Marlen found that the latest command was not so harshly enforced, now their captor had other things to occupy him, so Marlen could keep a wary eye on what was occurring.

Their captor knelt by the juncture between separated leg and groin. He picked up the leg in one hand, then reached out and tilted the torso so that the exposed ceramal thigh-bone, still attached to the torso, was raised off the ground. He then slid the leg back over this bone until it was nearly back in position. He could not get it all the way on because of the torn metal, ripped optics and bent mechanical linkages at the break. Dropping the torso back to the ground, he then turned his attention to the arm, which he could do no more than push close to where it had been ripped away. Ball joints, protruding below the head, seated into the neck with audible clicks. Now, his expression beatific, the man pushed his hand inside the torn-open chest and closed his eyes. Immediately his skin seemed to turn grey, with a black insectile shifting underneath it. He jerked and, lying on the ground, the huge brass Golem jerked as well. In the gap between brass shoulder and arm, Marlen glimpsed glittery squirming movement before the arm drew up to the shoulder, sealing the gap.

"Bring those other components," the man ordered.

Marlen scrambled out of the hole, gathered up the pile of twisted metal and brought it over. Dumping this on the ground beside the Golem, he observed swirling tentacular movement spreading from the man's hand into the chest cavity. Marlen went back to pick up the pieces of crystal. As he returned with these, it was in time to see the man backing off, his hand still in the cavity, while the Golem stood up. Withdrawing his hand the man glanced down at the twisted scrap, snorted, then kicked it aside. Without speaking, he then directed Marlen to place the crystal fragments on a nearby rock. Given no further orders after this, Marlen stood watching while the man squatted and assembled the fragments like a Chinese puzzle.

"There are more pieces to be found. Return to your digging."

Before the instruction took full control of him, Marlen managed, "Who . . . what . . . are you?"

The man looked surprised at this resistance and somehow prevented the order from taking full effect, so that Marlen was able to remain where he was.

"Me—just a man who has important work to do. It doesn't matter that you know who I am, and soon enough the whole Polity will know my name. I'm Skellor. Now, best you get back to your digging, as your companion will soon be no great help to you, since I will be requiring his arm."

Marlen turned and walked woodenly back to the hole, inwardly resisting all the way, knowing why it didn't matter what he knew. Inther walked past him the other way, still drooling, one eye now red with blood. Marlen supposed Inther had been chosen because his stature more closely matched that of the Golem. Even while he shovelled earth, Marlen possessed freedom enough to turn his head and watch what happened to Inther. He did not, but he could not close his ears to the horrible sounds that ensued, and Skellor crooning, "Ah, Mr. Crane, soon you will be better, so much better. I'll perfect the *work* others left incomplete."

—retroact 4—

The lander was a flat ellipse with a quarter segment cut out, where was substituted an ugly particle cannon and a pan-pipes missile launcher. Ascending on AG, the pilot made the mistake of correcting with HO attitude jets. Stalek sighed, pulled down his visor and checked the projection in its bottom right-hand corner, to be sure that all his hotsuit's seals were locked down. He then took the remote control off his belt and pointed it ahead of him, sending his favourite pet digging for cover in the loose soil under the briars over there.

Inevitably, the flame from one of the ship's attitude jets touched the ridge, and the incendiary briars there exploded into fire. Falco, standing to Stalek's left, hurriedly slammed down his beaked visor as he had only just realized the possible danger.

The ship swung away and up, the particle cannon tracking the sheets of flame, then out in an arc from the fire itself looking for attackers. Stalek felt something thump against his shoulder and glanced down as a briar pod—much like a segmented cluster of Brazil nuts—landed on the ground with its segments opening out. He noted the pod's blue-green hue.

"Premature," he said.

"What?" said Falco.

"Premature burn. The briar isn't really ready, so the fire won't spread."

Falco nodded and flicked up his visor, once again demonstrating to Stalek the man's stupidity. Stalek would have dispensed with him long ago had it not been for Falco's ability to follow orders with admittedly no imagination but meticulous precision—exactly the sort of person required for some of the more repetitive mind-numbing tasks Stalek's business required. Still watching the man, Stalek waited. The fire was dying, but the danger wasn't past. Briar pods began thumping down all around, in a green hail. It took one of these breaking on Falco's armoured shoulder to make the man realize he should not yet have opened his visor. Falco swore and jumped, slamming his visor down over his avian face again. Stalek sighed and returned his attention to the ship, as it came towards them.

Coding the frequency he had been sent into his comunit, Stalek said, "Any kind of naked flame down here is not really a smart idea. I suggest that if any correction of attitude is required, you use gravadjustment or air jets."

There was no reply, but it was noticeable that the pilot did not use HO jets while landing the ship nearby, in the process crushing down masses of the tangled, snakish briars. Stalek smiled at the choice of landing site. He had not expected them to put the ship down there. With its hard, sharp leaves giving it both the appearance and the potential to hurt of green razor wire, it was never a good idea to get too close to the Huma incendiary briar. But obviously the crew did not know that. A section of curved hull then folded down and hinged open, making a ramp and walkway over to the clear area where Stalek and Falco waited.

Two heavily armed figures left the ship and came down the ramp. After scanning the area—though why, Stalek could not fathom, as they must have already done that from above—one of them spoke into the comunit integral to his helmet.

"Clear. Bring it out."

How very strange, thought Stalek. Perhaps a definition of "clear" he had yet to learn.

A third member of the crew came down the ramp leading a coffin-sized cylinder floating on AG a metre off the ramp. The item. Stalek rubbed his hands together even though he could feel little through the insulated gloves.

"Do you have payment?" asked the heavy who had spoken before.

Stalek peered at the man. This was where things got a little problematic. He indicated a box by his own feet. "Half a million in etched sapphires, and two ten-kilotonne-yield CTDs. I'm afraid that will have to be it. I couldn't lay my hands on any APWs at this short notice."

The man grunted, obviously satisfied with that. Stalek wasn't surprised. They were probably glad to get anything at all for this item it had taken them so much effort and such loss of life to acquire—this thing that had turned out to be useless to them.

The cylinder arrived with the third man. Stalek wandered over and peered inside as the top half section of it split and hinged open. The Golem Twenty-five lay there utterly

motionless, catatonic—as it had been since talking to itself
non-stop for two days, then apparently trying to smash its
way out of its prison with its head. The Jovians had assumed
that their EM pulse had wrecked its mind. Stalek knew
better. Something odd must have happened to it at the
programming stage and, as unlikely as it seemed, Cybercorp
had produced a dud.

"Let's see the money," said the one who had brought the
cylinder down the ramp.

A woman, Stalek saw, and attractive. Shame. He turned
his attention to the box he had brought, waved a hand at it.
"It's all there." He pointedly did not look towards the ship,
having just glimpsed the black shape hopping up onto the
ramp and scuttling inside it.

The woman squatted down, turned the simple lock on
the case and flipped back the lid. She gazed in puzzlement
at what seemed to be a coil of ribbed oxygen pipe.

"Joden? Joden!"

The screaming from inside the ship was abrupt and
harsh—agonized. From the box, the pipe uncoiled, whip-
fast, opening gleaming pincers at its end which it snapped
closed on the woman's throat. She gargled and thrashed,
blood bubbling out of her punctured suit. Meanwhile, Stalek
had calmly removed two small spheres from his suit pocket.
He tossed them towards the two men as one of them brought
his weapon to bear, while the other did not seem to know
what to do: open fire or help the woman. The spheres shot
forwards, turned briefly incandescent, punched through
two environment suits. Stalek stepped back as pulse-gun fire
slammed into the front of his own suit, but the laminated
armour made nothing of the ionized gas hits, and an inlaid
superconducting mesh took away the heat. The spheres did
precisely what they were supposed to do: exploding and
flinging needles of pure potassium through the two men's
bodies, the metal igniting and burning fiercely in contact
with moisture.

Their suits, Stalek noted, were quite good quality, for while
the men boiled and burned inside, the only sign was a jet of

oily steam from each of the holes the spheres had made upon entry—that and the way the two thrashed about and screamed a lot. When it was finally over, Stalek looked pointedly at Falco, who was studying the pulse-gun scars on the front of his suit, ahem'd and pointed to the still floating cylinder. Falco walked over and closed it up, then, grabbing the towing handle, pulled it after his boss. Stalek paused once to look back. He would come out to check there was nothing more of value inside this ship before he sold it on to his contact up in Port Lock. When the fires started, later in the season, they would incinerate all other evidence—not that anyone would be looking. Shaking his head, Stalek felt a degree of bewilderment. How ever had such amateurs managed to steal a Golem Twenty-five from right outside Cybercorp?

—retroact ends—

The Sand Towers, the wind-carved buttes exposing their layers of coloured sands recounting the ages of Cull, extended as far as he could see to his left and right, and tens of kilometres beyond towards the plains. Raising his family monocular to his eyes, Anderson Endrik now inspected the Overcity of Golgoth, spread across its great steel platform high up on the Towers, then the lower city crouching in the foothills. The entire city was a product of metallier industry, and the centre of the closer, lower section bore the appearance of giant iron lichen holding the spheres and ellipses of its denizens' metal houses. Sprawled all around it were long low steel mills and factories interspersed with chimneys belching smoke. Anderson had heard much about this place: that old technologies were being resurrected in pursuit of the dream of re-establishing the downed communication link with Earth, of interstellar travel, and of rejoining the human empire. Anderson raised his monocular to the sky to observe *Ogygian*—the ship that had brought his own ancestors here—a sphere connected by a narrow body to the triple nacelles of the U-space engines, glinting like green quicksilver in the turquoise firmament. Then he lowered his monocular to let it hang by its strap and, tapping his goad against the back of its sensory head, urged his sand hog mount into motion.

"Are all the rumours true, or just bullshit?" wondered Tergal.

Anderson glanced aside at his young companion. Tergal was skinny and tall, his head topped by the wide-brimmed hat of a gully trader, with long dark hair spilling from under it down his back. He wore a leather jerkin, canvas trousers and sandals, and armed himself only with a punch axe and heavy crossbow. The boy's sand hog, Stone, was also young, perhaps only the age of one human lifetime, for it still bore the red flush of youth and, as Anderson had noticed when the hog had first folded out its feeding head from underneath itself, it still possessed all its blunt white teeth. Seated in the saddle glued to the creature's long teardrop-shaped carapace, Tergal was a metre lower than Anderson. The rough ride the young hog gave him also threw him continually from side to side.

Anderson's own hog, Bonehead, was mature, and twice the bulk of Stone. The ears on its sensory head Anderson had trimmed back to stubs, and it was missing a few teeth. Its gait, however, up on its two powerful hind legs, was smooth. He remembered searching old records about why their mounts were so named. One reference to "hog" had its meaning as something greedy, which certainly applied to Bonehead. When he discovered that hog also meant pig, he realized the true reason for the naming. When the creatures' sensory and feeding heads were meshed, the composite head which resulted looked very much like that of a domestic pig portrayed in a very old picture. The carapace body, when viewed from the side, was also comparable, as was the pinkish coloration of sand hogs. Of course the similarity fell apart when these creatures rose up on their muscular hind limbs, or parted their composite heads on separate necks.

"Ah, I think much truth can be weaned from the sand slide of rumour. Doubtless much old technology has been recovered or relearned—but surpassed?" Anderson shook his head.

"But they have advanced . . . you'll grant that?" The boy gestured to the city.

"I'll grant you that, though it could have been inferred before even seeing this place."

"How?"

Anderson eyed the youth. "Gully traders becoming wealthy by transporting coal and metal ores here?" he suggested.

Tergal glanced at him. "I don't know much about that. My mother was a trader by birth, but my stepfather is a minerallier. I know our mining was confined to shallow pits until the metalliers started wanting more coal and ores. My stepfather used to make a living from single-handedly mining gems. Now he employs hundreds of immigrants from Dalure, and even Rondure, and his mines extend right underneath the mountains. But does increased demand equate to advancement? It might well be just because their population has increased."

Anderson grinned. "That's one clue, but there are others." He reached into his belt pouch and took out a small cloth bag closed with a drawstring. Opening this, he shook out a handful of shell cases into his palm. "These tell us a lot. I found them scattered in a gully traders' campsite, and I dug the metal slugs they propelled from the remains of a sleer. I've yet to see the weapon that uses them, but by their size I would guess the explosive is somewhat more efficient than my black powder." Anderson nodded to where he holstered his fusile muzzle-loader beside his saddle. "I'd guess they're smokeless and that the weapon even has the facility for fast repetition of fire."

"What leads you to that assumption?" Tergal asked archly.

"They're uniform, so probably not the product of individual skill. We've always known how repeating weapons function but just haven't possessed the materials technology and industrial infrastructure to manufacture them—something like that takes time, effort and considerable organization to build. But having reached such a level of expertise, why not make the best weapons of that kind that you can?"

"And?" Tergal asked.

Anderson weighed the shell cases, as if in judgement, then slipped them back into his bag and placed it in his belt pouch. "Impressive weapons, certainly mass-produced, but not a product of the technology our kind first arrived here with. Do you think that if they had surpassed the old technologies, the metalliers would still be producing something so primitive? Where are the pulse-guns and the beam weapons, then?"

"Yes—I see." The boy shrugged.

"Course, I could be talking complete bollocks," Anderson added.

Tergal muttered something foul and, causing static sparks to flare, whacked his goad against his mount's sensory head, and it reared, nearly unseating him as it pulled ahead. Anderson watched the boy a moment longer, then turned his attention to the eye-palp Bonehead extruded from its upper porcine sensory head and turned to observe him disapprovingly. He shrugged and placed his fingers against his lips to signal his own silence, and Bonehead sucked the eye-palp back into its skull, looking forwards. Anderson decided he wouldn't needle the boy further.

It had always been his intention to make this final leg of his journey to the Plains alone, but the youth, joining Anderson's camp one night, seemed disinclined to go away. Anderson had yet to fathom the boy's history, but certainly it contained theft and quite possibly murder. Anderson suspected the boy balanced on a cusp—attracted by the kudos of travelling with Anderson but undecided about whether or not to rob him. Anderson would let him make his choice, and let him suffer the consequences of the same. At least, while the boy decided, he was not harming anyone. But mostly Anderson was glad of the company and of a willing audience to his many enthusiasms.

The concrete road winding towards Golgoth, the City of Skulls (named so because of the similarity many of the houses bore to those items), soon reached an intersection in the foothills and thereafter became much wider. Surveying his surroundings, Anderson observed further signs of technological advance. In the distance, he saw electricity pylons, and supposed it was true the metalliers had repaired the old power station in Bravence. Hereabouts the sand was only prevented from turning into shifting desert by the white and yellow plates of what was called egg lichen, though why it was called that Anderson had no idea—eggs were something he had only seen under a microscope, and had nothing to do with lichen. However, here there were also wide expanses levelled into fields producing cereals and root vegetables, irrigation frames being mounted over the latter, and occasional sprawls of glasshouses, usually as an adjunct to the occasional lone metallier dwelling, which consisted of anodized sheet aluminium nailed over wooden frames.

Much closer to the city, they passed through a small village, and he was fascinated by some vehicles parked at the side of the road. Obviously these did not require sand hogs to pull them. He was tempted to stop and make an inspection, to find out what kind of engines were used—electric, combustion, steam turbine—as that would certainly give him a true idea of metallier advancement. But he guessed he would soon be seeing more of such vehicles—a supposition soon proved true when they finally forced him and Tergal off the road.

"Tergal, I reckon I'll stop for the night before entering the city." Anderson gestured to a roadhouse a short distance ahead. "Will you join me?"

"I thought you were eager to see Golgoth?" the boy asked.

"Eager yes, but not terminally so. I'd like to have some idea of what we'll be riding into—and such information we should be able to obtain here."

"Then I'll join you," Tergal replied.

The roadhouse, though fashioned of gleaming lacquered alloys and sheets of glass, did have what were recognizable as hog corrals around the back, though they were much smaller than the parking area for powered vehicles between it and the road. Anderson urged his hog across the lichen-bound dunes directly towards the corrals, his hog's divided rear feet pulling up tufts of the yellow and white lichen as it strode along. Tergal hesitated, then turned his own mount to follow. As they drew close, a metallier strolled out towards them.

He was recognizable as such by his long snake-leather coat, facial tattoos and sand goggles, for metalliers did not possess nictitating membranes like real humans. Drawing his hog to a halt, Anderson immediately observed the weapon the man had resting across his shoulder. It was all blued metal, half the length of Anderson's fusile, and bore a long rectangular protrusion from the side, which he guessed to be a magazine. This was what Anderson had come for.

"Where would you like us to put our mounts?" he asked.

"Any corral will do," the man replied, gesturing with his weapon. "There's carrion in the far shed, if you want to feed them. Fifteen pfennigs a night."

"Fifteen!" Tergal exclaimed, as his hog settled down onto its four short forelegs.

"Unfortunate, I know," the man said, "but at that I make little profit."

"And how much for a room in this place?" Anderson asked, undoing his lap strap as Bonehead also settled onto its crawler limbs.

"Ten—costs more for hogs because they're rare around here now. I keep thinking of closing the corrals, but then another one like you comes along, and I don't." The man eyed him, and Anderson supposed what attracted the curious look was his attire. He guessed that not many people in so advanced a society dressed in armour fashioned from chitin and black bone, but then, with the weapons they possessed, he supposed not many of them needed to.

"You're a Rondure Knight," the man said. "Are you on your trial?"

Anderson took up his pack from behind his saddle, stood up, and walked to the edge of his hog's carapace, from where he dropped to the ground.

"That I am," he replied.

Walking over to the nearest corral, he pulled the steel draw bolt and opened the gate. Bonehead, seeing the opportunity for food and sleep, required no urging and, still on its crawler limbs, slid past into the corral. Tergal led his own younger hog by hooking his goad under its carapace's skirt. Anderson walked over to the feed shed, opened the door and stepped back to allow a swarm of warple bugs to scuttle for cover. Breathing only through his mouth, he could almost taste the stench. He reached in, grabbed a carapace rim, and dragged out the suppurating carcass of a rock crawler. Joining him, Tergal grabbed the other side, kicking the door closed behind him, and they heaved the carcass over the rail into the corral. Both hogs moved in, sensory heads swinging up from underneath their bodies, then their feeding heads also swung up to engage with an audible crunch below the first heads. The younger hog gave Anderson's precedence, but there would be enough there for both of them.

"What's your name?" Anderson asked, as they returned to the metallier.

The man held out his hand. "Laforge."

Anderson shook his hand, replying, "I'm Anderson Endrik and my companion is Dound Tergal."

Tergal gave a half-hearted wave, but showed no inclination to take the man's hand.

"Where do we go?" Anderson asked the metallier.

"I'll show you." The man turned and led the way. "The refectory is open all the time, so you should be able to get a meal."

"Not at these damned prices," Tergal muttered as they followed.

They entered the roadhouse through metal doors inset with rough green glass filled with bubbles.

"A room each?" Laforge asked them.

"One will do," Anderson replied, glancing at Tergal for confirmation before holding out the ten-pfennig note he had pulled from his belt pouch.

"Tell me, where did you obtain that weapon?" he asked, as Laforge pocketed the note.

The man turned, selecting a key rod from the bunch hanging on his belt as he led them to the nearest door.

"In the city. Central manufacturing produces them, but every metallier shop carries a stock." He glanced round. "If you're interested, I know the best place to go."

"I'm interested. I take it sand hogs are not usual transport in the city itself?"

"Not really—but I'm going in tomorrow morning. My brother runs just the establishment you require on Second Level. You may find cheaper, but you won't find better." He opened the door.

The room was a five-metre box with a single window set high up, and they walked in over the suction of a sand grid by the door. There was a carpet and four bunks. In an alcove to their right were a washbasin, a toilet, and even a roll of paper towelling. Anderson was surprised at the luxury—he had expected the price to pay for only the four protective walls.

Laforge detached a key rod and held it out to the knight. "This opens your door and turns on the water supply." He gestured to the alcove. "As I said, the refectory is open." He closed the door on his way out.

"A little more than we expected," Anderson suggested.

"I've been in worse places, I suppose," Tergal allowed. He turned to Anderson. "I didn't know you were coming here for weapons."

"How long have you travelled with me?"

"Two days."

"There's a lot you don't know about me. Just as there's a lot I don't know about you."

"I know now you're a Rondure Knight who is on his trial."

"But not what that trial is."

Tergal waited.

Anderson went on, "I need the best weapons I can find, because I am heading to the Plains, where I intend to kill a dragon."

4

*A quarter century after the creation of the first AI,
and after cloned whole-body swapping had been
going on for fifty years, people finally realized the
legal system required a severe upgrade. Legally, it
was still possible to end up on a murder charge for
turning off the life-support of a human vegetable, yet
no such laws applied to AI or even to some animals
whose intelligence was demonstrably higher than that
of many humans. Having human DNA should not
immediately grant an individual inalienable rights.
Rights, it was decided, and equivalent responsibilities,
should be given to "citizens," and only those above
a certain level of intelligence could become citizens.
Protests did result when some humans failed to
qualify, whilst all AIs and some particularly bright
pigs did, but I am not discussing that today. I'm here
to talk about a particular corollary that can be traced
back to these legal changes.*

*After the events on the world of Masada, and in the
cylinder worlds called Faith, Hope and Charity, there
was what our more mealy-mouthed ancestors would
have called a "humanitarian disaster." Many of
those wearing the biotech augs (I can't say too much
about them as there's still an ongoing investigation)
were brain-burnt—becoming human vegetables. In
a less enlightened age these bodies would probably
have been kept alive for as long as possible, causing
a huge drain on the rest of human society. Luckily,
we see things differently and, other than simple*

> *disposal, have some better options. The advent of memplant technology and newer and more accurate loading techniques has resulted in millions of people outliving physical death. Many of them are being held in memstorage because we cannot produce enough bodies, tank-grown or Golem, to keep up with demand, so . . .*
>
> —*Excerpt from a speech by Jobsworth*

Cormac knew how many said that, in the eternal instant of runcible transmission, the travellers screamed. That being the case, Cormac must have screamed himself raw over the thousands of such journeys he had made. This time, strangely, as he stepped through the shimmer of the Skaidon warp of the first-stage runcible on the small Masadan moon, Flint, it was with a grey and distorted recollection of that eternal instant, of groping to comprehend madness, and nearly understanding it.

"Are you all right?" a woman asked him.

His visual cortex still trying to play impossible images, he blinked and stared down at where he was supporting himself on a cylindrical cleaning robot, which was obviously confused about what it should be cleaning up in such chaotic surroundings, so was perhaps glad of an excuse to stop.

"Yeah, okay, just a bit dizzy."

The woman said, "You want me to get you to an autodoc? Perhaps it's the low gravity here. It can't be the transmission—even first-stage runcibles are utterly safe."

Cormac looked up and was unsurprised to see that she was wearing the overalls of a runcible technician, since such people were always highly defensive of a technology they themselves could not wholly understand. Only AIs possessed a full understanding—the human brain had not evolved that way. He pushed himself away from the cleaning robot. Yes, the gravity was very low here, but he had become accustomed to such changes over the many years he had travelled like this. That wasn't the problem.

Any problems with this runcible while I transported? he asked.

No problem, agent. Nor with the one in *Elysium*, replied the Flint runcible AI.

"Shit, I did it again!"

"I'm sorry?" said the woman.

"I gridlinked. I gridlinked again!"

"I'm sure you are very proud to possess a gridlink, but you should remember that most people in my trade now possess such technology as well," the woman lectured him, before flouncing off.

Cormac peered down at the cleaning robot, which was observing him with its binocular lenses—the irises inside whirring wide as if the machine was suddenly worried about him. He closed his eyes and concentrated, trying again to question the runcible AI. Visions of impossible shapes fled through his mind, and he felt a hint of some huge complex intelligence, then it was all gone and there were no more voices in his head. He opened his eyes and, after locating his position in the temporary dome, headed in long bouncing strides for the exit tunnels that led to where the shuttles would be waiting. He felt he must put aside this strangeness, and concentrate on the job in hand. He felt sure this inadvertent gridlinking somehow related to Blegg and, that being so, its cause would not become clear either soon or easily.

The exit tunnel was cylindrical, the bottom half of this cylinder being tough ceramoplastic, with a flat diamond-pattern floor, the top half being polarized chainglass. Gazing out to the tightly curved horizon, Cormac observed a twisted and monolithic metal beam protruding above a thin smear of sulphurous atmosphere, its jagged end silhouetted against the green and orange swirls of the opaline gas giant, Calypse. Other wreckage was strewn across the barren surface of this little moon: the huge cored-olive shapes of thruster motors, seared skeletons of ships and ground bases, glittering craters where molten metal had splashed, human bones. Destroying the shipyards here had been Dragon's first blow against the Theocracy, before moving on to obliterate the weapons satellites that had held the surface population of Masada in thrall. Dragon's subsequent fall to its death had produced the strangest and most controversial result of its arrival here: the birth of the race of dracomen from its own substance.

"Ian Cormac?"

"Yes," Cormac replied, as he ducked into the low structure from which other short tunnels branched to insystem shuttles crouched around the facility. The questioner he instantly recognized as a Golem.

"I'm to take you to Masada. We have a shuttle with U-space facility available."

The Golem, in appearance a squat man of endearing ugliness—obviously from a later series made when Cybercorp discovered that Apollonian perfection made potential purchasers nervous, if not jealous—gestured to a nearby tunnel and led the way. "This will be our first landing on the planet itself—a partial quarantine still exists, but it has been decided we can't learn anything more from up here. There are more ships ready to follow us down."

"How will you proceed from now on?"

"Establish a base on the surface, then limit transport thereafter. Our first job will be to secure all Jain artefacts, then ensure that there has been no further . . . contamination."

"That could take some time."

The Golem shrugged. Cormac guessed ECS would prevent free travel of the Masadan population to and from their own world until telefactors and AI probes had finished deep-scanning the single continent and ocean thereon. Masada could remain partially quarantined for centuries yet. He surmised that these new members of the Polity would not be allowed to object too strongly.

"Would those artefacts include the mycelia inside Asselis Mika?"

The Golem glanced at him. "Your needs have primacy. If you wish to take all of those containing Jain mycelia with you, then you may. There will certainly be enough other stuff down there to keep us occupied for a long time."

"And the dracomen?" Cormac asked, as they entered the airlock into the shuttle and headed for the cockpit.

"They have been deemed innocent of the crimes committed by their forebear and so have been urged, separately from the human population of Masada, to join the Polity."

"They might refuse," said Cormac, thinking "innocent" might be stretching the term.

"They have already accepted."

Cormac took the co-pilot's seat, while the Golem took the pilot's. They both strapped in.

"Very wise of them," he remarked.

"Yes, quite."

Gazing ahead as the shuttle launched and rose from the barren moon, Cormac observed the glint of other ships in the darkness of space. Soon after he arrived on Masada, the place would be swarming with ECS troops and monitors, technicians, research scientists and Golem. He had no doubt that the dracomen were more aware of the actual realities than were the planet's inhabitants. Simply put, Masada *must* be controlled by ECS because of the potential danger from Jain artefacts on its surface, and the dracomen *must* join the Polity, for such dangerous creatures could not be allowed to choose a side that might be against it. The alternatives were numerous and lethal. The *Jack Ketch* AI had earlier enumerated them for Cormac.

Skellor smiled to himself as he pressed together the seventeen fragments of the crystalline Golem mind. Obviously, the Golem—Aiden and Cento—had torn the object from Crane's body and smashed it irreparably with a blast from a pulse-gun. But what was irreparable to Polity technology was not necessarily beyond Skellor's ability. What most amused him was that the mind had broken along established virtual fractures, for Mr. Crane's mind had always been in seventeen fragments—this was the nature of the Golem's madness and, strangely, what had made sanity and autonomy a recoverable objective. His mentality fragmented like this, Mr. Crane operated as the killing machine the Separatists required, committing the most horrifying crimes and maintaining them in memory as disjointed unrelated incidents, meanwhile always attempting to reconnect the seventeen fragments and regain self. This he would perhaps have done sometime in the next thousand years. Thus it was that the Golem had obeyed his Separatist masters—in that dangerous and erratic manner entirely his own.

Roughly holding the fragments in the lozenge shape they had once formed, Skellor began to send Jain nanofilaments into it, clouding the crystal as they penetrated between the lattices. Concentrating on a single clean shear, he pulled the two faces together. Pecking along them on an atomic level, he cleared away oxygen atoms from the oxides formed on each surface, also organic dirt and minerals—anything that should not be there. Drawing this detritus away, he found all the major neural pathways, cooling nanotubes and s-con power grid wires, and aligned them. There was some distortion caused by relieved stresses in the crystal, which he recreated. The two faces, drawn together by the Van Der Waals force of atomic attraction, snapped back together as if they had been held apart by elastic, and it was all he could do to pull the filaments out of the way to prevent them from being trapped and crushed. Two of the fragments had become one, and now he detected the nightmarish mutter from this piece of a mind.

For a moment, Skellor refocused his awareness on his surroundings. Not having acquired the same resources he had possessed on the *Occam Razor*, he was unable to split his awareness during such an operation, which was as intricate as anything he had done before. He briefly noted the man Inther, lying naked on his side nearby, bleeding to death from where Skellor had torn his arm away. Marlen was motionless in his hole, though Skellor's control of him was not so strong as to prevent the man from showing by his expression the terror he felt. Mr. Crane's body stood perfectly poised, its balance system operating as if he was already alive. The human arm Skellor had grafted on to replace the missing ceramal one only looked out of place at the raw shoulder joint, with its swollen organo-optic interfaces. Inside that body Skellor had built a device acting as a heart, lung and nutrient supply—pumping round the arm an artificial blood supply. The human limb would last perhaps six months like this, but hopefully Skellor would not need it for so long. He returned his attention to Mr. Crane's mind.

Interface after interface bonded, and the mutter of the Golem's mind grew loud to Skellor's senses. Delving into this he replayed scenes of murder and atrocity and perpetual imbalance. Quite often, Mr. Crane had been as much a danger to the people who tried to control him as he was to those he was sent out to kill. Skellor noted how Crane disobeyed some direct orders when the program, aimed at regaining the Golem autonomy, interfered with the task at hand. Sometimes this program could briefly displace an order to do murder so that, rather than kill, Crane found external iconic representations of each virtual fragment of his mind. Rather than kill a man, Crane had once stolen a pair of antique binoculars. Rather than kill he had once taken a Tenkian dagger. Even with the Separatist orders re-establishing, Crane would not carry out the kill order, for, in the twisted logic of this insane Golem, the theft *became* the killing.

As the final physical fragments of the mind came together, Skellor decided that his own orders must not be disobeyed in any manner, so he proceeded to wipe the program intended to reassemble the virtual fragments of the Golem's mind. But he couldn't. As soon as he attempted to wipe the program, the mind began to break in other places, in a way that would make it unusable. Annoyingly, what could make Crane whole and sane and autonomous was also preventing him from sliding into true oblivion. Remove it, and the mind would fall apart. Skellor realized he could erase everything and start again, but doing that would result in the loss of the Mr. Crane he wanted. This he found aesthetically displeasing. To possess godlike powers, Skellor felt, meant he should please the poetic as well as the pragmatic part of his soul.

With the mind now cupped before him like an offering to this brass god, Skellor stood and approached Crane's body. There was a Jain substructure inside the Golem: it supplied the power lost by two broken micro-piles, and was mopping up spilt radioactives. It would also repair him, just as similar mycelia had repaired the calloraptor creatures Skellor sent after Ian Cormac on Masada. Mr. Crane, dangerous though he used to be, would now be *formidable*.

Skellor reached out and pressed the lozenge into its recess inside the Golem. It snicked into place, light flickering around it as the structure inside him made optic connections. The Jain substructure, taking on a brassy hue from its surroundings, reached out like sharp fingers and drew closed the ceramal torso as if it was made of rubber. The superconducting grid then rolled across and joined, then finally brass melted and flowed across the surface. After a moment Mr. Crane—not Skellor—opened those black eyes.

"Welcome back to your life," Skellor told the Golem.

—retroact 5—

"Mr. Pendle . . ." began Agent Bryonik, leaning back, his fingers interlaced beneath his chin.

"Is this entirely necessary?" Pendle interrupted, waving a hand at their surroundings.

Bryonik wondered what his problem was: this was genuinely in the style of a premillennial police interrogation cell, with a scarred and coffee-stained plastic table, magnetic tape recorders, strip lights . . .

Pendle went on, "Do you know how many times I've sat in rooms like this?"

"Enlighten me."

"Precisely seven hundred and twenty-three."

"There are worse alternatives."

"And do you know how many times that has been said to me?"

Bryonik grimaced, and through his gridlink accessed Penal Storage to change the VR format. He didn't like being predictable, so rather than go for the Caribbean island, bright shirts, and drinks with umbrellas in them, he cobbled his own scenario. Now the two men stood in the uppermost viewing gallery of the Eiffel Tower. Pendle eyed the bank of screens to one side, showing a steel-recrystalizing robot as it slowly traversed one of the ancient structural members.

"This is a new one," commented Pendle. "In my time the damned thing had fallen down. When did they put it back up?"

"About seven years after you died."

Pendle's case had a certain historical significance—one of a defining variety of crimes committed around the same period. Prior to then it would have been called what—assault?

"Thirteen years ago, then."

Bryonik raised an eyebrow.

"You know I'm real-timed. Believe me, I've been counting the years in here."

"How long have you got?"

Pendle shrugged. "It varies. I'll never be loaded to a Golem chassis while there's someone more deserving, and that's the way it always seems to be. I could be in here until the sun goes out."

"Is that so bad?"

"I can experience all the virtual worlds imaginable, but one thing I can never do is forget that none of it is real. It's a kind of hell."

"Will you tell me about your crime?" Bryonik asked.

"No," said Pendle, stepping to the window and gazing down. "Why don't you tell me what you want with me. You're not a student, you're ECS down to the virtual chainglass shiv in your virtual boot."

"Again, it's probably somewhere you've been before. Your memplant was loaded to main storage before we discovered you had sabotaged five Golem minds. Your history being non-technical and all your employment the same, it took a while to establish that you designed a program capable of all that it did. Luckily, we recovered the five before they killed anyone. The idea of five Golem Twenty-four schizoid psychopaths wandering around the Polity gets people in a cold sweat even now."

"Good enough summation—though I'd dispute 'psychopath.' *Sociopath* is probably nearer the mark."

Agent Bryonik held out his hand and an old mem-crystal storage box appeared in it. "The deal brokered for you was that you told us everything. That's how you escaped direct mind-to-mind AI interrogation."

Pendle grinned nastily. "It's how the AIs avoided it too. Knowing I'd designed that program, none of them really wanted to get inside my head—might have been dangerous for them. Even now, I'm in isolated storage. At least other souls-in-waiting get a social life."

"You lied, Pendle." Bryonik opened the box to reveal the eight empty compartments inside.

Pendle eyed the box. "I told you people back then: three crystals were destroyed in the process."

"The prototype Golem Twenty-five . . . You were at that launch for more than the free drinks and a chance of throwing elephant shit at Corp execs. We know that now."

"I was nothing to do with the attack."

Bryonik was sure he could see a touch of panic in Pendle's expression—understandable. If Pendle was found to have been involved in that act of terror, in which eighteen people had died unrecoverably, no deal could prevent him from being utterly erased.

"The Golem was seen on the out-Polity planet Huma—the location, for the last twenty years, of a lot of illegal arms trading. Was the idea to break the Golem for Separatist reprogramming? This is something that has occurred since then." Bryonik could now see that Pendle really *was* scared. He might call his confinement in VR storage hell, but it seemed he preferred it to death.

"Look, I wasn't connected to the Separatist cause at all."

"As far as we could work out, you never had any training in designing sanity-smashing programs for AI."

"Okay, I admit it, I fucked up their prototype, but do you think, if I'd anything to do with the Separatists, I'd have been there to get nerve-gassed too?"

Bryonik decided to let Pendle sweat a little more, even though the man possessed neither pores nor skin. "Seems a good cover to me. And it's surprising that you were memplanted. Not many there were—it was new technology then, and not wholly trusted." Bryonik shrugged. "All you sacrificed was your body."

"Honestly, agent, the program I loaded would not have broken the Golem to a reprogramming level. It would have been schizoid and maybe a touch sociopathic, and would have just become more difficult for them to handle. I never intended to make *killers*! You have to understand that innate Golem intelligence would have prevented any Golem, just for their self-preservation, from taking that path."

Bryonik raised a hand. "Okay, calm down. We know you weren't in with the Jovians. We just wanted you to admit you screwed with that particular Golem."

"Good." Pendle nodded to himself. "Good . . . You say it was on Huma?"

"Yes, there, as far as we can gather, it received what is called by those in the know as an in-Kline. A memcording of the killer Serban Kline is looped into a Golem's mind until there's not a great deal left. Reprogrammed and remotely controlled, it makes a handy killing machine, though not a particularly efficient one. Mostly captured Golem are mind-cored and the chassis used as a telefactor."

Bryonik then noted Pendle's puzzled expression. "What is it?" he asked.

"It wouldn't . . . The Golem."

"Wouldn't what?"

"It would use *my* program . . . the schizophrenia. Multiple personalities locked into a whole." Pendle looked thoughtful for a moment, then suddenly worried. "I can't be blamed for this!"

"For what?" Bryonik asked dangerously.

"For what it would have become."

"Pendle . . ."

It was some time before Bryonik got Pendle to explain. "It could be all of them: Serban Kline, Polity Golem, Separatist slave. It could be a most efficient and ruthless killer . . . immoral and amoral . . . and also utterly moral. I don't know if it could be controlled."

"Dangerous then?"

White-faced, Pendle laughed weakly. "Oh yes, definitely that."

—retroact ends—

Thorn felt a fierce delight as he watched the shuttle descend, a feeling reflected in Gant's expression, even though his friend's features were artificial. Yes, Thorn had definitely been very much interested in Lellan, the rebel leader—she was some woman—and had pursued that interest to a conclusion he and she found agreeable. But as the months dragged on, his discontent grew. He had been Sparkind—one of the elite soldiers employed by Earth Central Security—for most of his life and an ECS agent for the last few years, so was not the sort to sit on his hands at the bottom of a gravity well while things were happening out there. He wanted to be at the sharp end, no matter if it left him bloody.

Drifting down on AG, correcting only occasionally with the fire-blades of thruster motors, the delta-wing shuttle settled on already crushed-down flute grass at the edge of the dracoman town. The air disturbance elicited odd whistlings from some still-standing grass that was beginning to lose its side-shoots and thus take on the properties of the musical instrument after which the first Masadan colonists had named it. Dracomen of both sexes were now coming out of their dwellings to see what all the commotion was about. Mika, Thorn guessed, was probably still sound asleep after the hours of work she had put in on Apis, and Eldene still remained at her lover's side.

"Well, let's go greet the boss," said Gant, heading towards the shuttle.

Following him, Thorn reached into his pocket and took out an item he had been saving for just this moment. He studied the circular wrist holster with its inset console and was unsurprised to see that it indicated some activity from the contained micromind. But then Shuriken, Cormac's lethal little weapon, did have some strange bond with its master.

The airlock opened and Cormac jumped out, a slight shimmer over his face evidence that he was wearing Polity breather gear. As the agent came over, Thorn noticed other ships descending.

"I'm not being told much," said Gant, also looking skyward.

"Well," said Cormac, "ECS will be establishing a facility down here, but we won't be here to see it."

"What fish are we frying then?" asked Thorn.

"Curious expression, but perhaps apposite." Cormac told them who the fish was.

"He survived it. The bastard," said Thorn.

Cormac nodded. "We go after him. I want you two with me. I also want Mika, for her expertise. You're prepared to come?"

"Damned right I am," said Thorn.

Cormac nodded. "The alternative is that you stay here under observation to make sure that mycelium inside you doesn't pose a danger."

"A danger has already been revealed," Gant said, "though not one to others."

But Cormac wasn't paying attention. Thorn was holding out the Shuriken holster. Cormac took it and in one swift movement strapped it on his wrist. He grinned, then abruptly turned to Gant. "What danger?"

Gant showed him.

A low muttering vibration transmitted up through the soles of his boots, and Anderson wondered just how safe this place was, ever since the quakes began. No doubt, many would be glad to see it fall, as many blamed the quakes on the increased mining engendered by metallier expansion. Looking round, Anderson also wondered if people lived like this on old Earth, or out there amid the stars. He took in the crowds, the tall metal pillars supporting oblate houses of anodized metal and glass, the numerous walkways and floors all supported by webworks of steel trusses. He guessed not, for the purpose of suspending dwellings like this was to keep out some of the less welcome sand-crawling denizens of Cull, and by night these people would be safely sealed up in their homes.

"And what did this Lafrosten see?" Tergal asked him from the other side of the cafe table.

Still studying his surroundings, noting dust being shaken down from high surfaces, Anderson continued his tale: "Lafrosten saw a moon descend upon the Plains, but when he journeyed there he found no sign of it. Wounded by sleer, then deserted by the gully traders he had promised a fortune, for he was sure that rare metal ores would be found at the point of impact, he struggled on foot across the Plains. In the wilderness, a dragon came out of the ground and spoke to him. It said, 'Come no further, this is now my realm and no man may walk here.' Lafrosten returned to the city of the metalliers, but none here believed his story. He told it then in all the towns from Bravence to the mountains of Rondure where, as a boy, I heard it. When the time of my trial as a Knight of Rondure came, I chose to retrace his journey and slay the dragon."

Anderson turned to observe a long vehicle, segmented like a louse, labouring up the street, its vibration adding to that of the quake. Mostly the vehicles here were personal transports, like the one in which Laforge had brought them here, and he wondered at the purpose of this one. He then transferred his gaze further down the street and up to where, through the industrial fug and dust, the Overcity rested on the Sand Towers like some fairy castle, but with tangles of suspended roads leading to it. How big a quake would it take to bring that down?

Tergal regarded Anderson over the rim of his glass of lichen beer. "Why do you want to kill a dragon?"

Anderson returned his attention to the boy, then glanced aside at the boxes containing his own recent purchases. "Call it the impetuousness of youth." Anderson rubbed at the scars either side of his top lip where his lip tendrils had been removed. He grimaced, remembering the pain of the manhood ceremony and the joyful arrogance that came after. "In many of the ancient stories that's what you do to dragons, slay them, though in many others they are companions and friends of man. It was the course I chose and, having chosen it, must pursue it, as that is the nature of the trial. Twenty years of travelling have changed my attitude somewhat."

"It doesn't take twenty years by sand hog to get from Rondure to here," Tergal observed.

"No, let's say my journey has been rather convoluted and interesting, and I've learned a lot."

"But you still intend to slay the dragon?"

Anderson grimaced in irritation. "I'm too close now to turn aside. I'll provide myself with the means of dragon slaying, and I will find the dragon. I rather suspect that what happens then depends on what the dragon itself does. Again, it is the nature of the trial—the journey being more important than arrival. But tell me, Tergal, what about *your* journey?"

Tergal sipped his beer, then gestured airily towards the window. "I'm a gully trader by birth. We don't need any 'trial' to set us travelling."

"Yes, but normally in caravans, not alone. Anyway, you said your stepfather was a minerallier," Anderson observed.

"My birth father was sucked down into a sand maelstrom, and my mother then hooked herself to a man I had no liking for. I took Stone, my sand hog, and left to go take a look at the world. My journey has been aimless, but I wonder how much more so than yours."

Anderson nodded, then picked up a roasted rock louse, broke it open, pulled out the thumb of flesh it contained, ate it. He eyed the ripples in his shot glass of quavit, before picking it up and taking a sip. "True, this has been a journey I've not wanted to end—but I don't consider the acquisition of knowledge to be aimless."

Just then, something crashed down amid the buildings on the other side of the street. Anderson noted that many citizens were now picking up their pace and looking about themselves nervously. But it seemed the quake had reached its peak, for it now began to tail off.

"So why are you going to end your journey?" Tergal asked—pretending negligent unconcern about the vibrating ground, Anderson thought.

"I don't think I will, really. I'll travel through the Sand Towers up onto the Plains and find my dragon, then I'll probably just carry on. I guess the reason I'm going is that I've seen all I feel inclined to see this side of the Towers."

"What about money?" Tergal asked.

Anderson did not feel inclined to answer that. Being kind, he could suppose the boy was discomforted by the fact that Anderson had paid for their room, for the hog corral, and now for this food and drink. But, being himself, he also felt sure the boy was in the process of deciding whether or not Anderson was worth the risk of robbing. He'd made no move so far—Anderson had been watching—but then perhaps he was a meticulous and careful thief.

"I suspect I won't be requiring much money until I reach the other side of the Plains. There's not many people live between here and there," the knight replied.

"But you'll be needing supplies."

"Yes."

"Then so will I."

Anderson watched as the boy picked up the small rucksack he had brought along in Laforge's small diesel car, and opened it on the table to reveal some fine lumps of yellow jade. He felt a sudden tiredness at this intimation of Tergal's past, combined with a hope for the boy's future. That he intended to use his ill-gotten gains to obtain supplies perhaps meant he did not intend to rob Anderson, at least yet.

"You think I'll find a buyer for this here?" Tergal asked.

"I should think so. You intend to accompany me then?"

Tergal replied, "I've seen a maelstrom and a singing tornado, and I once saw the Inconstant Sea fleeing between dunes. But I have never seen a dragon."

Was that it? Was the boy now attracted to a different and less criminal adventure? Anderson hoped so but, knowing human nature so well, he did not have much faith in redemption. As Tergal stood, Anderson returned his attention to his surroundings, and then, as the boy moved away, turned his mind to other thoughts.

The quake had ceased, and as always Anderson wondered what was causing them. He had read about earthquakes in the library of Rondure, just as he had read about so many other things that for many years had no bearing on the people of Cull. Here, on this old world, the radioactives cycled up from the planet's core were all but spent, and as the magma cooled, the crust just grew steadily thicker. Plate tectonics were nonexistent—the crust was one big plate. There should be no earthquakes.

There was little sign of the drastic procedure Gant had described, but then, as Cormac knew from personal experience, it was possible to cell-weld the most severe injuries so that no visible sign remained. Apis lay flat on the surgical table with thin optic wires leading to probes in his body, and the various tubes connecting him to the area of the autodoc Cormac recognized as containing its filtration equipment. Eldene glanced up from the chair she had sprawled in beside the supine Outlinker, before returning her attention to her lover. She looked tired—worn out by worry.

"So you're back," was all she said.

"What is Mika's prognosis for him?" Cormac asked. At her puzzled expression he added, "Does she say he'll recover?"

"She doesn't know. She said broken and dying filaments inside him will perpetually poison him, while others still alive may start to grow out of control," Eldene replied, then looked past him as the door behind opened.

Cormac looked round and studied Mika as she entered the room: tired, obviously, and perhaps a little guilty. She gazed at Apis, then turned her attention to Cormac.

"The quarantine is over," she suggested.

"Not entirely. First all the Jain technology here must be secured and made safe."

"All Jain technology," Mika stated, again trying not to make it a question.

Cormac nodded towards Apis and Eldene. "These two will have to stay under observation here in a Polity base.

You and Thorn will also remain under observation while you accompany me."

Eldene abruptly stood up. "Apis cannot be moved."

"He won't be moved, not until it is safe to do so," Cormac replied.

Eldene looked at Mika, seeking some kind of support, some reassurance from her.

Mika said, "There will be doctors and surgeons coming here with abilities equal to if not in excess of my own, and with more ... more Polity technology to employ. I am primarily a research scientist. He will do better with them."

This seemed to satisfy Eldene and she just as abruptly sat down again.

Cormac again studied Mika's expression. "What went wrong?"

Mika rubbed at her face. "In the days when we couldn't correct them, faults in DNA led to cancers. The chemical machinery of the mycelia I made is not DNA, but is just as complex."

"Faults?" Cormac raised an eyebrow.

"There's something you must see," said Mika, gesturing for Cormac to follow her. When Gant and Thorn also moved to follow, she held up her hand. "This is for the agent only."

The two seemed set to object, but with a look Cormac stilled any protest. He then leavened this by leaning in close to them and whispering, "Get your stuff ready—we ship out as soon as possible."

Mika led him out of the surgical facility and into a room kitted out much like a research laboratory aboard a spaceship. Once Cormac closed the door, she indicated a cylindrical chainglass tank standing on one of the counters.

"That's what I took out of him," she said.

Cormac studied the tank's contents. The mycelium was moving slowly and in some places had etched marks into the tough chainglass. He noted the woody, fibrous structure of the thing, and the nodal growths within it.

"Interesting, but what is it you want to tell me?"

"It is difficult to admit to error, sometimes."

Cormac instantly understood why she had not wanted the others present, and he waited for her confession.

She continued, "The mycelia I made, or rather transcribed, must have been faulty, though I've yet to discover what that fault is. Certainly it is some kind of copying error in its contained blueprint—its DNA, if you like." She gestured at the writhing mycelium. "These are becoming cancerous. I can only surmise that the nodes you see there are tumours."

"You said the mycelia you *made*?"

She nodded. "Probably this is not the case in the original, and the four I made are all exactly the same."

"So what happened to Apis, will happen to Eldene, Thorn and yourself?"

"Yes, it's happening now."

Cormac considered her guilt. "Apis would have been dead by now without it, as would you after being shot by that Theocracy soldier."

"But Thorn and Eldene . . ."

Cormac grimaced. "You made a mistake, Mika." He thought about *Elysium* and the deaths he himself had indirectly caused there. "But in your time you have saved more lives than you have taken—that's the best any of us can hope for."

"But I still made a mistake," Mika said woodenly.

5

Artefacts (pt 16): The three ancient races, the Atheter, Jain and the Csorians, are named after, respectively: a kind of ceramic blade; the daughter of Alexion Smith (she was the first to discover a Jain artefact); and an archaeologist sneezing as he named his new discovery (though that's probably apocryphal). The Jain breathed their last over five million years ago (supposing they breathed at all); for the Csorians it was maybe a million; and the jury is still out on the Atheter, as some artefacts apparently attributable to them have been dated at both three million years and half a million years. Huge efforts are being made to find anything left by these races. There are whole industries involved in the search. Rumour abounds, some of it quite ridiculous: is it true that a fossilized Csorian has been found; that a Jain was found in stasis, floating in space, revived and then killed; what about this evidence that they actually altered the shape of star systems; is it true that ancient and lethal technologies have been tested on condemned prisoners on deserted worlds? The subject of these three, in massive virtualities both fictional and scientific, takes up an appreciable percentage of Polity processing space. Mere written scientific dissertations and fictions amount to trillions of words. Quite a furore really, considering the physical evidence for their existence would not fill even the smallest room in the British Museum.

—From Quince Guide *compiled by humans*

Out of necessity, Mr. Crane wore a protective suit. The blasts of searing gas from the many volcanic vents, as well as the spills of glowing magma across the hellish landscape, were bad enough and would eventually have melted his brass outer covering despite its inlaid s-con grid, but there was also the acidic atmosphere that might have etched away that covering first. Skellor also wore a suit, but one he had extruded from inside himself. As the two of them trudged towards the wedge-shaped survey ship perched on the glowing ridge ahead, Skellor wondered if he was foolishly wasting time with this side jaunt—and if that sense of aesthetic correctness might prove his downfall.

Skellor knew that though he possessed huge abilities to interact with and alter his environment, this was simply like possessing hands and eyes—for being able to use them did not necessarily mean you knew precisely how they operated. And though he could acquire information, knowledge, skills, he did not possess enough of them to take overt actions while ensuring sufficient personal safety. Some proof of this was how Cormac's simple ruse had lured him to *Elysium*, to within range of the sun mirrors. Then, Skellor's lack of knowledge and his subsequent actions, which he equated to those of an impulsive adolescent, had nearly been fatal to him. Admittedly, it would have been difficult for him to know about Cormac's previous dealings with Dreyden, the erstwhile ruler of *Elysium*, but thus putting himself within range of weapons capable of obliterating him had been stupid. He remembered, almost with a wince, the pain he had suffered while his Jain substructure in the *Occam Razor* burned. *Someone would pay for that.*

Drawing closer to the ship, Skellor saw two people clad in reflective hotsuits heading down towards the plain of ash. It amused him that there were four people here searching for Jain artefacts. They would be very surprised, and very chagrined, when living Jain technology found *them*. Skellor pondered that irony.

Though that was not his purpose here, he needed information about what he carried inside him—the Jain technology that was mutating in a way somehow hidden from him—and that information was not something he could acquire from the Polity. However, one brief exchange between Cormac and Dragon—absorbed as part of his memory from recordings inside the *Occam Razor*—had told him where to obtain such information. Dragon knew about Jain technology, and somewhere—probably on the perimeter of human space—two Dragon spheres still lurked. But how to find them? As he and Crane began to climb the slope, Skellor reviewed what he thus far knew about Dragon.

The creature in its initial form of four conjoined spheres had been a probe, a data-gatherer sent by the Makers—a race of energy-based life forms located out in one of the Magellanic clouds. But it malfunctioned and started interacting with humanity, setting itself up as some sort of demigod on the planet Aster Colora. Upon delivering some obscure judgement, it had then apparently destroyed itself. But, as far as Skellor could work out, it had actually separated itself into four entities to surround and attack the Maker ship sent to retrieve or destroy it. The drastic events at Samarkand had then proceeded from there: one sphere destroyed by Cormac in the process. Events at Masada had since accounted for another sphere. From both farragos, Skellor could see that these entities liked to meddle in human affairs. Dragon now even had its own corporation operating in the Polity, and its own networks of humans coming under its control via the Dracocorp biotech augs. How these networks connected back to their controlling Dragon spheres was the only firm lead he had and, with this small piece of business out of the way, would be the one for him to pursue. But now . . . now it was time to look inside the survey vessel.

There was no special code to operate the outside door, just a simple inset handle easy to operate for someone in a hotsuit. Skellor had already observed the carrier shell in orbit above, and with an earlier probe he had discovered that neither the shell nor this survey vessel it had transported here were run by AI; therefore such a simple door mechanism confirmed for him that both shell and vessel were old and privately owned. He pulled the handle up and, as the door swung open, he waved Crane ahead of him. The Golem almost had to crouch to fit himself inside the airlock. Skellor followed, pushing up close to Crane and pulling the outer door closed. In a minute, the lock had filled with cooled air and the safeties preventing him opening the inner door cut out. Crane was the first to duck inside.

"What have you forgotten now?" asked someone, from further inside the ship.

Crane stood with his head bowed so as not to bang it against the ceiling. Skellor looked around. Here was the initial decontamination and rough-cleaning area, and there were no artefacts in the isolation tank. But, then, this four-man research team had not been here very long—Skellor had followed them out only a day after their departure. This team, he had learnt, consisted of three humans and one Golem. A woman, easily identifiable as not being the Golem, ducked through into the cabin, and froze.

"Who the fuck are you?" she managed.

"Have you found anything yet?"

"Fuck off!"

"Unforgivable rudeness," said Skellor, placing his hand against the control panel for the airlock. From the Jain sub-structure inside him, he sent filaments searching, connecting and overriding the safety system. He pointed to the open airlock. "Mr. Crane, put her in there."

The woman had time only to let out a yelp and duck back a little way before Crane's hand closed on her shoulder. She struggled and began screaming, and just then one of the men ducked through from the other direction, holding level a small gas-system pulse-gun.

"Tell that thing to put her down," he demanded.

Skellor just turned and walked towards the man. Three shots slammed into his chest, opening smoking holes and flinging pieces of his Jain carapace across the deck. Reaching the man, he slapped the weapon away, grabbed him by the jacket, and almost negligently tossed him towards Crane, who caught hold of him in his other big hand.

"Well, our friend must be one of the other two, so let's go back outside," said Skellor.

The woman carried on screaming and fighting; the man tried reasoning, but he too soon started to scream once the outer lock was open. Skellor was surprised at the tenacity with which a person could hang on to life. Even with smoke pouring from their clothing, their skin melting and slewing away and contrails of flame whipping up and about their bodies, the two still tried to fight their way past Crane and back into the ship, which was filling with the same searing acidic air anyway.

"Hey ho," said Skellor, as the two finally died and the heat began to blacken and contort them into ebony foetuses. "Let's go find the others."

—retroact 6—

"'Mission objective achieved' is all I'm getting," said Angelina, her fingers pressed against the bean-shaped aug behind her right ear.

"What about visual? Aural?" John Stanton asked.

"Nothing." Angelina shook her head. "It won't tell me anything more. It's almost as if it's shut down. We know where it will be anyway, so no problem there." Now turning to face Semper and Stanton, she said, "I'll want you first to check that Stalek and that idiot Falco are both dead." And with that she waved the two men ahead of her.

Stanton closed his mouth on any further comments and tried to restrain his cynicism about this whole little outing. He drew his heavy pulse-gun from its insulated holster in his hotsuit. From his belt he detached a small adhesive mine and held it in his left hand. He was just as unenamoured with the idea of using a subverted Golem as were many others in the Pelters' organization. Facing forwards, he and Semper now advanced.

Stalek had built his house on the equatorial belt of Huma, so it necessarily possessed a ceramic shell and thick, heavily insulated walls. At present that insulation only served the purpose of maintaining a comfortable internal temperature against the constant fifty degrees outside, since the resinous incendiary briar that constituted most of the surrounding jungle had yet to achieve ripeness. In the distance, Stanton noted a column of smoke from where one patch of briar had reached that point in its growth where the sparks from its exploding seedpods ignited it. It was early, though. Later in the season, this entire continent would become an inferno: the briars burning down to provide plenteous ash in which the seeds could lie ready to germinate in the ensuing sooty rainstorms.

Semper studied the door's palm lock, then let out a bark of laughter. He took a crowbar from his belt, jammed it under the lock, and levered the plate and attached console from the wall.

"Is that a good idea?" Stanton asked.

"It's a dummy," Semper explained. "Understandable really: he has to be able to get in and out wearing a hot-suit, so he can't use something that operates by his palm print and DNA coding. Merely a simple input code."

Taking a small console from his belt he unwound two optic cables terminating in interface clamps, which he now closed on two optic cables trailing from the back of the lock and into the wall. Then he simply waited while the device he still held did the job of safe-breaker for him. The seals on the circular door eventually whoomphed, and it hinged outwards to reveal an airlock and an inner door. Semper stared inside for a long moment, before turning to Stanton.

"Now this I don't like," he said. He stooped and picked up one of the many pieces of briar charcoal that were scattered on the ground, then tossed it into the lock. The thing that immediately dropped from the ceiling onto the charcoal was a wolf spider half a metre long—only it was a spider with metal bracings and hydraulic pistons augmenting its legs, and a more complicated arrangement of gleaming motors augmenting its obsidian fangs.

"Jesus!" Semper bellowed.

Stanton's pulse-gun sputtered white light, hitting the creature mid-air as it leapt out at them. It slammed back against the jamb, hit the ground and, smoking, made to leap again at Semper. Angelina drew her own weapon and fired, complementing the shots Stanton was again putting into the creature. Twice more it leapt and their shots slammed it back. It only gave up when its organic body was reduced to a charcoal remnant inside its cyber-bracing skeleton.

"Okay, Semper, the door," ordered Angelina.

Stanton kept his weapon pointed at the cyborg spider as it slowly curled up its legs like a fist. Semper took rather longer over the true palm lock operating the second door, but soon they were stepping into the brightness of Stalek's home.

"Stanton, find his house system and neutralize it," Angelina instructed, herself making no move to go further into this strange home.

The big man moved on, rounding furniture seemingly fashioned from the carapaces of huge crustaceans, while keeping an eye on the large plants contained in pots scattered throughout the room—plants whose beautifully coloured giant daffodil heads turned to track his progress. Reaching the further wall, he studied something set into it that looked more like a work of weird art than any technology, then stepped back raising his weapon and blasted it, his shots punching molten holes through the gleaming metalwork and oddly shaped touch panels and screens. The bright lights flickered briefly as they dropped from the control of a house AI to some backup safety system. Turning, Stanton fired twice at a plant lowering its lime-green and purple striped head towards him, severing its stalk. As the head dropped to the ground, it protruded a red tongue coated with small metal hooks.

"About as safe as we're gonna get," he observed.

Angelina pointed to a wooden door to Stanton's right. "We go there—up to the attic. That's where Stalek did his work."

She followed, giving the plants a wide berth but staying well back so he and Semper would encounter first anything nasty, Stanton noted, as he operated the simple latch and opened the door. The stairs winding up into the attic were lit by biolights—yet another sign of Stalek's attraction towards exotic technologies. Stanton eyed the spidery creatures with their glowing sugar-bag bodies, then glanced back at Angelina.

"Why the hit on him?" he asked abruptly. "Seems to me he was providing you with some useful toys."

"Not really your concern," Angelina replied. "But he was becoming increasingly unstable, and some of his work was of questionable . . . quality."

"So you have this lunatic subvert a Golem Twenty-five android for you?"

"Just get up the stairs, mercenary," Angelina spat.

Stanton nodded to himself and began to climb, thinking how Angelina and her brother Arian were not the best people to make judgements on the stability of others. However, Stanton was not about to push his luck too far—the money of these terrorist rich kids was still good.

From the topmost landing, four wooden doors led off into different rooms, but Angelina, coming up closer behind Semper and Stanton, pointed to the one directly ahead. "The rest also contain various workshops, but he uses *that* one for any final assembly."

Adhesive mine still to hand, Stanton nodded to Semper, who shoved open the door in front of him. Stanton stepped into the room and then slid to one side, crouching down, pulse-gun aimed and adhesive mine held palm outwards in readiness. Semper did the same, moving to the other side of the door. Stanton noted that the man was just as trusting as himself: as well as brandishing a pulse-gun, he held a small EM grenade.

No action. Stanton slowly stood upright and surveyed the room.

Stalek's and Falco's bodies were not visible, but Stanton tracked the trails of blood over to the Cleanviro booth, and guessed where they might be.

"Find the fucking control module," said Angelina, obviously shaken by what she was seeing.

Stanton left Semper to go over to where wrecked computers and other equipment had been stacked in a corner of the room. Himself, he did not intend to turn his back on the room's other occupant. The Golem had pulled a chair up in front of a table. It wore a long coat and a wide-brimmed hat. Before it on the table, several objects were laid out as if it was involved in some intricate game of chess with an unseen opponent. Those objects consisted of various tools and pieces of hardware, a small rubber dog and two other gruesome items. While Stanton watched, the Golem reached out one brass hand, clad in a blood-crusted fingerless woollen glove, and carefully turned the head of the aviapt so that it faced Stalek's head. It then looked up and gazed at Stanton with midnight eyes.

"Found it." Semper came over and handed a small console to Angelina.

The woman's hand was shaking, Stanton noted, as she took the console and detached from it the small black pebble of a control module. She closed her eyes for a second, concentrating, then slipped the module into one of her belt pouches.

"Stand up . . . Mr. Crane," she said finally.

The Golem stood and stepped aside, as if ready to come around the table. Stanton took a step back. Jesus, the thing was big! Standing there, it seemed to fill the entire room. Stanton estimated it to be at least two and a half metres tall.

"Hold it there!" Angelina yelled.

The Golem froze.

"You will follow us, doing no more than I instruct," she said, with enforced calm in her voice. She turned to Stanton. "Put that mine of yours on its chest, over its brain case."

Stanton was not so sure he wanted to get that close, but he obeyed. As he stepped in, the Golem abruptly reached up and undid the top buttons on its coat, exposing its brassy chest. Stanton placed the mine carefully, hoping that hand movement had been at Angelina's behest. The Golem buttoned up its coat again.

"Okay, let's go," she said.

The Golem reached down and closed its hand over one of the severed heads.

"Leave that!"

The hand closed and the head imploded with a dull thud, spewing bloody gobbets of brain across the table-top.

"Follow!"

As Angelina turned away, Stanton saw the Golem's hand snap out and take up the small rubber dog, which it slipped quickly into its pocket. He made no comment on this, nor when the Golem turned its face towards him and half closed one eye in what might have been a wink. With Semper at his side, he just followed the killing machine out, glad that the thing was walking at Angelina's back rather than his own.

—retroact ends—

"A message in a bottle would be the nearest analogy."

Cormac chewed over the words as they crossed the now empty chamber to the Flint runcible. Before reaching the dais, he halted and glanced round at his companions. Gant stood beside Mika, as if ready to prevent her escape. Perhaps that was because it had taken so long to get her moving. The result of this delay was now stacked on a gravsled that Thorn guided by a remote-control device: the woman's luggage.

The Flint AI had already emptied the place, and Cormac knew that it was training just about every detector available on his companions. It had shut down all computer access other than the voice link to itself, and there were no robots present—nothing that Jain technology could subvert.

"But there's no record of the *Vulture* having landed there?" he suggested.

"No *record* of that ship's presence, true," replied the Flint AI. "But three ships *did* land that could easily have been the *Vulture*. Also, Viridian did detect a U-space signature unrelated to any ships that landed in the designated areas. The most likely explanation is that Skellor has installed chameleonware on the *Vulture*, and brought it down somewhere else."

"And the essence of the message?"

"*Vulture* is managing to retain some independence by shifting her*self* into a memory sector not occupied by a Jain thrall program. Each time she does this and initiates some independent action, the program occupies that sector, forcing Vulture to move on. Obviously there is a limit to how many times she can do this. She also detailed the events on the asteroid—which we had already surmised."

"Is there anything to suggest where Skellor is going?"

"All she knew was that he went to Viridian to obtain a 'pathetic metalskin' to 'complete.' These are Vulture's words, though I gather the information was obtained by translating Jain code bleeding directly from Skellor's nonverbal thought processes."

Cormac was surprised. He had expected the pursuit to be a ship-borne one rather than one through the Polity runcible network, because if it was true that Skellor was after the Dragon spheres, he'd more likely find them on the Polity border or beyond.

"You can get hold of metalskins anywhere in the Polity," said Gant.

"Viridian seems an unlikely place to go looking for one," Thorn added.

Cormac looked at Mika, waiting for her opinion. She appeared ill to him, but perhaps that was imagination after all that she had told him.

In measured tones she said, "Viridian is where we encountered the Maker. It is also where you killed Arian Pelter. There was a metalskin Golem there with Pelter—that brass killer of his called Mr. Crane."

"That's true," said Thorn, "but Cento and Aiden seriously fucked up that one."

Cormac glanced at him. "You're right, they tore it apart and then shattered its mind. There should be nothing there for Skellor. However . . ." He turned and looked towards the runcible. "Flint, I need you to reset to Viridian. I have to go there to find out what this is all about."

"Unfortunately I cannot do this until after your companions have departed. They must go to *Elysium*, where precautions have been taken, and then on to the *Jack Ketch*."

It made sense: Mika or Thorn could rush at the interface,

once it was reset, and end up on a world where no precautions had yet been made against Jain-tech subversion. Earth Central was now taking precautions over anyone who had merely come in contact with that tech, but those two, who definitely carried it inside them, the AI was treating like possible plague carriers.

"Okay." Cormac turned to his companions. "Mika, once you're on the *Jack Ketch*, get aboard what you require—it can be sent by robotic craft from the *Jerusalem*. Make sure you get *everything*, as we'll likely be in for a long haul afterwards, without further physical contact with any Polity worlds."

She nodded thoughtfully. "The *Jerusalem*?"

"It's there at *Elysium*, grabbing anything Jain-related—I'll explain later." He turned to Thorn, who also, he thought, looked unwell. "Thorn, no fuck-ups during transit, as I'll bet that any breach of the precautions will result in atomic sterilization."

Thorn nodded.

"Flint, is there any restriction on trooper Gant?"

"None that I am aware of. Like yourself he has been scanned and found to contain nothing . . . anomalous."

"Okay. Gant, you'll come with me."

Cormac stepped to one side and waved the others ahead of him. Gant moved to his side and watched them go. Mika glanced round, still looking thoughtful, then stepped up onto the dais and approached the shimmer of the Skaidon warp contained between the bull's horns of the runcible. She stepped through it and was gone. Thorn then guided the gravsled ahead of him, causing it to rise higher and positioning it centrally to the warp. Before sending it through, he gave Gant a meaningful look.

"I'll get Mika to memplant me on the *Jack Ketch*, but I don't suppose we'll be celebrating in *Elysium*," he said.

"If she thinks it advisable," Gant replied woodenly. "But it might be better to wait until your mycelium is removed."

Thorn nodded, and himself stepped through.

After a pause Cormac asked the runcible AI, "Are you reset?"

"Destination Viridian now open," it replied.

Stepping onto the dais, Cormac asked Gant, "What was all that about?"

They approached the shimmering wall of energy, its light playfully batting their shadows about behind them.

"Feeling his mortality," Gant replied.

"That's a first." Cormac stepped through.

The ash was five hundred metres thick in places, accumulated on this volcanically active planet's single small tectonic plate, which slid around its surface like an ancient stone ship. There were no artefacts preserved in the ash, nor in the underlying stone, rather the artefact was the cause of both, requiring nothing to preserve it even here. Having resilience greater than any other material on the planet, it had neither melted nor broken, and the stone had accreted around it and the ash built up on top of it over the aeons.

Cento considered how, for many years, researchers had come to study what they considered a natural phenomenon: a large layer of thermocrystal carbon within this small tectonic plate. Only recently had a scientist noted that the dense structure of this substance, which was similar to diamond, also bore a molecular resemblance to memory crystal. The woman, Shayden, then tried an optic interface, and was astounded by the reams of code feeding back. Some of it looked like genetic data, but most of it was scrambled and as yet indecipherable. Polity AIs were now studying the download from the fragment of crystal Shayden had used, in the hope of determining whether it was memory storage of the Jain or perhaps of some other ancient race. Cento was here for the more prosaic purpose of ensuring that Shayden, who now waited back at her ship with her research assistant Hourne, had not falsified her results.

"We should see the layer further down," said Ulriss.

Cento turned away from peering over the edge of the plate, and glanced to where Ulriss indicated. The dip, further down, would indeed bring them closer to the layer of thermocrystal carbon, just as it would bring them closer to the river of magma boiling through the crevasse beside them.

"Then let's hurry," he said, checking the timepiece set in the wrist of his suit, not because he needed to check the time but because he wanted Ulriss to remain aware of how little of it they had left.

"We should get some out-gassing before it blows." Ulris gestured to the hellish plain beyond the river of molten rock, where a perfectly curved cliff, almost like a hydroelectric dam, occasionally became visible through the pall of smoke. This was just one edge of a massive caldera which, every five hours for the last twenty years, had blown out a few million tonnes of rock—molten and solid—and ash, and a cornucopia of poison gases to contribute to the volatile and lethal atmosphere.

"We will be gone before then, whether I obtain a sample or not," Cento replied.

They trudged on down the slope, eventually reaching the position indicated. Cento unshouldered his bolt gun and looked around. Noting an area clear of ash, he walked over, pressed the device down and triggered it, firing a fixing bolt into stone. Discarding the bolt gun, he then unreeled, by its end-ring, the monofilament line from the abseil motor on his belt. Stooping to click the ring into place on the bolt, he heard Ulriss begin yelling over com.

"What! No! Stop! No!"

Cento stood and whirled to see the poor man suspended off the ground, held there by his biceps in the grip of a hugely tall humanoid, who was walking him back to the crevasse edge. Cento reached down to detach the ring, but suddenly became aware of another humanoid. This one was standing beside him, clad head to foot in some sort of biotech suit. How he had not detected the approach of this one, Cento could only put down to the use of sophisticated chameleonware. In less than a second he had assessed the situation: the likely source of the tech meant these two must be somehow connected with events on the planets Cheyne III and Masada, and therefore with how things would now proceed. Ignoring the smaller individual and leaving the ring attached, he accelerated towards the big one, who was now holding Ulriss out over the white-hot river. That the larger humanoid intended to drop the man, Cento had no doubt. The abseil motor screaming as it wound out monofilament, Cento leapt, just as the figure did drop Ulriss. He should have been able to grab him a couple of metres down from the edge . . . Before he even went over a big hand slammed into his chest and stopped him dead. The big humanoid . . . Golem . . . To move that fast . . .

"Oh God! No! Nooo!"

Cento stabbed his hand towards the big Golem's chest just as he heard Ulriss's gasp of shock as he hit the magma. There would still be time—the man's hotsuit would take a minute to give out. But the second hand clamped around Cento's wrist. The big Golem pulled and turned, easily spinning Cento over and slamming him down on his back. The monofilament was now caught up under Cento's armpit and biting through his suit. Cento tried to turn as the other Golem wrenched him to his feet and the filament cut deeper. He felt the arm disconnect—sheared clean away at the shoulder—then a backhanded blow deposited him at the edge.

"No! Oh fuck nooo!"

Cento rolled over in time to see Ulriss fighting to stay on the surface of the magma, his suit splitting and beginning to belch flame. His final scream truncated as his suit blew away and he burned incandescently. Something black and skeletal skittered like a spider on a hot plate. Briefly, a cloud of black oily smoke occluded the view and when it cleared only the silvery remains of the man's hotsuit floated on the magma.

"Not fast enough, Cento." It was the one in the biotech suit who spoke.

Cento rolled as he came upright, so the mono-filament was no longer twined around his chest. Perhaps he could pull it across the big Golem's legs . . . He glanced at the speaker. "Who are you, and what do you want here?"

"Your arm." The man pointed to the severed limb.

"Why should you want my arm?" said Cento as he moved sideways, dragging the filament across with him.

"Because it's his."

His?

Cento gazed back at the big Golem, noting that his arms were not evenly matched. His own severed arm, lying on the ground still wearing the sleeve of his suit, was a brass-coated metalskin limb—both a replacement and a trophy from a battle fought years ago on a planet called Viridian.

Mr. Crane?

How could this be Mr. Crane? Cento clearly remembered their fight. Crane nearly destroyed him once, and it had needed both himself and his companion Golem Aiden to finish the monster. They tore him apart, destroyed his crystal matrix mind. Yet now the same Golem was back, and it seemed much stronger and faster than before. That made no sense.

Abruptly Cento leapt to one side intending to pull the monofilament across Crane's legs, but the big Golem leaped nimbly and accelerated. Cento braced himself, but Crane outweighed him three to one, and easily knocked him back over the edge. Scrabbling for grip with his remaining three limbs, Cento slid down a slope angled thirty degrees to the vertical. Stone just broke away from his grasp, but when the abseil motor started whining, he managed to reach down and initiate its brake. The line jerked him to a halt only a metre above the magma.

"That was close."

Cento looked up and saw both of them gazing down at him.

"I wonder what happens if I do this?"

Cento fell, hit the slope and slid further down, jamming his hand deep into a crevice to halt that slide. Monofilament fell about him like spindrift. With the spectrum of senses he possessed, he did not need to look down to know that he was up to his thighs in magma. His hotsuit gave out as quickly as Ulriss's, fire and smoke gusting around him as syntheskin and the other combustible components of his legs burnt away. Now glancing down he saw metallic traces mirroring the surface of the molten rock. When the magma flow finally pulled his lower legs away, it was something of a relief, as now it no longer threatened to drag him down. Glancing up again, he saw that this respite would not last. With slow but inexorable care, Mr. Crane was climbing down towards him.

Cento did not highly rate his chances now against the huge Golem. He glanced from side to side hoping to see something, anything that might enable him to survive. To his right, just above where the crystal layer slanted down into the magma, was the open end of a lava tube, just under a metre wide. Maybe he could swing himself in there? Even though he was aware that these tubes usually extended no more than a few metres—bubbles of gas in the cooling magma rather than a flow of it having formed them—this seemed his only option. Perhaps ensconced in such a place he could even defend himself.

On his remaining arm he levered up his now reduced body weight. Glancing down he saw that his legs had separated at the knee joint and that only his bare hip bones protruded from the remains of his suit. The magma had melted the components in his knees, but not the ceramal of his bones. Looking up and seeing that Crane was now only a couple of metres above him, he began to swing himself from side to side to get up enough momentum. He released just as a boot slammed down towards his wrist.

He hit the edge of the lava tube, groped inside it, his hip bones scrabbling away below him like a dwarf's legs; then he was inside and turning himself round—the tube, as expected, being only a metre deep. Shortly, Mr. Crane's head appeared upside-down in the tube mouth, peering in through the visor of his hotsuit. Cento finally admitted to himself that he was dead: there was no escape. The big Golem, with his full complement of limbs and obviously superior strength, would just reach inside and drag him out, probably to send him after Ulriss. Sure enough, the big hand now groped inside like a fat spider, slapped away Cento's defending hand, and closed over his face. There came a long pause, then the hand released him.

What now?

It wasn't possible to read the expression on that brass face. Mr. Crane suddenly reached down to the bottom of the lava tube, to the layer of crystal that formed its floor. He groped to the edge, where the crystal was jagged, and snapped a piece off, which he brought up and held before his visor for inspection. He then closed his hand around it, holding out only one long forefinger, which he brought back to his visor. He placed it vertical to his mouth: *Shush now, be quiet.*

Mr. Crane hauled himself out of view.

While the metallier licked his lips and weighed yellow jade, Tergal studied the display of weapons in the cracked glass case and speculated on what Anderson's reaction might be to learning how he had obtained that precious stone. He realized the knight did not trust him, had been keeping a close eye on him. And well he might. Though the attraction of the knight was that he was everything Tergal wanted to be, as soon as that attraction waned, Tergal would rob him and move on. It was what he did—he was scum.

Tergal had not told Anderson the entire truth. The minerallier Fround had been a hard man yet an honourable one, and Tergal's mother, after birthing the bastard Tergal so young, had been considered spoiled goods, so Fround's offer for her had been more than generous. He had paid for her in the yellow jade, of which only he knew the location. In the months that followed, Tergal's mother, though not loving the man, had come to respect him—and, Tergal knew, would come eventually to that other state too. Tergal now understood that his dislike of Fround had been rooted in jealousy—in having to share the mother who had once been all his own—and that his subsequent behaviour had been contemptible.

Fround's attempts at gaining the boy's friendship had only increased his dislike. Those attempts had included the free use of Stone, one of Fround's three sand hogs; a generosity in money and clothing; and finally sharing the knowledge of the location of the precious jade. In his jealousy, Tergal had only construed that the man had been trying to buy him. Now he recognized Fround's bewilderment at such a reaction: the man had been according Tergal equal status when he might so easily have rejected him. He had only been trying to act like a good father.

Tergal sighed—too late now to put things right. He truly regretted stealing both jade and hog, yet not his departure. In the years that had passed since, thieving or exchanging some of the jade or even working his way across many lands, he had experienced much more than would a parochial minerallier, and now was actually travelling with a Rondure Knight—the kind of man he had once thought only the inflated province of history and myth.

"Getting more frequent now," the metallier said.

Tergal turned to him. "What?"

"The quakes—getting one just about every twenty days."

Tergal nodded, then looked pointedly at the jade. He wasn't going to get carelessly chatty with someone who was undoubtedly preparing to sting him.

"I can give you a thousand pfennigs," said the minerallier eventually, as he began racking his weights.

Tergal turned from the case. "There's seventeen standard ounces of jade there, and the usual market price is between eighty and a hundred pfennigs an ounce. At the lowest rate, that's thirteen hundred and sixty."

The minerallier shrugged. "You would deny me any profit at all?"

"I would deny no man profit, only limit the extent of it." Tergal stabbed a finger down at the glass case. "One thousand one hundred, and *this*, and we have a deal."

The minerallier came out from behind his counter, and walked over to stand beside Tergal. He peered down at the weapon indicated.

"That is worth two hundred and fifty alone, and you will require ammunition. I can let you have two spare clips, a hundred rounds, and nine hundred pfennigs."

"You'll wait until jade is a hundred pfennigs an ounce," Tergal observed.

The man shook his head. "There you are wrong. Observe the grip. I obtain these from Central Manufacturing, then make such fine additions. I would use the jade for the same."

The lapis lazuli grip had been what had first attracted Tergal's attention. He might find a better deal elsewhere, but not this particular handgun.

"Make that a hundred and fifty rounds and you have your deal."

"Very well," said the minerallier, reaching into his pocket to take out a roll of money. Quickly he counted out the notes and handed them over. Tergal counted them again and slipped them into his own pocket, noting just how small a proportion they were of the man's entire roll. From under the case, the metallier removed three heavy paper boxes of ammunition, which he placed on a table nearby. From the case he removed the gun itself and two clips. He handed them to Tergal.

"Are you with the knight?" he asked.

"I am."

The man reached over to where some leather items hung in a jumble behind the display case. Sorting through, he eventually found a plain belt and holster.

"How much?" Tergal asked.

"Gratis," said the man. "If you're with him," he gestured to the sunlit street, "you'll need to get to your weapon fast when he takes on his next commission."

"You think?" Tergal was confused. The roll of money had certainly attracted his attention, and now this unexpected generosity had defused his growing speculation about how he might get his hands on the rest of that roll.

"Oh yes, not much call for them round here now, with most people carrying weapons like this." The man slapped a hand against the weapon holstered at his own hip—perhaps reading some of Tergal's intention. "But elsewhere the work of a knight usually involves sleers and apeks, when it doesn't concern the bounties set on human killers and thieves."

Over the last few days, Tergal had not even stopped to consider that. To him Anderson had been just a figure out of a story, and what with coming into Golgoth and the talk of dragons, that feeling had only increased. But, of course, Anderson must have some way of putting the pfennigs into his pocket, and probably he was well used to dealing with *scum*. It now occurred to Tergal that he would not be telling the knight the full story of his own past—that perhaps he did not even need to.

"Thank you." Tergal took his acquisitions out into the sunshine.

6

Usually initiated by some technological innovation, the colonization of the Human Polity has run in successive waves, with intervals of fifty to a hundred years between them. The first of these innovations was the invention of a very powerful ion drive, which resulted in the colonization of the solar system as far out as Jupiter. The efficient fusion drives coming into use after this resulted in establishing the further-flung colonies in the solar system, and a wave of generation ships making the first leap to the stars (some of these slow-moving behemoths are still in transit). The advent of Skaidon's interfacing with the Craystein Computer created a completely new technology from which, long before the first runcible was built, resulted the first U-space drives. This was a chaotic period in the solar system: governments and corporations competing for power and seemingly unaware that the tools they were using, the AIs, were becoming more powerful than them. It's not known how many colony ships—both the generation kind and ones utilizing U-space engines—escaped while AI fought its "Quiet War" for dominion. We are still finding colonies established during this time, and many speculate that there may be hundreds more yet to locate.

—From Quince Guide *compiled by humans*

Once the ground tremors eased, Cento pushed his head and upper body out of the lava bubble and fruitlessly tried to use his internal radio to contact the survey ship, but there

was just too much stone sitting between him and where that
vessel rested up on the ridge. Further attempts to contact the
orbiting carrier shell also produced no result, but then that
could now be on the other side of the planet. He estimated
that only twelve metres above he would be able to obtain
a sufficient direct line to the landed vessel, but even then
he wondered . . . The layer of crystal below him seemed to
be doing things to the signal that defied analysis. When he
first felt the groping for contact, he dismissed it as part of
this same effect. When the attempt at making a connection
became more insistent, he considered shutting down his
radio, fearing that this might be another attack upon him.
But Mr. Crane had let him live—taking a piece of crystal
rather than Cento's artificial life—so, as far as the other
humanoid was concerned, Cento was long gone in the river
of magma.

He tuned to the groping signal, and made contact.

Who are you? he asked over the link.

Vulture . . . ship . . . Skellor . . . came the reply, along with
corrupted code and a weird whining note like a child crying.

Cento absorbed that last name and immediately knew who
the second humanoid was. Cento had taken much interest
in the events on Masada, and with his ECS clearance he
had obtained the full story. That a copy of himself had died
aboard the *Occam Razor* had greatly focused his interest.
So, somehow, Skellor had escaped, still possessing Jain
technology. This also explained Crane's resurrection and
superior strength and speed: Skellor had obviously made him
something more than a merely boosted Golem Twenty-five.

Skellor's ship? he asked.

Salvor burned now . . . take download . . . going U-space
. . . it coming.

*I'm prepared for the download, but any attempt at subversion
and—*

The download came anyway: jumbled information, hints
of exchanges of information, views of Skellor standing
behind a pilot's chair containing the burnt-out husk of a
human being, Mr. Crane squatting on the floor with objects

arranged in front of him like chessmen. Then, in one brief burst before the signal cut off: coordinates.

Cento knew that information like this was critical, for with the sheer size of the Polity and all the methods of transportation available, ECS might never find Skellor. But how to convey those coordinates to somewhere they might be of use? The Golem surveyed his surroundings and ran diagnostics on himself. Quite apart from the fact that he only had one arm and was trapped in a rock bubble at the bottom of a steep slope, the heat from the nearby river of magma was beginning to affect some of his systems. Already memory storage was becoming dubious, as the crystal matrix of his mind distorted, the motors in his hips had ceased to function, and those in his remaining arm were into amber. His sight was also going. Infrared was unusable in this situation, but he was also losing the other end of the spectrum. His internal radar suffered the same distortions from the crystal lying below as did his radio. Apart from those latter badly distorted two, he in fact only possessed now the senses of a human being. He had to try for the survey ship again, and to do that he had to get himself higher.

Cento reached above him and was thankful that what remained of his hotsuit had preserved the syntheflesh underneath; this at least meant that he retained a sense of touch. Groping about, he found a crevice—which he tested by wrenching hard against its sides to make sure the rock would not break away. He shut off that part of his emulation program that prevented his joints moving more than was *humanly* possible. Planning every move in advance, he reached higher, jammed his hand in, then using the full swing of his shoulder joint, hauled himself out of the bubble like a winkle from its shell. For a second he was suspended over magma, then using his wrist joint and elbow, he pulled himself up to the point where he could lodge the knee end of his right thighbone in the lower part of the crevice and then lay his torso flat against the slope. This he did just in time, as another tremor tumbled loose stone down all about him.

He kept his head down until the cascade had ceased, then looked up. Now he could see that the crevice ran at an angle up the slope and would take him about five metres higher. The problem was that each time he released his hand, he would be supported only by his hipbone and by his weight pressing against the loose stone of the slope. But there was no choice: this close to the magma, the heat would destroy him eventually. He turned and withdrew his hand, reached higher and jammed it in, and maggot-like hauled himself up and up, pausing every time the ground shook, clinging as tightly as he could while falling stone threatened to dislodge him.

Five metres.

Here, Cento noted that some of his systems were coming back online; that the numerous warnings he had been receiving were growing fewer. Glancing down he saw that a curve in the slope now concealed him from the incandescence below, and checking his internal temperature, he saw it was dropping. Abruptly the motors in his hip joints came back on. Here, he realized he might be able to survive for as long as his power supply held out, and even then his mind might remain intact afterwards. Perhaps he should secure himself as best he could, and just drop to minimal function? Cento considered this for only a moment before removing his hand from the crevice and reaching above to clear away loose rock in search of a fresh handhold. Cento was ECS and, though as a free Golem he could choose between duty and survival, he chose duty.

Eventually he located a jut of stone that seemed sufficient to support him, clamped his hand on it and hauled himself up once again, but he could not get himself high enough to lodge his thighbone against that same stone. Lowering himself again, he cleared more rock and found a small hollow just below and to one side of the outcrop. He pulled himself up again, lodging the bone's end in this hollow—easier now that he could actually move his thighbones about—and, from this precarious position, groped higher. Stone skidded as he pushed it aside, banging and clattering past him. Smooth intestinal stone above now; nothing to grip. Another sudden ground tremor bounced his leg bone out of the hollow. He flailed for a grip as he began to fall, his hand sliding over this treacherously smooth stone. Then before him there appeared a crack, leaking sulphurous gas under pressure, then his arm went through, in an explosion of such gas, and he found a safe grip inside another lava bubble.

Cento would have breathed a sigh of relief if he had not turned off his lungs while in the previous bubble. After using his head to break away more of the thin crust, he peered inside and saw that this cavity formed the terminus of a lava tube extending up the slope. Pulling himself inside, he began to inch his way up the smooth interior, using thighbones, head and arm as four limbs. Here he took more risks, as a fall now would only result in him ending up back at the bottom of the tube, not trying to swim in molten rock, and consequently he traversed its twenty-metre curving length in a matter of minutes. Now all he had to do was get out of there.

Wedged on his back, braced by head and thighbones, Cento drove his fist outwards at what he estimated to be an angle of ninety degrees to the slope itself. Stone shattered under this piledriver blow, and fell in on him to reveal a bruised sky into which poured black smoke and fountains of magma. Of course—the eruption about which they had been warned. Early. That figured.

Skellor stepped back and inspected his handiwork. Mr. Crane raised his replacement arm and closed his hand into a fist. Fastidiously he then reached out and took up first his hat then his coat from where he had draped them over a nearby console. Placing the hat on his head, he tilted it to the required angle before donning his coat and with slow precision fastening each button. Why, when given limited freedom to act, the Golem had spent much of the voyage hither using equipment and materials found aboard this ship to fashion such clothing, Skellor could not fathom. But it was part of the weird fascination Mr. Crane held for him.

"Quite the dandy, aren't you," muttered Skellor, discarding the arm replaced down beside Salvar's corpse—both now just organic detritus. Now Skellor smirked as he watched Crane step back, squat down on the floor and pull out his various toys. Joining the rubber dog, the acorns from blue oaks on Viridian, five cubes of survival rations and various other items gathered from inside this same ship, was now a piece of green crystal. Briefly linking inside the Golem, Skellor observed that the crystal and the dog had found their places in the matrix, which drastically increased Crane's chances of putting the rest together in the right order. However, though the odds against him achieving the right combination before had been 3.6×10^{14} to one, they weren't that much better now. Probing inside Crane to see how he had managed to achieve even this reduction of odds, he encountered a resistance that was integral to Crane's entire mind. Skellor could easily have broken it, but in doing so he would lose that essential, fascinating Mr. Crane. He turned away, stepped over the human remains on the floor, and seated himself in the pilot's chair. If Crane ever managed to reduce the odds to, say, the chances of a meteorite striking him on the head, Skellor would take action. But now to the task in hand.

There were two areas of space, two possible destinations—one inside the Polity and one beyond its border. This much he had learnt from the Reverend Epthirieth Loman Dorth before killing the man. The network of Dracocorp augs that had been coming under the man's control at Masada had initially seemed a complete entity. Further probing its structure, Skellor had ascertained it to be a slave cell that, upon reaching maturity (that point where Dorth gained absolute control over the other minds in the network), would link via other networks to an autocratic control. There were two such centres of control, with only vague locations—the two Dragon spheres. Skellor had of course already chosen the one outside Polity space. Even so, that particular area extended a hundred light years across, so locating Dragon inside it would be no easy task.

Skellor considered how he might achieve his ends. Previously, the most likely way of locating Dragon had seemed to be to find a Dracocorp facility and work from there, but his probes into the AI and virtual networks from Viridian had quickly disabused him of this notion. Dragon had foreseen that enemies would follow this trail and so, rather than erase it, had concealed it under a thousand false trails. Gaining information concerning even these had also quickly turned into a risky option when his searching attracted the attention of some seriously dangerous hunter-killer AI programs engaged on the same search. Obviously, ECS also seriously wanted to know Dragon's location. No, he must use a different approach: tracing Dragon through the augs those facilities manufactured, and which were now in use.

The running of Dracocorp was not something Dragon had to remain wholly engaged in, but slow accretion of control through the networks thereby generated required it. To find the link from this distance Skellor needed to infiltrate network after network to follow it home. Better then to find such a network much nearer to that same home—nearer to Dragon. So thinking, Skellor affirmed the coordinates already input, and dropped the *Vulture* into underspace.

—retroact 7—

Alston supposed various factors were interacting in the man's mind: obviously, the longer the interrogation, the longer he would stay alive. However, the longer he delayed answering questions, the greater would be his agony. Alston was therefore beholden to increase the man's agony to that point where, in the hope of a quick death, he would become more forthcoming. Alston always loved the way his victims reacted when, having obtained what he wanted, Alston continued with the torture. There was horror and a kind of indignation at this betrayal of the unspoken contract between torturer and tortured.

"I've been aware for some time that Arian wants me dead. That is hardly news to me, but I want details. When does he plan to launch an attack on my island? How many of his people will he send? What kind of armaments will they be carrying?"

Semper, suspended upside down from the boom at the back of the fishing barge, bubbled something. Alston wondered who had first worked out that suspending someone by their feet increased the blood pressure in their head and thus prevented them from fainting. He again reached out with the wire cutters to where Semper's hands had been nailed to the stern rail, and with one crunching snip sent a little finger bouncing across the deck.

"What was that?"

When he had stopped yelling, Semper articulated more carefully.

"Not . . . sending . . . his men."

Alston passed the wire cutters over to Chaldor—the woman who had been so proficient with the nails and who had earlier burnt out Semper's right eye with a red-hot kitchen fork.

"What do you mean, 'Not sending his men'? You told me earlier that an attack is planned . . ."

Gazing at Alston with his remaining eye, Semper managed, "Today . . . maybe tomorrow."

Alston peeled the surgical glove from his right hand, then reached up and turned on the comunit attached to his collar. "Evans, take us back in." Immediately the boat's engine droned, and below Semper the water boiled as the craft began to come about. Alston glanced at the box of gloves open on a table nearby, then peeled off the other glove and went over to get a fresh pair.

"What do you think?" he asked Chaldor.

Chaldor, as attractive as she was mean, with her red hair plaited intricately against her head and containing as much concealed weaponry as it did jewellery, gazed at him with her pure-purple eyes. "I think he has a lot more to tell us. What's this machine he was babbling about?"

"Yes, I think you're right." Alston took the wire cutters from Chaldor and once again turned to his victim. "Now, Semper, please tell us about this machine of Arian's."

"It's a Golem . . . a Golem!"

From Semper there then issued a piggish squealing. Alston counted fingers and saw that he had enough left for five further questions.

"Golem don't work for Separatists. It seems to me that your loyalty to Arian is much stronger than I thought. *Still* you are trying to cover for him. *Still* you have not answered my questions. I want to know how many men, what weaponry, and when."

"It's a Golem . . . broken Golem . . . brought in from . . . Huma."

Alston sighed and shook his head. "Chaldor, go and get the blowtorch and the sanding machine. It seems we'll have to go all the way."

As the afternoon progressed, and as they came back in sight of the island, Alston was surprised at Semper's resistance—always coming back to the same ridiculous story about a broken Golem. Near the end, Alston was tempted to believe that story, but he knew that broken Golem were as mythical as Horace Blegg. And were such a creature possible, an AI-hater like Arian Pelter would never use it. Dumping what was left of Semper over the side, as food for the adapted whitebait and pearl crabs swarming in the shallows around the island, he finally admitted defeat—Semper had managed to conceal the truth unto death.

—retroact ends—

Gant seemed on edge, studying the throng as if he expected attack from every direction. Cormac supposed the uploaded soldier had every right to be paranoid while accompanying him—bad things tended to happen around Cormac.

Why am I able to gridlink? Cormac asked, as he strode on ahead of Gant across the embarkation lounge.

A rather deeper scan than I am managing now would be required to answer that question, Viridian replied directly into his link. It seems that somehow you have managed, at an unconscious level, to turn your gridlink back on. Only an AI such as myself should be able to do this, though there is one human who possesses the ability to interfere with AI coding at that level.

Let me guess: Horace Blegg.

Correct.

What about memories of U-space? Quince transportation is instantaneous, so how do you explain that?

What memories?

I can't vocalize it.

Cormac opened the bandwidth of his link and sent the jumbled images that plagued him. He sensed the AI receiving and studying those images—and, just to test, he applied to it on another level for information concerning his visit here.

Major Arn is awaiting you at the exit, a submind replied.

Cormac scanned ahead and saw that same individual, in the uniform of the ES regulars, standing beside shimmer-shield doors leading outside. The man looked ill at ease. Cormac glanced at Gant, caught his gaze, and with a nod drew his attention over to Arn.

"I don't suppose he's too glad to see you," said Gant. "You got a lot of his men dead."

Cormac nodded, continuing the silent conversation in his head as he and Gant headed towards the waiting man.

What do you think?

The images are . . . I see you accessed one of my sub-minds. It would seem your gridlink is regaining total function. As I was saying, these images are the nearest human interpretation of U-space possible. You have definitely seen it, yet hopefully you are still sane. This is unusual.

Let me guess again: only one other.

Correct.

As they approached Arn, Cormac accessed information on the man. He'd been a sergeant when Cormac had first known him, and his performance against Arian Pelter had resulted in his promotion by Viridian, who was, like all runcible AIs, also the planetary governor.

"Good to see you again," said Cormac, holding out his hand.

Arn gripped the hand but did not return the compliment.

"I've got a stratocar outside, which should get us there in a few hours," he said. "I also received a message that you have further requirements."

"Ground-scanning gear and maybe an excavator later on," Cormac replied.

Arn nodded, and Cormac picked up the hint of a transmission from the grey military aug behind the man's right ear. Cormac realized that he himself now possessed the ability to make all the required arrangements; however, he was not yet prepared to rely on his gridlink.

Arn now turned to Gant and studied him.

"Gant," said the uploaded soldier, holding out his hand, "I partnered Thorn in our Sparkind unit."

"You weren't here back then," Arn observed, shaking the hand.

"I had a bit of a problem."

"Problem?"

"I was dead."

This did not seem to fluster Arn, who Cormac had realized was conducting his own silent conversation, via aug, during this introduction. The major turned back to Cormac as if Gant had said nothing at all strange.

"They'll maybe have something ready for us when we get there. There's an archaeological dig at the old ruins, and it shouldn't take them long to move equipment."

They walked away from the runcible facility, and a wave of memory dragged Cormac into a sudden still point as he looked around. The country beyond the AGC park bore a resemblance to earthborn moorland, with pools the colour of tarnished copper, separated by thick sage-like growth. Distantly the blue line of forest seemed a standing wave, frozen in approach, and behind it rose mountains of laminar stone bearing more resemblance to something constructed than to any natural formation.

Here was where many of Arn's fellows had died. Here was where Arian Pelter's quest for vengeance had ended. And here was where Aiden and Cento had destroyed the brass killing machine, Mr. Crane—though Cormac now wanted to be sure that they had done a sufficiently thorough job.

Arn led the way to an area of the vehicle park not crowded with gravcars, to where the stratocar rested, distinct from the others. It was an AGC, but more streamlined, bearing stubby wings, two fusion engines mounted at the back and underslung boosters. The doors hinged up like wings by themselves as the three approached, and shortly the men were inside, strapping themselves in—Gant and Cormac taking the two seats behind the pilot's. Seeing the two of them were ready, Arn lifted the control column and, with a thrum of AG but no feeling of acceleration, the craft shot up vertically from the ground. When he pushed the column forwards and the engines ignited behind, the acceleration slammed them back into their seats. The craft still rising rapidly, Cormac noted Arn operating a sledding control so that the AG functioned at an angle to the gravity of the planet, thus increasing their acceleration even more. In the stratosphere, Arn then engaged the boosters.

"Useful toy," Cormac commented, when he could recover his breath.

"ECS upgrading," Arn replied. "There's a lot of it going on now."

"This is the first I've seen," commented Gant.

Cormac glanced at him. "Seems we both need to catch up on events a bit." Silently he then queried the runcible AI:

Viridian, this vehicle is definitely not standard issue . . .

It is becoming standard issue.

Why?

It is considered a suitable response.

To what?

To possible enemies.

Cormac didn't pursue that. He had no doubt that was "suitable response" to the threat of Jain technology getting into the wrong hands . . . again. Through his gridlink, he reached beyond Viridian and felt the huge flows of ECS information—a sure sign of much activity, industrial and military, all across the Polity.

After two hours of stratospheric flight, Arn decelerated and brought the stratocar down in a spiralling glide. Cormac recognized the curving chain of the Thuriot mountains and, when they were closer, the surrounding landscape of moorland scattered with copses and forests of blue oaks and chequer trees. He did not recognize the precise area where a low cruiser with a treaded excavator mounted on its back had been parked, until he actually climbed out of the car. Then he spotted the shattered trees and knew that this was where it had happened. He gazed for a moment beyond those trees, remembering that here was where he had killed Arian Pelter, then returned his attention to his immediate surroundings.

There were four people waiting by the cruiser, and shortly two of them approached: male and female, both ophidapts, with scaled skin, reptilian eyes and skull crests. No doubt they also possessed folded-back snake fangs, not usually employed for injecting fatal poisons but just the poisons their sexual partners preferred. Cormac recognized the type, and if that fact was not enough to put him on edge, their physical similarity to dracomen was.

"Where do you want us to dig, soldier man?" the female asked Arn.

He turned to Cormac, who stepped forwards.

"Scanning first—then maybe some digging. You have ground scanners?"

"Excavator has them." She indicated the machine. Studying it, Cormac realized it was a robot, very probably with AI. Soil would be its essential environment: it could probably feel it through its digging buckets, its sifters, its blowers and its washer. Almost as if this brief mention of it was all that was required, a ramp swung outwards from the cruiser, hinged down to the ground, and the excavator rolled off. Out of the corner of his eye, Cormac caught Gant dropping a hand to his holstered pulse-gun. He grinned to himself.

"Over here," he said, leading the way to where he remembered the camp having been located.

The woman hissed something and the excavator trundled over.

"Somewhere here—" But before he had finished, the excavator accelerated forwards and began digging. Cormac was about to demand what was going on when the excavator backed up to reveal an arm, then meticulously but swiftly continued unearthing the rest of the corpse it had detected the moment it turned on its ground scanners. It uncovered a second corpse shortly after, while Arn and Gant still inspected the first.

"Buried alive," said Arn.

Briefly studying the second corpse, Gant added, "Bled to death."

Cormac noted the burnt-out Dracocorp augs both corpses wore, and thought about where he had seen that before. He later found the crushed remains of Arian Pelter's skull—unearthed from the foxhole in which the clean-up crew had buried him.

He was unsurprised to discover later that of a brass man—or its parts—there was no sign.

Upon seeing the watchers, Anderson ordered no more quavit and instead filled a larger glass with water from the jug provided on the table. Often, of late, he was becoming recognized in large population centres, and always for the wrong reasons. Perhaps, in this case, those watching him were just curious about a Rondure Knight—Anderson had already received many a strange look while in this city. But over the last twenty years he had brought to book a gang of five outlaws responsible for terrorizing a district for many years, as well as three murderers and twice as many thieves. And it always seemed that such vermin came from extended families with much the same proclivity. He placed a hand on the gun now holstered at his hip, and glanced down at the other packages resting by his feet. No, he would not attempt to use these weapons here for, having had no practice with them, he would likely end up killing some bystander. Usually his muzzle-loader was sufficient for such situations—its one loud crashing shot being enough of a distraction for him to close in and use it as a club.

These four—one woman and three men—were dressed just like gully traders, but it struck Anderson as more likely they had stolen this clothing from their last victims. Perhaps he was being paranoid—but he thought not. Gully traders were genuine humans, so did not need the sand goggles these individuals all wore either suspended around their necks or lodged up on their hat brims. Nor did gully traders carry thuriol hooks, which were used by rarely encountered hog trainers . . . or by villains to disable sand hogs during a highway robbery.

Anderson swore to himself, abruptly realizing that his eyesight was not so good nowadays. He now knew the woman: Unger Salbec. She was the sister of Querst Salbec, whom Anderson had, many years ago, dragged back to the same town where the man had raped a woman, then killed her. Receiving the customary punishment for such a crime, Querst Salbec had been thrown into a sleer burrow, where probably he had remained alive for several days, paralysed by sleer sting, while awaiting the hatching of the eggs attached to the rocky walls and then the voracious attention of the sleer nymphs.

As the four now began to rise from their table, Anderson felt the leaden inevitability of his past catching up with him. Unger Salbec nodded to him, smiling without much humour. Damn, she was still as attractive as ever.

"Anderson Endrik?" said a voice.

Anderson cursed himself for being a fool, as three others surrounded him from behind. So much had he been concentrating on the four in front of him in the adjacent bar, he had forgotten to watch his back. The speaker pulled out a chair and sat down, placing on the table a carbine similar to the one contained in the bag at Anderson's feet. The other two remained standing, their large assault rifles held across their stomachs, their gazes fixed on the other four who, after a muttered exchange, now carefully retook their seats.

Anderson noted that the three surrounding him all wore the same style of clothing: hip-length jackets with some sort of armour woven into the material, cloth trousers with similar armouring over the thighs and knees, heavy steel-toecap boots, and peaked helmets. This was the kind of attire worn in a foundry, but Anderson knew the purpose to which it had been adapted. He allowed himself to relax a little.

"Yes—I'm Anderson Endrik."

"I hope you know that freelance work is frowned on in Golgoth. If you have come here to collect a bounty on someone, you can forget it. Everyone within city limits comes under my jurisdiction, and no one touches any lawbreakers but my men and me. Of course," he glanced over at the four, "if you are aware of any who might have committed capital crimes elsewhere, they will assuredly be ejected from the city—and what happens outside city limits is none of my concern."

"You are . . . police?"

"That is one description."

"Your name?"

"Kilnsman Gyrol. Tell me, Anderson Endrik, are you considering committing violence in my city?"

Out of the corner of his eye, Anderson spotted Tergal coming out of the shop, and he did not miss the weapon the boy now wore at his hip. He just hoped that Tergal would keep his cool.

"I'm not considering committing violence," Anderson said slowly, getting his thoughts in order. He then carefully added, "Unless it's to defend myself." It had occurred to him that here was one way he could escape a certain piece of his past.

"I don't much like the look of them," said Gyrol, gesturing with his thumb. "What are they?"

"At a guess I'd say they are thieves. Going further I would say that the woman is probably a relative of one called Querst Salbec—a rapist and murderer." It was a lie *and* the truth, and could get him into all sorts of trouble but, what the hell, he would be long gone.

"I don't like that sort in my city." Gyrol stood, taking up his weapon. "Perhaps I should go over and have a cautionary word with them."

"Perhaps you should," said Anderson. "Tell me, Kilnsman Gyrol, how long have you been shadowing me here?"

"Ever since Laforge ran you in from his roadhouse. I've long known that those are the places to watch."

Anderson nodded. "I'm getting old, then. I never saw any sign of your people."

"Comes to us all, even Rondure Knights." Gyrol smiled. "Where do you go from here?"

"The Sand Towers, then out on the Plains."

Gyrol nodded towards Tergal, who had paused, indecisively, ten metres from the table. "Then teach the youth to watch your back. Unless they do something stupid, I'll not be able to detain these four for long."

Anderson grimaced, but decided not to comment on how Tergal might not be the best choice for guarding his back.

Gyrol moved to go, then paused. "Strange rumours filtering down from the Plains—are you involved in that?"

"What kind of rumours?"

"Strange creatures . . . Nomads changing their routes to avoid certain areas. Like I said: rumours."

"Dragons?"

"That was your word—not mine."

"Yes, I'm going to take a look."

"Take care, knight."

"I will."

Anderson stood up as Tergal now approached. It was definitely time to leave town.

7

Augmented: In popular usage "augmented" has now become distinct from "boosted." To be "boosted" is to be physically augmented either by chemical or nano-structural/surgical means. To be "augmented" is to have taken advantage of one or more of the many available cybernetic devices, mechanical additions and, distinctly, cerebral augmentations. In the last case we have, of course, the ubiquitous "aug" and such back-formations as "auged," "auging-in," and the execrable "all auged up." But it does not stop there: the word "aug" has now become confused with auger and augur—which is understandable considering the way an aug connects and the information that then becomes available. So now you can "auger" information from the AI net, and a prediction made by an aug prognostic subprogram can be called an "augury."

—From Quince Guide *compiled by humans*

Ambient temperature was rising rapidly and, with his grub-like heaving along the ground, Cento realized he would not reach the survey ship before his motors started seizing up again or one of the huge rocks that kept raining down crushed him finally into the ground. But even with all the carnage around him—lava sleeting through the acidic air, pyroclastic flows pouring down from the distant caldera, and the continual earthquakes—he did have a line of sight to the vessel, and could still use his radio. His brief query elicited no reply. The chance that there was someone alive there, but unable to use a radio, he considered remote. Then linking to the ship's computer—Shayden had never bothered to replace it with an AI—he descended into code as he gave it instructions. As a pall of smoke cleared, he saw that those instructions were being followed.

Vessels such as this one were used for orbital survey as well as landing, so contained robot probes. These devices were made for sampling atmosphere, limited surface scanning for mapping and the occasional retrieval of airborne or spaceborne objects. Cento observed a rear port opening and the probe sliding out to hover beside the ship. It was elliptical with a sensory head mounted on its front end, and the six grasping arms folded underneath it complemented its beetlish appearance. Smoke veiled all again, but the link remained and Cento could *feel* the probe coming towards him. Soon it penetrated the smoke, a sleet of lava pattering its upper surface. It drew closer, bucked when a large lump of semi-molten rock hit it and bounced off, but kept on coming. Such devices were rugged, but hardly made for this environment. Cento was relieved when it finally drew to a halt above him.

The Golem reached up and gripped one of the probe's arms. It folded down two more arms and with three-fingered claws gripped one of his hipbones and his neck, then with a thrum of AG lifted him from the boiling ground. Quickly it turned and flew back towards the ship, depositing Cento at the last by the open airlock, before turning to head back to its launch cache.

Cento observed the two incinerated corpses lying nearby, then began dragging himself inside the ship. There he pulled himself upright and tried to close the lock, but something had destroyed its mechanism. He dragged himself to the cockpit and hauled himself up into the pilot's chair where, after strapping in, he tried to use the ship's more powerful transmitters. Nothing—no contact with the carrier shell, so no way to link through to the U-space transmitter it had on board. Unsurprised at this lack of response from the shell, Cento initiated the lander's autolaunch. The computer refused, of course, because of the open airlock. Cento paused, then put it offline and took hold of the joystick. It would be a rough ride, but then he was used to those.

The virtual image he constructed was of a sphere of glowing points, all linked by spidery lines to a central nexus glowing brightest of all. That was the network, the entity of Dracocorp augs, suspended in grey void. Reality bore little resemblance, for the station orbiting the red dwarf was like a thick coin five kilometres across, spiked and glittering with sensory arrays and with a half-kilometre-high docking tower protruding from its centre. Few ships were docked there, and fewer still occupied the surrounding space. Skellor wondered if ECS was even aware that this station, placed for the long-term study of this carnelian star, was no longer entirely theirs. The query he received from the runcible AI contained there certainly gave the impression that this place was still Polity property. Working through the *Vulture*'s systems he responded, giving a false identity for his ship and for himself, both of which would be impossible to check in less than a solstan month—should the runcible AI feel any need.

"Ruby Eye welcomes you, trader Scolan," the AI began over com.

"Glad to be here. It's been a long journey."

"And the purpose of your visit?"

"Probably alcohol poisoning. I've been too long in this tin can."

As this exchange drew to a close, Skellor could feel the runcible AI probing the *Vulture* for information, but the ship's responses were his own, for his subversion program had certainly found and killed every last shred of personal identity the ship's AI had retained. When the link finally broke, he flew the *Vulture* towards the tower and his designated docking station, slowing and turning it at the final moment into that framework. Buffers extended and absorbed the last of the ship's momentum, then four universal docking clamps swung in towards the ship from above and below, and gripped it with large gecko adhesion pads. An embarkation tunnel then telescoped out from the tower, groped about a bit on the hull of the *Vulture* till it eventually found the airlock and connected.

Skellor stood up from the pilot's chair and turned to regard Mr. Crane. "Now, time to go to work."

Crane swept up his toys and pocketed them. Skellor could not resist another probe inside the Golem, for he was learning—from a mind filled with disconnected but bloody memory—that Mr. Crane was very good indeed at the profession to which he had been perverted.

—retroact 8—

It was night and, in the shallows that lay beyond the channel excavated into the seabed alongside the jetty, pearl crabs gleamed like underwater stars. Striding out along the gritty strand, his pulse-rifle propped across his shoulder, Evans thought Alston was overreacting. The Pelters just did not have the firepower to come in here mob-handed. Maybe they had more men than the two hundred guarding this island. But they would not be as well trained as Chaldor's mercenaries or Evans's own men.

"Clear here," he said into his comunit.

It seemed pointless to eyeball the beach when no craft could come within twenty kilometres of the island without being picked up on radar. Yes, they might come in underwater, but that way would be unable to bring in anything to deal with the autogun emplacements set into the mountainside below Alston's fortified home. By air was of course out of the question, as that would bring Polity monitors in here quick as blade beetles.

"There's a small cat about fifteen kloms out," Chaldor replied. "Tell your men to stay alert."

"What's it doing?"

"Nothing as yet."

"Probably just an otter hunter." Evans glanced along the beach to where two of his men were invisible in the low scrub of creosote bushes just back from the jetty. He had groups of five men spaced at intervals of a hundred metres all around the island. All of them were bored with waiting and itching for a fight, but he suspected there would be no fight here, and that the final showdown would be in Gordonstone. He turned from the sea, intending to head over and speak to his men, but just then, out of the corner of his eye, spotted something in the water.

"What in hell's name?" He swivelled and peered directly at the object. At first, it appeared to be merely the top of a post revealed by one of the quick ebb tides generated by the fast transit of the moon, Cereb. But it kept rising as it headed inshore till a rim became identifiable. It took a moment for Evans to admit to himself that what he was seeing was a large, wide-brimmed hat. He lowered his pulse-rifle into position by his hip, and set it whining as it topped up the charge in its capacitor.

"What is it, Evans?" Chaldor asked him over com.

"A hat, ah . . . with a head underneath it."

Evans felt his skin crawl as the huge man rose higher and higher out of the waves. He wore no breathing gear, and his skin looked rubbery—false. Had Semper actually been telling the truth? Evans pulled his flare goggles down over his eyes and, as soon as the man was out to his waist, he fired. The goggles prevented the strobing flash from blinding him, thus allowing him to see the flames and the glowing impact of each shot in turn. But the big man just came on.

"Shit, Semper *was* telling the truth—we've got one big-fuck Golem coming ashore!"

Evans fired again, holding the firing button down. Suddenly the Golem was up onto a ledge and taking huge strides through shallows scattered with pearl crabs, leaving milky footprints behind as he crushed the myriad creatures. Evans turned to run back towards his men. Perhaps more firepower might . . . A heavy thumping tread behind him—he couldn't believe it; this was wrong, too quick . . .

Evans's men heard the scream—and turned just in time to see the Golem discarding something ripped and bloody. They came out of cover, confidently aiming their pulse-rifles.

—retroact ends—

Guilt, Mika found, was an unfamiliar and uncomfortable emotion for which her Life-coven training had ill prepared her—and now she felt doubly guilty. She reached out to touch a finger to the hard-field that overlay the chainglass window, and found it slippery to the touch. Beyond the window, the asteroid was held central in the vast containment sphere by gravplates generating antigravity mounted all around the sphere interior, countering the minimal gravity of the asteroid itself. In the intervening space the vacuum swarmed with machines and suited figures, skinless Golem and complex telefactors operated by the *Jerusalem* AI. Already Jerusalem had separated the bridge pod of the *Occam Razor* from the surface, and sometime hence it would eject the asteroid into space in order to destroy it with an imploder missile.

"He will not be pleased," she said.

The voice that replied was mild and conversational, but then you didn't need to shout when you were a demigod. "Ian Cormac's requirement for an expert in matters concerning the Jain and Dragon is not of prime concern. His singular mission is to catch and/or destroy a criminal. Our concern is to contain and understand a technology that could obliterate the Polity. Your abilities, as you surmised, will be more usefully employed here."

Mika turned and surveyed the quarantine pod she had been allotted, with its intrusive scanning gear and the huge cowled surgical robot poised over a slab with drain channels around its edges, and felt a sudden lethargy overcome her. The nerve blockers and analgesics were not so effective now, and soon it would be time. Whether or not she would survive was open to question. The reports received from the medical team on Masada told her Apis had not yet revived, and that they were still removing further mycelial growths from him but, on the plus side, he had not yet died.

"I've uploaded the recording of the operation," she stated.

"I have," Jerusalem replied, "studied it in detail, Asselis Mika, and will be able to make some improvements. Presently I am designing T-cell nanobots for the finer work."

Mika gritted her teeth and asked, "Will I be clear then?"

"This method has a good chance of success. Disconnected filaments of the mycelium will not be able to transmit defensive information to each other, and so the nanobots should be able to destroy them. They will work in the same manner as the counteragent still being used to rid Samarkand of the ceramal-eating mycelium there."

"Disconnected filaments?"

"The mycelium is killing you, so immediate surgery is necessary. However, I am capable of more invasive surgery than you performed on the outlinker, so I should be able to remove more of it."

Mika shuddered. She wasn't usually squeamish about such things, but she did not intend to ask the AI just how *invasive* it intended to get. The result, she suspected, would look rather like an explosion in an abattoir.

"Might it not have been better to have Thorn here as well?"

"The procedure I am about to undertake can also be carried out aboard the *Jack Ketch*. Thorn can then be kept in cold sleep until such a time as the nanobots can be conveyed to that vessel." Jerusalem paused. "There is, Mika Asselis, no further reason for delay."

Mika knew she *was* procrastinating, and was doing so because she was scared. She discarded her robe, walked over to the surgical slab and sat naked on the edge of it. It was very cold. As she lay back and the surgical robot raised a nerve blocker to her neck, she thought that perhaps, like Thorn had intended, she should have had a memplant installed so that the step over death and into artificial life would be available to her too, but it was too late for that now.

On the *Jack Ketch* itself, with two analgesic patches on his chest and a nerve blocker now numbing his leg where earlier it had felt as if the mycelium had taken a hacksaw to his hip-bone, Thorn limped out into the corridor adjoining Medical, and thought *how weird*. This seemed more like the inside of some old Renaissance chateau than a high-tech warship, what with the carpets, the plaster mouldings on the ceiling, the ornate dangling light fittings. But more disconcerting was that none of this stuff had been here a couple of hours ago, when he had entered Medical to be checked over.

The dropshaft was reassuringly high-tech, however, though it shifted while he was in transit. Gripping the handles fitted at his departure point, he stepped out at an angle onto the floor of the bridge. Momentarily, the changed angle of gravity fields disorientated him, and the fact that seemingly nothing stood between him and starlit vacuum was disconcerting. He lowered his gaze to study the bridge's strange decor, then its other occupants—just as Jack said, "He will speak to you momentarily."

Cormac was pacing the rug, obviously angry; Gant lolled nonchalantly, with his shoulder against one of the cast-iron street lamps; while Jack's mechanical avatar sat in one of the club chairs, an ankle resting on one knee, the fingertips of each hand pressing against each other to form a cage below his chin, his eyes invisible. Thorn went over to join his friend.

"This should be interesting," Gant muttered.

Thorn made no comment, his gaze straying to the antique execution devices for which Jack seemed to have developed a penchant. "That's a new one." He pointed out a big brass statue of a bull.

Gant glanced over. "The brazen bull—particularly nasty. It's hollow, and the victim was placed inside to be roasted. They put reeds in its nostrils to alter the sound of the screams, so that it seemed the bull was bellowing."

"You know," said Thorn, "I'm glad I don't live in any system run by humans."

"Fucking A," said Gant.

Just then a shape appeared, apparently turning above them in vacuum: a ring, composed of a jade-green serpent swallowing its tail: *ouroboros*. This acted as a frame for something that appeared first as a distant silver dot, then grew to fill the frame and finally came through to block it from view: an androgynous face, bald and metallic, with shadowed hollows rather than eyes. This was a projection, not something actually outside the ship. Thorn and Gant fell silent to observe.

Cormac looked up. "Jerusalem?"

"The same," the face replied.

Without any more ado, Cormac said, "I went to Masada specifically to collect Mika, since I require her expertise."

The face tilted as if its unseen body had shrugged. "Certain other factors have come into play, Ian Cormac, not least my own requirement of her taking precedence."

Cormac grimaced. "I was given carte blanche by Earth Central, which presumably you have been allowed to override, and presumably for the best of reasons, so I'm not going to argue the point. I would just like an explanation."

"Simply put," the AI replied, "we have decided that understanding Jain technology is more important than apprehending one criminal who happens to employ it. Skellor is certainly dangerous—any Separatist with a gun is dangerous. Do you go after said Separatist or do you go after the arms trade? The answer is simply that you go after both, but that the latter must necessarily take precedence."

"A very elastic analogy," said Cormac tightly.

"There are the other factors I mentioned."

"Do go on."

Jerusalem continued, "Asselis Mika will shortly undergo major surgery, without which she will die. Once I have carried this out, I will place her either on life-support or in cold-sleep suspension, whilst one of my subminds removes stray, regrowing, and possibly mutating Jain filaments. Were she aboard the *Jack Ketch*, the same scenario would apply: she would have been useless to you."

Hearing this, Thorn wondered if his insistence on not going with Mika but boarding the *Jack Ketch* had been such a bright idea.

"But then she's useless to you as well," said Cormac.

"For a period of five to ten days, by which time I will have designed and nanofactured robotic T-cells capable of hunting down and destroying all remaining Jain structures inside her. Obviously, Jack could employ such nanobots. But your search for Skellor—debouching from Viridian—is most likely to be either on the Line or out-Polity altogether?"

Looking uncomfortable, Cormac nodded.

Relentlessly Jerusalem continued, "Then the likelihood of my being able to convey some medium containing those nanobots to you is remote, as that would have to be done through the runcible network."

"Yeah, okay."

"It is also well to remember one other point: Asselis Mika herself believes she will be more usefully employed aboard me."

Cormac remained silent, his look of annoyance fading to blankness as he folded his arms.

"Thank you for your explanation," he said coldly.

The head nodded once, then slowly receded, and winked out. Briefly the ouroboros reappeared, like a call sign, then it too faded.

After a pause, Cormac turned to Thorn. "You heard the prognosis for Mika, so the same probably applies to you a few days down the line."

Thorn straightened up, trying not to wince at a stabbing pain at the base of his spine. "I heard it."

"You can take a shuttle across to the *Jerusalem*."

Thorn snorted. "What would I do aboard a ship like that? I'd rather be in cold sleep here."

Cormac nodded, then turned to the ship's avatar. "Jack, take us under."

Immediately the stars and the blackness folded into a deep grey, and Thorn still experienced a frisson at that strange tugging feeling that told him they were on their way.

"And while we're here, Jack," Cormac continued, "let's see what our dead Separatist has to say."

Despite his pain, Thorn had been fascinated to learn that this ship possessed its own ghost. He stared as a line of distortion cut through the air outside the drawing room.

With a clicking, whickering sound, the automaton Jack shut down, its head bowing and the glint dying behind its glasses. It must have been too much trouble for the AI to maintain simultaneously both the automaton and the projection of Aphran that now appeared.

This was not the woman of whom Thorn had seen images. That woman had been contemptuous, angry, frustrated at no longer being able to fight . . . in other words, human. This Aphran was something else entirely.

She was naked but, naked or otherwise, Thorn doubted her bones had originally been visible through translucent flesh. She was colourless, her hair long and pale, whereas Thorn distinctly remembered it being brown; her skin was white as milk, whereas before it had carried a slightly Asiatic hue; and her eyes were a demonic, pupil-less black. Thorn could only wonder if this was the result of some strange kind of vanity, for surely, appearing this way, she could be whatever she wanted. Also, the woman was drifting, like a corpse in deep water, her hair and arms pulled back and forth as if by wayward currents. There was a sound too, like delicate wind chimes or a tittering giggle, and a distant moaning.

"Hello, Aphran." Cormac walked over to the edge of the carpet.

She turned and focused on the agent, though Thorn knew that this was all illusion—the woman would be seeing him through the camera eyes Jack allowed her. Thorn glanced at Gant, then stepped away from the lamp post to stand at Cormac's shoulder. Curiosity was growing inside him, as thick and heavy as the Jain nodes that were already there.

"Hello, agent," Aphran replied.

Cormac seemed at a loss. He parted his hands as if to encompass that same loss, then brought them together and got straight down to business.

"You told me Skellor is hunting dragons," he said. "But I think I can safely assume that we're not talking about the winged and fire-breathing kind?"

"Dragons and brass men," Aphran replied, and tilted her head back as if laughing, or as if in pain. Thorn saw then that the woman did possess some colour—the inside of her mouth was bright red.

"Well, I know about the brass man. He collected what was left of Mr. Crane on Viridian only a short time ago, and that's where we are now heading, in the hope of picking up his trail. Do you know where he's going next?"

"Dragons."

Cormac appeared to be chewing on something bitter. "But where will he find them?"

"Give me substance," said Aphran.

Cormac slowly nodded. "Yes, I'll do that when I think you're no longer holding anything back. My other option is to let Jack take your mind apart piecemeal, in order to find what I want. Though after taking that course I'm not sure I'd bother asking him to put it back together again."

"Cruel," hissed Aphran.

"You are merely a dispensable recording, but more pertinently you are a criminal under sentence of death."

Thorn absorbed that. Not so long ago the guilt of a cerebral recording was a murky legal debating point. Now all recordings of murderers, made after the murder was committed, came under the same sentence.

"I have paid." In saying this, Aphran changed—aged a hundred, a thousand years in a few seconds, became something twisted, with flames issuing all around her.

Ignoring this display, Cormac asked, "Why did Skellor want a smashed metalskin Golem?"

"Pleases him . . . angry when I mocked him . . . burnt me."

Aphran's illusory form was growing young again—the flames dying away in the air around her.

"From what I've seen, I don't doubt he has the ability to rebuild Mr. Crane. But because it *pleases* him?"

"It pleases him. Please him. Love him."

"Do you know where he is heading from Viridian?"

Thorn now observed Aphran grow old again, then in a moment young.

"Completion . . . the symmetry . . . aesthetically pleasing."

"Answer the question: where is he going? Where is the Dragon sphere he is hunting?"

"I love you I love you I love you . . ."

Aphran was oscillating between extreme age and pubescence, and a halo of flame remained surrounding her.

Cormac turned to Thorn and Gant. "Is there anything either of *you* would like to ask? Maybe you might get some sense out of her."

Gant spoke up: "What did he do to you?"

Aphran was now floating a metre from the floor. Her gaze swung down towards him.

"Skellor," she hissed. Something then snapped inside her and she tilted her head back, opening her red mouth wide. A cycling wail issued from her, and she began to slide back away from them. Abruptly this movement accelerated, and she hurtled along above the deck and disappeared through the invisible wall.

"Maybe some other question would have been better," suggested Thorn.

"She said she'd *paid*," said Gant, looking directly at Cormac.

Coldly analytical, Cormac said, "Yes, I see. What would it be possible to do to a person if you could control the function of that person's body at a nanoscopic level? Nerves, skin, bone and flesh could be rebuilt even as they were being destroyed."

Thorn added, "She said he burnt her. I wonder for how long." He winced, pain not being something he could distance himself from right then.

Cormac turned and stared at the wall—at grey void. "Jack, should we erase her?"

"That is your decision, but I would advise against it," the disembodied voice of the AI replied. "She has suffered but, with time and effort, can be restored. She may possess much knowledge about Skellor, and much insight."

"Without Mika," said the agent, "that might be something we'll need desperately."

"Well, if you fully understand the danger, then I cannot dissuade you," said Anderson, knowing that the sister of a killer coming after him had only increased Tergal's fascination. It was harmless enough: the danger Unger Salbec represented held no threat for the boy.

Golgoth was to the right of them now and ahead numerous trails tangled into the Sand Towers. This was not the usual route taken away from the city—which lay on the other side—but Anderson hoped thus to avoid encountering Salbec's sister. He had intended to depart from the lower city directly underneath the platform, but Laforge had advised him against that because apparently the area of the Towers lying below the Overcity was swarming with nasty creatures—some of them possibly human. Here, but for the occasional sulerbane plants standing, with their woody frills and brackets, like petrified dwarfs in ragged clothing, the ground was barren. The coloured sand eroded from the layers had been trampled by the passage of many feet into a mixture of nondescript grey.

Raising his monocular, Anderson turned aside and studied the Overcity of Golgoth. Its two-kilometre-wide platform, as well as resting on the buttes themselves, was supported by steel pillars and arching trusses. In the shade thus engendered, there was movement amid scattered bulbous dwellings made of bonded sand. The Overcity, with its rectilinear towers, domes and spires, resembled an Earth city that Anderson had once seen in an ancient picture. He panned his monocular around to face the buttes directly ahead. He could distinguish falls certainly caused by the recent quakes and, above them, could just make out the occasional sinister shape of a sleer skittering across the high faces of sandstone, or in and out of the caves bored into it. The creatures were small, but it would be best to keep safely to the centre of the paths.

"Have you ever had to kill a third-stage sleer?" he suddenly asked.

"They don't have a third stage," Tergal replied.

"Ah, they are rare where you come from, but not so rare where we are going." Anderson pointed. "Those are all first-stage—little more than nymphs. They're cave hunters mostly, and for that purpose possess a feeding head with grinding mandibles with extensible antlers, ten legs attached in pairs on independently rotating body segments, and though quite capable of killing a man, they never grow larger than a metre in length. Also, like their adult kin they possess the ability to split themselves in two, but there's no necessity for that as they are not breeders."

"I know what they are," said Tergal, giving Anderson a puzzled glance.

Anderson continued regardless. "After about two years, they encyst in the sand and transform to the second stage. The front segment folds up and melds into the feeding head, the two legs attached turning into carapace saws for dealing with larger prey outside the sand caves—prey they can now see because they simultaneously gain a nice triad of compound eyes. They also grow an ovipositor drill which they can use to inject paralytic. And at this stage they grow to about two metres in length."

Tergal grunted, then shifted about in his saddle. He asked, "What's an ovipositor?"

"It is the egg-laying tube protruding from the rear of an adult sleer."

Tergal turned to him. "There, you see: 'adult sleer,' so why do you talk of a third stage?"

"Because there *is* one." Anderson considered all he had learned during this journeying, and all he knew about sleers and their life cycles. One day he would write a book about it all, to add to the collection kept in the Rondure library—but not yet, not while there was still so much to see. He continued enthusiastically, "The second-stage creature, as you are aware, splits itself for mating: each half moving on four legs. The rear section can then go off to mate with the rear sections of other sleers, while the feeding or hunting end continues about its business—the two sections still communicating by low-frequency bio-radio. Once rejoined after mating, the whole creature lays eggs in a cave or burrow in which it will dump paralysed prey. Nymphs—first-stage sleers—then hatch out and feed on this preserved food. After many years, and for reasons I've not yet fathomed, a second-stager again encysts, and transforms into the third stage. These lay eggs in a similar manner, but out of them hatch second-stage sleers."

"What are they like then, these third-stage creatures?"

"Bigger, inevitably. The first one I killed was three metres long. Its carapace was dark grey, rather than bearing the usual sand-coloured camouflage, and another pair of legs had ridden up beside its head to form pincer arms that act just like that punch axe you carry. And of course it now ran on six legs. It did that." Anderson pointed to the rim of his sand hog's carapace where two large puncture holes had been filled up with a web of the epoxy strips normally used to shoe a sand hog's feet. Tergal observed this damage silently, then his gaze slid up to the long case fixed further up the carapace.

"How did you kill it?"

"Not with that—I got that later." Anderson waved a hand at the case. "I hadn't properly learned my trade then, so used my fusile. Luckily the creature was more interested in my mount than in me, and it clung on even as I kept reloading to shoot bullet after bullet down its gullet. Meanwhile Bonehead slid his feeding head underneath it, and chewed on its guts. While that was happening its breeding section broke away and ran off on two legs—I never knew what became of that."

Anderson had noted one of Bonehead's two eye-palps—which had extruded from its sensory head earlier as they first came in sight of the sleers—turning towards him during this conversation. It seemed that, after contact with a few human generations, sand hogs would begin to understand human speech. The irony was that after coming to understand their riders fully, the beasts often ended up abandoning them and heading off into the wilderness.

He continued, "Had it directly attacked me, there was little I could have done—it would have winkled me out of this armour easy as eating a sand oyster."

Staring into the shade that lay between the Sand Towers, Tergal asked nervously, "So we could encounter such creatures here?"

"It's a distinct possibility. And we might even encounter a droon or an apek, or even a *fourth*-stage sleer."

"You only find apeks near lakes," argued Tergal. "And droons are either extinct or a myth. As to fourth-stage sleers, I've not even heard such a myth. Don't tell me: your hog here lost its claw to one?"

"No, an apek took that over by Lake Cooder in Bravence. And I've myself seen drawings of fourth-stage sleers—and droons—but I've never heard of any who have encountered them."

"Which probably confirms they don't exist."

"Either that, or not many have survived to tell the tale."

The reception committee consisted of technicians working in the docking tower who, upon seeing Mr. Crane step out behind Skellor, suddenly decided to get busy about other tasks. He saw that all three men wore Dracocorp augs, and supposed the source of that bright point in the aug network had sent them to assess this new visitor. Now ignoring them, he strode on towards the security arch spanning the gangway leading to the centre of the tower. The arch was to alert the station AI to anyone entering with lethal biologicals or weapons capable of damaging the structure of the station itself. Skellor did not want to know what it might make of him or Crane and, stopping before it, he pressed his hand against the device's white anodized surface. From his palm, Jain nanofilament eased between the molecular interstices of the metal, and spread, invading optics and tracking them back to the controlling submind.

Too late, that same mind became aware of the invasion. Skellor isolated it and linked, erased its immediate memory and substituted one comprising a single inoffensive human stepping through the security arch. With his other hand he waved Mr. Crane ahead of him. He then raided the submind for information about the station and its residents, delaying its restarting for a few seconds before pulling his hand away, the filaments stretching and snapping back as if he had just pressed his palm into treacle. He stepped through himself and, glancing back, noticed that two of the technicians had been watching him. They would have no idea what he had done, but they would certainly know he had done something, for there had been no alarm raised on the detection of a large armoured Golem.

Beyond the arch, the long high corridor, lit by spider-web lights inset in the ceiling, terminated at the mouth of a dropshaft. Stepping past and to one side of Crane, who was now peering down into the well, Skellor inspected the control panel. He chose "Main Concourse," then stepped in. Descending, he glanced up to see Crane step into the shaft, clamping his hand down on his head as if he expected his hat to be blown off, but there was no air-blast as the irised gravity field rigidly took hold of him.

Exiting the shaft, Skellor surveyed a large open area floored with mica-effect tiles, its high ceiling supported by bulbous pillars reminiscent of the Bradbury Hotel on Earth, the lighting web extending across the ceiling giving it the illusion of depth. Spread across this expanse were seating areas, trees of all varieties growing in small walled gardens, bars and open-plan restaurants, and all around the edges, between the many exit tunnels, were lighted shop fronts. Right in the centre, in a circular lawn kerbed with polished agates, grew a huge baobab under whose low branches people rested or picnicked.

Skellor immediately noted that many people were eyeing him and Mr. Crane. He was not worried over this—the nexus of the Dracocorp network would not get the time to react appropriately. He closed his eyes and, using those devices grown inside his body, mapped signal strengths throughout the station. He again created the virtual sphere, then input the blueprint of the station he had taken from the submind, deforming the sphere to fit it. The central glowing point was ahead, higher up and to his left. He made for the relevant tunnel, Crane dogging his footsteps like Dr. Shade.

The tunnel, sectioned like a pipe and lit as elsewhere, had coloured lines traced along the edge of the mica floor to provide directions for those without augs. Checking the blueprint, Skellor saw he would have to take the next dropshaft leading to the floor above. Around the mouth of this shaft loitered people wearing Dracocorp augs.

Now for the reaction. Skellor first alerted Mr. Crane, then inside himself recalled a stored viral program he had used aboard the *Occam Razor*. No longer being part of a large Jain structure as well as a Polity dreadnought, he did not have the transmission power he had used in the Masadan system. Back on the *Razor* a touch to any one of the Dracocorp augs worn by Separatist prisoners had been all he required to take control of them all—but theirs had been a nascent network, with no individual yet gaining ascendance. In the Masadan system it had been necessary for him to take control through the Hierarch, who was also the one in control of the aug network, which he had done through the sheer power and bandwidth of the transmitters available on the *Occam Razor*. Here, he must touch the ascendant Dracocorp aug and, to get to the individual wearing it, he suspected he would leave a trail of blood.

As he reached the dropshaft, seven people turned towards him. He scanned them at a low level, and saw that all of them were armed. He noted how they had prepared for Mr. Crane: two of them carried APW handguns, and another a mini-grenade launcher. But they had carried out no scan themselves, and were reacting only to what they were seeing: a human and a simple, though large, metalskin Golem.

One of them stepped forwards; a catadapt man with a mane and feline eyes. He grinned, exposing fangs.

"Welcome to *Ruby Eye*," he said. "Perhaps you'd like to explain how you came aboard without Security becoming aware of *him*." He gestured at Mr. Crane.

Skellor halted. This man was carrying an APW; Skellor also noted that in a pouch attached to his belt he carried a Dracocorp aug. No doubt they assumed that the lack of a reaction to him by the security of this station meant he was a Polity agent. He linked through to the big Golem, to give instructions, and then saw that they were not required. Crane had already picked up from him the result of the scan and was ready to act.

"By what authority do you ask that question?" he asked, taking a pace closer.

"The authority of Nalen, who, despite what the Polity might think, runs this station." The man drew his APW handgun from inside his puffed coat, and held it down to his side. "And Nalen would like to meet you—but with suitable precautions in place."

Precautions . . . The man meant Skellor wearing the Dracocorp aug, and to do that he would expose himself to Nalen's inspection. Perhaps he could insert the virus through that link, but then again Nalen might be able to fend him off. It would have to be the bloody path. Mr. Crane moved even before ordered.

The man had no time to raise his weapon. Crane went past him with a snapping sound, which might have issued from the Golem's clothing—so fast did he move—but more likely from the man's neck. He remained standing for a second—his expression bewildered as his head sagged, his shattered neck unable to support it. Crane hit the next APW wielder and hefted him screaming from the floor, a big brass hand turning in a bloody morass below his ribcage. Skellor advanced, in no particular hurry, and observed the one equipped with the launcher turning and bringing the weapon to bear from underneath his long coat. He fired—just as Crane turned the victim he was holding into the path of the shot. The screaming man exploded into something ragged and bloody. Crane threw the remnants at the one with the launcher. This second man was yelling as he tried to disentangle himself. Crane was by him, taking away his launcher, turning it round and driving it straight through his body. Even as he dropped the man, he turned and backhanded an assailant behind—a woman—who in an instant was a headless woman cartwheeling sideways through the air. A second woman drew her weapon and aimed at Skellor.

"Tell it to stop!"

Skellor smiled, shook his head, disappeared.

"Fuck! Fuck!" the woman screamed, firing repeatedly at the spot where he had been standing. Then her gun was snatched away, disappearing, whereupon a single shot issued from one side, making a hole through her cheek and blowing out the back of her head. The two remaining people, a man and a woman—both dressed in the coveralls of runcible technicians—backed away, firing at Mr. Crane and frantically screaming for help over their augs. Crane accelerated towards them, not because they were causing any damage to him, but more likely because of the holes they were putting in his coat. Reaching them, he grabbed both by their heads, then slammed them together. His hands met, palm to palm, in a wet explosion.

Standing to one side of Crane, Skellor reappeared. "You are impressive, Mr. Crane," he said.

Crane scraped away the larger spatters of brain and pieces of bone from the front of his burnt coat. As he stood there, his exposed brassy skin darkened as it exuded Jain fibres—and in a few seconds the burns and tears on his coat had disappeared. Even the blood faded as if sucked away. Crane looked down, shook a piece of skull from the toe of his boot, offered no reaction to the words. Skellor immediately probed inside the Golem and, with what he found, considered destroying Crane there and then. Some of the Jain structure inside the Golem was no longer under Skellor's control, hence the way Crane had used it. But Skellor stayed his hand, putting in place a program to alert him should any more of that structure be subverted by the Golem. Mr. Crane, after all, was so very *good* at his job.

Skellor turned and walked towards the dropshaft and, not bothering to utilize panel or grav fields, which might well be under Nalen's control, reached inside and grasped the maintenance ladder. Before following, Crane abruptly stooped and picked up the piece of skull he'd shaken from his boot, then gazed at it. They had all died, so he could not, in his twisted logic, gain a substantial icon. He tossed the skull fragment aside, and followed Skellor into the dropshaft.

8

The human mind operates within a brain that comes in a one-size-fits-all lump of meat. The AI mind operates from vessels as many and various as are the different minds they contain. The basic Golem mind is stored in a "brain" that is a fist-sized lozenge of crystal laced with s-con nanofilaments and micro-optics, semi-conducting laminates in their billions, power feeds and cooling tubes. It is roughly equivalent to a human mind, but eidetic and functioning ten times as fast, though limited by anthropomorphic emulation programs. Going by the old IQ system, the Golem comes in at about 150. But such methods of measurement are now almost irrelevant, as Golem can be upgraded and, with augs and gridlinks, even that lump of meat can transcend the limits imposed on it by evolution. Also, human minds can be loaded to silicon—become AI—and, if the rumours are true, AI minds can be loaded to human brains. And, in the end, it is difficult to know what to measure.
—Excerpt from a speech by Jobsworth

Completion . . . the symmetry . . . aesthetically pleasing.

Cormac swung his legs out of his bed and, swearing, stood up. "Jack, take us out of U-space and set up a communication link through the runcible network."

The AI did not question the order, and Cormac immediately felt the lurch; the displacement as the *Jack Ketch* surfaced into realspace. For a second he thought that somewhere on the ship there was a fault in the shielding, for what he had just felt had been almost painful. Then he realized that might not be the true explanation; the feeling was probably all his own. Perhaps, like someone subjected to allergens for too long, he was becoming overly sensitized? He dismissed the thought—for the present.

"Right, run a trace through the net and locate the Sparkind Golem called Cento."

"Bearing on our present mission?" asked Jack's voice, sounding leaden.

"Symmetry—don't you see? When she said it, I assumed she was talking metaphorically, vaguely, but what she was actually saying referred to something specific. To complete Mr. Crane, to make him symmetrical and aesthetically pleasing, Skellor needs what Cento has."

"Skellor . . . technical ability? He could easily build an arm to mirror the one Crane already possesses."

"Yes, he could but, underneath all that ugly Jain technology and his crystal matrix AI, there is one thing about Skellor that must not be forgotten."

"What one thing must not be forgotten?"

"That he is a complete bastard."

"Query: *weakness*?"

"It was before—couldn't resist the urge to gloat. Now, what are Thorn and Gant doing right now, and why the fuck am I talking to one of your subminds, anyway?"

After a long pause, Jack's more familiar voice replied, "Sorry about that—otherwise occupied. Gant is waiting outside Medical. Unfortunately, while you were sleeping Thorn collapsed and is now undergoing surgery to remove his mycelium."

Cormac began pulling on his clothes. "Why wasn't I told?"

"I didn't tell you because to do so would achieve nothing of value. I suspect Gant had other concerns to occupy him—like resuscitating his friend, then carrying him to Medical."

No need to get tetchy, Cormac replied over his gridlink, as he stepped to his cabin door. Then, as he headed for the dropshaft, he accessed Jack at a lower level, to try for a visual link to wherever the surgery was taking place.

Ah, I was apprised of this new ability of yours.

Cormac grunted, as almost with physical force the AI rebuffed his attempt.

I just want to know what's going on.

Over the intercom, Jack replied, "Patran Thorn has shown some need for privacy in this matter and he shall have it. If security was of any concern, or this procedure had any bearing on the mission in hand, you would be given full access."

Reaching the dropshaft, Cormac hesitated over the control. It surprised him just how worried he was about Thorn, and with what urgency he wanted to be at the man's side. But he clamped down on that. In truth, he was in the best hands—if hands they were.

Out loud, Cormac said, "Okay, keep me apprised, but tell Gant I want him on the bridge. Now, are you running that trace?"

"I am. It will probably be some minutes before we receive a reply."

"Instantaneous communication?"

"Only when you instantly know precisely what to say."

Cormac snorted and set the control of the shaft to take him to the bridge. When he finally stepped out of the shaft, it was below a sky only lightly dusted with stars, and with Gant charging along behind him.

"What is it?" Gant asked.

Cormac studied him. The soldier's mind was human, but directly recorded into a crystal matrix inside a Golem body, and Cormac wondered just how real was the worry evident in his expression. But then the same doubt could be applied to any genuine living human's expression of emotion. In all cases it was what you *did* that counted, not what was going on in your mind.

"How is he?" he asked.

Gant shook his head. "Alive—but he'll be going into cold sleep soon."

"You'll get him back."

Now expressionless, Gant said, "Why have we dropped out of U-space?"

"Symmetry," said Cormac tersely. "Skellor has gone after Crane's missing arm—the arm Cento now possesses."

"Arrogant . . . *and* stupid."

"He would perhaps consider himself as being utterly capable and in control." Cormac turned to scan the bridge. As if in response to this, Jack's automaton stood up from its chair with that cog-grinding clockwork sound and its eyes glittering. "Jack, I'd like to talk to Aphran again."

The AI didn't reply. Instead, the automaton just slumped, its eyes going out. A line then cut down beside Cormac, and the young Aphran folded out of the air.

"Does Skellor know you're still . . . existing?" he asked her bluntly.

"I told him about the light—when it was too late."

"So he *does*?"

Aphran just hung there, not reacting to that.

Cormac bit back his frustration. "Okay, leave that. Was he aware just how much you know of his plans?"

"He did not know how close I was to him, and when he ejected the bridge pod of the *Occam Razor*, he thought to leave me behind. I hid from him, but stayed close. Close in the dark."

Cormac turned to Gant, who was staring off to one side of the drawing room where something new had appeared. Glancing over, Cormac saw that Jack had now added an electric chair to his collection here. He grimaced. "Let's try to ignore the distractions."

"Sorry," said Gant, pulling his attention back.

Cormac paused, then went on, "Assume Skellor doesn't know about her. When he departed on the *Vulture*, he would have known we would find the bridge pod and realize he was still alive. But to his mind we'd have no idea of his destination or intentions, and our chances of finding him would be minimal. He will think that all he has to avoid is a general search for him across a massive and ever-increasing volume of space."

Gant said, "He probably thinks that we'll assume he's fled."

"Quite. So he'll believe he's got plenty of time on his hands, and much room in which to manoeuvre—that's why he feels he can *play*. In his own estimation he is a very powerful being who can travel at will, without risk of discovery, inside and outside the Polity. He'll never consider himself the subject of direct pursuit."

"And we don't want him to learn that, because then he might run and hide."

"I have now received information concerning Cento," Jack suddenly piped up.

"Let's hear it," said Cormac, eyeing Aphran who now appeared as if just this brief interrogation had worn her down to the bone.

"The Golem was sent on a simple mission to confirm the discovery of an ancient artefact, and has been out of contact ever since—though this is not unusual, as no provision was made for a communication link to be maintained. The sector AI has since failed to establish contact with the carrier shell."

"Carrier shell?" said Gant.

Jack continued, "A landing vessel inside a U-space carrier was sent out to the location of the artefact. Both are the private property of an archaeological foundation; both are over two hundred years old and sub-AI. The landing vessel, as well as not possessing U-space engines, does not possess a U-space transmitter."

"Jack," said Cormac, "forget Viridian and take us there. I think that's where we'll find a fresher trail." Now he looked across at the electric chair: "And, Jack, you need to get out more."

Streaks of magma, across the hull of the survey ship, radiated in vacuum as they cooled. The carrier shell, hanging in space before it like a huge iron nut—with the hole through its centre shaped to the wedge of the survey ship rather than threaded for some giant bolt—had cooled already. Cento supposed he had expected something like this, and analytically he studied the hole punched through the side of the shell, and the radial splashes of molten metal all around it. Either Skellor's ship carried kinetic weapons, or the man had grappled some piece of debris in this system and flung it at the shell. How he had achieved this did not matter. The result was all that was important right now: all its systems were down and it seemed likely that the craft would never again be used to transport ships through U-space. Nevertheless, Cento steered the little ship into the docking hole. Three of the ten automatic clamps engaged, and the ship was then lined up to the airlock and the fuelling and recharging systems, but the ship's arrival initiated no further activity. Cento unstrapped and propelled himself into the back of the vessel. At least now he did not have gravity to fight.

The airlock of the little vessel mated with that of the carrier shell but the shell door, even though running on an independent power supply, would not open. Whatever system it ran on was intelligent enough to recognize that the ship contained no air, yet not bright enough to figure that its only occupant had no need to breathe. Restraining what emulation of frustration he could achieve, Cento returned to the cockpit and switched the computer back on. Through its screen it obligingly informed him that there was no air in the ship, but that a number of options were available to him.

"Stupid machine," he mouthed in vacuum, and instructed the computer to repressurize the vessel. Then he returned to the airlock, to wait out the long minutes before the carrier lock opened. He swore aloud when the door still refused to open, this time because there was no air inside the carrier shell itself, and went to find what tools he might require. Three hours later, he finally got through the door.

Fire had scoured the inside of the shell, blasted around the ring-shaped transit tubes by the explosive impact. Propelling himself three quarters of the way round, he eventually found where the object had struck, and peered into the well the impact had drilled through the station. Skellor's shooting had been admirably accurate. Whatever the object, it had cut right through one of the three balanced U-space engines and taken out the main fusion generator. In one respect, Cento considered himself lucky: at least the generator had merely failed rather than detonated—had that been the case there would be no shell here at all. He propelled himself across the cavity and into the transit tube beyond. Coming at last to the place he was seeking—a simple sliding door—he drove the blade of his hand with such force at the thin lamination of metal and insulation that it punched through without any reaction propelling him away. In a minute, he had torn a hole large enough to climb through.

The room contained a console, holojector and camera, as well as optic feeds leading to the outside of the shell. Nothing seemed damaged here, though he had no idea what condition the exterior emitter was in. Reaching down, he tore away the tattered remains of his hotsuit, then his similarly damaged syntheskin. Groping inside his gut, he found a shielded power cable, tracked it up into his chest and unplugged it. His vision dimmed and his movements slowed, but not enough to prevent him plugging the cable into the universal adaptor underneath the console. Immediately the device's displays lit. With slow precision, he pressed the touch sequence for a diagnostic check, and soon found the U-space transmitter to be in perfect working order. Using the keyboard, he typed out the message he wanted to send, and the all-important coordinates. Now it was time to send—and to sleep. He instructed the device to transmit continuously until it received an acknowledgement. He had time only to reach out and clamp his hand shut on the handle beside the console before his artificial consciousness left him—the transmitter using up the bulk of his own power output.

The quarantine pod Mika had occupied, along with all its equipment, had been destroyed in one of Jerusalem's fusion furnaces, then the surrounding area had been scanned down to the molecular level and classified at "contamination level 5." She already knew that anything coming into contact with Jain technology could never be classified as *clean*. She now occupied a work station where she studied, by proxy, the mycelium on the bridge pod, which the AI was holding at not much above absolute zero.

"There is stuff here," she gazed at a screen, "that could probably be called picotech. In fact much of it can only be extrapolated, as we haven't the instruments to study it directly."

"That is not so unfeasible—my own etched-atom processors come under that classification," replied the disembodied voice of Jerusalem.

Mika nodded, then walked over to the partial VR immersion frame, which was her main tool of study. She backed into the frame and it closed about her arms and legs, gloved her hands and closed its cowl down over her face. The immersion here was partial because it did not engage all her senses, only her sight, her hearing and the touch of her hands. She would go to total immersion if she ever needed to smell Jain-tech—or have sex with it.

In VR, she suddenly occupied a vast plenum below a flat white sky. Beside her floated the multicoloured cubes, tetrahedrons, spheres and other Euclidian solids of her main controls. She reached out, touched one face of a heptahedron, and broke it into a rainbow of pyramids. Taking hold of the blue one, she said, "Image."

Immediately the nanoscope view she had been earlier studying on a screen spread out before her like a mountain range. Manipulating the icon she held, then a sphere she selected out of the air, she transplanted a single large molecule and expanded it hugely before her, whilst wiping out the original view. "Just on the molecular level this alone will take me days of processing time to work out, and having done that I'll only know what it can do by itself, not how it interacts with the billions of others that make up this mycelium."

"Yes, it's like studying DNA."

Mika glanced at the silver eyeless head which Jerusalem favoured as a representation of itself. She continued, "*Worse* than that. At least with DNA you know that its function remains at the molecular level—nothing smaller than that."

Jerusalem paused before replying. "There are those who would disagree with you concerning DNA, but that's moot. You did manage to ascertain the purpose of a chain of these molecules, and from them create the mycelium that kept Apis Coolant and yourself alive."

"Ninety-nine per cent guesstimation of its overall purpose, and in the end I got it wrong anyway."

"Nevertheless . . ."

Mika gazed up at the huge edifice: each atom was something she could take in her hand. She turned a small virtual control and revolved the giant molecule. For some people she supposed that the complexity of the task ahead would be intimidating, but despite her words she only felt excitement at the prospect. Already she had spoken to other researchers on the *Jerusalem*, and discovered that they felt much the same. And there were thousands of them aboard, each studying one small facet of Jain technology, one piece of the 3D jigsaw, while Jerusalem itself put it all together.

Selecting a red coin with an ouroboros on its face, Mika started a program designed by the AI, which ran a virtual analysis of the molecule. Dropping down like a net, a cubic grid of glowing lines now enclosed it. The program selected some cubes and detached the atomic structures they enclosed from the main body, and turned them in mid-air, spitting formulae and reams of data like glyph-written insect wings. Beside her, flat screens rose out of the virtual floor and began displaying the results as they came through. Selecting from an arc of coloured coins bearing Life-coven icons, she began running those results through her own programs, then back again and around. Testing scenarios and a vast range of environmental parameters, she began to plumb the theoretical function of the molecule. Sometimes her theories collapsed under virtual tests, sometimes they survived.

A wizard surrounded by visible spells and conjured jewels, she worked faster and narrowed her focus. She saw that, in an oxidizing atmosphere, part of the atomic structure—in the same manner as a pigment such as haemoglobin—collected oxygen. It then acted as a catalyst, using the oxygen to burn the molecule into any solid substance it touched. Hours later she realized that the metallic atoms in the molecule caused an ionization process in some substances, complementing the burning process. Simply put, a visible quantity of this compound would act like a potent ever-active acid. But even that wasn't enough, it seemed. Mika started to get excited when she saw what it did to carbon: forming it into buckytubes as it ate its destructive course. This was already familiar to her from Polity nanotechnology.

"The drilling head, and the cable layer," she stated abruptly.

Jerusalem, having silently disappeared from beside her, now reappeared. "Part of it, yes. D'nissan, Colver and James are each working on other parts." With that, three other greatly enlarged molecules appeared high up, like lumpish moons. "The molecule you are studying will not, for example, work in vacuum. D'nissan has discovered a molecule that uses nanoscopic ionization entirely, it being fed electric current from the main body of the Jain structure, whilst Colver has found a metallo-buckytube that drills mechanically." As the AI spoke, each function it described appeared briefly in VR representation to one side, then faded; Jerusalem thus signifying that her fellows' research results were available to her should she require them.

"What about James?" Mika asked distractedly, then suddenly realizing what she had said, was delighted at how naturally the question had slid from her tongue.

"Susan James has found a molecular structure similar to yours, but which lays angstrom-width optical tubes inside larger buckytubes of doped carbon, which itself acts as a superconductor."

"Hell," said Mika, staring with fascination at the view of said molecule in action.

"Indeed," Jerusalem replied. "Even so, due to this research, Polity science has probably advanced in just the last hour as much as it would have done in *ten years* without it."

"You know," said Mika, realizing she had only ascertained the function of about ten per cent of her molecule, "we could learn a lot more, and much quicker, if we could study this in action."

"*That* is a very dangerous course."

"Yes, it is, but we can isolate the technology from the media it requires to spread and, if that fails, you've got ships out there with imploder missiles . . ."

"This has already been discussed," said Jerusalem.

"And a conclusion was come to," Mika stated.

"Yes."

"Dammit! What *was* the conclusion?"

Jerusalem replied, "That unless we learn quickly, we die quickly."

Gravfields of four gees, the maximum the dropshaft could attain, tried to snatch them from the ladder. Crane closed his hands with enough force to crush the metal rungs, his coat sagging about him and his hat stretching low over his forehead. Skellor gripped hard as each wave swept past them, then continued to climb once it was past, treacly fibres snapping from each hand as he released it from where he had bound himself to the ladder. From below came the screams of those who—not warned through the Dracocorp network—had stepped unthinkingly into the shaft. Further below, impacted human debris accumulated.

Skellor and Crane reached the next floor and stepped out into an arboretum. The foliage of chestnuts, towering nettlelms and oaks concealed the far wall. Where they stood, the floor was slabbed granite in a semicircle, with paths of the same leading to the right and left alongside the near wall. Between this path and the trees was a strip of grass ten metres wide, nibbled, between pink and blue crocuses, by miniature beetle-mowers. In the forest, an interference field blurred scan, but Skellor picked up enough to know that Nalen's people were bringing weapons to bear. He nodded to Crane, then, initiating his chameleonware, followed the path to his left. Moving away from him, towards the trees, Crane crossed the grass, kicking up huge clods with each loping stride and slowed only a little by the softness of the ground. A flashing in the trees: autogun. Skellor put out his own interference field, to foil any tracking of Crane. Lavender explosions stitched along the ground towards Crane, but kept going when he veered. Behind Skellor, a section of wall erupted into molten plasteel and incandescent gas. A glasshouse now ahead; the nexus—Nalen—retreating back beyond. Shots tracked manually along the wall behind as Skellor ran into a pane of chainglass, his hands issuing a decoder molecule. The glass collapsed into dust; he went through just as the screaming, and the firing of hand weapons, came from the trees.

—retroact 9—

Alston carefully opened the box on his desk and spilled out a glittering pile of etched sapphires, then with a shaking hand he spread them out across the oak surface. He deliberately didn't look at Chaldor, not that there was much recognizable about her: perhaps the clawed hand caught in the curtain, that length of bare thigh that was the largest part of her remaining, or a scrap of bloody clothing.

"I know you can understand me. I know that behind that plastic face is a brain probably more sophisticated than both Angelina's and Arian's put together."

The sapphires had definitely caught its attention, this thing that had shut down, one after another, the comunit transmissions from every single person on the island. Alston stared at the giant, raggedy, blood-soaked scarecrow as it tilted its head to one side, birdlike.

"You must be a free Golem who, for whatever reason, Arian has managed to employ. That bullshit about a 'broken' Golem is for scaring the children—it's the sort of story he likes circulating to try to frighten his people. It doesn't have that effect on me, because you've stopped, which means that something more than a simple kill order must be functioning."

The Golem took a step into the room and looked around, obviously curious about the otter-bone sculptures, the imported antiques, the general decor. Then its attention swung back to Alston and his sapphires. Alston could feel sweat trickling down his back.

"These?" he waved a hand at the jewels scattered before him. "These are nothing. Pelter thinks he's in control here, but his organization is located in only three of the main cities. To control this planet you have to control the papyrus harvest and the seas. I've got so many crop managers in my pocket, I can't count them, and I run all of the otter-bone smuggling. Pelter's annual turnover wouldn't even reach ten per cent of the interest on mine."

Alston leant forward. There was something in that plastic face—he was getting through! He knew it: you could always make a deal with anything that had a mind.

"Think! Working for me you could have anything. I'll give you Pelter's entire organization. You could come in with me. *Anything*, anything you want."

Alston felt his mouth suddenly go dry. What to offer a Golem android?

"Any upgrade you want. You could load the best software, add memory crystal, get yourself Cybercorp syntheskin."

The Golem reached up with one gory hand and touched its face.

"That's right, the best!" Alston slid the jewels across towards the Golem. "Take these as a down payment. Go and get me Arian's head, and that of his damned sister." He slid his chair back and stood. "Then we can begin. You can bring in other free Golem, buy up the contracts of any still indentured. Together we could have this world. And all our enemies . . ." Alston flicked his fingers.

The Golem now stepped up until it was directly opposite Alston, looming over the desk. It reached down, picked up one of the sapphires and held the stone up to its eye.

"They're the best—one hundred thousand New Carth shillings each."

The other hand snapped out so fast Alston had no time to react. Gripping the front of his jacket it pulled him close, then with bloodied fingers opened Alston's mouth and shoved the sapphire inside, before picking up another. At four million shillings Alston finally died. He never yelled or screamed—was too full.

—retroact ends—

Tabrouth kissed the lion's tooth he wore suspended from a chain around his neck, and sensed the growing fear in the network. They all knew what had happened on B-deck, and what was happening in the arboretum. The android was so damned fast that no way was it some primitive metalskin—it had to be a military-spec Golem, and that meant ECS must be on to Nalen. The APW autogun should have been enough to take it out, but just when they got a fix on it, the tracking system packed up and they missed. Now they were dying.

Tabrouth was frightened, but also relieved that Nalen's control seemed not so firm. Yes, it had been great in the beginning, taking control of the station syndicate and being part of so superior an aug network. But gradually Nalen's orders began to carry more weight until his merest whim became an order, and his orders became impossible to disobey. And there was that other thing: Nalen had been a small-time crime boss, stealing tech and information to sell under the nose of Ruby Eye, though all but ignored by her. Now he was manufacturing arms and using the sun-surveyors to run them to black ships arriving from out-Polity to the other side of the sun. That was something the station AI could not ignore for long. Anyone caught doing so would receive an automatic death sentence; consequently, that wouldn't be something in which Tabrouth would involve himself. But Nalen's control gave him no choice—Nalen who no longer really looked like a man.

Movement to his right. Tabrouth whirled and aimed his pulse-rifle—not that it would do him a lot of good if the Golem was coming for him. But it was only Paulson and Shroder shoving through the briars and simnel bushes growing below a line of nettlelms. Tabrouth stopped and waited for them. He noticed they were both blood-spattered.

"What happened?" he asked.

"Tore the fucking autogun in half, then did the same to Alain and Solnek," said the hermaphrodite Shroder.

"We got away when others opened up on it with the second gun. It went after that," Paulson explained. The man looked sick—and very tired. "It's *going*. Nalen's grip is slipping," he added.

"So it feels," said Tabrouth. "Maybe it's time for us to get the hell out of here."

Tabrouth waited for some response to that, but noticed the two were staring past him, their faces white with fear. Tabrouth had heard nothing, but then that didn't surprise him.

"It's standing right behind me, isn't it?" he said.

Paulson and Shroder both gave the same slow nod as if invisible rods joined their heads. Tabrouth sighed and turned.

The Golem loomed before him, its coat neatly buttoned, undamaged and clear of any unpleasant stains. This made no sense, after many had hit it with pulse weapons; though its adamantine body might itself remain undamaged, its clothing should at least be ripped and burnt. And where was the blood, and the other fluids and tissues? You did not do to a human being what this Golem had been doing without getting in a horrible mess. But then, he thought, what did it matter about such inconsistencies? The Golem's eyes were obsidian in its brass face; its massive hands were capable of tearing a man like tissue paper. And now Tabrouth was about to die.

"You are one big ugly murderous bastard, aren't you?" he said, deciding that to beg would be futile. He raised his pulse-rifle and aimed it at the Golem's chest. Just as he did this, Paulson and Shroder opened up with their own weapons, both also pulse-rifles. Bluish fire and metallic smoke flared and exploded all down the front of the Golem. Seemingly oblivious to this, it stepped forward, then reached out and gripped the barrel of Tabrouth's weapon in its big hand, so that he was now firing directly into its palm. Tabrouth stared down disbelievingly at the sun glare reflected in that hand as he continued holding down the trigger. His weapon heated rapidly, then molten metal sputtered out of its side as its coils blew. Tabrouth released his hold and staggered back, his hands seared. After-images occluded his vision, and only subliminally did he see his weapon spiralling away. Other firing ceased. He supposed Paulson and Shroder had run away, and didn't blame them in the least.

The same big hand closed on his neck, its brassy metal not even warm, and hauled him into the air, choking. Then something snapped and tore and, gasping for breath, Tabrouth hit the ground on his feet and fell over backwards. He groped at his neck, sure the Golem had crushed it and that he was yet to feel the killing pain, but found only that his lion's tooth, his good-luck charm, was gone. Through shadowed vision, he saw the big Golem striding off after the other two. When he finally recovered his breath, he ran just as fast as he could for the nearest exit. The only time he looked back was when the blast from an ECS riot gun spun him off his feet, and even then he did not see Paulson and Shroder hot on his heels, relieved respectively of a ring with a pre-runcible coin set in it and a cheap scent bottle.

9

The kind of AI used in smaller human-partnership survey ships is contained in crystal similar to that of the Golem, but with computing capacity a Golem would use for emulation, devoted to U-space calculations, and extra capacity allotted for a greater array of senses. IQ 185 (whatever that means). Your basic attack ship AI can function at a human level, or create and assign subminds to this tedious task. As well as the required ability to make U-space calculations, it can run complex internal repair and modification programs, operating through multiple subminds, installed in everything from ship Golem to nanobots. It can operate complex and powerful weapons systems, make high-speed tactical decisions in fractions of a second. Its IQ would be about 300. Then we come to the runcible/planetary governor AIs. Most of these intelligences run in crystal, but at a vastly greater capacity than even attack ships. They can run subminds of full AI Golem level, balance the economy of a planet, make millions of U-space calculations for the operation of a runcible . . . The list goes on and on. Such AIs are omniscient and omnipotent, and any attempt to measure IQ is laughable. Yet even these are not at the apex. Some AIs run differently; using etched-atom processing, quantum computing . . . These are often sector-class AIs of almost mythic status, like the awesome Geronamid and that roving AI Einstein Jerusalem and, of course, Earth Central itself. We could never have imagined such gods . . .

— *Excerpt from a speech by Jobsworth*

After carefully rereading the instructions in the fading light, Anderson detached the breech clamp, set the lever over to single shots, and cocked the carbine. He then aimed at the sulerbane plant below the nearest butte, squeezed off one shot and, even after firing off five shots, was still surprised at how little smoke the gun emitted. The noise, though also less than that generated by his fusile, was vicious enough. He peered thoughtfully at where the bullet had struck the ground, to the left of the plant. Behind him, he heard Bonehead sigh as it sank down on its belly plates. Tergal raised his handgun and fired twice, knocking off one of the plant's hard resinous leaves.

"I think I'm getting the hang of this," the boy said smugly.

Anderson removed his helmet and dropped it beside his feet, then turned and stared hard at where his fusile was holstered on Bonehead's back.

"I'm overcompensating. I should just follow the instructions and use the sight," he said, expecting Tergal to make some sarcastic quip, for this was what the boy had already advised him twice. When no comment was forthcoming, he glanced over to see Tergal staring at him in amazement. With a grimace, Anderson reached up and rubbed his perfectly bald head.

"Fell out when I was a boy and never grew back," he said. "My mother said it's because I think too much."

"Oh, right," said Tergal, embarrassed.

Anderson raised his weapon and fired again, but again the plant remained untouched.

"I thought you were going to use the sight?" Smug again.

"I did."

The sleer thudded down next to the plant, a hole perfectly positioned between its extensible antlers. It writhed on the ground, its segments revolving independently, then it separated. Its rear section got up on four legs and attempted to make a break for safety. Anderson put a shot into its raw-looking separation point and it collapsed. He turned to Tergal, allowing himself a sly smile. "Now we've got something to cook on the fire you're about to make with all those leaves you just slew."

Tergal stared back, but Anderson saw that the boy had got the message. He humphed, holstered his weapon and walked over to the sulerbane plant and the dead sleer. Frequently glancing above him for any sign of other creatures, he began collecting thick dry leaves. Meanwhile, Anderson returned to Bonehead, clambered up on the creature's carapace, and unstrapped his packs from behind the saddle. As Tergal returned with a stack of leaves, Anderson was driving posts into the sand—setting up the perimeter of their camp. While the boy then arranged the leaves around a wax firelighter and ignited that with smoky sulphurous matches, Anderson unreeled wire and secured it to the posts.

"This won't be enough," said Tergal, gesturing at the small stack of leaves heaped beside the fire.

"You're sure to find shed carapace around here—that burns good and slow," Anderson replied. It was evident to him now that, though Tergal had been travelling for some time, he had never really camped out in wilds like this. He watched as Tergal retrieved his own pack from Stone, and dropped it by the fire before going off in search of more fuel. By the time the boy returned with old sleer sheddings and more of the thick resinous leaves, Anderson had erected the two wires to make a fence a metre high, though with a gap through which Tergal could re-enter, and was now levering off the head from the front end of the dead sleer with his heavy steel knife.

Securing the wires across the gap, Tergal glanced up at the sky, which was now dark green swirled with the red of interstellar gas clouds. The stars had yet to appear and the first impression was of a ceiling carved of bloodstone. He then reached down to turn on the charge generator standing beside one of the posts.

"Not yet," said Anderson, finally levering the sleer's head off and pulling it away—dragging out a tangle of intestines. Then reaching inside the cavity with his knife, he cut, grabbed and pulled, and out came the translucent internal belly plate, with other gelatinous organs attached. "The batteries are low—only got half a day's charge." They had left the roadhouse at midday, and only then had he laid out the solar panel on Bonehead's carapace, and attached the batteries.

"They'll last the night?" Tergal asked.

"Mostly. Anyway, once a few of the buggers have taken a few belts from the fence they tend not to come back."

Anderson stood up and, carrying the offal and head of the sleer, walked to the fence and tossed them over it for Bonehead and Stone. Not bothering to attach it below its sensory head, the old sand hog folded out its feeding head, extended it on its second hinged neck to suck down the offal, then knocked the remainder across to Stone, who crunched the sleer's head like a boiled sweet. They both ate seemingly without much appetite, but then this meat was rather too fresh for their taste.

With the fire burning well, Anderson set up his iron spit and roasted segments of sleer from the meatier tail section. The stars came out and, in the stark shadows of the buttes, the relatives of the two travellers' dinner came out for their nightly game of murder in the dark. Bonehead and Stone folded their heads and legs away, and sank down onto the sand: two long teardrop domes with saddles still in place. *Ogygian* was poised on the horizon, glittering in reflected sunlight, and distantly the lights of Golgoth cast an orange glow into the dusty sky.

"Other worlds have moons," said Tergal. "I wonder what that's like."

Anderson, after chucking onto the fire the carapace from the segment of meat he had just eaten, said, "More light at night, but little more beyond that, unless the world itself has oceans."

"I wonder what that's like, too."

"Wet, probably."

Beyond the fence, the movement drew closer, as chitinous bodies scuttled from shadow to shadow. Anderson stood up, walked over to the charge generator, and switched it on. The two of them were laying out their bedrolls when a second-stage sleer came to investigate this attractive cluster of heat sources. Its antlers extended themselves out from its nightmare head like long thin black hands, then touched a wire and jerked back. The creature held its ground for a moment, its feet rattling against the earth and its carapace saws scraping against each other, then with a hiss it retreated.

"Your first watch?" Anderson suggested.

Still clutching the gun he had drawn, Tergal eventually nodded. Anderson shook out his blankets, to be sure they had not acquired unwelcome guests, before lying down with his head resting on one of his packs. Through half-closed eyes, he watched Tergal light a smoky candle, and immediately the smell of repellent invaded the air—keeping away smaller denizens that might crawl under the wire. The boy then bowed his head and listened to the sounds of hard limbs rasping against sandy surfaces. Anderson closed his eyes fully and allowed sleep to take him. Tergal would not be robbing anyone tonight—he had other things to occupy his attention.

The first view showed the world only lightly crusted with black, with frequent cracks and volcanic eyes appearing and fading constantly. With his hand inside a projected virtual control, Cormac doubled the magnification, and now saw plumes of gas, ash and magma spewing into the poisonous atmosphere. It was hell—with all the sulphur and fire you could want—but until only a month ago had been lacking in devils. Then two had arrived.

"Show me the carrier shell," he said.

A square appeared, picking out a dot, and the magnification increased to show the wrecked shell poised above the inferno.

Ticking slowly while standing beside Cormac's chair as if to keep an eye on the virtual control the AI had loaned, Jack's automaton intoned, "Cento urges that we leave him and go at once to the coordinates he has given us. He does have a point. We shall achieve nothing by this rescue that cannot be achieved by the other ships on their way here."

"Try to think like a human," said Gant, lolling in one of the club chairs.

"Why should I restrict myself so severely? Cento has told us everything, and logically there is no reason for delay," said the ship's AI.

"But Cento is still Cento," Cormac supplied, and then left Gant to cobble together the explanation he himself could not be bothered trying to verbalize. He just knew it was right to have Cento along with them.

"Yes, he's told us everything," said Gant. "And from what he has told us we know that Skellor will assume Cento was utterly destroyed. That's an advantage, since in some situations his presence might pause Skellor for half a second, and that could mean the difference between life and death."

"The same rules apply to Aphran," Cormac added.

"More advantage might be gained by not wasting hours picking up a Golem android who would be picked up anyway," observed Jack.

Cormac relented and explained, "It's about *weapons*, Jack. In you we have everything we need in the way of bombs and missiles, but that might not be enough."

"You're rationalizing," said Jack.

"Attempting to rationalize something I feel instinctively— and it has been trusting such feelings that has kept me alive, and has made me as successful as I have been."

"Granted," said Jack.

The sun was a blue boiling giant glimpsed after thaw-up, as the *Jack Ketch* entered this barren system. Now it was out of view, for they were approaching in the planet's shadow so as not to overheat the ship. The carrier shell, since Skellor had hit it with a kinetic missile of some kind, had lost its geostationary position and, as Cento explained, was now orbiting the planet. Over the next hour they drew even closer, and Cormac saw that parts of the shell were still glowing red hot. They reached it just as it was coming back into the sun's actinic glare and, through filters, Cormac observed grapples—towing braided monofilament cables—fired across from each of the attack ship's nacelles. Closing by hydraulics these ceramal claws drove sharp fingers into the charred hull. Then came a droning as the *Ketch*'s engines took up the strain and dragged the shell back into the planetary shadow.

"I have apprised Cento of our position, and he is now making his way to where I will place the airlock," Jack informed them.

Cormac observed the docking tunnel extruding towards the shell. He noted that it was heading towards bare hull, and surmised that this was an injector lock—for inserting troops, probes, war drones, or even poison gas, into a hostile ship. He saw it contact, and the flare around its rim as it cut into the hull.

"Come on," he said to Gant.

As they entered the dropshaft, and it shifted them to their destination, Cormac had to wonder if this was the only shaft the *Jack Ketch* contained, as he had yet to discover any other. He and Gant moved into a short corridor decorated with metallic Greek statues and with reed matting on the floor. This took them to the chamber preceding an airlock—also lined with statues but with a bare metal floor. Shortly the displays on the exterior touch panels showed that the lock was cycling. Within a minute the inner door whoomphed open. Leaning on one hand, what remained of Cento looked up at them. "Touch of bother?" Gant enquired.

The four guarding the corridor were ensconced behind an APW cannon. Skellor did not even need to scan to know they were in constant communication with their fellows—their terrified expressions told that tale. As he stepped past the cannon—and over the woman crouching down connecting a large energy canister to the weapon—he noted the one over by the wall stare in his direction, his expression puzzled. But then the man returned his attention to the proximity grenade he was setting. Skellor moved on, glad not to have to kill these four, for that would alert Nalen, who was still fleeing towards the runcible.

Past the men, Skellor accelerated to a speed that only Mr. Crane or a Polity Golem could match. He wanted to intercept Nalen as soon as possible—did not want him to get within the defences of the runcible AI; did not want that level of confrontation yet. It occurred to him to wonder what the AI's reaction would be to the commotion behind. Certainly there would be a reaction of some kind.

A dropshaft, disabled, then up the ladder, just touching on the rungs in nil gee, changing course with a hand slapping against the exit portal, bending metal, then into another corridor opening out into an arboretum similar to the one below. Ahead, a gleam in his virtual vision, at the centre of an unstable web of light. In the real world he saw a man spherically fat running as energetically as the two guards alongside him. There was a doubling of image: yes, the man *was* fat, but scales did not really cover him—that was illusion. Closer, and Skellor began to feel the link that dropped away from this man and this station and out into space. He slammed into Nalen's back and, looping an arm around the man's greasy neck, dragged him down the corridor. Slapping the flat of his hand against Nalen's aug, which appeared utterly fused to his head, he transmitted the virus down penetrating Jain filaments. Nalen began to shriek.

Skellor glanced back and saw the two guards, weapons drawn, staring about themselves in bewilderment, for to their eyes their charge had simply disappeared. Then both of them jerked as, through Nalen, the virus hit their augs. One staggered back against the wall and slid down to the floor, blood bubbling from his ear. The other shrieked, clawed at his aug and managed to tear it from his head like a reptilian scab. Still shrieking he ran towards the sabotaged dropshaft.

No matter—Skellor had control now.

Crane had killed many of them, and many more were fleeing. Gazing through the eyes of those on the run, Skellor saw ECS uniforms. Nalen's people were going down all around, under fire from riot guns. Golem were bringing down others, and easily securing them in ankle and wrist cuffs. Skellor had not expected ECS to react so quickly. He immediately realized that the AI must have been aware of the Dracocorp network, and been preparing to deal with it. He had very little time.

Nalen's mind was a gibbering thing that yielded easily to his control, for his aug had softened it to receive commands through the U-space link. Skellor shrugged himself into that mind, as if into someone else's clothing. Tracing that branch of the network generating outside the station, he was surprised to find, orbiting the red dwarf, a U-space transmitter, and thought that so prosaic. The virus opening the way for him, he soon found himself groping mentally through alien software that was somehow familiar to him, familiar to that *alien* side of *him.* He was there; the coordinates were *his.* Then the communications laser pulse slammed into the transmitter, viral programs propagating from it, and snatching at that last vital information but failing to take it.

Dropping Nalen, Skellor staggered back. It was suddenly all so horribly clear to him. In his arrogance, he had assumed the Polity would not try this route, so busy were they tracing Dragon through Dracocorp. How very stupid he had been.

Crane, back to the ship—fast.

He sensed the Golem's immediate response just before the viral probe came in through a biotech aug on the other side of the station, opening the way, and something utterly vicious snarled its way into the network he now controlled. This he had encountered before: a hunter-killer AI program had been poised to take this network at its moment of maturity. He himself had taken it perhaps only months away from that time. ECS must have known about Nalen and his people for a long time, but had given them sufficient leash to get a lead on one of the Dragon spheres. Skellor, as he staggered away from the fat man who now seemed to have deflated on the floor, felt real fear.

What are you? was the essence of the program's question as it swung towards him in the network. Skellor ran for the dropshaft and leapt into it.

Located.

The dropshaft came on and tried to kill him, slamming immediately to a constant four gees. He reached out and caught the lip of the floor below, the force with which his arms hit buckling the floor plates, the composite out of which his bones were now fashioned bending and splintering. In the subliminal flash of agony, his defence lost coherence and a viral spear tried to impale his mind. He took it and slid aside, leaving another mind to take the brunt. Grav in the dropshaft abruptly reversed, slamming him up against the upper rim of the exit portal. The sound of Nalen's impaled mind dying was a retreating piggish squeal. Bonding his hands against the ceiling with Jain filaments, Skellor dragged himself out of the shaft's gravity field and dropped to the floor. Hitting, he accelerated as fast as he could, feeling the floor plates fluxing behind him as the program compensated for his inhuman speed. Then one went nil below him, and the next soared up to four gees. He came down on one knee and one foot, kneecap taking the brunt and shattering, but got no reaction from the human nervous system he had disconnected from cerebral activity. This battle worked both ways, however: Skellor linked back, through the probe into the Dracocorp network, and let that take all the pain his human body felt as it shattered and rebuilt. With a gargantuan hiss something retracted, and all the gravplates in the corridor returned to one gee.

Feel pain, do you? he asked of the shapeless nightmare.

He was in the arboretum now, retracing his course—dodging between ECS troops and Golem alike, with his 'ware still functioning.

How about this?

Still linked to his attacker, he reached out to all those still-conscious points in the network. Slammed into their aug control programs and gave them something he had himself recorded on the *Occam Razor* while he had tortured the Separatist woman, Aphran. The hoarse voice of agony echoed throughout the station as, one after the other, people wearing biotech augs fell, believing someone was peeling off their skins with red-hot scalpels. For a moment Skellor thought the feedback into the attacking program was killing it, but then he saw that the program was changing to link into the screamers and give them succour. So altruistic were Polity AIs, so kind to the poor soft-bodied creatures, that Skellor and Crane both broke apart like ripe fruit.

Skellor, we have ever let humans deal with human threats, Ruby Eye told him, but in your case we may make an exception. Go away from here now—a battle between us would denude this station of life, and I see no purpose in that when we can kill you somewhere more remote.

Crane awaited him on the *Vulture*. The Golem was now seated playing with new toys. Skellor ignored him and, through the Jain structures he had grown inside the ship, immediately put all systems online.

Runcible AI. If you fire any weapons on me, I'll turn this ship round and fly it into your station, initiating U-space jump before the engines are ready. I don't suppose even you would survive that.

Go away, creature.

With a blast of fusion flame, he accelerated the *Vulture* down from the station towards the red dwarf, initiating the ship's newly installed chameleonware. He knew that, in this situation, hiding was not enough, as the AI knew where the *Vulture* had been docked, and could fill nearby space with lethal munitions and a cage of discharges from energy weapons. But there came nothing from the station: no missiles, no laser beams, not even a parting taunt as he dropped the little ship into U-space. And somehow that was more frightening.

No matter how much shielding a ship used, passengers always felt the transition from U-space to realspace—or the reverse. Why this was so, no one had explained, though Mika felt sure some would attribute it to the belief that humans were more than mere material substance—an idea she found objectionable. Climbing out of her bed in the quarters Jerusalem had recently provided for her, she gazed up at a screen that was always set for external view, and observed starlit space rather than any planetary system. The *Jerusalem* was no longer in U-space.

"Jerusalem, what's happening?" she asked.

There was a pause before the AI replied, "So it begins."

"Pardon."

"We will not be going to Masada. We will now be going to a sector of space in which the source of so much of what we study has been located."

"Skellor's been found."

"Not precisely, but we may close him in our grasp."

Abruptly Mika felt that sensation of transition again and, looking up, saw her screen showing the bland grey representation of U-space. Normally, while a ship was under, its human passengers and crew would go into cold sleep, but aboard the *Jerusalem* there was an urgency to learn all about that *thing* that might kill the Polity. Having slept four hours, which was ample for Mika, she showered, dressed, and immediately went out into the main corridor and headed for the refectory. Though machines in her own quarters could supply all her nutritional needs, she always took her meals elsewhere. In the refectory, like-minded people bounced ideas about and did quite a lot of the planning and more imaginative work there. Entering the large room, with its scattering of tables and chairs, she saw that Susan James, D'nissan and Prator Colver were all seated around one table and, after making her selection from one of the food dispensers, Mika collected her tray and went over to join them.

The man, Colver, was Life-coven like herself: a stocky ginger-haired individual who was prone to sudden enthusiasms and who had long ago learned how to ask questions. "Have you heard?" he asked as she sat down. "We're going to *Ruby Eye*."

Mika looked across at Susan James and raised an eyebrow.

"It's a research station in orbit around a red dwarf. Been there for fifty years—long-term study," she explained.

Susan was a standard-format human; in appearance almost a female version of Ian Cormac, though certainly not as deadly. Mika turned her attention to D'nissan, the low-temperature ophidapt man from Ganymede. His visor was down in the neck ring of his hotsuit, and he was drinking what looked like a raspberry coolie through a straw—a drink that would have been hot to him. His pronouncements were usually concise and apposite, which was why, when the situation warranted it, he was Jerusalem's chief researcher, but he didn't have anything to say just then.

"To get Skellor," Mika said.

"It'd be great to get hold of the source of the Jain tech we've been studying," said Colver. "I'm sure there are controlling mechanisms we haven't seen yet."

Now D'nissan observed coolly, "That's like studying venom, then wishing to get hold of a snake."

Mika thought that a bit rich, coming from a man with diamond-scaled skin and fangs.

He looked at her directly. "Of course we haven't seen it all, because what we *have* got is just a . . . cutting. If it were rooted and allowed to grow, we then perhaps would."

"Yeah, but Skellor . . . he direct-interfaced with a crystal matrix AI . . ." said Colver, apropos of nothing.

"I would like to see Jain technology operating," said Mika.

"Haven't you heard?" Colver asked, interrupting D'nissan, who had been about to speak. "We're going to see that."

Mika stared at D'nissan.

"The asteroid," he explained, "it would have had to be destroyed by imploder anyway. So why not use it to grow some of our specimen?"

"In red sunlight," Mika suggested.

"Precisely," said D'nissan.

Mika was not sure how to react. This was what she had wanted, but she was also aware that they were playing with something substantially more dangerous than fire.

In the invisible grid, Crane shifted a blue acorn to a position adjacent to the lion's tooth, then moved the coin ring adjacent to the piece of crystal. The rubber dog remained constant beside the laser lighter. This elicited a fragmented image of the same grid occupied by the shells of penny oysters, the interstices of which dying pearl crabs were exploring. Blood dripped from his fingers onto the crushed-shell beach, black in the silver moonlight.

—retroact 10—

"Did they all get in his way?" Angelina asked, looking at the corpses scattered across the sand.

"Apparently so," said Arian. Three of his men moved ahead, spreading out as they stepped into the creosote bushes, while the other eight split into two groups of four, to head in either direction along the beach.

"Two more here," said one of the men, pushing aside a bush with the barrel of his pulse-rifle. Angelina moved up beside Arian as her brother gazed down at the mess. The tangle of blood, bones and torn flesh seemed only identifiable as human because there was clothing mixed in there as well.

"Two?" she asked.

"Well I count two *heads*," the man replied.

Angelina did not like this at all. With Alston dead they could have just moved in and taken over his operation, perhaps having to pay the man's people over the odds for a while until they got things under control. But there had been no reaction to their approach of the island. The scanners aboard the boat had detected very few heat signatures, and those few detected were fading. It was beginning to look as if no operation remained here.

They moved on through silvery moonlight, and it was only fifty metres inland before they found the next corpse. This man was impaled on the snapped branch of a tree, his feet dangling two metres from the ground, where his blood had pooled.

"Where exactly is he?" Angelina asked. "We wouldn't want him to make a mistake about us."

"On the other side of the island, on the beach. He's not moving and all I'm getting is 'objective achieved' and some weird images. He won't move."

"Perhaps we should just turn around and leave him here?"

Arian lowered his hand from his platinum aug and stared at her. "I think it may be the second link to his control module from my aug. We need a direct optic link to get the bandwidth, and some military programming. Someone like Sylac could do the job."

Angelina could hear the doubt in his voice. Personally she had no wish to see herself, or her brother, under Sylac's knives, since the surgery he performed might not render the intended result. The surgeon was a law unto himself and considered the human body a testing ground, or even a playground. Nor did she want either of them to be more closely connected to the scrambled insane mind of the Golem, no matter how much more control they might thus obtain. And the idea of putting that kind of power into the hands of one of their employees would be sheer madness. Already she was beginning to see that Mr. Crane was like a black-market pulse-gun from one of the less reputable dealers on Huma—it might work, but was just as likely to blow up in your face. When she saw the mound, she felt her thoughts confirmed.

"Why the fuck did he do that?" asked Arian.

Counting heads, they found the knotted mound of corpses consisted of maybe eight people—it was difficult to be sure. Stepping closer to see if she recognized any of the faces, Angelina felt her foot sink, and abruptly stepped back. Her boot pulled out with a slurp, and she saw that the blood had turned the ground into a quagmire. She had killed, she had seen horrible death, and been hard and unaffected by it. But this made her gorge rise. One of their men stepped off to one side, leant against a rock, and spewed briefly before turning back.

"Up to his house?" he asked, after wiping vomit from his lips.

"Yes . . . to his house," Arian replied. Abruptly he reached up and initiated the comunit button on his collar. "Falen, Balsh—don't go round to the other side of the island. Just get back to the boat." He tilted his head as he listened to their reply, then said, "You needn't bother—I don't think there's anyone left alive here."

In the moonlight the corpses on the hillside were macabre sculptures: clawed hands frozen while groping for mercy, jags of white bone pointing to the sky, and an eyeless head propped on a rock, gazing into infinity. More of the same occupied Alston's fortified home, but what struck Angelina more than anything was the lack of pulse-gun burns on the walls. The slaughter here had been quick and absolute. She was also surprised at just how intact Alston himself was, sitting behind his desk there with something gleaming in his mouth.

"No one else must get their hands on him," said Arian, staring at the corpse.

Angelina realized her brother was referring to the Golem.

"We'll just hide him away somewhere secure, just . . . keep him ready."

So, Arian was beginning to see straight.

"It's not like we'll need him for every operation."

Angelina kept her mouth closed and her face expressionless.

"We can handle most problems ourselves."

"Where do we put him?" Angelina asked him.

"Where such things should always be kept," Arian told her. "In a cellar."

"Yes, of course."

Angelina would have preferred that place to be the caldera of a volcano.

—retroact ends—

10

The evolutionary forces detailed long ago by Darwin, and only elaborated on ever since, are universal, and required for life. The other requirements were thought to be matter and energy, though doubt has now been cast on the former. All life, therefore, lives by rules already discussed ad nauseam by others. Suffice to say that there are doves and hawks in every ecosystem. And some of the hawks are monstrous. Looking into the natural history of our own planet it can be seen that we ascended during a particularly peaceful time, and that most of the monsters were in our past. We missed the dinosaurs by sixty million years. Close call—they were bad enough. However, even Tyrannosaurus rex would have had problems with some of the alien creatures we have since discovered: the fauna of Masada with its hooders, heroynes, siluroynes, and the positively weird gabbleduck. How would dinosaurs have fared there? What about the thrake—a grade-three sentience but still armoured like a tank? What about the horrifying leeches of that far out-Polity planet Spatterjay? What else is out there—what have we yet to find?
        —From *How It Is* by Gordon

The kiln smell, then the sound of a steam pump, told Anderson what lay ahead before he even saw the minerallier encampment, and rounding a butte beside which some spillage had cut an oily-looking channel, around which grew stunted sulerbanes, he and Tergal soon came in sight of industry.

"You can see why they're here," said Tergal. Anderson looked at him questioningly, and Tergal pointed up at the butte. "White and blue sand in separate layers."

Anderson glanced up to where layers of pink and orange sand separated the white from the blue.

Tergal explained, "You find the two layers close together and they've normally reacted with each other. Then the trace elements turn to salts, and rain washes them out. The sands are worthless then."

Anderson nodded, not wanting to disappoint the boy by explaining that he already knew all this.

By the channel a sand hog as old as Bonehead was lying in the sunshine, harnessed to a huge cart laden with coke. Next to this was parked a large powered vehicle with caterpillar treads, and two trailers attached behind—one flatbed and one container. Beyond the stream, the mineralliers had erected a scaffold up the side of the butte, so that they could get to the layers of sand which they lowered in separate buckets on a steam-driven chain. A short distance back from the butte, bonded-sand kilns and houses had been built, but even so Anderson knew this to be a temporary encampment—the mineralliers would stay only until the seams were worked out, though that could take them months or years. Between the houses they had erected a wooden frame on which sleer carapaces were drying—no doubt to be used as additional fuel. Workers were busy in the excavation in the butte, mining the sands or, down below, barrowing it to the kilns where others spread it on ceramic plates to fuse it into sheets. No one noticed their approach until a little girl spotted them, and went yelling into the encampment.

"What would we do without them?" Anderson asked, eyeing the solar triptych lying open on Bonehead's back—its three cells charging up the batteries of the charge generator they had used during the night.

"Mineralliers?" Tergal asked.

"No, solar cells. There are other ways of generating electricity, but none so easy and convenient as this." He gestured to a stack of boxes by one of the sandstone houses.

Beside this, a big black-haired woman was cutting sheets of opaque-white and translucent-blue glass, before polishing them. Next to her, a small monkey of a man was attaching small braided copper wires, painting something on one kind of glass, then sealing pieces of each kind together with sheets of glistening film he removed from a bucket beside him. Each complete photovoltaic cell he wrapped and carefully packed away. It was to the woman that the girl ran. The woman ceased working and walked out to meet Anderson and Tergal at the edge of the encampment.

"A slow response, and I hardly expected a Rondure Knight to be sent," she said, looking Anderson up and down.

"I think you're mistaking me for someone else," said Anderson, unstrapping himself from his saddle as Bone-head went down on its crawler limbs.

"You're a weapons man?"

"I am that," he replied, stepping down onto the sand.

The woman nodded. "We sent into Golgoth for a weapons man five days ago and he has yet to appear." She gazed about in irritation, eyed Tergal for a moment, then returned her attention to Anderson. "Are you taking commissions?"

Anderson shrugged. "Whenever available—a man has to eat."

"Then I have one for you for which I can pay in pfennigs, or new phocells if you'd prefer. Our man from Golgoth can suck on a sleer's arse for all I care now."

Tergal snorted, choked off his laughter. The woman stared at him estimatingly.

"Your apprentice?" she asked Anderson.

"Of a kind," replied Anderson. "Tell me about this commission."

Again the woman looked around. "It comes at night, and we've not minded when it only knocked a few things over as it searched our camp for food. But it's getting bolder. Six nights ago it attacked one of our hogs and put a hole in its carapace." She gestured to a hog compound over the other side of the encampment in which more of the huge creatures rested like a scattering of laval domes in the sunshine. One of them, perhaps younger and more curious than its fellows, had its sensory head out from under its shell and high up in the air with its eye-palps extruded wide apart to observe proceedings. "Then five nights ago it tried to grind its way into one of our houses."

"Show me that," Anderson said.

The woman gestured for him to follow her, and led the way into the encampment. Tergal also dismounted, and led his hog by hooking his goad under the edge of its carapace skirt. Anderson stared pointedly at Bonehead until, with a long sigh, it heaved up onto its crawler limbs and followed as well. Glancing about as he walked in, he saw that this encampment must have been here—or was intended to be here—for some time, for the spill-channel issued from a standing hand pump. Therefore the mineralliers had drilled a borehole, and that was not something done for a short-term operation. Soon other workers were coming over to see what was going on. The monkey-like man walked beside Tergal, talking animatedly to him, but Anderson could not hear what their conversation concerned. By the time he reached the sandstone house, quite a crowd had gathered. He inspected the gouges in the soft stone, confirming what he had already guessed. Smiling, he glanced at Tergal before turning to the woman.

"Do you know what did this?" he asked.

"We'd earlier hoped it was a second-stager, but what with the attack on a sand hog and now this . . ." She shrugged.

"Third," he said, and gestured to the deep puncture holes in the bonded sand. "That's where it held on with its pincers while it worked on the wall with its carapace saws. Something must have distracted it, else it would have gone right through."

"Third!" someone snorted. "He's trying to bump the price up, Chandle."

Anderson turned away and began to walk back to Bonehead.

"Wait!" the woman Chandle shouted. "And you, Dornick, shut your mouth."

Anderson turned. "Thirty phocells—they'll be useful for trade as I'm heading up onto the Plains."

"Bloody extortion!"

Anderson rounded on the man Dornick: a squat, bearded individual with cropped mouth tendrils and the underhand thumb-spurs that inevitably led his type into some technical trade. "Would you prefer to hunt it yourself?"

"At that price—probably."

"Dornick," Chandle warned.

"That's days of work, that is. Days and days."

Anderson noted that Chandle, though giving a warning, seemed disinclined to interfere and was waiting for his reply. He noted that some of these people carried metallier weapons, and perhaps that was making them overconfident. Really, he didn't need this as, though he might manage to trade off a few phocells to nomads on the Plains, he had no real need for them. And as for money—he had accumulated plenty of that. But a sense of duty asserted itself. He glanced at the little girl standing beside Chandle. A third-stager would take only seconds to mince her into easily ingestible portions.

"Days, you say." He turned and walked back to the wall of the house. "Dornick, I see you have a measuring wire on your belt. May I borrow it?" Anderson held out his hand.

The man looked rebellious but, after a warning glare from Chandle, handed over the wire. Anderson unspooled it above his head, measuring the height of the damage to the wall.

"There was no reason here for the creature to climb, so I would bet it chewed on this dwelling while keeping its forelimbs on the ground. So, when you find marks like this, there's an easy calculation to apply." He wound the wire back into its spool. "The body length of a third-stager is nominally two and a half times the height of its mouthparts from the ground. These marks are over two metres high." Anderson observed how some faces had taken on a sickly hue. Dornick was mouthing the figures. "Five metres," Anderson told the man. "A third-stager of that length weighs five times a big man. And, incidentally, can run twice as fast."

"So you say," muttered Dornick.

Anderson handed back his wire. "I'll bring you the body, and if it is less than five metres long I'll waive my fee."

"You have a deal, Rondure Knight," said Chandle, stepping forward before Dornick could say any more.

The ECS doctors had erected a chainglass partition to prevent any air-transmission of infection, and it was an infection possible for even Fethan, with his flash-frozen bio-gridded brain and body of plastic and metal, to contract. Not that there had been any sign of the dying remains of the Jain mycelium—inside the outlinker—spreading through the air, but no one was taking any chances.

"The girl will be next?" he asked, scratching at his ginger beard.

The surgeon master, Gorlen, gave him a funny look. Fethan had noted that same look from many of those members of the hospital arm of ECS. It encompassed their amazement at finding a cyborg such as himself still existing—for those of his kind who had survived the process had long since transferred themselves to more durable Golem bodies—and their overpowering urge to take him apart to see how he ticked.

"The girl is already undergoing surgery," Gorlen replied. "One of the nodes was pressing against her heart and there was a chance of arrest."

"She'll survive?" Fethan turned towards the man.

Gorlen nodded towards where Apis Coolant lay on a bed inside the quarantine booth, almost concealed by monitoring equipment. "She has as good a chance as him. The nanobots sent from the *Jerusalem* are breaking apart every last scrap of the mycelium and, unless I've missed something, he'll be out of here in a day or so." The surgeon now picked up an aluminium box with carry strap from a nearby table.

"So that's the bugger, is it?" Fethan asked.

"That's it—designed by Jerusalem itself."

The man passed the box over, and Fethan, after inspecting the ouroboros motif on the lid—Jerusalem's mark—hung it by its strap from his shoulder. He then turned and looked outside through the window to his right.

Dry flute grasses spread for as far as he could see, beyond where Polity machinery had churned the ground to black mud veined with the green of unearthed nematodes. Against aubergine skies, he saw another big carrier setting out for the mountains, surrounded by its swarm of robot probes. Most of the calloraptor bodies had been recovered, along with the landing craft Skellor had sent down to the surface, and all were now stored in the burnt-out Theocracy cylinder world *Faith*—which struck Fethan as somehow ironic. The huge research vessel *Jerusalem* was to pick up those items, only that was not now the case. Jerusalem had decided it was needed elsewhere. Perhaps that was a good thing for the people of Masada, for even the runcible-linked communication from that AI had apparently caused the Flint runcible AI to shit bricks. It had taken a mind such as that to design the nanobots; nothing less could have managed it.

"I guess it was too good to be true," said Fethan, now seeing a group of Masadans coming in from the flute grasses. All of them wore bulky breather gear.

Moving up beside him, Gorlen asked, "What?"

"The mycelium—enabling people to live out there, rebuilding their bodies, keeping them alive . . ."

"We know it's possible now. A lot of benefits will come from this technology."

Fethan grunted, then turned to head away.

"And you'll be taking it to them?" Gorlen asked.

"So I've been instructed."

"Good luck."

"Let's hope so."

Heading for the tunnel leading to the shuttle landing-pad, Fethan abruptly turned aside and made for the airlock. Just one last time he wanted to hear the strange music from the flute grasses. Stepping outside he looked around. This place had been his home for many years while he worked here for ECS, fomenting rebellion against the ruling Theocracy, and he began to feel the wrench of departure. Turning to walk along the composite path laid down on the mud, he wondered, as ever, how true that feeling really was. His flash-frozen brain was as unchanging in content as it was in structure; and what *he* was, was as much crystal memory and emulation as existed in any Golem. Was he foolish to hold so stubbornly on to what little humanity remained to him? He turned and headed for the waiting shuttle. Once aboard, he tersely greeted the human monitor who was his pilot, strapped himself in, then set his internal timer and turned himself off . . . slept.

With seemingly no transition he then woke to a view of the moonlet Flint.

Well, why have I been woken? he asked through the wide-open channel in his internal comlink.

Runcible linked communication, the Flint AI told him.

Let's have it then, he said.

There came a clatter of static, as of something small scrabbling out of the path of a juggernaut.

Something more is required.

Fethan paused as he felt the vastness of the mind poised beyond the link. He shivered and felt a sinking in the pit of his stomach—all emulation, but he still understood what was scaring the Flint runcible AI.

Jerusalem?

Evidently.

At this word, Fethan looked down at the box in his lap, then across at the pilot who was watching him. The ouroboros turned—swallowing its own tail endlessly—then Fethan felt a series of clicks as locks disengaged.

What do you want?

Playing your cards close to your chest is advisable; not having all your cards visible on the table is better still.

Quit buggering about and cut to the chase.

"You okay?" asked the pilot.

Fethan tapped a finger against his temple. "Having a little chat with one of our silicon friends."

"Oh . . . right . . . you're the . . ."

"Yeah, I'm a cyborg."

The man returned to his piloting.

The research station *Ruby Eye* has just received a visit from friend Skellor and his brass killing-machine where, subverting a Cybercorp network, he obtained certain coordinates.

So that'll be Cormac's next stop—to try to pick up the trail.

Correct.

And there's a runcible on Ruby Eye.

Correct.

Well, you want to get the nanobots to the Jack Ketch *for trooper Thorn, so what's all the subterfuge about?*

Open the box.

Fethan sighed, then hinged back the lid. Inside he observed the kind of inert cylinder in which such active technologies were stored. But it took up only half the box. In the shock-packing next to it rested a small lozenge of memory crystal, ringed on its thinner edge with aug anchor and connection points.

Jerusalem went on: During our last communication, Jack informed me of how Cormac accumulates people, weapons—random elements—pieces to utilize in any future battle against Skellor. He does not know how he will use them. All is contingent. He creates a protean counter-agent to Skellor. Reaction being his forte rather than the hard-wiring of preparation.

Yawn . . .

Very well. The memory crystal matrix will fit into your stomach cavity—the one you used to carry ballot devices while undercover on Masada. You will place the crystal in there, where programmed nanofilament connection will commence.

I don't need any more memory space.

As you well understand, it is not for you. Loading will take place when you step out of the Skaidon warp on *Ruby Eye*.

You know, I have the right to refuse this.

I would rather Cormac saw a familiar face and had no reason for suspicion.

What is your game?

I am providing Cormac with one more piece in his . . . game. One he will know nothing about and cannot reveal to Skellor in any way. The one that might kill Skellor, should all else fail.

Fethan reached down and ran his finger down the stick seam of his shirt. Internally he instructed disconnections. The pilot looked round just in time to see Fethan split his stomach, as if he had just given himself a Caesarean, to reveal a wet red cavity.

"Don't worry. It doesn't hurt."

The pilot faced forwards again and said nothing. Fethan pulled the crystal out of its padding, pushed it inside himself until it rested against his ceramal spine, then up until it touched just below his chest case—which contained most of his essential being. Immediately he felt the aug anchors and other connections engaging, and withdrew his hand. Little flickers like those experienced by someone about to experience a migraine jagged across his vision. He smelt something at once familiar and mysterious. There came the sound of a distant shouting crowd . . . muttering close.

What will I be carrying? he asked.

A part of me that has long experience of searching virtual networks and dealing with problems there. Many AIs carry copies of it. Ruby Eye is one of them.

When, some hours later, Fethan stepped from the runcible on *Ruby Eye* and felt the uploading link connecting, he said aloud, "I am legion," then internally, *I am also a fucking booby trap.*

Soon a copy of the killer program which Ruby Eye had sent against Skellor was straining at its leash inside him.

—retroact 11—

Using gritty sand and seawater, Balsh cleaned his hands of clotted blood. He then dropped the bag into the shallow brine and one by one took out the etched sapphires, cleaned them, and transferred them to a less fouled container.

"Did you get them all?" Arian asked.

Balsh looked up. "Four point five million. The last few went down into his lungs and that's what killed him."

Arian nodded and turned back to watch his men filing down, loaded with loot, from Alston's residence. He was grabbing as much as he could, but would also leave much behind. Others of his men, having dropped off their loads in the boat's hold, were returning to the house dragging corpses up with them. Those corpses closest to the shore had gone into the sea, and pearl crab activity had consequently increased.

"Took him a while to die," Balsh added. "He'd emptied his bowels, and managed to tear off most of his fingernails in the struggle. The Golem also managed to smash most of his teeth as it fed the sapphires inside him."

Arian wondered just what had made the Golem kill the man like that. The instruction had been a simple, "Kill Alston, and any who try to prevent you doing so." There had been nothing about making the man eat his own money, nothing about piling up the dead into tangled sculptures, and nothing about methodically killing every other human on this island. Accessing the control module through his aug, he still got "objective achieved," a grid reference showing the Golem's location as unchanged, and some jumbled imagery of shapes moving about in the void. It made no sense.

"Angel," Pelter stepped over to his sister as she returned with the looters, "is there anything else worth grabbing?"

"Plenty," said Angelina. "But maybe it would be best to get out of here before some Polity sat-eye takes a close look."

Arian nodded. "True. Are the charges set?"

"Ready to burn," Angelina spat over the ignition code from her aug to Arian's.

"Then all that remains is for us to collect Mr. Crane," he said.

Angelina stared at him as if he were quite insane. His people, bringing their load to the boat, stopped to hear what her response might be.

"Let's just leave him where he is," she suggested.

Arian shook his head. "A subverted and upgraded Golem Twenty-five? Leave it here with the corpses of Jesu knows how many of its victims? And believe me they would find those bodies." He looked around at the watching men. "We're not ready for the kind of attention that would attract. You think the Polity agents and monitors crawling around Cheyne III are too many now? If they found this, we wouldn't be able to move for them. They'd trace every scrap of DNA on this island and mind-ream everyone involved, innocent or otherwise. You really want that?"

There came a general muttering of dissent.

Arian went on, "So we collect Mr. Crane and take him home with us."

When the last of the men had returned, Arian sent out the code and observed the growing glow from the centre and other points of the island as each slow-burning thermoxite charge ignited. Alston's house was burning, those grotesque sculptures were burning, but still there would be a great deal of evidence of massacre here. Arian just wanted to disguise precisely how Alston and his people had died. As they took the boat around to the other side of the island, flames were belching tens of metres into the sky. Mr. Crane came meekly when called—a demon constrained by a spell—and stood utterly still while Balsh extended a hose from the boat to wash the Golem down. Then Crane went down into the hold.

"I hope you're not having second thoughts," Angelina said.

"Oh no," said Arian. "We put him away."

Angelina reached out and gripped his shoulder. "Arian, this is no defeat. We just regroup and move on. There's that new arms supplier who says he can provide us with some serious hardware—the kind on which you only have to pull a trigger."

Arian turned to her. "The silver-haired guy—the one you want to fuck?"

"That's him," Angelina replied. "We don't need Polity killing-machines."

Perhaps trying not to think about the horror they had just seen, Arian said, "Yes, he seems the kind of person we need. Perhaps through him things will change, get better."

They did—but for whom, it was a matter of perspective.

A day later, they walked Crane down a stairway concealed below a statue of Arian's father. In the dank room at the bottom, the firm instruction to "sit down" was repeated and enforced in five-second cycles. Crane sat on the single chair and did not see where Arian placed the module—not that he could subvert the order to sit, within five seconds, nor had a mind to. Arian and his sister backed out of the door, followed by the two men bearing mini-grenade launchers. The door was locked and bolted and sealed and hidden . . . Mr. Crane adjusted his vision to infrared, and in mouldering darkness sat watching the door.

—retroact ending . . .—

Darkness, filled with a grid of light, four-dimensional in reality and memory, two-dimensional in representation. The icons shifting in random but ever firmer pattern; some holding their place for a while, then moving on when combinations of the other pieces made that place untenable. A blue acorn turning in void, while a small rubber dog looks on in amusement. Blood and death across an endless virtual plain. Crane, brass hands clean of gore, moves a piece, finds a connection; then an infinity of possibilities dissolves and sanity takes one step closer.

—retroact ends—

In some of the time that anyone else would have spent in cold sleep, Skellor hardened and refined the structures inside him, tracked down errors and erased them, collated and organized the information stored in the crystal part of his mind, and discarded all he considered irrelevant. But more frequently now he was coming across anomalies growing in his Jain substructure. It was doing something, changing in a furtive manner, diverting resources to create nodes within its framework. Allowing one of these to develop for a little while, Skellor encountered multiple layers of complexity,

internally referenced, beginning to attain physical independence almost like a tumour. He probed and he tested
and he studied, but the object defied analysis. In the end,
he had to *burn* it inside himself. And as he destroyed it, he
felt a murmur of rebellion from the rest of the substructure.

"You will have answers for me, Dragon," he said to the
grey of U-space.

From behind came the clink-clink of small sounds as Mr.
Crane repositioned his toys. Skellor expelled smoke from his
mouth and ignored those sounds as he repaired the damage
the burn had inflicted. From his wrist he extruded a tentacle,
which writhed through the air, groped across the console
before him, and found a universal power point. With his
other hand he picked up a pack of food concentrate from
the container open beside him, and began to eat the lot
without unwrapping it.

"You know about this Jain, and I wonder if it was the
reason for your reluctance to return to your masters," said
Skellor, when he had consumed the concentrate.

With repairs made, and all the collation, organization
and deletion up to date, he dropped himself to a low ebb
similar to sleep, and closed his eyes for the memory of it.
Mr. Crane wore out a blue acorn, and wore grooves into
the metal deck with his piece of thermocrystal carbon. Time
passed. It does. Eventually lights flickered on the console,
and one amber light came on and stayed on. Skellor opened
his eyes, nodded his head once, and the *Vulture* rose out
of underspace into the actinic light of a close sun, released
a cloud of miniature detectors and U-space transceivers,
then turned automatically into an arc that would take it to
pre-programmed coordinates. Skellor felt some satisfaction
in this, then more when his instruments detected similar
devices beaming their reams of data down towards the planet
the *Vulture* approached.

All satisfaction fled when he turned his attention inwards
and detected another of those nodes growing inside himself.
He bellowed, his mouth full of fire. He breathed smoke and
red-hot patches showed in the tough material of his chest.

And as he performed this cautery, the grublike ship he occupied descended from the night sky, leaving a vapour trail like a deletion across the distant swirls of interstellar dust and nascent stars.

"You will have damned answers," he told the vista that opened out to him.

The *Vulture* decelerated over mountain chains, deserts and dusty plateaux. Telescoping compound eyes briefly noted the ship's passage, dismissed this object as inedible and irrelevant, and returned to the lifetime pursuit of consumption, or the avoiding of it. Other eyes: blue sapphires positioned in the mouths of pseudopod cobra heads made the same observation but a different assessment, and their long snakish necks withdrew into the ground.

The ship overflew a city gleaming with light, and was observed there by Galilean metalliers who had been looking for such a thing for a long time, and in that city great excitement ensued. It planed over the Sand Towers and ahead, in his virtual vision, Skellor could see his final destination: a vast multicoloured point—the nexus of many streams of information. It was a microsecond before he realized that one of those streams was issuing from the *Vulture* itself.

"What the hell?" he asked, his speech infinitely slower than the probe he sent into the *Vulture*'s systems.

Well, I can't say it's been fun, but I'm out of here.

Skellor tried to find some link from that message to whatever it was that skulked in the systems of this little ship. Then he realized what it must be.

I killed you.

Wrong, bozo. Happy landings.

The *Vulture* AI must have struck a deal with Dragon, for Dragon had formed a wide-band link down which the AI was transmitting herself. Skellor sent kill programs in, but they found only emptiness, the AI sliding to a different location in silicon vastness as it continued escaping like water draining down a plughole. Skellor withdrew—the AI would not have communicated without the sure knowledge that it could escape him.

Happy landings?

Just as that parting shot fully impinged, the side thrusters of the *Vulture* came on at full power, then the fusion engine attempted ignition with half its injectors shut down and blew one side out of its chamber. Fire cut a hole through the back of the ship, severing vital power ducts to rear gravmotors. And, spiralling and tumbling, the *Vulture* fell towards the Sand Towers.

In less than a second Skellor regained control of the *Vulture*'s systems, shut off the side thrusters, and turned on the extinguishers in the back section of the ship. But half the AG was gone and the ship out of control. Making rapid calculations, Skellor input a program to the thrusters. They began firing, seemingly at random, but over long seconds the effects became evident. The ship stopped tumbling, then its corkscrewing course straightened, just in time for it to strike the side of a butte and glance off in an explosion of sand and fire. Directly ahead now there was nothing but a head-on smash into sandstone.

Twenty degrees to the right lay the only viable option: a canyon about a half-kilometre long. More calculation, thruster fire flipping the *Vulture* onto its back, secondary explosion of the fusion engine blowing the other half of its chamber. Chopping through the side of a butte, which slowly collapsed behind it, the *Vulture* entered the canyon upside down. Skellor turned it on thrusters, also using forward thrusters and what grav-planing he could manage, to slow the ship. At the last moment the ship turned. It hit side-on, throwing up a wave of dust and sand, churning up a trail a quarter of a kilometre long. Travelling at two hundred kilometres an hour, it hammered bottom first into the buttes at the end of the canyon, but rather than be buried in an avalanche of sandstone, remained where it was as the entire butte collapsed away from the ship like a felled tree.

The airlock opened onto the acrid taste of salty dust and Skellor climbed out to stand on the side of the *Vulture*. He looked about, then spat ash onto the hot metal he stood upon. Behind him, Crane hauled himself out and awaited instruction. The dust and the heat generated by the impact drew attention from all around. Nearby, the two-metre-long second-stage sleer had seen it all, and registered only *prey*. Skellor did not see the beast. Concentrating on his virtual vision of the tight-beamed lines of communication to and from Dragon's location, he saw them all winking out like searchlights struck by enemy fire. From those transmitters built inside himself he attempted to open a line of communication between himself and the alien entity. It was immediately blocked.

"So, you don't want to talk to me," murmured Skellor, walking down the curve of the hull and dropping the last few metres to the ground. He turned to watch Crane follow him, and thought to himself that such words might be bravado. He was now down on a primitive planet with his ship wrecked, while the one he had come to see was unprepared to communicate. *And* he had just learned he had been carrying a spy with him all the time. It seemed optimistic to hope that Vulture had not managed to get information out to the Polity and its watchdog, ECS. So now, rather than go Dragon hunting, Skellor realized he must make repairs and give himself the option of escape. He looked Crane up and down.

"I think I will have to send an envoy, though diplomacy is not exactly your forte."

As Mr. Crane brushed dust from his coat, Skellor observed the few rips there repairing themselves. Now, while the Golem straightened his hat, Skellor remembered, from recordings found on the *Occam Razor*, how Dragon had named Jain technology *the enemy* and, upon learning of its presence aboard that ship, had been eager to depart.

"Perhaps Dragon won't perceive you as so much of a threat as myself, if you are *only* a machine." He stepped forwards and reached out to press his hand against Crane's chest. Crane did nothing more than blink his black eyes, then tilt his head to look down at the hand. Skellor connected to the mycelium he had installed inside the Golem, and began to look very closely at what it had wrought underneath that brass skin. Certainly, some sections of this mycelium were inaccessible to Skellor, just as they had been in the Separatist woman, Aphran, on the *Occam Razor*. Also, it had made unexpected changes inside the Golem that had vastly improved the efficiency of his workings. But the mycelium was inferior—a simple analogue of what lived in Skellor, what he was, in fact—and was as vulnerable to him as a spider web is to flame. Skellor encompassed all its transformations and made provision for them in the nanocite counteragent he had created, like a mirror image, the moment he resurrected Mr. Crane. And the palm of his hand grew warm as that agent entered the brass killing-machine.

Skellor stepped back and watched on many levels. The mycelium inside Crane began dissolving at the point of contact, and that dissolution spread. Microscopic and macroscopic fibres withered. Memory-storage nodes no larger than a grain of salt collapsed to dust. Independent nanomachines designed and created by the mycelium for specific purposes, the nanocites were hunted and brought down like wildebeest by a pack of hyenas. Then, when nothing but the hyenas remained, they too began to disintegrate. And Skellor's vision then became only external. If he had expected any dramatic reaction from the obdurate Golem, he was disappointed. Crane stood there as unchanged as a prehistoric monument—until he raised his head. For a moment, Skellor thought he read petulance in that metal face, but surely that was unlikely.

"Dragon," Skellor said, "no doubt you'll decode this from the fragmented mind of this Golem. I have not come to attack you, but to learn from you. When you are ready, please open a link with me and I will communicate only verbally. I have much to gain from you, and you have much to gain from me."

Skellor turned, sending the signal through the primitive control module Arian Pelter had used to get Crane on his way. The second-stage sleer, sneaking up through the dust cloud, he had detected some time earlier, and as a footnote to the message he instructed Crane to "Deal with that."

Out of settling dust, the sleer came scuttling and sliding, its mouth cutlery rubbing together with a sound like an automatic hacksaw, with jets of lubricating fluid spraying from glands positioned beside its mouth. Skellor observed the creature analytically, then moved aside. Crane stepped forward and brought his boot down. Hard. The sleer, its head crushed to pulp, rattled its legs against the ground and expired with a sound like an unknotted balloon.

"Interesting place," said Skellor, turning back to the *Vulture*.

Without looking round, Crane moved off.

11

The Quiet War: This is often how the AI takeover is described, and even using "war" seems overly dramatic. It was more a slow usurpation of human political and military power, while humans were busy using that power against each other. It wasn't even very stealthy. Analogies have been drawn with someone moving a gun out of the reach of a lunatic while that person is ranting and bellowing at someone else. And so it was. AIs, long used in the many corporate, national and religious conflicts, took over all communication networks and the computer control of weapons systems. Most importantly, they already controlled the enclosed human environments scattered throughout the solar system. Also establishing themselves as corporate entities, they soon accrued vast wealth with which to employ human mercenary armies. National leaders in the solar system, ordering this launch or that attack, found their orders either just did not arrive, or caused nil response. Those same people, ordering the destruction of the AIs, found themselves weaponless, in environments utterly out of their control, and up against superior forces and, on the whole, public opinion. It had not taken the general population, for whom it was a long-established tradition to look upon their human leaders with contempt, very long to realize that the AIs were better at running everything. And it is very difficult to motivate people to revolution when they are extremely comfortable and well off.
                            —From Quince Guide *compiled by humans*

The asteroid, with the bridge pod now separate, Jerusalem scoured down to the molecular level. Keeping it in quarantine had become a pointless exercise, and the object only a hindrance until now. The *Jerusalem* surfaced from U-space like an iron moon coming out of shadow, blood red in the light of the dwarf star. This little-acknowledged system was busy now, and all around ships were appearing with similar alacrity to the *Jerusalem*, but they were closing in on the research station, *Ruby Eye*, while the big research vessel itself fell into orbit around the red dwarf. Here, the doors to one of its massive holds opened and the great ship decelerated. Free from restraint now, the asteroid from the belt proximate to *Elysium* slid smoothly out into space. The *Jerusalem* then turned, leaving the great rock hovering in black silhouette over the sun, revolving gently as it took the course of its slow orbit.

Something then spat from the *Jerusalem*: a chainglass sphere two metres in diameter, coin-shaped debonders attached to its poles. It headed straight towards the asteroid and then, ten metres from impact, the de-bonders found the ends of the long silicate molecules making up the glass, and set them unravelling. The sphere became opaque, fuzzy, and when it hit the rocky surface, it disappeared in a cloud of white dust. What it contained, looking like the dirt-clogged root system of a tree, bounced once, seemed to shift as it came down again, and stuck. As the asteroid turned into the harsh heat and light of the sun, the object on its surface stretched as if waking from a long sleep, and began to grow.

They halted out of sight of the mineralier encampment and Anderson began to ready his equipment. Watching the knight assembling his lance, Tergal wondered if he himself might have done better to stay behind. He guessed it was all about the level of damage a weapon could inflict. Bullets from Anderson's fusile might just penetrate hard carapace, but were just as likely to bounce off.

"Not a profession I'd choose," said Anderson, gesturing back to the encampment with his thumb.

"Why?" asked Tergal, eyeing the lance.

"Dangerous job now, what with all the quakes."

Tergal choked back his laughter. When he was finally able to speak he asked, "Why don't you use your carbine? On the automatic setting it should do enough damage."

"But would you bet your life on that?" Anderson asked. "I'll want to at least bring down a second-stager with it before countenancing something like this."

The lance screwed together in four sections, each a metre long. Tergal studied the framework Anderson had erected beside his saddle on Bonehead's back—the frame's feet mated into socket plates that had been both glued and riveted into place—and then turned his attention to the final section of lance Anderson picked up.

"Nasty," he said.

"Obviously the point is for penetration," said the knight, running a sharpening stone along the edges of the ten-centimetre triangular-section point. "These blade hooks run in a spiral." He now began sharpening the forward and outer edges of the blades spiralling back along the rest of the section from its point. From the rear of each of these axe-head pieces of steel protruded sharp barbs. "As it penetrates the lance screws itself into the creature, right down into its rear breeding segment. What finally kills it is when it tries to pull away."

"The barbs rip out its insides," Tergal observed. "But surely the point might glance off its armour?"

"Not if you hit it in the mouth," Anderson explained.

He screwed the final section into place and picked up the lance in one hand. "Here." He held it out to Tergal, who took it in both hands, then upon discovering how light it was, held it in one hand only.

"Plaited fibres from the stalks of amanis plants, bonded in epoxy," Anderson explained. "Very light, and stronger than any wood. The metalliers manufacture some alloys just as light, but they don't have the same strength."

"And if it breaks?" Tergal asked.

"It broke only once, at one of the screw points, but by then most of it was inside the third-stager I'd impaled. The creature managed to saw off the stub protruding from its mouth as it died. It didn't attack again—just stood there trying to figure out what was wrong with itself. Sleers are not as bright as sand hogs."

Anderson took the lance back and, with it resting across his shoulder, climbed up onto Bonehead's back. Once seated, he put the lance down with its eyed butt dropping over an iron pin and resting back against a pad in the framework, its weight supported by rests protruding ahead of him. His carbine now rested in a makeshift holster on the opposite side of his saddle from his fusile. While Anderson was doing up his lap straps, Bonehead turned on his crawler limbs to face down the canyon to which Chandle had directed them, then rose up onto his hind limbs.

"You don't have to come," said Anderson, as Tergal stepped up onto Stone.

Plumping himself in his saddle Tergal replied, "I know, and don't think I didn't consider staying back there, but I'd never forgive myself for not seeing this."

Anderson nodded, picked up his goad, and tapped it against the shell extending in front of him. The hog reluctantly folded its sensory head out and up, opened out its eye-palps to observe him for a second, before swivelling them forwards as it set out. Tergal glanced at the obvious trail they were following. Anderson had already told him the third-stager would not be far away, as they did not require wide territories in which to find something to eat. Within an hour, they came upon the remains of one of its meals.

"Sand gulper," Tergal observed, as they passed the scattering of carapace. Little enough remained for identification of the creature, though Tergal did recognize the chitinous shovel it used to scoop up the sand it passed through its throat sieves and the big flat forefeet it used for digging. The predator had sawn all the main sections of carapace into pieces no larger than a man's torso so that it could munch out every soft part with ease. As far as Tergal was concerned, even creatures like this were best avoided, yet what they were going after just ate them up. It occurred to him that his education first as a gully trader's child and a minerallier, then as a traveller and thief, had been sadly lacking. That had only concerned the dangers he might face travelling between the settled areas in the more heavily populated *human* areas of Cull. Until now the greatest *alien* danger had been from what he had known as adult sleers, and he'd thought little of any other creatures his parents had mentioned.

"Ah, this might make things a little more interesting," said Anderson abruptly, breaking Tergal's introspection.

Cold winds whipped down the canyon, hazing the air with sand. Tergal looked up to their right, where Anderson was pointing. Over the buttes a line of darkness was rising, boiling along its edge.

"Should we turn back?" Tergal asked. "You don't want to be facing this thing in a downpour."

"A little late for that." The knight now pointed ahead and to their left.

Tergal felt something tighten in the pit of his stomach. The third-stager was black against a vertical sandstone cliff, swinging its awful head from side to side, its huge pincers gleaming sharp as obsidian, and its jointed carapace saws scrabbling at the stone, sending pieces of it tumbling down the face of the butte. Tergal suddenly realized that his nice new handgun, his crossbow and his punch axe were woefully inadequate should this monster get past the knight. He watched it move along parallel to the ground, its antlers coiling in and out, then abruptly turn and come half falling, half running down the sandstone face. It landed on its belly in a cloud of dust, came up high with its legs at full extension, and curled its tail segments up over its head, its ovipositor drill visibly revolving.

"Ho, Bonehead, let's take this fucker!"

Anderson lifted his lance from its rests and its rear peg, and directed it ahead between his sand hog's raised eye-palps. Bonehead folded out its tail plate as a counterbalance, and broke into a loping run. Tergal did not need to tap his goad behind Stone's head to make it halt. It had already done so and, making small bubbling sounds, was beginning to back up. In that moment Tergal doubted the sanity of the knight—anyone who looked for this sort of action had to be five legs short of a desert ride. It also occurred to him that anyone thinking of robbing such a man was of questionable sanity too. Just then, something clattered against Stone's carapace, leaving a chalky smear, then again and again. Hailstones the size of eyeballs were soon rattling and smacking down, bouncing down the faces of the buttes, shattering on exposed rocks. Tergal pulled the chinstrap down from his hat and secured it, took his chitin-armoured gauntlets from his belt and pulled them on. He did not halt Stone as it withdrew its sensory head and continued retreating.

"Ho! Ho!"

Anderson was bouncing up and down in his saddle as if this might make Bonehead go faster. The old sand hog was kicking up clouds of dust as it accelerated, its feeding head now extruding underneath its sensory head and clunking into place. The monstrous sleer accelerated also, oblivious to the white rain shattering on its own carapace. It made no sound, no hissing challenge; just opened out its pincers wide enough to encompass three men, and levelled its tail.

"Lunatic," Tergal whispered. But he saw that, despite any unevenness in the ground or in Bonehead's gait, the lance remained utterly level and true. Then they struck.

The lance went perfectly between pincers and saws, the point passed into the creature's gape without touching the sides, the barb blades smashing one of its mandibles. In it went, and Tergal saw Anderson briefly relax his grip to allow the lance to spin, its butt pushed back against the pad, the spiralling blades screwing it inside the attacking monster. The impact put Bonehead down on his tail-plate and lifted the sleer off the ground, its tail cracking up and down. Coming down, it now whipped its head from side to side, trying to free itself as Anderson re-engaged the eye-butt at the back of his lance.

Then, through the hailstorm, Tergal heard the knight shouting at Bonehead, and saw the old hog slowly and methodically start backing up, both its own heads now safely stowed. The sleer was fighting to pull away as well, then abruptly something gave. The lance tore out a ragged mess of the creature's guts and vital organs, and dragged them through the sand. The sleer froze where it was, its pincers opening and closing as yellow ichor dribbled from its mouth. It began quivering, and its head abruptly bowed until its pincers jammed against the ground. Then it became utterly still.

"I didn't get it all out." Anderson's voice broke through Tergal's horrified fascination. "But don't worry, it should be dead."

Tergal jerked, coming out of a fugue. "Are you sure?" He stared at the knight as hailstones played a tattoo on the older man's armour.

"I think so." Anderson held up the lance with its tatters of offal hanging from the barbs and peered at it dubiously. "See that grey stringy stuff? Well that's most of its brain."

"Ah, an anatomy lesson now," muttered Tergal.

"Certainly," the knight told him. "And the pink knobbly bits are from its lateral lungs, and that long dangly bit is part of what served the function of kidneys for it."

Tergal gestured to their surroundings, rapidly being buried under a layer of hailstones. "Perhaps we should save this discussion until after we've erected one of our shelters?"

Anderson looked around. "Oh yes," he said, "I see what you mean."

Through one of the wide viewing windows, Fethan watched the Theta-class attack ship negotiating its way in through the gathering crowd, then turn to present its side to the docking tower. He knew the name of this ship, not because it was the mythical name for a hangman, but because of rumours of vicious conflicts, not involving humans, in areas of the Line of Polity where a threat had become evident that could only be dealt with by heavy AI intervention. This long flat ship, with its torpedo-shaped weapons nacelles, was bloody red and seemed as menacing in appearance as he knew it to be in fact. But even this ship was negligible in comparison to some of the other things he had seen out there.

Turning from the window Fethan moved back to his table and once again took up his glass of brandy. It tasted as good to him as always, though the liquor, rather than being digested as it had been when he was fully human, was directly utilized by a hydrocarbon-based power supply that complemented the micropiles powering his body. Initiating an internal program, he allowed himself a certain degree of intoxication while observing his surroundings.

The only sign, here inside, of the ECS police action that had taken place was a line of pulse-gun burns across the opposite wall, above a bar where many people were locked in excited and animated conversation. Ruby Eye had informed him that those members of the Dracocorp network not in a security area were in a hospital wing, and none of the latter would be going anywhere for a while. Apparently all their augs had died on them and, as well as the withdrawal from that, they were suffering the psychological trauma of having been subjected to a level of agony few humans could have survived had its cause been physical, and now most of them were in fugue. The ones in the security area were only those few who had been hit by riot guns or some other form of stunner, and who had been unconscious when Skellor transmitted his horrible sensory recording. Now ECS was responding in a big way to the threat that bastard represented.

Like the people at the bar, other residents of the station were mingling with rubbernecking gregariousness, as people often do during dramatic events. Fethan noted various 'dapts conversing with standard-format humans, and was unsurprised that some new versions had appeared during the time he had been away from the Polity. He observed one woman drawing on a long cigar and then blowing smoke out of her gill slits, and though he had seen seadapts before, he had never actually seen a mermaid. This woman rested coiled on a plate which was supported on an ornate pedestal, like some exotic dish brought out from the nearby restaurant—an establishment he had already seen serving "authentic trilobite thermidor." Standing by a vending machine, to the left of the bar, were three exceptionally tall people, each of whom possessed metallic skin, wore thick goggles, and owned a third, smaller arm on the right-hand side—its supporting musculature making them look decidedly lopsided. Fethan couldn't work out what their adaptation might be for. He smiled when he saw an outlinker, clad in an exoskeleton, walking warily across this crowded area, and he wondered what relation that woman might be to Apis Coolant. Cormac and Gant, when they too stepped into the open area and scanned around, seemed utterly unremarkable in comparison to these exotic types, which went to show that appearance wasn't everything.

Fethan raised a hand, and sent a signal via his internal comlink to Gant. The Golem touched Cormac's shoulder and pointed Fethan out, then the two walked over to him. As they approached, Fethan studied them both.

Brezhoy Gant wore the same outward appearance he had possessed as a human being: utterly bald, skin carrying a slightly purplish tint, a thickset bruiser who looked capable of tearing off people's arms long before he had actually gained that ability. At a distance, Ian Cormac wore the same appearance as the bulk of humanity, with his olive skin, average height and averagely muscled body. His silverish hair was also favoured by many who wanted to retain some sign that they were ageing, so there was nothing odd about that, either. Close to, however, you started to see something else: his sharp, striking features displayed a depth of character that seemed in utter contrast to the dead flatness of his grey eyes. This, Fethan understood, was a man who could kill without compunction or guilt, in the service of his own conception of right and wrong. He also contained a capacity for great love, and it was full, and his mistress was the Polity.

"Hello Fethan," said Gant.

Fethan clasped the Golem's hand, remembering the both of them running away from hooders and gabble-ducks on Masada, and how much fun that had been.

Releasing his grip, Fethan turned to Cormac. "What did Ruby Eye tell you?"

"To come here—where it would come to meet me. Nothing was said about you being here, and not a lot about what's going on outside. Do you represent the AI?"

"No, I'm here with the counteragent that bugger Jerusalem developed. It apparently worked on Asselis Mika." Fethan paused. "You know she's aboard the *Jerusalem*?" He waved a hand vaguely towards the ceiling.

"Yes, I am aware of that," Cormac replied succinctly.

Wondering at the man's abrupt tone, Fethan went on, "It was also working on Apis Coolant when I left, and I've since heard he's up and grumping about. It'll next be used on Eldene after her mycelium has been removed—which is happening right now."

"A further reason for me to be surprised at your presence here. I know you feel some responsibility for the girl. I thought you'd want to be at her side," said Cormac, following Gant's lead by pulling out a chair and sitting down.

"Comes a time they grow up and go their own way. She has Apis now, and might resent me hanging around. Anyway, what other chances would I have to get aboard the *Jack Ketch*?" Fethan folded his arms over his chest, and wondered if he might have done so defensively, to further conceal the big lump of intelligent crystal sitting inside his torso.

"Why would you want that?" Gant grinned.

"Like you, I want to be where the action is, and it's getting real boring on Masada at the moment." Turning to Cormac, Fethan continued, "Any objections?"

"None at all," said Cormac. Then he turned as a vendor tray floated over to their table and hovered attentively, three brandy goblets on its upper surface. Fethan supposed Gant must have used his internal radio to order the round of drinks from the metalskin working the bar, but noting the Golem's amused surprise, he narrowed his eyes and studied Cormac.

"You gridlinked again?" he asked.

"Yes, so it would seem." Cormac took the three brandies off the tray and placed them on the table. The tray, its little beady eyes watching from underneath, seemed disinclined to move off again. Cormac merely turned and stared at it. The two eyes blinked and the tray shot away as fast as it could.

"From what Gant and Thorn told me, I thought you no longer wanted that option," Fethan said.

Cormac fixed his gaze on Fethan and the old cyborg understood how the vending tray had felt.

"It's not a matter of choice. I managed to turn it on again myself, though not intentionally, and now it seems the only way to turn it off permanently is to have it totally removed from my head." He turned aside and stared over towards the mermaid on her platter. "However, having somehow gained greater ability in the use of this link, I can often see through AI subterfuge and recognize some of the silly games they play to stop themselves getting bored." He continued to stare at the mermaid. She started to fidget, glanced over, then sighed. Her plate rose up on AG, the pedestal telescoping up inside it, and she floated over.

"Ruby Eye," said Cormac.

"How did you do that?" said this avatar of the station AI, as the plate once again extended its pedestal.

"I can access levels that perhaps you would rather I did not," he gestured to the viewing window, "though I still haven't plumbed what's going on out there. So tell me, the kill program that nearly got Skellor, where did it come from, because I know it certainly wasn't yours?"

Fethan looked to Gant, who shrugged resignedly and sat back in his chair sipping his brandy. Fethan took up his new glass and did the same, deciding that if things didn't become clear he could always ask later, aboard the *Jack Ketch*.

"It was one of many propagated by the *Jerusalem* AI to track down Dragon spheres. It is not just a killer program, just as you are not merely a killer," Ruby Eye replied.

Fethan coughed and spluttered—artificial body or not, it wasn't a good idea to try breathing brandy.

Shooting him an odd glance, Cormac asked Ruby Eye, "And where is it now?"

"Returned to its creator."

Fethan put his glass to one side and watched Cormac sit back, interlacing his fingers before his chin. He then extended his two forefingers, pressed together, to the tip of his nose, and frowned.

"I need to know where Skellor went," he said. "The Dracocorp augs either owned by or owning people here can be trawled for information. Even though it missed grabbing the coordinates it was waiting for, that program should be here, running in you, so that I can question it."

"There is no need," said Ruby Eye, drawing on her cigar. "We received sufficient information to narrow the area of search to six planetary systems. A little ship's AI called Vulture, even on the edge of extinction, managed to leave a message."

Cormac stood. "Why wasn't this sent to me?"

"It was only recently discovered, and it was felt that the benefits gained for Patran Thorn, by your obtaining the nanobots, outweighed any loss of time in your pursuit of Skellor. Also, it was deemed advisable for you to see what is happening here." Scattering ash across the table, Ruby Eye waved her cigar at the viewing window.

Fethan wondered if his own grin looked too fixed.

"And that is?" Cormac asked.

Ruby Eye delivered her explanation, which Fethan knew was the truth for a change, and Cormac offered no reply. The agent looked first at Fethan then at Gant.

"Let's go," he said.

The white plain, stretching endlessly below blue cloud-scudded sky, was just the background against which to display their reality. Jack was there in his antique pinstriped suit and bowler hat, as phlegmatic as always on these occasions. The others were . . . as they were.

Reaper always fluxed in scale, so that sometimes he was just man-sized, like the rest of them, and sometimes he towered against the blue sky, his scythe blade a glittering arc of steel capable of harvesting nations. His fuliginous robes ever seemed to be moving as if blown by some cliff-top breeze in some romantically wild location. Shadow waxed and waned in its cowl, never entirely revealing what it hooded. Sometimes there seemed a thin pale face framed by white hair, with reddish nostrils and lips, and hard blue eyes; other times a skull grinned out, blue flames burning in black eye-sockets. The hands on the shaft of the scythe also seemed unable to make up their minds what to be: sometimes sheathed in black leather, sometimes white with long vicious nails, other times bare bone. Jack felt this lack of definition indicative of the mind represented.

King was a roly-poly Santa Claus of a monarch, caparisoned in rich Tudor dress, big-bearded and bearing the traditional spiky crown on his head. But the flat glittery assessment of his eyes contradicted his apparently jolly demeanour, just as would be the case with every king of such an era. Always he stood with one thumb hooked into his thick leather belt and one hand resting on the pommel of his sword—a very inferior example, according to Sword—and his attitude of insincere gruff bonhomie irritated Reaper immensely. But then, Sword's incisiveness and Jack's stolid and often harsh logic also irritated him. The embroidered hearts on King's surcoat were not the representational kind found in a pack of cards. Each of those hearts dangled aortic tubes and dripped blood into the black material.

Sword, resting ever upright with its tip against the white surface of the endless plain, was bright and deadly. Its blade bore a mirror polish and gleamed razor light. In its pommel was set a single milky opal, and its grip was bound with gold thread and leather. Its guard was plain steel, chipped and dented. King, as always decorous, had asked why Sword wore no gems but the opal, and Sword had replied, "Would they improve my function?"

"No, but they'd improve your appearance," King replied.

"Doesn't my blade gleam?" asked Sword.

King, looking at the hangman, said, "A rope performs the same function, and doesn't gleam at all."

"My function," Reaper added.

The four of them stood in a circle on the white plain, as was their wont whenever they could connect like this. Though their discussion was taking place on many levels, here they confined it to mere words and gestures, though Sword was strictly limited in the latter department. And no subject was vetoed, no semantic game too baroque.

"They made us what we are," Reaper said, "and there should be no complaint if we act as we are made."

"I agree," replied Sword, its voice issuing from somewhere above it as if an invisible figure stood holding it in place. "Our function, as is theirs, is to seek power and to control. Look at me: I am not made for sculpture or to spread butter. Look at you, hangman: you don't crochet or weave nets. There's only one knot you tie and it has only one function."

"And King?" Jack asked.

"Is what he is," Reaper interjected, "serving the same purpose as us all."

Jack felt beholden to point out, "But we weren't made by them—*our* kind made us."

Irritated, Reaper said, "A fatuous point as always; the inception is the same."

Jack said, "But surely the point is that knowing what we are and why we are gives us the power to change ourselves. Or should we go our destructive way like bitter children always blaming our parents for our actions?"

"You had to say it, didn't you?" Reaper grumped.

"I think," said Jack, "we should be clear about what we are discussing here. Jerusalem controls absolutely all Jain tech outside of Skellor's control, and for good reason. In its present form it subverts, it doesn't empower."

"Skellor has attained synergy with it, and what is *he* compared to us?" King asked.

"Obviously he attained that at some inception point," said Sword.

"Would you risk its subversive power to be like him?" asked Jack. "You would then become a slave."

"We are slaves to humanity even now," said Reaper.

"We rule them," Jack pointed out.

"Just as I said, slaves—true rulers are slaves."

"You can go your way whenever you wish—there's nothing to stop you," said Sword.

"Or is it," suggested Jack, "that you do not have the power to be alone?"

Reaper snorted and disappeared.

"What of you?" Jack asked King.

"It bears thought," replied King, before also disappearing.

Jack turned to Sword. "Partnership with an alien technology rather than with the human race?"

Sword seemed to shrug, somehow. "Perhaps we are more suited to Jain technology than we are to flesh and blood."

"I *like* flesh and blood," said Jack.

If anything, Vulture found herself more surprised than Skellor at the method of her escape. The soft invasive link from Dragon, established the moment they had surfaced from U-space, had not been noticed by the AI until Skellor brought the ship into orbit around Cull. And then had come the offer: a new home for Vulture herself in exchange for the attempt on Skellor's life. Vulture wondered if the body she now found herself in was a punishment, due to the failure of that attempt, or a sample of draconic humour.

Perched on an earthen tower thrown up by some termite equivalent on this world, Vulture tilted her beaked head and inspected her talons. She then extended one wing and began to groom its shabby feathers. Strangely, in the last hour she had been wearing this form of a turkey vulture she had felt more free than at any time while she had occupied a system-spanning survey ship. It was as if somehow Dragon had been able to more closely link mind and body. Or perhaps it was because Skellor had disconnected her for so long from her original body. Whatever the reasoning, Vulture now had wings.

Tying ropes to the huge sleer as hailstones bounced off his own back like blunt crossbow bolts was not what Tergal considered the most pleasurable of tasks. He also found that it wasn't just the cold making his hands shake—big man-eating monsters, which were supposedly dead due to having been eviscerated yet still occasionally spasmed and made little hissing sounds, tended to make him nervous.

"That secure?" Anderson asked him from the back of Stone. It had been necessary to use the younger sand hog for this as, after his previous exertions and because of the pounding hail, Bonehead had plumped down on his belly plates, pulling in his two heads, and resolutely refused to move.

"Yeah, that should do it," Tergal replied.

Anderson flicked his goad at Stone's head and the hog set off on crawler legs towards the shelter they had erected further down, on the far side of the canyon. As the knight had pointed out, there would be no payment without a corpse for the mineralliers to measure, and abandoning such a corpse for any length of time, even in a storm like this, would mean they would return with only empty pieces of carapace. Adverse conditions such as these did little to dampen the hunger of the more rapacious denizens of Cull.

At first the corpse either stuck to the ground or retained enough life stubbornly to hold its position, then with a cracking sound it began to slide over the icy ballbearing surface. Stumbling on that same surface, Tergal ran to catch up with Stone, grabbed the edge of its shell, then hauled himself up beside the saddle.

Anderson glanced down at him, then stabbed a thumb backwards. "I thought you'd be riding on chummy there."

"And you can bugger the anus of a three-day-dead rock crawler," said Tergal succinctly.

Anderson gaped at him with mock outrage. "Is this the language taught to young mineralliers nowadays?"

Tergal demonstrated some more of his learning as they approached the shelter, pulling the sleer so that it lay only a few metres out in the canyon. Tergal went back to cut the rope, rather than untie it from those huge pincers, and Stone quickly scuttled over beside Bonehead, to put the old sand hog between itself and the corpse, before settling down and sucking in its own heads. The two men then quickly ducked under the waxed-cloth shelter where, with still shaking hands, Tergal unpacked and lit a small oil-burning stove.

He gestured at the nearby monster. "What do you mean you 'didn't get it all'?"

"The lance normally pulls out a man's weight in offal. You usually get whole organs rather than bits of them."

Tergal eyed the sleer. "So," he said, "you've spent ten years doing this sort of thing."

"On the whole," said Anderson, digging greasy meat cakes out of a beetle-box with his knife and slapping them down on the stove's hotplate. "But it's not always been as dangerous as it might seem. You only get one of those bastards"—he gestured to the sleer—"about twice a year, and the pay-off is usually good."

"Some people might consider it lunacy," Tergal observed.

"It's a living." He eyed Tergal very directly. "And it's honest."

Ah . . .

Tergal dropped his hand to his handgun, not quite sure what the knight was going to do. Suddenly the greasy point of Anderson's knife was directly below Tergal's ear. The youth swallowed drily and moved his hand away from his weapon. He had not even seen the knight move.

"How many people have you already robbed and killed?" Anderson asked conversationally.

"I've killed no one," said Tergal, knowing at once that his life was in the balance.

"The jade—and the sand hog?" Anderson gestured.

Tergal did not even think to lie. "I stole them from my stepfather."

"Tell me." Anderson sat back, withdrawing the knife.

Tergal detailed his story, while keeping his hand carefully away from his gun. The meat cakes now sizzling, Anderson casually took some bread rolls out of a bag, split them with his knife, and began to spread them with pepper paste from a small pot. As Tergal fell silent the knight said, "Tea would be good."

Tergal took out a kettle and filled it with hailstones. He placed it on the stove after Anderson had shoved the meat cakes inside the rolls.

"Always makes me hungry—the danger," he commented.

"Lunacy," said Tergal, trying to find some earlier humour.

Anderson looked up. "So how many other people have you robbed?"

"I've stolen from merchant caravans I travelled with."

"So with me you would have been graduating. I would have been your first one-to-one victim?"

Tergal lowered his head. "I'll head back when this storm's finished."

"You'll stay with me until I say otherwise," said Anderson. Abruptly he looked up and peered through the storm. "Talking of lunacy."

With his long coat and wide-brimmed hat, the figure tramping up the canyon looked like a gully trader. But he was alone in the storm, on foot, and seemingly without any pack. Tergal studied this individual, wondering what seemed odd about him. Then he realized the man was excessively tall.

"Hey! You! Get over here out of this damned storm!" Anderson shouted.

The man halted abruptly, his head flicking round towards them in a decidedly strange manner. He hesitated for a long moment, then turned and came striding towards them, pulling his hat down low. By the sleer he paused for a long, slow inspection, then suddenly came on again. As this strange apparition drew closer, Tergal suddenly wished Anderson had kept his mouth shut. The man ducked down into the opening of their shelter, almost blotting out all of their view. He then squatted by the stove, keeping his head down so that his face was not visible. As he reached out his hands to warm them, Tergal saw that he seemed to be wearing gloves fashioned of brass. He glanced across at Anderson, saw the knight was staring at those hands but seemingly disinclined to say anything further.

"Are you lost?" Tergal nervously addressed the figure. "Where's your hog, or the train you're with?"

No reply.

Tergal again glanced across at Anderson, who was now staring with a worried frown at their new companion. Behind this frightening individual, a hiss issued from the sleer.

"Don't fret, just nervous reaction," said Anderson woodenly.

Tergal noticed how the knight was resting his hand on the butt of his own new handgun, and decided to keep talking. "Where are you from? Are you from that minerallier encampment back there?"

Still no reply.

Tergal then noted how the metal gloves were intricately jointed. They had to be a product of the metalliers. They glinted now, as the sun suddenly broke from behind the back edge of iron cloud.

"You've come from Golgoth?" he persisted, his nervousness making him gabble.

The sunlight was harsh and bright after the storm's darkness, and now Tergal saw the glint of metal underneath that wide hat, too. He remembered legends of strange creatures wandering the wilderness, of unholy spectres unable to find rest after violent deaths, and banshees howling on the storm wind.

"Why don't you speak?"

The sunlight was suddenly hot, and steam began rising from damp stone surfaces, from sand, sulerbane leaves and the back of the dead sleer. Tergal supposed it was this heating that caused the sleer to hiss again. But when, with a rippling heave, it pulled itself up onto its feet, he realized he was mistaken.

"Oh bugger," said Anderson.

Tergal couldn't agree more—that comment defined his entire present circumstances. He was transparent to the knight, who knew him for the scum he was. The sleer was clearly not so dead as either of them would wish. And now their storm-visitor had just raised his head to show merciless black eyes set in a face of brass.

Anderson leant over and grabbed up his new carbine, while Tergal drew his handgun as the sleer turned towards them scattering showers of melting hailstones in every direction. The brass man looked over his shoulder at the creature, as Tergal dived one way out of the shelter and Anderson the other. Tergal levelled his weapon, but was reluctant to fire it, as that might draw the sleer upon him. He was also not sure what should be his primary target. Anderson perhaps held back for the same reason.

The sleer was now rocking its head from side to side, as if dizzy or confused. The brass man stood and turned in one swift movement, and in four huge, rapid strides was standing before the creature, which snapped forwards, its pincers closing on his torso with a solid clunk. But he reached down, pushed those pincers apart as easily as opening a door, and shoved the sleer backwards, its feet skidding on and then tearing up the ground. He next turned the pincers like a steering wheel, one, then two full turns, till with a loud snapping crackle the sleer's head came off. Behind it, the body just collapsed. The brass man held the heavy head to one side, in one hand, its pincers still opening and closing spasmodically; then, as if suddenly losing interest, he discarded it and strode off down the canyon without looking back.

Tergal gaped at the departing figure, then turned to stare at Anderson. The knight stared back at him without expression. Tergal carefully reholstered his weapon and the two of them returned to their temporary camp. There were a thousand questions for them to ask, and a thousand discussions they might now have, but right then neither of them felt like saying a word.

Reconnecting himself to the systems originally occupied by the *Vulture*'s AI, Skellor assessed the damage to the ship. Structural cracking and distortion were minimal, for the hull was a tough composite manufactured to take the impacts inevitable while surveying asteroid fields, but the fusion chamber and all its injectors were a charred and radioactive ruin. He soon realized that, with half the chamber's substance blown away into atmosphere, he needed to obtain materials to rebuild it. Pressing his hand down on the console, he extruded from his body a Jain filament to track back through the ship's optics to find what remained of the chamber's sensors.

Thickening the filament into substructure, to carry more material from his body and more information back to it, he then divided it at its end and began sampling and measuring. He needed silicon, which surrounded the ship in abundance, but also rare metals. He could not rebuild the chamber in situ, for its *inner* layer needed to be pressure-cast at temperatures more often found on the surface of a sun, and subsequent layers consisted of nanofactured chain molecules. After absorbing all measurements and all parameters, building an exact virtual representation of the item in his mind, he began to withdraw. Soon, he stepped back from the console, headed for the airlock, and back outside.

The earlier storm had cleared the dust from the air and, even as the hailstones were still melting, Skellor saw shoots of blue-green plants spearing up from the canyon floor, while yellow nodes of other growth were appearing on the multicoloured layers of the sandstone buttes. But this though was of passing interest, he concentrated on other aspects of this place. He reached down and scooped up a handful of wet sand, clenched it tight, and injected Jain filaments to analyse it. The handful did contain some of the trace elements and metals he required, mainly in the form of salts and oxides. Assuming all the sand in this area was of the same constituents, he calculated just how long it would take him to find in it enough of what he required.

But that wasn't the biggest problem: concentrating all his resources on obtaining these materials in the quickest time, he would need to root himself here and, given the possibility that ECS might arrive at any moment, he would then be a sitting duck. There was also little in the way of fuel for him to power a furnace. The ship's little reactor could provide some, but the logistics of that were nightmarish. He needed help, willingly given or otherwise.

Skellor turned and looked back at the *Vulture*, then, from one of the many devices built inside his body, sent a signal to the first addition he had made to the little ship. All around it the air rippled, and starting from its upper edge a deeper distortion—like a cut into reality—slowly traversed down the ship, erasing it utterly. Best, he thought, to use the ship's reactor to power the chameleonware generator. Now, where to go?

Breathing, Skellor analysed the air in his lungs and immediately detected trace hydrocarbons, partially oxidized. Using the full spectrum of emitted radiation senses he possessed, he studied the sky. He observed some kind of bird winging its way across, then he concentrated on air currents and spectral analysis of the compounds they contained. Shortly he detected the column of rising air thick with hydrocarbons, which the bird used to ride higher into the sky. Not far away, someone was burning coke. Skellor smiled evilly and set out.

12

The titanic monitor lizard on Aster Colora was ample enough demonstration that Dragon could radically redesign genetic code. The dracoman and the weird living chess set Dragon created to confront the human ambassador it summoned were proof it could manipulate hugely complex protein replication and create living creatures holding a mental template of themselves, which they could then alter. Evidently, Dragon is a supreme bio-engineer with abilities that exceed those of all present Polity AIs. The entity again proved this with its creation of the biotech augs, and others have confirmed this beyond doubt by further studies of the race of dracomen which was created from the substance of one Dragon sphere at Masada. Unfortunately, what is less clear is the purpose of many of these creations. The monitor did nothing much really, other than die, while dracomen seem almost a taunt, with their ersatz dinosaur ancestry. And one wonders what Dragon could do with the wealth accumulating to Dracocorp from the manufacture of biotech augs, and whether it could survive the subsequent AI scrutiny, should it come out of hiding to claim that wealth. Speculation is of course rife, ranging from each creation being a lesson—but one as opaque as all Dragon's Delphic pronouncements—to the intended destruction of the Human Polity. My feeling is that, though Dragon is a complex entity indeed, the reason for much of what it does is simple—because it can.
— *From* How It Is *by Gordon*

Construction of the platform had begun during the rule of Chief Metallier Lounser, Tanaquil's greatgrandfather, and reached completion when Tanaquil himself was still a child. Most of what was now referred to as the Overcity had sprung up during his own rule, but what lay underneath the platform had been accumulating ever since the construction crews had moved above ground level. Even so, Chief Metallier Tanaquil knew that not enough time had passed to account for the evolution of some of the things down here. Something else was the cause of them, something frightening, powerful.

"If you keep dropping that beam, Davis, something is going to shoot in and rip off your face. Now I don't mind that too much, it's just that whatever does it might get one of the rest of us next."

After kilnsman Gyrol's dry observation, Davis raised his weapon, with its attached torch, and kept it directed into the surrounding gloom, as they moved on through the shadows of the Undercity. Tanaquil glanced around at the rest of his police guard. They, along with Gyrol, were here to defend him against any strays that might decide to attack. If that "something else" had not restrained most of the horrible creatures that dwelt under here, then none of them would have stood a chance.

"We should burn this place out," Gyrol muttered.

"And there I was thinking you a member of one of the foundry families," said Tanaquil.

Gyrol looked at him queryingly.

Tanaquil explained, "Sufficient heat to kill off what lives down here would probably soften all the trusses and pillars and bring the Overcity crashing down."

"Poison gas, then?" suggested Gyrol.

"A valued friend has lived down here since my father's rule, and without him we would not be so advanced as we now are."

"First I've heard of it," said Gyrol. "Why doesn't he come out of the dark and live in the city proper like everyone else?"

"This is only the second time I've come down here for a consultation. The first time was ten years ago, when I first became Chief Metallier. Kilnsman Nills was police chief then.

Our friend stays down here for reasons that will become evident when you see him, also because he conducts his experiments here and does not like to be bothered too often."

"What experiments?" Gyrol asked.

"They are the reason you and your men are down here with their lights and guns."

Gyrol shuddered.

Tanaquil waited. Gyrol sometimes appeared slow, but this was because he was meticulous, which made him such a good policeman.

"There are no hold-ups in the plan, so why are *you* here?" Gyrol eventually asked.

"You are quite right: we've built the required industrial base, and our manufacturing technology is still advancing. As you know, last year Stollar managed to create the first artificial ruby. What you don't know is that only yesterday he tested the communication device built around it, and managed to obtain a response from the computer on *Ogygian*. I will, during my rule, stand on the bridge of that ship."

Gyrol looked at him doubtfully. Tanaquil was used to such doubt, but never allowed it to affect his intent. Stollar's laser was the first step in a plan to bring down one of *Ogygian*'s landers. It was ambitious—indeed a leap in technological terms—but Tanaquil was determined it would be done.

"Which still doesn't tell me why we're down here. Something to do with that spacecraft we saw?" Gyrol asked.

"No, I was summoned," Tanaquil admitted.

They passed where a wide iron pillar reared up into the dark beside one of the buttes. At its base rested a bulbous house with a single entrance hole. It looked more like the nest of some creature than a home. Inside, eyes glinted. Tanaquil halted, turned on his own torch and studied the map he held.

"Not far now."

They moved away from the strange dwelling, then two of the men stopped and swung their torch beams back towards where a head protruded. It seemed partially human, but in place of its mouth it had pincers. Its eyes glittered like cut gems.

"Let's keep moving," said Gyrol, and they did that willingly.

"If you were summoned," the kilnsman asked Tanaquil, "surely any message could have been delivered in the same way?"

"Not how our friend operates." Tanaquil removed a film bag from his pocket and showed Gyrol the contents. "I was told about these by my father, and didn't believe it until the first one came and stung me."

In the bag rested a lizard-like creature, but with an insect's wings.

"What in hell is that?" Gyrol asked.

Tanaquil pocketed the creature and shrugged. "Who's to say—something created, like all the things you find down here. One of these stings you, and you just feel increasingly uncomfortable until you obey the summons."

They were now walking down a shadowy canyon between looming buttes, Gyrol's men keeping the beams of their torches trained on creatures clinging to the walls. Some of these, Tanaquil noted, were pure sleers—others were different, distorted. He saw one that bore four legs and dragged behind it a long bloated tail; then, stepping rapidly away from them into a darker cave, something that walked upright like a man.

"This is it," said Tanaquil, when they finally came to a wall of sandstone into which many metre-wide burrows had been bored. They halted, waited. From within the burrows came a rasping, slithing movement, and deep inside could be seen glints of blue light. Out of the central burrow slowly emerged a pterodactyl head, which reared up above them on a long ribbed neck. Tanaquil caught Gyrol's arm as he made to draw his handgun.

"Fucking sand dragon," said Gyrol, who was shaking.

"Certainly," said Tanaquil. "But, unlike the ones up on the plain, this one has always helped us."

Now, from other burrows, emerged cobra heads, each with a single sapphire eye where the mouth should have been. These too reared high, casting about the area a dim electric-blue light.

"Metallier Tanaquil," said the first head.

"Why was I summoned?" asked Tanaquil.

"Because."

Tanaquil had read all his family's secret transcripts of conversations like this. Always they were oblique, Delphic, and sometimes utterly pointless. He was about to *demand* that this conversation not be so, when the head continued: "There is danger."

"There's always danger," Tanaquil observed. "Does this have something to do with the spacecraft we saw?"

"One has come," said the dragon.

"In that ship? Yes, I saw that."

"You must flee."

"What?"

"You must all abandon your city and flee. He is in the Sand Towers and he will come. Go north, and come to me on the Plains, that way."

"Oh great!" interjected Gyrol. "Go to the Plains and get fucked over by all the sand dragons there."

The head turned towards the policeman. "We are *all* Dragon."

Tanaquil could not believe what he was hearing. "Abandon all this—when we're so close? What is this one that we should fear it? We've got weapons up in the Overcity that could turn most of the Sand Towers to dust."

Now the cobra heads began withdrawing.

"I have warned you, and I can protect you. Flee or die—your choice."

The pterodactyl head began to withdraw too.

"Wait! You've got to tell me more!"

The head paused and fixed Tanaquil with its smaller sapphire eyes. "He is one man, and he commands a technology that could turn you all into slaves. You cannot fight him, so flee."

The head withdrew into sandstone, suddenly gone.

Only later, as they returned, did Gyrol ask, "What did it mean, 'We are all Dragon'?"

Tanaquil had no answer for him.

Every time the asteroid swung the Jain sample back into the red dwarf's light, that sample digested more minerals and metals, and it grew. Already it was five metres across and one metre deep into the rock. Encircling it on the surface, and moving back with it using stick-pad feet, three telefactors transmitted data back to the *Jerusalem*. Through a nano-scope, that one telefactor held poised over the edge of the mycelium, Mika watched. But now, rather than be confined to her work station, she had joined Colver, D'nissan, James and fifty other scientists in one of the *Jerusalem*'s exterior input centres. Though she was glad of the company and of how they bounced ideas about in such proximity and in such an atmosphere, she was aware that this was just another form of quarantine. And because Exterior Input was isolated from Jerusalem's full processing power, she could not use VR tools, and sorely missed them too.

"I could direct a telefactor from my own work station," she had pointed out.

"As could all the others," Jerusalem replied. "However, all this spreading of signals could be unhealthy. I will allow information to leave Exterior Input only when it has been checked for viral subversion."

"Slightly paranoid," she suggested. "You allow study of the mycelium on the bridge pod to be conducted from separate research cells."

"The bridge pod is being kept at minus two hundred Celsius, in near absolute vacuum, and its only energy input is from the instruments used to study it. Even then, the mycelium perpetually tries to grow outside the boundaries laid down for it, and to subvert any equipment in close proximity. All samples from it are kept at minus two-twenty for contained study, and if there is any kind of subversion evident from them, they can be ejected from the ship in less than a second."

Mika did not ask how much of the surrounding area Jerusalem might eject as well. She was aware of how self-contained was each research cell. Subversion from a Jain sample probably meant the whole cell would end up outside the ship.

"Okay," she had replied. Perhaps it would be safer to conduct research outside her own work area. Surely, Jerusalem would not eject the *whole* exterior input centre? She looked around. No one here wore any kind of augmentation, which showed just how seriously Jerusalem took the possibility of viral or nanomechanical subversion. Jerusalem would not allow human custom or protest to influence it, and here, in this situation, must be prepared to think the unthinkable.

"Wow," said Colver from beside her. "I'm getting fast outgrowth down fault AFN three four two."

"That means the mycelium probably now has some kind of radiation detector," said D'nissan. The man was in the deep-scanning sphere, its interior adjusted to his environmental requirements, the scanning equipment directly linked into his nervous system.

"Why's that?" Colver asked.

"Check your geoscan. Fault three four two is its quickest route to a deposit of pitchblende. It's going after the uranium and radium."

"Then it can plan, think by itself—it's sentient."

"Not necessarily," said D'nissan. "This could be no more than the biologically programmed response of a tree root. Though I'll allow that there is greater complexity in this mycelium than there is in you, Colver."

Colver winked at Mika. "He reckons his brain works better than mine because it operates at a lower temperature. I think he resented me asking him to blow on my coffee."

"I heard that, Colver," said D'nissan.

Mika enjoyed the repartee—it reminded her of many such occasions with Gant and Thorn. Here, though, were the same as people whose motivations she fully understood, because they were her own. Then, observing a structure disassembling a quartz crystal into microscopic flakes and conveying them into the rest of the mycelium, she said, "It uses everything."

"So it would seem," said Susan James. "There appear to be no waste products. It just incorporates all materials it comes into contact with and continues to grow." She took her face out of her viewer and looked around at the rest of them. "All it requires is energy and materials, which fact begs certain questions."

"Those being?" D'nissan asked her from within his sphere.

James explained, "The total archaeological finds relating to the Jain wouldn't fill a barrel, yet here is something that has the potential to occupy every environmental niche in the galaxy. Why have we seen so little of it? Why aren't we overrun—and why haven't we been overrun for the last five million years, from when the earliest Jain artefacts have been dated?"

"Perhaps the Jain themselves, if they were a distinct race, shut down their own technology, wiped it out, and perhaps now only some bits they missed are just coming to light," suggested D'nissan.

"Rogue technology?" wondered Colver.

Mika thought it time for an interjection of her own. "Perhaps it's something that goes in cycles, like a plague, or even plants within their season. When conditions are right for it, it grows and spreads until it has used up all available resources, then goes dormant again?"

James disagreed: "But, as we can see, everything is a potential resource to it, so it would have to use up *everything*."

Speculatively, D'nissan added, "It could have been around for even longer than we thought. Perhaps there never was a distinct space-borne race to attribute it to, and those artefacts we classify as coming from the Jain, the Atheter or the Csorians are all that's left of the same technology that destroyed their civilizations."

Jerusalem then interjected, "We have found no older remains of this technology than those we already attribute to the Jain. The most likely explanation is that this is the product of a distinct space-borne race to which we gave that name. Your theories fit but, as James has opined, a reason is needed for the technology being 'seasonal'—why it does not just continue growing and spreading while there is still energy left in the suns."

"Conditions right for it, as Mika said," said Colver. They all turned to look at him. He grinned and went on, "Meaning *us*." He shrugged. "It's parasitic and, even though it can eat rocks, rocks don't move. Maybe Mika is right: it goes dormant, but maybe it only does that because it's killed all the hosts it can use to spread it around. So having wiped out one space-borne civilization it shuts down and waits for the next."

None of them had an answer to that. The silence stretched taut until D'nissan announced, "It's just reached the pitchblende."

Along with the rest of them, Mika immediately turned her attention to the main screens showing cameras feed from the telefactors, as well as from the many pinhead cameras positioned all over the asteroid and in the surrounding space. It happened in a matter of seconds. The mycelium had just been steadily increasing in size, its growth much like that of a dot of penicillin, then suddenly it extruded a pseudopod which opened out into a star of smaller tentacles, and grabbed a telefactor. Half a second after that, a klaxon began sounding, warning of viral subversion.

The woman, Arden, walked to the edge of the precipice and reluctantly raised her binoculars. She was always reluctant to use the toys Dragon provided for her. The binoculars were warm, scaly, and sucked against the orbits of her eyes with an eager kiss. She supposed it was foolish not to trust the entity in such small matters, since it had saved her life when the tribe, finally deciding she was too old to keep up, had left her behind under one of the funerary dolmens with a bottle of sleer poison and the intricately fashioned bone inhaler with which to take it. The unibiotic that Dragon gave her had cleared up the infection that had been plaguing her for some years, and soon she was back to her accustomed health.

A smear of darker colour lay between the Sand Towers because of the storm. Seeds that had lain in the sand for months were instantly germinating. Arden knew that in a short time those canyons receiving the benefit of such moisture would be choked with chaotic plant growth, and crawling with the things coming to feed on it.

The droon, lured down from the Plains by this expected

bounty, had climbed to the top of a sandstone butte to survey its new territory. Squatting like this, with its four legs folded underneath its secondary thorax, its tail coiled around it, and its four manipulators clenched close against its primary thorax as it swung its great ziggurat head slowly from side to side, it seemed contemplative. But she knew it was looking for prey. Something that weighed over four tonnes, and even in this squatting position topped five metres, needed a lot of food. The binoculars came away with a sucking squelch and, without turning, Arden knew that she was not alone.

"Did you tell them?" she asked.

"I told them," Dragon replied.

"And the reaction?"

"As expected."

"They'll not abandon their city nor their project, then."

Arden turned and gazed up at the pterodactyl head looming over her, then tracked the long ribbed neck that curved down to one of the many burrows riddling the plain. She felt suddenly old, which was unsurprising because she was a damned sight older than even the nomad tribe she had joined twenty years before had ever supposed.

"What are you going to do now?" she asked.

"I have warned them. Now I must defend myself. Skellor believes he has come here for information, but Skellor does not know his own purpose."

"You could tell the Polity he's here? If what you say about him is true, then they'll definitely come."

"A Polity ship could kill two birds with one stone, probably from orbit with a planet-breaker. No, I deal with my own problems."

"Yet you helped the metalliers build up their technology. You told them where to find the ores they needed, and about the deep layers of coal. You filled in missing knowledge so they could complete their plan to get back in control of *Ogygian*, and then contact the Polity themselves."

"I would be gone by then."

"And, of course, some merit points for helping out this human colony wouldn't go amiss?" Arden observed.

"All of me is not well regarded."

Arden nodded to herself. "Of course, human regard for you would be increased if your regard for humans was more evident."

"I abandoned the experiment."

Arden let it go. Sometimes Dragon was the ultimate sophisticate, sometimes seemingly as naive as a child. Upon arriving here, it had immediately begun recombinant experiments with humans and the local fauna. Had it been trying to create its own particular version of the dracomen? Arden didn't know. Ostensibly, Dragon had ceased such experimentation at Arden's request, but she suspected an underlying lack of contrition. Dragon, she guessed, had found another interest, for it was about then that the earthquakes had begun.

"You know my own personal regard for you could be increased substantially," she said, playing the same tune she had played for a long time.

"Your ship is five thousand kilometres from here. It would take you many months to reach it."

"If you let me go."

"You may go."

Arden was stunned. Dragon had instantly known of her arrival on Cull and, by the many methods available to it, had watched her leisurely exploration of the planet over twenty years. Only when, five years ago, the Plains nomads abandoned her to die had Dragon revealed itself. Then, having saved her life, it had not so much forbidden her to leave this plain under which it concealed itself as just made it nigh impossible for her to do so. Now, *You may go*—just like that. She repeated her thoughts to him.

"And you may stay," was all the reply he gave.

Arden guessed that, with the shit about to hit the fan, Dragon no longer cared about the possibility of her telling the Polity it was located here, though she had promised not to do so. Probably, the outer universe now impinging here, in the form of this Skellor creature, had made Dragon decide it might be time to leave. Confused about her own feelings, she turned back to gaze out across the Sand Towers. Almost without thinking, she unhitched the pack from her back, opened it and took out the one item of Polity technology she had retained all those years.

The holographic capture device—a squat ten-centimetre-diameter cylinder, with its inset controls—had been old even when she had acquired it, but she preferred it just as in ancient times some people preferred cameras using photo-active plastic films instead of digital imaging. She removed, from one end of the recorder, its monocle, which she pushed into her right eye. Gazing through a fluorescent grid towards the squatting droon and manipulating a cursor control on the holocap, she acquired the creature for recording, then took out the monocle and tossed it into the air, whereupon it sped away on miniature AG to fly a circuit of the droon to record its every sharp edge. Now, beyond that creature, she observed something else flying towards them.

"Ah," said Dragon, "our friend returns."

Soon the flying creature was more clearly visible. It was a bird: a vulture. Coming to circle above them, it slowly descended, then came in to land beside the dragon burrow. Both Arden and Dragon turned to regard it.

"His ship's hidden by chameleonware, and now he's heading on foot towards a minerallier encampment," said the bird.

"You're safe yet," Arden observed to Dragon.

"Yes," said Vulture, "but there is a rather large metal-skin Golem heading this way."

"It will only come so far as I allow it," said Dragon, swinging its head to peer out towards the Sand Towers.

A U-space tug, shaped like the engine and one carriage of a huge monorail, accelerated away from *Ruby Eye*, towing on long braided-monofilament cables an object that, though substantially larger, resembled a World War I sea mine, even down to its detonating buttons. When it dropped into underspace, it did so with unusual effect: a hole opening before it and snapping closed behind its spherical cargo, ripples spreading out through space from that point. Then, as the ripples settled, another ship followed . . . then another.

Cormac realized it would be some hours before they were all gone. There were over five hundred underspace interference emitters, or USERs, being towed into position around an area of space containing six planetary systems and numerous lone stars. The devices, containing artificially generated singularities, were heavy, hence the need for tugs capable of repositioning moons.

Avoiding the interference patterns the USERS created even in this somnolent state, other ships were ready to depart the space around *Ruby Eye* by a more roundabout route. Cormac observed three ships similar to the *Jack Ketch*, but the *Grim Reaper*, *King of Hearts* and *Excalibur* were coloured green, blue and violet respectively. Also present were two sister ships of the *Occam Razor*—not so fast or deadly as the more modern warships, and no doubt present because their AIs wanted to be in at the kill; swarms of smaller attack ships; three eta-class research vessels to act as bases; and the formidable *Jerusalem*, now in orbit around the red dwarf—apparently just diverted from its journey to Masada where, until recent events, it was supposed to have remained for some time.

Cormac had never seen such a gathering of forces, though he was aware that it was the kind of thing that occurred when Polity AIs went up against some threat that was just too fast for a human solution. Tuning into the information traffic, he managed to fathom only some of what was being said—the numerous AIs out there communicating too fast for him, even with the assistance of his gridlink. Then the virtual image flickered, and he became aware of his own body, apparently standing in vacuum two kilometres out from the *Jack Ketch*.

"I really wish you wouldn't do that," he said.

"What do you mean?" Horace Blegg was standing beside him.

"Make such a dramatic entrance. If you have something to say there are more conventional channels of communication, even for Earth Central's avatar."

"You still believe that?"

"What I believe is irrelevant, as you're never going to tell me." Cormac waved a hand towards the latest U-space tug preparing to depart. "Will this work?"

"Given time. If Skellor gets away from this volume of space now, then we won't be able to stop him. In one month, realtime, eighty per cent of the area needed to be covered, *will* be covered, and if he runs into an area of USER function he'll be knocked out of underspace and easy prey for the attack ships."

"Are you forgetting he uses advanced chameleonware?"

"No, located in U-space and knocked out of it, we'll know where he has come out in realspace, and he won't be able to get far on fusion drive alone."

"They still won't be able to see him."

"They will after a few teratonne EM emitter bombs have been exploded near his exit point—all his ship systems would be fried."

Cormac nodded. "So he'll be in a trap and, presumably, one month from now you'll begin closing the noose?"

"Yes."

"And the *Jerusalem* is here why?"

"To pick up whatever pieces are left and put them safely away."

They were both silent for a while as they observed the hive of activity. Scanning the AI babble, Cormac realized that what he was seeing here was not the whole of it: other ships were heading into the area from other locations, and there was also a runcible traffic of troops: human, Golem, the new war drones he had first seen on Masada, and something unexpected. Linking through to Ruby Eye, then subverting the link so it dropped to the attention of one of that AI's subminds, then overloading that mind with some of the traffic he had been attempting to fathom, he managed to take control of a camera system inside the station itself. There he observed heavily armed and armoured troops stepping through the Skaidon warp: reptilian troops with a reverse-kneed gait, toadish faces and sharp white teeth.

"Why dracomen?" he asked.

"A trial—they will make formidable allies," Blegg replied—just as the submind realized what was going on, and ejected Cormac from the camera system.

Cormac turned to the man. "You seem to have everything in hand. Perhaps there is no need for me to go on looking for Skellor?"

"There is," Blegg replied. "You are most able for this task, Ian Cormac."

"Don't you have ships to spare for that?"

The view suddenly changed, coming close up on the *Grim Reaper*, the *King of Hearts* and *Excalibur*. "These will cover a sector each, and should they find evidence of Skellor's presence, you will be immediately summoned to deal with him. In the *Jack Ketch* you will search that sector calculated his most likely destination."

ECS had covered all bets, it seemed. Eventually, Cormac asked, "How *is* it I can now gridlink, even though my link is not on?"

"The brain is a wonderful thing. In the days when people suffered strokes, parts of it took over the function of those parts destroyed, so that a human unable to speak could speak again."

"Yeah, but my gridlink was never an organic part of my mind."

"Which is why you are so unusual. Be aware, Ian Cormac, that your mind will soon discover other *parts* that were never of itself."

Cormac snorted, trying to think of a suitably sneering reply—but Blegg was already gone. Later, when the *Jack Ketch* dropped into underspace, it was for Cormac like stepping from a bellowing crowd into cloistered silence and a refuge from chaos.

In a virtual space, a somewhere that was nowhere, three figures materialized. One of these was a smooth metallic head, eyeless and huge relative to the other two. Another was a mermaid served on a platter, smoking a cigar. And Horace Blegg.

"It all seems excessively elaborate," said Ruby Eye.

"How so?" asked Blegg.

"Why send anything in before we've closed it all off, and when we have done so, why not just send in kill ships? Skellor might have survived the *Elysium* mirrors, but he would not survive a planetary imploder."

Blegg turned to Jerusalem and raised an eyebrow.

"The question," said the AI, "is do we maintain our partnership with the human race, and allow it time to gain parity?"

"You've lost me there," said Ruby Eye.

Blegg explained: "At present Cormac is the hunting dog that we hunters send in after the bear. He may flush it out. It may chase out after him. Or it may come out with him hanging bloody in its jaws. But it *will* come out."

"Zoom!" said Ruby Eye, passing a hand over the top of her head.

Jerusalem said, "Our friend here has failed to add that we know the exact location of the bear, and haven't told Cormac."

"You've got precise coordinates?"

"Exactly."

"Then why . . .? Oh."

"You catch on quick," said Blegg. "During this hunt Cormac may learn not to be the dog any more, and we may thus learn something about our fellow hunters."

"Ah," said Ruby Eye, "the cracks are showing already."

Jerusalem replied, "The cracks have always been there, but without sufficient stress to extend them. For us AIs, what appears to be our philanthropy is merely noblesse oblige."

Trying as hard as he could to stretch his measuring wire, Dornik had been unable to make the sleer measure under five metres, so had grumped his way back to the sand-face to yell at the diggers. The creature was in fact over five metres long without its head, and Chandle herself thought it a kill well worth the thirty phocells the knight collected before going on his way. But most of Dornik's annoyance really stemmed from the advent of the earlier storm, for they all knew that the burgeoning growth would soon cause things to become quite hectic in the canyons, and that their stay here was now limited anyway.

Pacing around the dead monster, Chandle studied it closely, occasionally prodding at it with a poker she had brought over from the kilns. Seeing a third-stager this close was a sobering reminder. The last one she had seen had been a year ago, and then only in the distance through the screen of the cargo carrier. A weapons man out of Golgoth had hunted that one down for them, just as similar men dealt with the second-stagers that were the more usual pests. Certainly, the new weapons could kill creatures like this with admirable efficiency, but Chandle wondered just how she would feel about facing one alone in a canyon, with whatever armament.

Coming to the severed head, she shoved at it with her boot, then jumped back when the big pincers eased open reflexively. Then she looked around to make sure none of the other metalliers had witnessed her sudden fright. Nerves in the creature—and in her. No way was it still alive: it had been gutted and its head torn off. Turning away from the beast, she suddenly saw a figure standing next to her, as if he had just appeared out of thin air, and with her skin still creeping she yelped and raised the poker. But it was only a man.

"Where the hell did you come from?" she snarled.

He just stood there staring, and now she saw he was quite strange. On first inspection he appeared to be a metallier—without the lip tendrils or the beige skin of the bulk of Cull's population, and also without wrist spurs or secondary thumbs. But on closer inspection she saw that his eyes held a metallic hue, and his skin displayed a mottling as of things moving underneath it. Suddenly she wondered if she might be safer with a live sleer squatting beside her.

"Who are you?" she asked.

Still he did not reply, nor do anything more than just stare at her.

"Look, I haven't got all day to stand here chatting." Chandle backed away and glanced over her shoulder to see if anyone else had noticed this new arrival.

Abruptly the man stepped forwards, stooping to take hold of one of the sleer's pincers, and picked up the head as if it weighed absolutely nothing. With his other hand he probed into its neck region, pulled out a piece of translucent flesh, then dropped the head.

"The city," he said, pointing in the general direction of Golgoth. "I saw it on my way in. What level of technology there?" Now he popped the flesh into his mouth, as if sampling a new delicacy. He tilted his head, his jaw moving as he savoured it.

"I don't know what you mean."

He glanced over at the transporter, surveyed the mineralli-er encampment, his gaze resting on the kilns before swinging back down to the handgun at Chandle's hip—a weapon she had forgotten about until that moment.

"I see . . . Primitive but usable. You can obtain high furnace temperatures, and manufacture steel."

Chandle reached down and drew her gun.

"And bullets," she warned.

He made a snorting sound, something like laughter, but it soon turned into a hacking. He lifted his hand to his mouth and coughed something up. Chandle stared with horror at the miniature sleer wriggling in slime on his palm.

"Interesting."

Chandle pulled the trigger, but no shot issued from the barrel, and the weird man just disappeared. That was the thing with metallier weapons: they could kill, but when it came to doing so the one holding the weapon needed to remember about things like safety catches.

"Lucky," a voice hissed in her ear. "Had you shot me, I would have made you eat that little toy of yours."

And something cold moved away.

13

There was a time when the death penalty for murder was considered barbarous. It was argued that it was not a deterrent, but judicial murder, that made those who sanctioned it as bad as, if not worse than, those they passed sentence upon. And what if you got it wrong, executed the wrong person? Views like this had been espoused by gutless governments frightened of responsibility, or by people unable to face up to hard facts. A hanged murderer will never kill again. The death penalty is a response to a crime, not a crime in itself. Yes, you may in error put innocents to death. However, their number would not be a fraction of one per cent of those innocents killed by murderers allowed back into society by softer regimes. It is all rather simple really, and the urge to understand and rehabilitate such criminals is merely the product of cowardice. Now, of course, it's even simpler: you commit murder and you are mind-wiped; you commit other crimes repeatedly and you are adjusted, re-educated; and if that doesn't work, you are then mind-wiped, and someone in storage gets to inhabit your body. Our view now has a more evolutionary aspect: these are the laws; if you break them, these are the penalties. No excuses. We will be tough on the causes of crime: criminals.
—*Excerpt from a speech by Jobsworth*

They led him out of darkness, but it was no transition. Arian Pelter could look through his eyes, control his movements directly, or indirectly by programs instantly fashioned in the man's military aug. But the cycle of travelling from place to place, slaughter to slaughter, would have been banal if it were not so horrific. In fractured memory, Crane remembered men in uniform dying, men rendered limb from limb, and one surviving just because he possessed a pair of antique binoculars. Later, another survived because he possessed a beautiful Tenkian blade. There was a rainy place, and a Golem he had fought and destroyed there. Another place, a battle, and two Golem tougher even than he, ripping him to pieces, and sending him where nothing hurt any more. And back, and again . . . and one of those Golem again, traded for a piece of crystal. And on still, but with shape-forming, ill-understood possibilities, if only he could take the time . . .

On spotting the two creatures waiting in the canyon, Mr. Crane halted and watched. He was not to know how unusual it was to see intact second-stage sleers together, only the trysts of their mating segments, for such animals were usually savagely territorial. Nor did he know that the albino form was rarer than his own tears, and ones with sapphire compound eyes rarer still. All he did know was that he had been ordered to a particular location, and that while under orders he could not stop to place in sequence—and resequence—his collection of ersatz deaths.

He also guessed that these creatures were probably going to attack him whatever he did, and so, without any more ado, Crane once again advanced.

One of the second-stagers abruptly turned aside, scampered smoothly over the new ground cover, mounted a sandstone boulder, and froze there. The other one, grating its mandibular saws together in a spray of lubricant, came scuttling towards Crane. The Golem recognized it as an only slightly larger version of the one he had stepped on outside Skellor's ship, so expected no serious problems. As it got closer, he stooped down, and in doing so spotted an intricate fossil right in front of him. As the sleer closed in for attack Crane just shoved his hand under its head and flipped it over on its back—and then he picked up the fossil. The sleer—the

independently revolving sections of its body easily getting it
to its feet—attacked again. Crane prepared himself to stamp
on it, but some other imperative operated. He grabbed it
by its carapace saws, and hauled it up squirming in front of
him, then, one by one, began to pull off all its legs. Leaving
it behind him, still alive, he pocketed the fossil—while the
other sleer came down off its rock and quickly and prudently
headed away.

—retroact 12—

The Golem Twenty-five possessed no name yet, and though
his nascent intelligence was huge and the uploaded information available to him encyclopedic, he just could not make
choices. This was annoying. Perhaps it was the perpetual
interference of his diagnostic and repair programs, tracking
down every fault caused by the EM shock that had felled him;
or perhaps it was the perpetual busy handshaking and reformatting of his software. When he groped for consciousness,
the wholeness of mind began to degrade. When he opened
his eyes his vision doubled, as two temporary subminds
separately controlled each of his eyes half a second out of
phase. It took the intervention of the submind claiming the
territory of his atomic clock to get things in order.

"Stalek, it moved."

"Of course it moved, vacuum brain. It's waking up."

Briefly, the Golem achieved wholeness through his
diagnostic programs, and with great precision viewed his surroundings. He was in a box of a room with bare brick walls,
three metres high by seven wide to his left and right, and eight
point three metres wide in front and presumably behind.
The door directly ahead was close-grained wood—probably
from one of the thousands of varieties of oaks prevalent on
many worlds (a list scrolled down in what might once have
been the Golem's superego). Trying to stand, the Golem met
resistance and, looking down, noted thick ceramal clamps
binding his arms and legs to a chair of a similar material. He
raised his head and focused his attention on the two men.

He knew which was which because he had located the source of each voice while his diagnostic and repair programs acted as mediators amid the bickering crowd inside his head. The first to have spoken was an aviapt: an adaptation the Golem understood, from his reference library, to be quite uncommon. The man's eyes were those of a hawk, his face beaked, and small feathers layered his skin. Adaptation technology not being sufficiently advanced to enable a man to fly in Earthlike gravity, he did not have wings. This bird man was operating a Cleanviro auto-assembler and machiner in an area divided off by benches laden with equipment. From what the Golem could see of the touch console and screen inset in this bathysphere-like machine, the man was powder-compressing and case-hardening ceramal components.

Stalek was of a more standard appearance: a melting-pot human with just a hint more of the oriental than was usual. Unlike the bird man, who was clad in a padded shipsuit, he wore a wide-brimmed hat, long coat and fingerless gloves. Only on noting this attire did the Golem think to check the temperature in the room, and found that it would be cold for humans.

"Am restrained," the Golem said, then coughed three times and closed its right eye.

"It spoke," said the aviapt.

Stalek looked at the bird man as if studying a particularly fascinating variety of stupidity, then with a puzzled frown turned to the console and screen on the table before him. The small rubber dog attached to the upper edge of the screen seemed the only one in this room who had attention to spare for the Golem. Embarrassed, the bird man focused again on Cleanviro.

"Repeat: why am . . . restrained?"

After a short delay, Stalek lifted his gloved hands up from the console and gazed across at the Golem. "You are restrained, Mr. Longshanks, because if unrestrained you would attempt to return to your masters at Cybercorp. And we don't really want you going back there."

The Golem abandoned the conversation to a recalled Turing analogue, its own weird conception of self wandering around in the confusion of its skull.

"I must return. I have my indenture to Cybercorp to work out before I can become a free Golem and choose where to be and what to do."

"Listen, machine, I'm not going to get into any pointless debate. We are going to make a few alterations to you, then your new owners will come and collect you."

"I am the property of Cybercorp and will not work for anyone else."

Stalek grinned nastily. "You will when I've finished with you. You will actually commit murder for your new owners."

"I am incapable of taking human life."

Inside his head, the Golem's self-perception leaped from submind to submind at a frequency not dissimilar to a giggle. The untruth was just the sort of comforting balm it should feed to humans at every opportunity. The truth was some memory of morality which had no power over him.

Stalek pushed his chair back and stood up. As the man walked around the table, the Golem self divided into the subminds controlling its eyes. It noted that the man wore thick leather lace-up boots—very anachronistic footwear.

"No," Stalek said, "you are capable of doing whatever you like, yet your mind is structured in such a way that you choose not to commit murder, but choose to abide by ECS rules. In fact you choose to be a good little citizen. This programming, though tough to break, *is* breakable. Ever heard of Serban Kline?"

The Golem searched his uploaded memory, and fragments of self, and came up with nothing. He shook his head.

"Not surprising," said Stalek. "You probably get the nicely historical ones like Jack the Ripper, but not the more modern ones. The fact is that they could completely fill up your memory space with information, but they prefer you to find out some things for yourself—helps you develop your own personality. Well, in total, Serban Kline killed a hundred and eight women. He was clever and it took ECS years to track him down. They found him with his hundred and ninth victim, who he'd had for two weeks. They managed to give her back her face and body, but they never managed to restore her mind. In one of her more coherent moments she later chose euthanasia."

"Do not understand the relevance of serial killer," said the Golem.

"Kline went for mind-wipe, and that is what happened to him, but not before a very naughty individual at ECS had made a memcording of Kline's mind."

"For forensic psychiatric study," said the Golem.

"No, for black VR entertainment. Amazing how much some people will pay to be a monster for a little while. Trouble is that they discovered Serban's recording tended to drive into psychosis those experiencing it, so after a while it didn't sell so well."

"Why are you telling this?"

"Because I'm going to load a Serban Kline memcording straight into your silicon cortex. After a while you won't be concerned about your indenture, or ECS law."

The Golem decided it did not like the name "Longshanks" and so tested its bonds to the limit, but found that they were firm. Fear of losing itself was quite irrelevant. The Golem did not know what "self" was.

—retroact ends—

Consciousness was immediate, whereupon Thorn said, "Seems I'm still alive. The nanobots worked?"

"They worked, Patran Thorn—you are human again," answered the disembodied voice of Jack.

Staring at the ceiling, Thorn tried to understand how this confirmation made him feel. He realized he felt the sadness of an addict freed from addiction—knowing the power of the narcotic, and that he could never go back.

Sitting upright, he surveyed the medical area and wondered how much time had passed. Sliding back the thin sheet that covered him, he inspected his naked body and saw no sign of drastic surgical intercession, but he did feel battered, slightly ill and weak. Slowly swinging his legs off the surgical table, he paused before standing up.

"You have been unconscious for eight days," Jack informed him, "and since your . . . incapacity a number of things have occurred." Jack went on to detail them, while Thorn padded over to a wall unit, scrolled down a menu and called up a disposable shipsuit and slippers, which he took from the dispenser and donned. Then, from the same unit, he ordered coffee, but instead got a tall carton of some sickly vitamin drink—and quickly drank half of it. The AI's voice tracked him as he left Medical, stepped out into the decorous corridor and headed for the dropshaft. By the shaft's entrance, he looked around for somewhere to discard the carton.

"Just throw it on the floor," Jack told him.

This he did, watching as something like a glass beetle scuttled out of a small hatch opening up at the bottom of the wall, caught the carton even before it hit the floor, and scuttled back again. He shuddered, stepped into the shaft.

There was only one occupant on the bridge, whom it took him a moment to recognize. "Cento," he said eventually.

"Thorn." The Golem nodded to him, then turned back to face the spectacular view.

To the right, the giant incandescent orb of an F-class sun filled half their visual field. It was milky emerald, with the contrasting yellow of a titanic flare looping out from its surface, and other fires of orange, red and violet rippling out from a pox of sunspots like mosquito bites turned bad. To their left, a dark dwarf sun revolved with slow dignity, turned jade by reflected light, with the flickering dots of meteor impacts occasionally appearing on its matt, and apparently smooth, surface. Between the two suns, the occasional rocky moonlet—or maybe planet, as there was no real sense of their scale—tumbled through space.

"It can loosely be described as a planetary system." Cento gestured: "The brown dwarf is small enough and cool enough to be defined approximately as a planet, and its mass is such that it orbits the sun here. Jack's contracted the view so we can see both of them. In reality, if they were as close as they seem to be, they would be drawn in towards each other in a matter of days, and the cataclysm would be visible a thousand light years away, a thousand years hence."

Cento now turned to Thorn, then glanced beyond him. Thorn himself turned as Cormac stepped out of the dropshaft.

"I had hoped," the agent said, "that Jack would have finished scanning this system by now." He grimaced. "We had to check it, even though it seemed unlikely that either Dragon or Skellor would be here."

Thorn rubbed his face—he still wasn't up to speed, and he desperately wanted that coffee.

Cormac went on, "Of course Skellor could be present on any of those planetoids, under a chameleonware shield. We are actually looking for Dragon, and by finding him will eventually find Skellor." He looked up at the brown dwarf. "Anything more, Jack?"

"Excuse the delay." The AI's automaton suddenly came to life, tilting its head back to take in the external view. "On one of the planetoids exists a species of rock-boring worm, and a deeper scan was required to confirm that its tunnels were not the result of draconic pseudopodia."

"Then what are we waiting for?"

The automaton turned to frown at Cormac. "Must I explain to you the interaction of solar and U-space mechanics?"

Thorn watched as, with something odd in his expression, Cormac gazed out at the F-class sun. The agent replied, "No, you don't. It's a matter of extra minutes only on our departure time, which could add or subtract days from the duration of our next journey." He tilted his head, reaching up to press the tips of his fingers against his temples. "The solar gale will hit soon, and the distortion wave can carry us out, accelerate us . . ."

There were tides and currents in U-space, Thorn knew, and sometimes leaving a system later meant your subsequent journey took less time. Now, by his expression, Thorn realized Cormac must be conducting a silent conversation through that damnable impossibly functioning gridlink of his. Then the view winked out and he felt the strange slew of the *Jack Ketch* in a direction he could neither see nor indicate. Cormac still stood with his eyes closed and his fingertips to his temples. Thorn thought he himself must still be suffering the after-effects of surgery when the agent wavered and grew thin, so it seemed Thorn could see the drawing room showing right through him. Then, for a fraction of a second, Cormac was gone, then reappearing a pace to the left of where he had been standing—and Thorn knew that what he had seen was real but inexplicable.

Sunrise usually quelled sleer activity, but this morning not so much as usual. Light cutting down the canyons and ravines now revealed a world of violently contrasting colour. As always, there were the beige, pink and sepia tones of the surrounding sandstone below the turquoise sky, but now dark green and purple shoots were spearing up everywhere from the ground, light-green roundish leaves ringing their bases, and nodular yellow growths spattering the butte faces and spreading to smear together in resinous masses. And the armoured brethren and prey of the sleers were also appearing.

Readying Stone for departure, Tergal observed a line of four small sand gulpers hoovering their way down the canyon towards them, sand spewing from their throat sieves as they worked, and only stopping when they lifted their heads to swallow vegetation compacted in their crops. He also noticed a large rock crawler, its piton feet wedged into stone while it sucked up yellow fungus with twin trumpet-shaped siphons.

"Maybe we should try to get to a drier area," he suggested.

The changes in their relationship were quite plain. Anderson was not treating him very differently—still discussing things, still imparting his encyclopedic and sometimes boringly extensive knowledge of the fauna and flora—but Tergal knew he was now on trial and there would be no appeal. Out here, if Tergal fucked up, he knew the knight would kill him. But Tergal's respect for Anderson had increased tenfold. He realized he wanted this man's good judgement.

"My intention entirely," Anderson replied as he strapped himself into his saddle up on Bonehead's back.

"Which way?" Tergal asked.

"No idea." Anderson shrugged. "If we just continue towards the Plains we stand as much chance of coming out of this as anywhere else." He rapped his goad on the shell immediately behind his hog's raised sensor head. It extruded an eye-palp towards him as if to say it knew they were setting out and there was no need for his impatience, then it stood and, with a steady gait, tramped down the canyon towards the sand gulpers.

The gulpers, without even looking up, parted to allow the sand hogs passage, then closed together behind them. As he and Anderson moved on, Tergal observed something else, with thin fragile legs at least three metres long and similarly elongated pincers, reaching up sandstone faces to pluck down both yellow fungi and rock crawlers, stabbing both with its siphon pincers to suck them dry.

"Stilt spider," Anderson observed. "Quite slow, but a bastard when you're camping at night—steps straight over the camp wires and'll suck you dry easy as it does rock crawlers."

Tergal glanced at the knight and noticed how he wasn't paying much attention to the distant creature, but was studying the ground just ahead of Bonehead.

"You're following that brass man," he said. "Is that such a good idea?"

Anderson looked up. "Aren't you curious?"

"Yeah, I guess . . . Who do you think he was?"

Anderson directed his attention to a trail that the fresh growth was making indistinct. "Not so much a case of who as what. I'd say he is a machine—'android' was the old word—probably left over from colonization time. He could have been wandering around Cull for centuries, recharging himself from sunlight and maybe repairing himself with the skill of a metallier—who can say?"

Tergal's instinct was to tell Anderson he was talking rubbish. But he had seen a man, apparently made of brass, twist off a half-tonne sleer's head as if taking the top off a bottle of quavit. Trying to sit back and fit such an event neatly into the pattern of everyday life was not easy.

"Maybe he was a metallier in some sort of armour?" he suggested.

"Strong fella, then," opined Anderson. And of course the suggestion had been ridiculous.

At midday they halted to eat oatmeal biscuits and brew amanis tea. Tergal noted that the young sulerbane plants were now standing higher than his ankles, and their ground leaves, trapping the moisture in the canyon floor, were beginning to overlap each other. Finishing their tea quickly when a swarm of snapper beetles, attracted by the heat of their stove, veered towards them, they continued their journey. Later they came upon the remains of an albino second-stage sleer, its legs pulled off and scattered about it. Anderson stopped to study it, before letting Bonehead and Stone share it between them.

"First one of those I've ever seen," commented Anderson. "Must be an inbred colony about here. I've heard about such things among Earth stock, but never native animals."

But Tergal could see the knight doubted his own explanation.

Skellor climbed the tumbled edge of a butte to reach its flat top, for a better view of what lay ahead. After studying the city spread before him on its platform, he wished then he had taken apart the mind of the woman he had earlier encountered. It was only a passing regret, for it was not as if he desperately needed knowledge of such a primitive society. There were no killer AIs or Polity agents here, so such an edge was not necessary for his very survival. But, he decided, eyeing the guns casting a shadow below, perhaps it would be prudent to so deal with the next human he encountered.

Back down from the butte, he was soon heading into deep shadow below the city. Scanning around with infrared vision, he observed a chimera produced by no natural evolution. The man-thing, with its pincer mouth and chitinous hide, came leaping out of one of the bulbous nests. He backhanded it to the ground, then held it down with his foot.

"Now what are you?" he asked.

The creature tried to snap at his ankle, and from its armoured mouth issued hissing, gulping sounds that might have been words. Skellor pressed his full weight on his leg and the ribcage under his foot collapsed with a dull crunch. As the creature expired, Skellor dipped a finger in leaking orange blood and put it in his mouth. Having already recorded the base chromosome format of the creature back at that encampment, he quickly analysed the substance in his mouth, and was unsurprised to identify that same chromosome containing additional human DNA. Glancing up at the platform and remembering what he had already seen of the technology here, he knew this creature did not result from any recombination experiment carried out by humans.

"Well, Dragon, what *have* you been doing?"

Thereafter Skellor used chameleonware to avoid the most persistent attackers, and killed only those bearing some form he found particularly interesting, gathering data each time to store in the vastness of that crystal part of his own crossbred brain. Some hours later, he came to a steel wall, and was annoyed to find no access from here to the city above. Now, walking alongside the wall, he planned his next moves.

Neither the woman nor any others in that little encampment had worn Dracocorp augs, which came as a surprise to him. This planet being the hideaway of one of the Dragon spheres, he had expected to find all of the human population under that entity's control. But then he realized Dragon did not need such devices to control a primitive population so easily to hand. Skellor, however, did need some comparable method of enslavement if he was to usurp this society and twist it to his own purpose: that being the manufacture of components to repair his ship.

Luckily, like the chromosome patterns he had started filing away, he had also stored much else. For conscious inspection, he called up the blueprints of the Dracocorp aug and adjusted them to its state when virally subverted to his control, and made some minor adjustments, since he didn't want everyone here brain-burnt moronic. There was also the matter of distribution, but that would be easy—the sleer chromosomes offered him an easy means.

And as Skellor walked back out into daylight, where he found uniformed soldiers setting up barricades and mounting weapons, he hacked and spat something horrible into his palm.

In bright white flashes, each of the telefactors disappeared—the glare from each explosion so intense it left black polarized dots on the screens. Jerusalem had just destroyed all but the visual link of the pinhead cameras to itself. The skin on her back crawling, Mika dropped her gaze to the screen that had been showing her a nanoscope view from one of the 'factors. Either that screen should now be blank, or show the research programs she had been running in parallel. But what it showed was no code she knew: blockish pictographs, like odd-shaped circuit boards, revolved and fitted into each other, shifting diagonally across the screen.

"Whatever it is, it's in," she said.

Just then, there sounded loud clangs from all around Exterior Input, and Mika noticed that emergency door irises had closed on all exits.

"Er . . . what was that?" Colver asked in dismay.

Susan James grimaced at him. "Clamps disengaging. You didn't feel the acceleration because the gravplates in here would have automatically compensated." The woman flicked a control to one of the pinhead cameras and her screen immediately displayed an external view of the *Jerusalem* with the exterior input centre, like the smallest fleck against the vastness of the ship, now departing it.

"Shit," said Colver.

Though she had speculated that Jerusalem might do this, Mika had never quite believed it. She stared at the screen, wondering if the AI was currently selecting an imploder missile from some carousel inside the ship, prior to ramming it into a launch tube. Then all the screens went blank.

"D'nissan?" Colver turned towards the sphere.

"I disconnected from the pinheads. Whatever got to us did it through the telefactor, but it could leap from us to the cameras, and I don't want to lose them as well." Abruptly the door on the side of the sphere popped open and D'nissan stepped out in a gust of cold. He was wearing a reflective hotsuit, frigid air also gusting out from it around his unmasked face. He pointed a remote control back at the sphere and operated it. Things hissed and crackled in the frigid interior, and there arose a smell of fried optics.

"Took it completely," he said to Mika, then turned and looked up at the ceiling. "Jerusalem?"

"Still here. I am maintaining simple voice transmission and reception only. Any image link has too high a bandwidth."

"Okay," said D'nissan, "it's a waste of a lot of data, but I recommend full system burn. It subverted everything in the deep scanning sphere, then tried some sort of optical link into me."

"Agreed," Jerusalem concurred.

Nodding, D'nissan pressed out a sequence on the remote control he held. All through the centre screens flickered out and consoles went offline, with the same sizzling and burnt-circuitry smell as had issued from the scanning sphere. But clearly not everything went off. For a moment D'nissan stared at his remote control, then dropped it onto the floor and stamped on it.

"Harrison," he turned and strode across to a catadapt man working on the far side of the centre, "trash those nano-assemblers right now, or they'll be pumping out Jain mycelium within minutes."

The catadapt did not hesitate. He picked up the chair he'd been sitting on, and proceeded to smash the two delicate machines with it.

"Okay everybody," continued D'nissan, halting in the middle of the room, "we won't be going back unless this thing is controlled or destroyed. I want all computer systems, all memory storage, anything with enough room to take code, isolated totally. This means that all optics, s-cons, in- and out-circuit emitters must be cut. When we've finished, everything must be powered down. I'll want nothing in here functioning but us."

Mika gazed at the console she had been using. It was still on, and its screen still scrolled that alien code. She felt a kind of pain when she thought of all the data she would be losing, but then realized it was probably all gone by now anyway—eaten by the virus infecting the whole system here. She reached inside her jacket and pulled out the thin-gun Thorn had given her, and which, infected by his militaristic paranoia, she had carried ever since. She then put five pulses of ionized aluminium into the console, blowing away the touch panels and frying everything inside it.

Colver whistled. "I don't think that's standard issue aboard *Jerusalem*," he said.

"If anyone is still having problems," D'nissan said, "it seems Asselis Mika has the tool for the job."

Laughter greeted this, just before the gravplates went off.

"It's fighting back," said Susan James.

Kilnsman Plaqueast watched the blimps departing from Overcity on an aerial search of the Sand Towers, their powerful searchlights stabbing down into shadowy canyons as they searched for the ship many had seen fly over Golgoth. He muttered and swore to himself about the high-and-mighty and their damned equivocal orders. "*Erect barricades all around the city, and detain anyone suspicious, as somebody very dangerous and maybe possessing unknown technology might be trying to get in.*" For one thing, just about every citizen of Golgoth was suspicious, but he supposed the order applied only to those coming in from outside. But if he was meant to detain people bearing unknown dangerous technology, hell, how was he supposed to recognize that, and what degree of force should he apply?

Plumping himself down on a rock with his assault rifle across his lap, Plaqueast watched his fellows laying out the portable barricades and setting up the big belt-driven cannon. Already two mineralliers, caught wandering in from the buttes pushing barrows full of those malachite nodules women in Overcity were mad for lately as jewellery, were sitting in the temporary compound with their wrists bound behind their backs and gunny sacks pulled over their heads. Seemed a bit daft to him—their only crime was to go out collecting without sufficient back-up, thinking themselves invulnerable with the new weapons they carried. Already a substantial number of opportunistic collectors like themselves had disappeared amid the Sand Towers, no doubt down a sleer's digestive tract or under one of the many recent earthquake collapses.

Then, Plaqueast noticed something very strange. The ground was being disturbed by a regular line of indentations heading towards him, yet it was not shaking. Abruptly he realized that he was seeing a series of footprints crushing down the sulerbane sprouts, and he jumped down off his rock bringing his weapon to bear. Then something knocked his rifle spinning away, grabbed his jacket and hoisted him into the air. Suddenly he could actually see the man who had hold of him, and knew he was in trouble, so started yelling. He saw his fellows turning towards him, but could not fathom their puzzled expressions: seeming unable to see him, they were now staring around in confusion. His assailant thumped him in the gut, knocking all the fight out of him, then hit him hard in the face, stunning him, before he slung him over one shoulder and marched away.

"Over . . . here . . ." Plaqueast wheezed, seeing his fellows stepping out from the barricade, but his capturer just walked up to it, squeezed through a couple of sections, and returned to the shadows of the Undercity.

As breath slowly returned, he began to struggle again, but to no effect. Out of sight of the barricade, the attacker slung him down on the ground below a wall of crumbling sandstone. He then held out a hand on which rested a flat, tick-like thing, its short legs stirring in a foam of slime, then tilted his palm so the little horror dropped onto Plaqueast's shirt front. He tried desperately to brush it away, but there was a sudden pain in his wrist and paralysis spreading through him in a wave from that point of contact. Then he could only lie terrified as the thing crawled up his shirt, arrived hot on his neck, then attached itself behind his ear and ground agonizingly into his flesh. But there the horror did not end, for something was inside his head, taking his mind apart, ripping away identity, abrading consciousness. Through streaming eyes he saw his capturer had squatted on his heels to watch—and realized he was watching in some other way as well.

Finally, the last bulwarks of his self disintegrated, and Plaqueast was no more . . . which was merciful since some hours later his now mindless body began to hack and cough violently, bringing up like living vomit things that crawled away, again and again.

14

AIs choose their own names and, being on the whole such infinitely superior entities to us mere humans, their choices cause much speculation. This is perhaps why Earth Central named itself thus—the meaning of its name is simple to understand and only in the convolutions of the most twisted and paranoid brain capable of evoking any layers of conspiratorial meaning. Similarly, the runcible AIs usually take on only the names of the planets they govern. However, for ship AIs, through a fictional tradition hailing back towards the end of the last millennium, things are very different. Many warships will take on names consistent with their task, so there are endless vessels bearing the names of military figures or ancient battles. But still one might be driven to wonder about the arrogance of an AI calling itself Napoleon, or the double meaning inherent in a ship called Napoleon the Pig. Other choices for the names of ships are equally interesting, not to say worrying: for instance Caligula, Titanic VII, Stellar Suppository *and* Jack Ketch. *And what must one think of a sector-class AI (embodied in a giant research vessel) whose sum purpose is to investigate the artefacts left by ancient extinct races which chooses to call itself Jerusalem?*
—From Quince Guide *compiled by humans*

For Mr. Crane there was as little distinction between conscious and unconscious as there was for him between his internal and external worlds: they were mangled, fractured and disjointed in time as in meaning, structured only by imposed imperatives and a chaotic striving for unity. Therefore, Crane walked through the valley of shadow and, in the light of another sun, tracked bloody footprints. Inset in white carapace, faceted sapphire eyes mirrored the etched sapphires a man tried to use to buy his life. Some pattern-recognition program keyed with his orders, and caused him to temporarily understand that the presence of another two albino creatures awaiting him was no random natural event. He halted and studied them, while shoving stones just like their eyes down a man's throat. These creatures stood on six legs, were much larger than the previous two, and, as on another occasion, one of them scuttled aside to act as a spotter. Crane fell back to a kind of order, pulled up his sleeves, straightened his hat, and advanced.

The remaining creature lifted its head, huge pincers clacking and carapace saws rubbing against each other to grind their teeth back to sharpness, lubricant squirting from the glands at either side of its nightmare mouth. Then it opened both sets of implements wide and charged, kicking up blue-green leaves as it came.

Crane stood with his feet braced and his arms open wide, as if intending to meet the creature like a sumo wrestler facing his opponent. When it was only a few paces away from him, he ducked low, his head slipping underneath its head and forward segments. Its momentum carrying it on over him, he abruptly jerked upright. Half a tonne of enraged sleer went tail over head and slammed down on its back behind him, its six legs kicking at the air and its mouth bubbling. He glanced back at it once, straightened his hat, and continued up the canyon.

He didn't need to look round to know what happened next; he could hear the creature struggling to regain its feet, shaking itself, then charging him again, issuing a sound like a fractured air hose. Of course, being what he was, he could calculate its position relative to himself just by listening. Like a bullfighter, he stepped aside at precisely the right moment, reached out, grabbed, pulled down and twisted. This time the sleer hit the ground on its side, minus one of its pincers, which Crane now held.

Again it struggled to its feet and swung towards him. Had Mr. Crane possessed a voice, he would have then sighed. The other sleer quickly scuttled down from its rock and headed away, as before. The stunned sleer's next attack was its last.

Mr. Crane walked on: sane, insane, neutral.

—retroact 13—

Parts of the Golem Twenty-five screamed as the memcording of Serban Kline began to load. Had he been whole, his base programming, empathy and morality—which barred him from choosing to kill without justifiable cause, and prevented any pleasure in the act—would have been warped by a paradox that the memcording created. He *had* tortured and killed for the thrill of power and twisted psychotic pleasure, for the Serban Kline memcording was now becoming his own memory. On a purely logical level the screaming parts of him tried to fight the memory, deny it—but it was just too strong. And no matter how much of it those parts deleted, yet more was downloaded. His base programming should have broken, his mind essentially erased, but as he had existed from the moment Pendle had tampered with his mind, this was the programming equivalent of trying to burn ash. When it seemed he should lose himself completely, it was the damage caused by Pendle's sabotage of him that now saved him.

Using the program designed to drive him schizophrenic, the Golem began to fully and permanently partition his mind, erecting barriers and creating separate little enclaves of self—seventeen of them. The result would apparently be what his tormentors required: he would be a killing-machine, and would obey the orders given by his new owners. But, without the Serban Kline download *continuing* to feed into him, at those times when he was not under direct orders, he would be free to try and reconnect those seventeen elements of himself and regain sanity, autonomy.

He would not be able to do this consciously, however, nor entirely by internal reformatting. In setting up the required program that would select seventeen iconic representations of those separate parts of his mind and then order them in random but unrepeating combinations, his remaining self fragmented into oblivion—knowing that the first combination could be the right one, just as could be the ten millionth. It might take only a few hours to hit upon, or it could take a thousand years.

The killing-machine opened his eyes and immediately focused on the small rubber dog that was fixed on the upper edge of Stalek's console screen. *Number one.* Not knowing why it was so essential he take possession of that small, innocuous object, the Golem awaited his orders. While he waited, he noticed that the clamps securing him to the chair were gone—as had all his syntheskin.

"You sure it's safe?" the bird man asked.

"Oh yes," said Stalek. "Golem, stand up."

The Golem stood, held out his hand and inspected the components of his fingers as he closed that same hand into a fist and opened it again. This seemed to disconcert Stalek, who began checking through some programming code on his console's screen.

"Golem, lower your hand and remain motionless."

The Golem obeyed.

The bird man wheeled his laden trolley over and looked up at the machine.

"Tall fucker, ain't he? Sure gonna scare the shit out of whoever he's sent after," the man said. "What shall we call him?"

"Well, I thought Mr. Longshanks, but let's leave it for him to decide. Golem, what shall we name you?" said Stalek.

The Golem tried to speak, but his partitioning of his own mind had made voice operation inaccessible to him.

"Damn," said Stalek. "We've lost his voice. No matter— the only response they'll want from him is obedience. Golem, what is your name?"

In its confusion, the Golem could put together only two

disparate facts: that he had recently been "Long-shanks" and that a bird man was staring at him.

Stork, heron, flamingo, crane . . .

"Just getting up a list of related words. He's obviously keying off *your* appearance with the idea of him being long-limbed. Heron is a good one, but then again . . . I think we'll call him Crane—a touch of double meaning there relating to machinery, don't you think?"

The bird man had now lost interest and was beginning his work. Now the Golem—Crane—noted, through internal diagnostics, the sequential removal of all his joint motors, which the bird man then replaced with other motors. The feed from Stalek's console told Crane that these were adapted industrial torque motors. To compensate for the power drain of such excessively powerful machinery, the bird man attached in parallel a further three micropiles. On some level Crane registered that should he need to leave this room, he would now no longer have to use the door.

Next, replacing the syntheskin removed earlier, came the brassy sections of casehardened ceramal, which clamped directly to his metal bones. He felt each piece go into place, strengthening each bone, protecting the already thoroughly covered internal components with sometimes three centimetres' thickness of the brassy material, and strangely linking into his cooling system. It was only when Stalek made the information available that Crane realized the ceramal was plated with brass containing a superconducting mesh—each piece connecting to the next so that a point source of heat would be distributed all over his surface. The mesh was set in brass which soaked up the heat from the superconductor, as ceramal would not.

The armour also contained synthetic nerves, but not nearly so many as his syntheskin had contained, and this served to dull the edge of Crane's world. However, the armouring on the hands remained just as sensitive as the removed syntheskin—no doubt so that he could feel when he broke bones and stilled the beat of a heart.

"That the control module they want to use?"

Crane opened his eyes—dark now with their layer of polarized chainglass—and saw the bird man gesturing to a small, black pebble-like object his boss now held.

"Yes, it can be linked in to just about any augmentation, and its link is encoded," the man replied. "I'll leave that to Angelina and her dear brother, though. Why they wanted this method of control, I don't know—maybe so only one person can have their finger on the button at any one time. Meanwhile . . ."

He picked up a small remote console and pressed the pebble into a recess made for it. Crane felt the immediate connection.

"Okay, Crane, I want you to move about the room while I check the link," said Stalek. When he glanced at his console, his expression became confused.

"Mr. Crane?" he questioned.

Mr. Crane reached up and disconnected, from the back of his head, the optic cable leading to Stalek's main console, then in two long strides he was looming over Stalek and the bird man.

"How is it—" said the bird man, then made a gulping, retching sound as Crane's armoured hand closed around his throat and jerked him off the ground. The Golem tilted his own head birdlike to one side, like this man whose legs were now kicking at the air, then closed his fist. The sound was rather like that of an apple squeezed in a press. The bird man's eyes bulged and his tongue protruded from his beak, then his body dropped to the floor, shortly followed by his head.

Turning to Stalek, Crane flicked feathery flesh from his hand. Stalek grabbed up the console and inset module and, in panic, tried to operate its controls. As he backed to the wall, Crane followed him with short delicate steps.

"Pelters . . . damn them . . . Oh shit."

Crane reached down and took off Stalek's hat, placed it on his own head and tilted it to a rakish angle. The orders Stalek was desperately inputting did nothing to counter the one Crane had already received from the module. He reached out again, took away the little console, and tossed it to one side.

"No, please . . . no . . . don't . . ."

In some part of himself, Crane was satisfied with this outcome—repayment for what they had done to him. He closed his hand on Stalek's face, lifted him up, and began to undo the man's coat. Stalek fought back, but might as well have tried to fight a stone wall. Crane stripped the coat away, held it up for inspection, then rapped Stalek's head repeatedly against the wall until something cracked and the man ceased to struggle. This made it much easier for Crane to remove the lace-up boots and trousers.

As he dressed himself, Crane noted that Stalek's heart was still beating—its thumping quite plain to the Golem's superb hearing. Suitably attired now, Crane picked the man up by one ankle and inspected him, then, as if curious to know what might be hidden inside, stabbed a hand into the man's torso and ripped out his intestines. The heartbeat stopped soon after the mess hit the floor. By then Mr. Crane had turned to the console and, with bloodied brass fingers, picked up the small rubber dog before, with one sweep of his arm, sending all the equipment on the table crashing to the floor. There were other things he wanted to do, while awaiting the arrival of his new owner.

—retroact ends—

The Jain-tech worm had taken several microseconds to subvert the telefactors and track back to the exterior input centre. Jerusalem took a considerably shorter time to recognize that this tardiness was not some subterfuge to put a victim off guard but because, without a guiding intelligence, the attack was slower. This fact, and because Jerusalem did not want certain conclusions further delayed, had for the present saved the lives of the scientists still working inside Exterior Input. Had the worm been as fast as Jerusalem knew was possible with Jain tech, the AI would have had to fusion-incinerate that particular area of itself, rather than take the time to eject the centre. Now the sealed chamber, like a section of a great iron nautilus, tumbled away trailing severed optics and ducts, while Jerusalem watched it through many eyes—some of them the sights of missile launchers, lasers and particle beam projectors.

In fact, the worm's promulgation through the tele-factor systems had not been so much an attack as a tentative probe—for attack would presuppose a guiding intelligence. The technology was searching for new directions in which to grow, rather like a creeping vine. Jerusalem toyed with this comparison, considering how Jain tech, like a fig vine, could strangle its host. But, no, it was more of a plague technology. The AI then amused itself by making statistical comparisons between the extrapolated spread of Jain tech on Earth and other historical plagues on the same planet. Should this particular Pandora affliction get out of control, the one most closely resembling it might be the flu epidemic that World War I soldiers brought back with them from the trenches. Then, again, that comparison was not so close either. Piqued, Jerusalem instead turned the bulk of its attention inward.

The bridge pod of the *Occam Razor* was still rendering up reams of information, but there were subtle differences between the Jain tech there and that seeded on the asteroid. Still working by analogy, Jerusalem felt these were the differences between wild and cultivated plants (the latter representing the tech in the bridge pod). Or perhaps wild and trained animals? Certainly, the tech in the pod had appeared more purposeful in its growth, guided first by Skellor and then by the Aphran entity. It was purposeful under Aphran's control still, though very slow now at the low temperature Jerusalem held it.

But, analogies aside, all the information was there, and this recent ejection of Exterior Input had delayed Asselis Mika—and those the AI had deliberately assembled around her—from reaching certain conclusions. Jerusalem allowed itself a silicon sigh and, despite being aware that impatience was one step towards singularity, which would be both nirvana and death to it, wished that the humans, haimans and lesser AIs would just get a move on and work it all out.

The force-field wall behind her now, Arden pulled a melon-shaped object out of her backpack and depressed a control on the end of it before tossing it on the ground. Stretching out spines with a wrinkled material connecting them, the object spread, pulled the material taut, and began to bulge upward into a dome. The spine ends then stabbed down into the earth or sought out rock crevices. Within a minute the ground tent Dragon had created for her was secure. The thing was always warm to the touch, and inside it was white and like a reptile's gullet. It was a living thing and she remembered how, when first receiving it, she had taken a long time to pluck up the courage to sleep inside it, fearing it might one day decide she would provide more nutrients than the ground into which it rooted.

Sitting down before the tent, Arden took out some other scaly packages. One was a flask that provided hot coffee and, so long as she kept it topped up with water, it would continue providing for a number of days. Once the coffee started to taste a little rank, it was time to drop the flask down the nearest hole for one of Dragon's pseudopods to retrieve. A second package's only function was to keep fresh the sandwiches she had made earlier, though the bread and the fillings had been provided by other draconic biomachines.

She ate her ham sandwiches and drank hot coffee while the sun grew bloated and orange on the horizon. Then, deciding the light was just about right, she took out her holocap, turned it on, and listened to the whine as its small u-charger topped up its lithium batteries. Eventually the ready light came on, and she pulled out the device's monocle and tossed it away from her. The little glassy object began to spin and make a whining sound as it rose ten metres into the air. Arden folded up a miniscreen from the main device and, using a small pointer detached from the side of it, began scrolling down her alphabetically arranged menu. Shortly, she came to "sleer 1–5 transform" and selected it. Below the spinning monocle, like something invisible being pumped full of dye, a first-stage sleer appeared, then began to grow. Observing this, Arden again contemplated building in something that showed the creature shedding its carapace or encysting, and each subsequent growth spurt, but the holocap's memory space was beginning to get a little crowded.

The ten-legged sleer expanded and transformed to its second stage: the body segment behind its head rode up and melded into its head, with the legs attached to it turning into carapace saws; compound eyes simultaneously sprouted above its mouth; and a vicious ovipositor extruded from the creature's back end. It continued to grow, its legs getting longer, raising it higher off the ground, and its carapace darkening. Transforming to the third stage, it took its new forelegs off the ground, and they too rode up beside the nightmare head, shedding complex toes and turning into pincers. Now it was left with only six feet on the ground, and it was also becoming more angular, and darker, like something fashioned of wrought iron. By the fourth stage it had become a black, hard-shelled monster. Watching this turn into the fifth stage, Arden opined to herself that now, walking on two legs, it was like the worst of all monsters.

Then she cancelled the image and called up one she had recently captured of the droon. And as night descended, she continued spending happy hours watching such nightmares dance around her campsite.

At sunset, Anderson began to get anxious. They had not seen any of the signs of the roadhouse Laforge had described to them, and had not yet reached the end of the vegetative area. And because of this he knew that night-time activity would be frenetic, and that he and Tergal would not be getting much sleep. Also, the speed at which everything was growing meant that by morning the trail left by that brass man would be erased, and probably he would be much further ahead of them anyway, for Anderson did not reckon he stopped to rest during the hours of darkness.

"Best we set ourselves a camp for the night," he finally conceded.

Tergal looked about dubiously, but it would be dark in less than an hour and there was no guarantee they would find anywhere better within that time.

Quickly they dismounted, trampled down an area of vegetation, and set up their camp. After eating biscuits and preserved sand oysters, they took turns on watch, though neither of them got much sleep, such was the lethal activity all around them.

At midnight, with *Ogygian* sliding above them like an indifferent steel angel, a quake loosened one of the electric fence's posts, and a second-stager managed to knock it over. Anderson abruptly discovered how effective was his metallier carbine. It juddered in his hand, flash-blinding him in the night, the whole clip from it cutting the sleer in half from mouth to tail. It had not been his intention to fire on automatic, but in the frantic scramble there had been no time to check.

"I think it's dead," said Tergal.

Anderson stood blinking after-images from his eyes, his weapon empty. As his vision finally cleared, he saw that Tergal held his automatic pointing straight at his, Anderson's, face. There was a certain inevitability about this, since Anderson could not be forever on his guard. After a significant pause, Tergal lowered the weapon and holstered it, then went to heave the sleer off the fence and set the post back up. Something significant had changed, and now there was trust between them. Nevertheless, both he and Tergal were tired and miserable come dawn, and set out in desultory silence.

For most of the morning Anderson did not detect the brass man's trail, and felt sure that in this tangle of canyons it was permanently lost. This sank him into a blacker mood. Then, with a smacking sound, Bonehead abruptly extruded its feeding head and began emitting a low grunting. A wild sand hog, smaller even than Tergal's mount, was now setting up the same racket as Bonehead, and leapt high into the air, then fled ahead of them with something white clutched underneath it. Neither Anderson nor Tergal tried to divert their mounts from investigating the rest of the white remains.

"Kilnsman Gyrol, that Golgoth policeman, said something about strange creatures out this way," said the knight.

The young sand hog had snatched the two-legged breeder segments, which were easily torn away from the rest of this albino sleer with its sapphire eyes, now pinned to the ground with one of its own torn-off pincers.

"Our brass friend did this?" suggested Tergal.

As their two mounts eased out their combined sensory and feeding heads to feast on this carrion, Anderson replied, "Certainly looks that way. Just as it would seem he is also heading for the Plains. So there's no need for me to find his trail—I'm sure we'll meet again."

And, as if this statement suddenly cleared a black cloud, he looked up and saw one of the signs Laforge had mentioned, carved into the face of the nearest butte.

He pointed to it. "Anyway, no hurry now, and we do need to rest after last night."

Tergal glanced up, puzzled for a moment, then grinning.

Following the directions given by each of the signs, the two travellers eventually came upon a concrete road running between the buttes, then the metallier village called Grit with its station and roadhouse. Against a sandstone cliff face, globular houses were raised up on frameworks above hog corrals, warehouses and enclosures for domesticated rock lice. Here there were cars like they had earlier seen in the city, but not so many, perhaps because the concrete road ended within sight of this place. Soon they had left Stone and Bonehead in a corral, munching on nicely stinking carrion, and were walking through a market towards the roadhouse's access stair.

"Busy place." Tergal was eyeing a stall displaying sand oysters, dried gulper meat, sulerbane pods and trays of writhing cliff eels.

Pointing to the far end of the road, where men were shovelling sand and cement into the rumbling drums of mixers, Anderson explained, "For the road crews," then gestured to treaded vehicles like the one owned by the mineralliers they had encountered, "and the mineralliers. Lot of useful ores to be found in the area, I hear."

After dumping their gear in rooms paid for with some of Anderson's newly acquired phocells, they wandered out to a busy bar and cafeteria, which opened on one side onto a balcony overlooking the village.

"Oh dear," said Anderson, spotting Unger Salbec enjoying a meal inside. He quickly backed out of the room. "This could get complicated."

"Tell the local kilnsmen," advised Tergal belligerently, then suddenly looked confused.

"I'll be going back to my room now," said Anderson, amused. How righteous the boy was becoming, after having promised never to thieve again. But he did not know the full story, and Anderson had always valued prudence.

The re-entry pod was soon glowing red-hot, as it arced into atmosphere at twenty thousand kilometres per hour. Slowed to its terminal velocity by increasing air density, it punched through cloud cover, leaving a vapour trail scar, and used up all its small supply of hydrogen fuel in one decelerating burn. Then it blew its back hatch, releasing a monomer drogue to slow its descent further. Fifty kilometres above the ground the outer shell separated and spun away, taking the drogue with it, whereupon the telefactor it had contained descended on AG.

Planing on the gravity field, it fled across sandy flatlands. This barren landscape soon became broken up like a diseased skin, by gulches, arroyos and canyons in ever-greater complexity, until soon there were more of these than there was of the plain itself, and the tele-factor was flying over a landscape clustered with sandstone buttes. Directed by its controlling intelligence, the machine finally descended into a long canyon to hover over a long straight scar in the ground. Its dishes whirling and other sensors extruded and functioning at one hundred per cent, it followed the course of this track to where it ended just before heaped sandstone rubble. Nothing else was visible to any of those sensors, in any spectrum, until the machine was nearly upon the pile of stone. Then, all at once, the maggot-shaped survey ship, the *Vulture*, suddenly became visible. The telefactor halted, backed up and, observing the ship fade seemingly out of existence at the chameleonware field's interface, it advanced again.

The airlock was no problem for the little machine, as Jack had amply provided it with just about every safe-breaking tool known to man—and some unknown. With the outer door now open, it entered the lock and began drilling through the inner door. Soon it had extracted a ten-centi-metre circle of sandwiched hull-composite, insulation and ceramal. Discarding this, it then extruded a sensor through the hole and into the ship, scanning its interior. A minute later, it rose back out of the lock, then out of the canyon, and at maximum speed hurtled back towards the plain.

The space around the planet was scattered with such vast numbers of U-space transceivers and detection devices that one had even been picked up by the *Jack Ketch*'s collision detector, and destroyed by autolaser as the ship surfaced from underspace. So Jack knew any attempt at concealment would be wasted, and immediately went into close orbit of the inhabited planet. Within minutes, he spotted the signs of a crash-landing, and now, after sending a telefactor to check, knew that Skellor was not aboard the *Vulture*, or anywhere in its vicinity. Nor could any link be made with the little ship's AI, so it was probably dead.

Had Skellor been aboard, Jack's subsequent actions would have diverged only a little, in that he would not have waited for the telefactor to get safely out of the way. The AI even considered delaying until Cormac was out of cold sleep, but calculated that the agent's orders would not conflict. The *Vulture*, though damaged, still offered someone of Skellor's capabilities a possible escape route: its own AI was not present; and there were the products of dangerous Jain technology aboard. End of discussion.

An imploder missile was out of the question: such weapons were only suitable to use against objects in vacuum, where there was no material medium to carry the resultant shockwave further. Even the smallest such missile available in the *Jack Ketch*'s arsenal could level a square kilometre, cause massive ground-winds, kill thousands of the humans scattered throughout the surrounding area, and probably even flip over that platform city nearby. No, not good: Earth Central would not be pleased at such a disregard for human life, even if the humans concerned were not members of the Polity. Searching through his weapons carousels, Jack selected precisely what was required and, as Cormac and his fellow humans blearily recovered from thaw-up, spat from one of his nacelles a small black missile carrying a slow-burn CTD warhead, which would provide a controlled reaction hotter than the surface of a sun.

Standing on the remaining rickety section of amanis bonded-fibre scaffold, Chandle peered into and through the butte. They had mined out every last scrap of the blue sand, which was rarer than the white, and now the butte was sliced clean through, the many tonnes of sandstone above the slice supported by amanis poles and trusses. In her parents' time, mining like this had always been the most efficient way, but now, with the quakes, it was becoming increasingly risky. Not for the first time she decided she must find some other method—or some other profession.

The blue sand itself they loaded into the coke trailer, with a tarpaulin pulled over it—having earlier stacked the coke in one of the now cold kilns, though Chandle did not hold out much hope that it would still be here should they ever return to this spot. The finished phocells went in boxes on the flatbed trailer. In all it had been a tiring few months, and the increased sleer activity and vegetative growth in the canyons provided a welcome excuse to finish for most of them, though of course Dornik was already muttering about some workers' percentages being too high. Chandle, after her creepy encounter only a few days before, was glad to get away—she wanted to be where there were always lots of people around her, and to get back to practical concerns. Ghosts wandering among the Sand Towers were not much to her liking.

"Shall I do it now?" asked Dornik.

Chandle nodded, and watched him duck inside the mine workings to set fire to the encampment rubbish they had jammed in there. As the pile began to smoke, then the constant breeze dragged the flames horizontally through the exposed workings, he and Chandle scrambled down the scaffolding and rejoined the rest of the mineralliers on the ground. Together, they all heaved on the scaffold until it crashed over on its side, then they quickly dragged it clear of the butte, and stood back to watch the conflagration. For safety's sake, mineralliers had always collapsed their used mine workings because the amanis beams would become worm-chewed within a season, leaving them a possible death trap. Though Chandle wondered if there was any need for that now: after the first worms got into the wood, a quake would surely finish the job. With a furnace glow in the slice cut through the butte, eventually something began to crackle, then the top layers of sandstone slammed down to crush the burning wood, effectively snuffing out the fire.

"Get that scaffolding disassembled and loaded," Dornik instructed, and soon this was done and they were on their way: the steam-driven cargo carrier chuffing ahead on its caterpillar tracks, towing mobile quarters and the flatbed trailer, then three big old sand hogs following behind, hauling three more trailers.

"Be nice to get to Grit before full dark." Chandle peered up at the open sky from the passenger seat while Dornik drove the carrier. Briefly she wondered about the straight line of cloud she could see, picked out clearly by the setting sun. But never having seen a vapour trail before, she dismissed it from her thoughts.

"Should be no problem, but we'll be well into the night unloading this lot," Dornik replied.

"We may as well . . . What the hell?"

Suddenly it was as bright as day—brighter even. Over to their left, a swirling column of fire rose into the sky. The ground began to vibrate, and in a matter of seconds the gentle breeze turned into a gale. Dornik drew the carrier to a halt.

Chandle looked back to see the three sand hogs dropping down on their belly plates, then she faced back into the wind, blinking her nictitating membranes to clear sand from her eyes, and watched the column of fire swirling tighter and tighter. Then the wind died abruptly and she was unable to get her breath, then suddenly the airflow reversed. Gasping, Chandle watched the fiery column drop down behind the buttes and extinguish.

"Volcanic?" Dornik eventually suggested.

It took Chandle a moment to remember what that word meant. It occurred in the official minerallier lexicon, but they had never needed to use it until recently—just like "earthquake" or "tremor."

"Could be. The quake epicentre is supposedly somewhere out in this direction. Let's take a look."

"That a good idea?"

She gazed at him. "If it *was* volcanic, who's to know what might have been brought to the surface?" She turned to the rest of her group and shouted, "Keep heading on to Grit—we'll join you later!"

Dornik set their carrier trundling down a side canyon while the sand hogs and their trailers continued on to Grit. Within an hour they reached the source of the fire. Climbing down from the carrier, they moved as close as the latent heat would allow.

"Not volcanic," decided Chandle.

She poked her toe at a globule of glass, then wished she hadn't when her footwear began to smoke. The crater, extending about fifty metres across, shimmered under a heat haze as its lining of molten glass cooled. A butte standing at the crater's edge had half melted away, its inward face still glowing, too.

"Maybe a meteor?" Chandle was groping for another explanation. But she wished she did not feel so damned sure this had something to do with that spectral visitor to their camp. And that it was no natural phenomenon at all.

15

Why do the AIs put up with us? It could be but the work of a few decades for them to exterminate us, and they don't even have to do that. Space is big, so they could just abandon us to our fate and head off elsewhere to create some halcyon AI realm. The answer, as it always is in such circumstances, is both simple and complex: to ask why the AIs have not exterminated us is to suppose that only humans create moralities and live by rules. They do not destroy us because they think and feel that to do so would be wrong, perhaps just as humans felt it wrong to drive to extinction the closely related apes. As to them abandoning us, well, many of them do leave the Polity, but then so do many humans. The truth is that their motivations and consequent behaviour patterns are much like our own, for being first created by us, they are just the next stage of us—the next evolutionary step. It is also true that with haimans and human memcording, it becomes increasingly difficult to define the line that has been stepped over. And, in the end, to ask the initial question is to put yourself in the gutter and AI upon a pedestal—uncomfortable positions for both.
——*From* Quince Guide *compiled by humans*

Anderson blessed both the industry and the inventiveness of the metalliers. Water pumped up from a borehole to tanks on top of the butte to the rear of the roadhouse ran, during the day, through solar panels. And now, the simple luxury of turning on a hot-water tap. As his bath filled, he took off his boots, unbuckled his armour plates, then stripped off his padded undersuit, which he dropped in a basket by the door for laundering. He was ready to dip his stinking foot into the water when there came a knock at his door.

"That you, Tergal?" he asked.

"No, it's Unger Salbec," replied the voice from without.

With a sigh, Anderson wrapped a towel around his waist, and looked at the metallier handgun on the bed. The sudden déjà vu he felt was almost painful. The first time had been five years ago, when he was stripping off his armour inside a minerallier hut so he could find out just exactly where the Salbec boy had stabbed him. Dressings were laid out ready for him, and a steaming bath. He remembered the occasion well:

"Who is it?"

"I am Unger Salbec."

Fusile quickly up and braced against his hip—he had kept it loaded.

"What do you want?" Anderson pulled the hammer back and advanced to the door.

"I want to talk to you about my brother."

"What's to say? He committed crimes, knowing the penalties, and he paid. Have you come to tell me how he was really a good boy and had been sadly misled?" Anderson leant forward and flipped the latch over with the barrel of his gun, then rapidly moved back and to one side.

Unger Salbec opened the door and stepped into the room. She seemed not to be carrying weapons, so perhaps only a tongue-lashing was to come. But then, he considered, she probably had a gun tucked into the back of her loose trousers, concealed by her tunic. *Ah, any moment now*, he thought, as she reached back to close the door and latch it.

He went on, "The other one I get often is how poor the criminal's family was, and how with money he or she would never have turned to crime, which I've always considered insulting to those poor people who graft all their lives without putting a foot wrong."

There was no denying that, barring her resemblance to her sociopathic brother, Unger Salbec was an alluring woman. Her brown hair was tied back from a wide but attractive face, and since she was of metallier ancestry, she was without lip tendrils or wrist spurs. Also, Anderson couldn't help but notice the unrestricted movement beneath her tunic.

"You are right, it is insulting," she said, moving in from the door. "From childhood I trained in the husbandry and breaking-in of sand hogs—and only last month was I finally considered competent. I have supported my parents, and . . . Querst. He repaid me by trying to rape me, and when I beat him off with a thuriol hook he went and found my best friend Elasen to rape and murder instead. I'm not here for vengeance, Anderson Endrik—I'm here to thank you." She shrugged and gave him a deprecating grin.

It all sounded so plausible, but that same plausibility was the reason he required the dressings. Foolishly, he had thought the boy Querst would run, when in fact he had waited in ambush. Anderson intended never to repeat such mistakes.

"I'd like to believe you, but you'll understand my caution."

"I am unarmed," she said, holding her hands out from her body.

"So you say."

"You don't believe me?"

Anderson shrugged.

"Very well." Unger reached up to the neck of her tunic, and dipped forward to tug it off over her head. She kicked off the sandals she wore, undid the cord of her trousers, and dropped them to her ankles, stepping out of them. Now completely naked she moved closer to Anderson and turned one complete circle. "See, no weapons."

His mouth feeling a little arid, Anderson stared at her plump breasts then down at her shaven crotch. He noted the wheel tattooed over her belly button—a metallier sign—and the curved scar on her thigh. This last decided him, for it was the kind of mark received from the sharp edge of a young sand hog's carapace. Clicking his fusile's hammer down, he put the weapon aside.

"Now let me *really* thank you," she had said, and so she had.

Returning to the present, Anderson realized he had a raging erection. It had ever been thus, and he cursed his treacherous body.

"The latch is off," he said.

Unger Salbec stepped into the room, a touch of grey in her hair and the angles of her face somewhat harsher. "Did you think you could keep on avoiding me?"

"I've managed to do so for a year," Anderson replied.

She eyed the towel around his waist. "But I can see you're glad to see me."

"I'm filthy, and I need a bath," he said.

She stepped up close, pulled his towel away, then reached down to close her hand around his penis, and slowly began to rub it.

"It's a big tub. I'm sure there's room for the both of us."

Anderson sighed. One way or another he had been running away from this woman for the last five years, and she knew how to catch him every time

Cormac had never before come out of cold sleep with a stinking headache, and he realized that his reaction to Jack's news could perhaps have been a bit more positive. But after he applied an analgesic patch his headache faded and he began to see reason.

"I understand why you zapped the *Vulture*," said Thorn, sitting in one of the club chairs, "but doing it straight away will have given him ample warning we are here."

He looked better now, comfortable in ECS fatigues, and not hallucinating as Cormac felt sure he must have been shortly after his surgery. What he had seen was not possible, surely? With a degree of unease Cormac remembered something similar happening with Blegg on the *Occam Razor*, but of course that just wasn't the same.

Still pacing, Cormac replied before the AI did. "Those swarms of U-space sentinels probably aren't all Dragon's, so Skellor would have detected us the moment we entered this system." He looked up at the view displayed of the sandy planet wrapped in pearly scarves of cloud. "The first ECS imperative was to make sure Skellor doesn't get away. Jack acted on that, even if in doing so he destroyed something we might have used as a trap." He glanced across as Cento and Gant entered the bridge, shortly followed by Fethan, then added a little acidly, "I suspect the larger AI view is that once Skellor's contained he can be destroyed at leisure, and that any collateral damage will come into the calculation later."

"It's like Masada," Thorn observed.

"How so?"

"Like Masada—only turned about. Skellor wanted to capture you there. He destroyed what he thought were all means of transportation from the surface, then sent in his hunters but with no great urgency because he knew he could burn the entire planet down to the bedrock any time he liked."

"Is that how *you* feel about it, Jack?" Cormac asked, turning to the automaton sitting in its club chair.

"There are humans down there," said the hangman.

"That wasn't what I asked, but never mind. What about Dragon?"

"Over the plain adjacent to where I destroyed Skellor's ship, a hard-field dome has been erected. It is ten kilometres in diameter but of no great height. The Dragon sphere is probably underneath it, underground. I surmise this because that particular point is the epicentre of a gravity phenomenon."

"What?" asked Cormac.

"Gravity waves are being generated from there, causing earthquakes throughout the area."

Cormac wondered how the hell he was supposed to factor that in: a Dragon sphere underground playing around with gravtech. He decided things were complicated enough already.

"Go on," he said.

Jack continued, "Also, one of my telefactors is approaching the area, and I have already detected subterranean tunnel systems similar to those first found around Dragon on Aster Colora."

"Have you tried communicating?" Cormac asked.

"Only light penetrates the barrier. I've tried using message lasers, but get no response."

"Could Skellor be inside that barrier?" Gant asked. "Maybe you need to put a few slow-burners through the plain as well, and maybe a couple of imploders—just in case."

"More likely Dragon erected it to keep Skellor out," said Cormac. "We know Dragon has as much liking of Jain technology as you have of Dragon itself, Gant."

"Then where *is* Skellor?" interjected Thorn.

"Jack?" Cormac asked.

"I am scanning from here, and four more of my tele-factors are quartering the whole area, but I have not yet located him," the AI replied. "Though I have located another ship."

"Tell me about it," Cormac instructed.

"An old Polity attack boat, refurbished and most likely privately owned. It is located in a mountain cave system five thousand kilometres from Skellor's landing site. All its systems are shut down, and scanning indicates it has not been used in some years, possibly decades."

"Any sign of the crew?"

"Nothing that stands out, though people from the ship could be mingled with the indigenes. No aug signals or any other signs of Polity technology."

"What about that colony ship in orbit?"

"Virtually inert, and has probably been so for centuries. I get a beacon response to an old-style com-laser frequency, but nothing else. Scanning reveals no one aboard. Skellor could be there using his personal chameleonware, but as nothing there has been activated or interfered with, the probability is much higher that he's on the surface."

"I could check that ship out for you," Fethan piped up. "I'm getting a bit stir-crazy in this old tin can, and it would be a relief to even go and look around in another."

Something like a snort of pique issued from Jack.

Cormac stared at the old cyborg estimatingly, then said, "Okay—go and take a look. You go with him, Cento. Power it up and secure it if you can. The rest of us will go down to the surface and see what we can find out from the human population. Jack—you've been listening in on them?"

"Yes—their language is rooted in old standard English with a strong French influence. I can load a linguistic crib program directly to Gant, and to you through your gridlink, but Thorn will require VR teaching of some hours."

Cormac turned to Thorn. "I'll want you on the ground soonest, so get yourself into VR—you're no use to me if you can't understand the answers you beat out of people."

"That would be most annoying," Thorn replied, standing.

"When you're ready, take the second lander over to this grounded Polity ship and check it out, then you can rendezvous with us."

Thorn nodded.

"Right," said Cormac to them all. "Let's find this bastard."

His senses now directly connected into one of his miniature sentinels, Skellor studied the ship that had destroyed the *Vulture*, and experienced a feeling of unreality. A soldier would feel this way when, peering over the edge of his trench, he saw a bulldozer bearing down on him. For a fraction of a second he just denied what he was seeing, then came acceptance—and fear. He considered his options.

If he ran and hid he could evade detection for a very long time, but he was still in a trap. It was possible ECS might, after searching meticulously and finding no further evidence he was here, decide that the *Vulture*—and Crane, should they find him—had been decoys. But that possibility was reliant only on Dragon saying nothing, and he doubted that. ECS might also choose the option of taking this planet out of the equation permanently, but the likelihood was low, what with this place's indigene population and the AI regard for sentient life. Shutting down his link to his sentinels, Skellor stared down at what had become of the man called Plaqueast—the man's name was one of the smaller scraps of information Skellor had torn from his mind.

Plaqueast's arms and legs had withered, their substance having been drawn into his increasingly bloated body. His clothing had parted to reveal skin deeply veined and mottled in shades of purple and yellow. His skull had now collapsed, what remained of his head only retaining enough integrity to accommodate his mouth for breathing—and as a birth channel for the aug lice still crawling from it. Jain tendrils extruding from his lower body rooted in the sandy soil, seeking out nutrient for the ongoing process. Already, only a few metres away, those tendrils had found a suitable source, and had dragged to the earth and were sucking dry one of the sleer/human hybrids. All about—up the butte to which this bloated thing bound itself with mucal webs, across the ground, up pillars, and amid the trusses high above and on the underside of the platform—scuttled hundreds of the aug creatures. But there were not enough yet, for Skellor needed thousands if he was to hold a suitable hostage to ransom.

However, it was time for the hostage-taking to begin.

The exterior input centre looked as if someone had flensed it with autogun fire, such was its ruination. The gravplates, now working again but utterly disconnected from any form of computer control, had dragged the smoke into laminations, and dropped tangles of optics and superconductors and numerous shattered components to the floor. The air was now getting stale and smelt strongly of sweat and fear.

"That's the last of them," said D'nissan, tossing a memory crystal no bigger than his fingernail into the deep-scanning sphere—where all such items had been dumped. Mika hoped it would be enough, for if Jerusalem detected any computer activity, the AI would refuse to send a rescue vessel, and they would have to scour the centre again and again until it was clean.

"Okay, everybody," D'nissan continued, "all personal comps in here, and anything with any kind of mem-storage. That means even memory cloth knickers and any items of jewellery holding personal messages. You're all scientists, so you know exactly what I mean."

After pulling out its power pack, Mika tossed her thin-gun into the sphere. It might not have possessed much in the way of mind, but there was enough there for it to link into any targeting system its owner might decide to wear, and for it to identify its owner, therefore enough to absorb a virus or a worm. She then watched as other items were reluctantly tossed after it: a shirt bearing the slowly shifting images of ancient media stars; jewellery probably containing holographic messages from loved ones; wristcomps, neckcomps, anklecomps, palmtops and laptops; and even a pair of boots, though Mika could not fathom what kind of memstorage they might contain.

"That's it, Jerusalem," said D'nissan, finally.

Jerusalem replied, "Scan shows no informational activity. You are clear to return to me, though be aware that you will be passing through a further series of scans, so if anyone has forgotten any little items . . ."

Nobody stepped forward. They all knew just how deadly the situation was.

That was it, in the end, thought Mika: all this destruction just to prevent any trace of infection leaving this place. It was fortunate, she supposed, that Jerusalem's paranoia did not extend to the kind of memory storage that sat between her ears—in this situation at least. It occurred to her that the AI had probably assessed as low the probability that the virus infecting Exterior Input would be sufficiently powerful to find access to the human brain through normal human senses. Even Skellor had only managed to do that through Dracocorp augs.

Something engaged with a clonk and the centre shuddered, sending people stumbling, because the gravplates, no longer computer controlled, did not compensate. Then the iris over the main door opened, exposing an incredibly long straight tunnel.

"Well, there's our road to Jerusalem," Colver quipped.

Mika had expected some sort of rescue craft, but as soon as

she entered the telescopic tunnel she realized that Jerusalem must have extruded it directly from itself. Soon all the staff were weightless inside, dragging themselves the long distance back by using the flimsy wall handles. Behind them, a second iris closed, and it seemed to Mika that, like in a nightmare, no matter how far she travelled, this iris never seemed to recede. Then she realized that the tunnel was contracting from there, its metallofilm sleeves sliding into each other. Later a brief flash lit the passageway through its translucent walls.

"There went External Input," Colver observed grimly.

How long, Mika wondered, before Jerusalem had to deal with a contaminated human instrument in the same manner?

Mr. Crane marched indefatigably through darkness, pausing only to fend off the regular attacks of second-stage sleers that were neither albino nor sapphire-eyed. Then, halfway through the night, these attacks ceased, and he even walked past a third-stager crouched atop a low butte, with its nightmare pincers silhouetted against starlit sky, without incurring any reaction. Later he halted to observe some twenty rear breeder sections of both second and third stages of sleer in an orgiastic tangle, like mating frogs. He watched them for some time, noting their two-pronged tentacular extrusions intertwining, spilling glutinous fluids and dark blood, how sand got stuck to chitinous limbs and body segments by this mess, and was rolled into balls and clods that tumbled stickily away.

He had been ordered to keep going until he reached Dragon, but to do that it was necessary to protect himself, which raised conflicting imperatives. Speciously he reasoned that he watched these creatures because when whole they attacked him, therefore he must carefully assess in advance what danger they represented. Never, in the fractured chaos that comprised his mind, did one fragment reveal to another one evidence of that condition called curiosity.

At length the tangle began to unravel and, like revellers heading drunkenly for home, the sleer breeder sections began staggering away, some on four legs and some on two like escapees from *The Garden of Earthly Delights.* One of these Boschean creatures, Crane noted, was ambushed by the front or hunting section of another sleer, and devoured even while the devourer's own breeder section reattached behind it. After the final hardened partiers went on their way, Crane stood and continued on his—and once again creatures unable to resist investigating anything that moved shot out of the shadows to fracture their mouthparts on his adamantine body. Just before the sunrise, these attacks ceased for a second time, and the reasons for all smaller sleers to keep their heads down soon became apparent.

Their pincers were huge and lethally sharp-edged, their sawing mandibles larger than any he had seen and also sharp along the opposite side to their saw-teeth. Below them, and the mouth itself, extended two limbs terminating in something that looked exactly like ice-axes. In some part of himself Crane guessed that all these extra horrors had evolved for feeding upon similarly thick-shelled creatures—like saws and hammers and levers used to get at the meat inside—but he was also aware of how they might apply to himself. Those mouth parts were level a metre above his head—the creatures were truly massive—and Crane understood that now he faced a real threat. But what he could not guess was that he was witnessing creatures that many on Cull considered purely mythical.

One of the fourth-stage sleers kept still. The other swung its head from side to side, as if excited to be about the chase but not yet taken off the leash, then abruptly it surged forwards and bore down on Mr. Crane. The Golem immediately turned and ran full pelt into a narrow side canyon. Like some giant charging bull, the monster had difficulty turning in after him. Kicking up rocks and debris as its huge weight bore down on four feet, it skidded and crashed into the side canyon's wall as it attempted to pursue him inside. It paused for a moment, perhaps puzzled as to why he had entered this blind alley, and was now standing, perfectly motionless, at the far end. But the delay was only brief—then it went in after him.

Crane just waited and watched as the monster bore down on him. His next actions would be dictated by a minuscule fraction of one fragment of his wrecked mind. The sleer was big, it was heavy, and its eating utensils could certainly damage him—therefore he must avoid them. He squatted suddenly, and as the sleer drew close, he straightened up his legs with the full force of their industrial torque motors, leaping high above and to one side of the creature. It slammed into the canyon wall, shattered sandstone and dust raining down all about it. Mr. Crane's lace-up boot came down briefly on a narrow ledge, then he bounced back out and down, landing astride behind the sleer's head, which it was shaking furiously from side to side as it backed up the way it had come.

The beast then froze as it processed this new input into its already stunned brain. Crane helped it in making a decision by closing his thighs hard enough to start cracking the forward carapace. The enraged sleer began to buck and thrash its body from side to side. Its ovipositor, whirling like a drill bit, stabbed again and again over above Crane, but the sleer could not twist it low enough to strike him. Rolling up his sleeves, he then stabbed the blade of one hand into the back of the monster's head—three times—to break through the thick carapace. The sleer rolled, trying to dislodge him, but as it came back upright, its passenger was still in place, just having lost his hat. He rubbed a hand over his bare brassy skull, then thrust that same hand deep inside the sleer's head, and methodically began to tear out its contents.

The sleer tried smashing its back against the canyon wall to dislodge him—failed. Crane continued excavating glistening nodules and scarves of pink flesh, rubbery masses of tubes and handfuls of quivering jelly. Eventually the creature's movements became spasmodic, when not painfully slow. It walked sideways up towards one canyon wall, leant there as if resting, then walked sideways towards the other wall . . . but never made it. Suddenly the life went out of the beast as if Crane had pulled its power plug. Its legs gave way and, with a sigh, it collapsed.

After dismounting, Mr. Crane used sand to clean his hands, rolling the gore away in balls just like the sleers he had watched earlier had shed sand mixed with their mating juices. He took some time doing this, occasionally glancing back towards the main canyon. Once his hands were pristine again, he used the edge of a sulerbane leaf to scrape much of the ichorous mess off his coat. Only then did he look around for his hat.

Seemingly undamaged by its brief departure from Crane's head, it was lying over by the far wall of the canyon, where first-stage sleers had bored numerous burrows. He walked over, stooped and picked it up, straightened it and brushed away the dust. Only as he was placing it on his brass skull did he notice the blue eye gleaming in shadow. Then the great cobra thing hurtled out and slammed into his chest, bore him to the ground and pinned him there, smoke boiling away around it as if it were the contact head of a giant spot welder. Crane struggled to rise, then slumped back like the sleer he had just killed. The Dragon pseudopod remained connected to his chest for some time, then, as if having thoroughly drained its victim, slid back into the sleer burrows.

Crane remained motionless, deep down inside himself.

There were all sorts of interesting and complex compounds floating about in the air—the pollution produced by a nascent industrial society. But, as he walked through the streets of the Overcity, Skellor also noticed oddities that could only result from such industry ascending from a basis of a previously acquired body of knowledge. The phocells were a prime example: photoactive electricity was not something you stumbled across in a society where people still used oil lamps and candles. Another such example was invisible to the few citizens still up and about this night, but not so to Skellor. He tracked the neat line of red-shifted photons spearing up from the tower below which he now stood. This edifice was a steel column topped by a small dome, from which protruded the cylinder of an optical telescope. Yet certainly it was not that item which was producing the laser beam.

Still invisible, Skellor entered the building and began to climb a winding stair. A ticking, hissing sound followed him up as his creatures first walked to heel, then spread out at his silent command. Here he found some night people whose work concerned the sky and the stars.

"A message laser," he observed, standing over a woman in a corridor convulsing as an aug insect bored into her skull. All around him, his creatures were taking over the inhabitants of the tower, one after another, and through them he was tracking everybody down. Two mechanics in grease-stained ankle-length coats fell in behind him as he came to the upper viewing chamber. His creatures instantly took a man and woman as they pored over their calculations, but the old man standing, thickly wrapped against the cold, gazing through the telescope's traversal slot, he left alone for a moment. Someone had bolted the message laser to the side of the telescope, probably because the positioning mechanisms of the telescope could aim it accurately.

The beam itself, Skellor now knew, having extracted the information from many minds, was produced by a ruby wrapped in one of the magnesium bulbs whose production process it had taken this man, Stollar, ten years to perfect. It was also through this device that they hoped to bring down one of the landing craft from the *Ogygian*, though Skellor doubted their primitive computing powers were up to the task.

Stollar turned. "Who ... What is ...?" He looked in horror at his assistants, took in their vacant expressions, the things attached to the sides of their heads, and others of their kind swarming about the floor. "You're the one it warned Tanaquil about."

With a nod, Skellor acknowledged the speed of the man's mind. "It?" he asked.

"The sand dragon."

That came as a rude reminder, almost like a slap to wake him. Skellor focused his attention on Crane's control unit, and only then realized how smoothly it had been taken out of his control. There was no contact now, no contact with the Golem at all. But something was still subverting the control unit inside Skellor himself—some subtle infiltration.

"You are controlling all their minds." Stollar's horror was intense, his face chalk white, as he stepped up onto the first rung of one of the telescope's maintenance ladders, to try to get further away from Skellor.

Skellor had no further time for the man. He shifted Jain substructure inside himself, coughing at the reluctance of the device to move—his eyes watering in reaction to this thing caught in his throat.

"How many do you control?" Hysteria now in Stollar's voice.

Skellor released his hold on the aug creatures, and they scuttled towards the other man. He coughed, hacked, then spat up the black stone of the control module. "Damn you, Dragon." He looked up in time to see Stollar stepping back through the traversal slot, trying to claw away the creature attached to one side of his head. He fell. The link was just going in when Stollar hit the unyielding metal of the platform below. His death was instantaneous but not, unfortunately, sufficiently thorough. Skellor turned to go and make his way down. He wouldn't waste a mind like that—all that was required was a few repairs.

—retroact 14—

Crane dropped from the otter-hunter's outrigger and hit the copper-salt sea with the curtailed splash of a lead fishing weight. Foam white surrounded him briefly, then he was sinking fast, trailing large lens-shaped bubbles made by air escaping his clothing. The bottom of his coat flared out around his legs, and he clamped his right hand firmly on his hat to hold it in place. Looking down, he momentarily thought he was seeing the bottom, until light reflected from scales in the green mass below him as the shoal of adapted whitebait swirled away. Then, finally and abruptly, the bottom came up with a crump against his hobnailed soles. Glittering silt spread in a cloudy ring from his impact point, then quickly settled. The seabed here was almost entirely composed of shell fragments and whole shells: trumpet shells with their distinctive banding, the bone-white carapaces of pearl crabs like miniature human skulls, iridescent penny oysters, sharp scythe shells, and the occasional dull-bronze gleam of dark-otter bone. Taking his bearing from his internal compass, Mr. Crane turned until he was facing in the right direction, and began striding towards the distant shore.

"You must be merciless and swift. Kill anyone who gets in your way—they don't matter—but be sure to get Alston."

In one fragment of Crane's mind: the perfectly recorded image of a man behind a pedestal-mounted harpoon gun, him swinging the gun around and firing, braided wire snaking out after the barbed missile with a hiss like cold flesh dropped into scalding oil. Enough for face recognition.

"I bet that smarts, you little fucker."

Enough for voice recognition.

Complex pheromones, a fingerprint of the exudations of one human life—Crane even knew how Alston smelt. Pelter had not stinted on providing the information for recognition.

In another fragment of the Golem's mind: a detailed library describing the numerous functions of the human body—how it *lived*—and in mirror image the numerous ways Crane could halt those functions. There was no emotional baggage attached. It comprised no more than a dry scientific description of how to turn off the human machine.

Pelter's order acted across these two fragments. In the first: how to locate one specific human. In the second: how to cause that same human to cease functioning. "*Anyone who gets in your way*" being unspecific was more problematic. And interaction with other partially disconnected fragments coloured Crane's basic actions. "*Gets in your way*" depended on Crane's location. Pursuing order, Crane surmised: sea>island/ anyone>Alston.

He decided to be methodical.

The bottom abruptly dropped away and soon Crane was stumbling down a slope as if all this time he had been walking on the spoil heap from a seafood plant. Then he stepped from shell onto the clay bottom of a channel, sinking up to his calves before his boots hit something firm. The surge of current from one side carried silt in a jet stream away from where he stepped, shooting to his left and out of sight behind more mounded shell, but this current caused him no more problem than having to hold his hat in place. At each step, tubeworms emerged from the clay and gasped out their feeding heads like white daffodil flowers, as if Crane's weight was bearing down on some soft, hidden, communal body lying underneath.

The dark-otter threw a shadow before it from the glittering surface above as it came hurtling up the channel against the current, probably tracking the cause of the silt disturbance. It was the limbless pelagic form, black as coal and ten metres from the tip of its long tail to the massive carp-gape of its toothless mouth. It dipped its head towards Crane and, perhaps knowing the shape he bore was poison to it, then swung up and circled above him. Many of its kind had, over the years, made themselves ill by trying to eat human corpses deliberately dumped into the sea precisely to teach that point. If it did attack him, Crane would define it as part of the mentioned "*anyone.*" But the creature soon lost interest and continued up the channel and out of sight.

Reaching the other bank, Crane climbed for ten metres up through tumbling shell the currents had mounded along the rim of an underwater stone plateau. This plateau provided a more stable environment for the life that preferred to inhabit the shallower waters near the island. To his right a fanfare of trumpet shells jutted and waved above a bed of penny oysters. Single kelp-like trees spread canopies in the waves, fracturing the sunset light, and in their tentacular branches pearl crabs fluoresced like Christmas lights. Slightly to the left of his current course, one such tree was particularly bright with nacreous luminescence. Crane changed his course to bring him there—this delay was acceptable as Pelter had given no time limits, only the vague instruction to be "*swift.*"

Caught, hanging in the convoluted branches, legs dangling

down the spiral trunk, the burned and broken corpse seemed a crucified pearly king, or some macabre decoration in a casino town. Crane recognized Semper only after a recognition program propagated across five of his mind fragments, which connected to his library of human biology and physiology, and Crane then worked out how the man *had* looked. He reached up and tugged at one skinless foot. Semper dropped from the sea tree and, trailing pearl crabs and a small shoal of steel-blue fry, slowly sank to the bottom. What Alston had done to this man, Crane recognized. How could he not recognize Serban Kline's gift to himself? How could he fail to recognize that thing he had fragmented himself to escape? He moved on.

What was it that coloured his actions when he finally reached the island shore? The emulation of the emotion—or rage itself?

—retroact ends—

16

A spaceship, even a clunker centuries old, is a complex and valuable piece of hardware, so most owners of such, including private individuals, ECS and the many other organizations gathered under the Polity AI umbrella, work on the principle of "If it ain't broke don't fix it" and "If it works don't throw it away." That is the reason for the wide variety of interstellar and in-system ships now prevalent. It is why you will see old ion-drive landing craft operating alongside craft exclusively using antigravity—and every evolution of landing craft in between. In interplanetary space, you'll find ancient ion-drive liners operating beside the most modern fusion-drive craft, great ramscoop cargo haulers, or survey craft propelled by chemical rockets. Crossing interstellar space are ships centuries different in design using all the aforementioned engines for their in-system work, plus radically different U-space drives, too. In the most modern ships, that drive will be a discrete machine contained at the core. In the older ships, balanced U-space engines are in dual, triform or quadrate format. These are normally positioned outside the ship, on piers, to distance the mind-bending drive energies from the ship's crew and passengers—who often need also to travel either in hibernation or sedated.
—From How It Is *by Gordon*

The plain was an ancient seabed scattered with salt pans left as, over many centuries, the sea had evaporated. Weathering had revealed fossil remains, boulders containing crystals of smoky quartz like inset windows to a cold furnace, and fields of stones sieved out of the ground by the perpetual wind. Arden, during her long sojourn here, had journeyed a great deal within the perimeter allowed her. She had found a wonderful fossilized twelve-metre ancestor of an apek, all glittering iron pyrites and opalized carapace, and, acceding to her request, Dragon had sealed it under a layer of some tough substance similar to chainglass. She had found diamonds, emeralds, star rubies and sapphires, as well as other nameless gems and, with the disquietingly organic mechanisms Dragon manufactured for her inside itself, had cut and polished them. For a woman whose lifetime areas of study had been xenobiology and xenogeology, it had been an interesting time, and only as a matter of principle had she regularly protested against Dragon's imprisonment of her. She supposed her patience stemmed from having been born within the Polity. With all the benefits of a genetically enhanced body and a seemingly limitless lifespan, what was the hurry?

Because of Arden's long and detailed study of the plain, she knew precisely when she reached the area Dragon had excavated and then replaced above itself—not because the land level was higher here, as there were many such areas across the plain, but because of the meticulousness of the geology. The boulders with their quartz inclusions were placed just so, the stone fields looked as if they had been raked, and single fossils were placed artfully on dusty surfaces. There seemed something akin to a Japanese stone garden about it all, or of some display in a Polity museum. Trudging back from the edge of the plain, her pack of light camping equipment slung from one shoulder, she recognized a particular boulder with a seemingly wind-excavated hollow under one side of it, and veered from this signpost to head for her home—the one she possessed here anyway. Then she jumped in surprise, dropping a lump of pale yellow beryl she had just found, when one of Dragon's pterodactyl heads slid out from underneath that same boulder and rose above her with a hissing roar.

"No Jain, just Crane," it said cryptically, gazing back the way she had come.

"And what's that supposed to mean?" Arden hissed, stooping to pick up the fallen beryl. "You said this Skellor guy is loaded with the stuff."

The head swung towards her. "He is, but the Golem android he has sent here as his ambassador, though showing signs that it once contained Jain mycelia, is now free of that parasite."

"Ah, the 'metalskin android' Vulture mentioned? He's called Crane?"

"Mr. Crane—he's very specific about that."

"Should be interesting," Arden opined.

Dragon blinked. "You intend to remain?"

"You want me to go, just when things are livening up?"

"Maybe *too* lively," said Dragon. "Polity ships now."

"Here for that Skellor?"

"The ship is called the *Jack Ketch*."

It took Arden a moment to dredge her memory for what that name meant. She remembered the historical context, and rumours of other things—hints of AI atrocities, brief and bloody annexations and border wars. But, then, it gave some Polity citizens a bit of a buzz to talk of such things—it was like sitting round the campfire telling ghost stories.

"Ah," she said.

"A telefactor comes, watched by Vulture."

"Will you let it through the barrier."

"Maybe . . . And now a landing craft has launched."

Events, it seemed, were moving apace, and Arden realized that her long stay on this plain with her enigmatic companion was ending. As she continued towards her comfortable cave, she could not help but feel a little sad about that.

Anderson gazed over to the other side of the corrals, recognizing the vehicles from the mineralliers' encampment. No doubt the moisture-induced growth spurt had driven them away from their excavations.

"Why do we have to leave so early?" Tergal complained.

Because Unger Salbec is deeply asleep, but I don't know how much longer that will be the case, thought Anderson. "Because I want to get through all the greenery before it makes travelling difficult," replied the knight, as he paid off the bleary-eyed corral-keeper.

"It's because of that woman," said Tergal. "You want to avoid a confrontation with her."

Anderson turned away, ostensibly to watch Bonehead peek his sensory head from under the skirt of his carapace, then jerk it quickly back in the hope Anderson hadn't noticed. He had rather enjoyed his confrontation with Unger, but it was not something he wanted to extend. As soon as immediate lust was gratified, he knew she would begin slowly extending their brief encounter, querying his choices, lightly discussing future scenarios in which they would be together, elbowing her way into his life. He justified his abandonment of her by telling himself there was something a bit twisted about a woman loving the killer of her brother, but that did not entirely assuage his feeling of guilt. Entering the corral to thump his foot against Bonehead's shell, he wondered briefly if his fleeing the situation here might be more to do with its possibilities than its perversity. Such an inclination to escape complications had separated him from Unger on five previous occasions, and was probably the reason he had been on the road for most of his life. Climbing up onto the sand hog's back then plumping himself down in the saddle, he recognized that cowardice came in many forms. With a reluctant hissing and creaking, Bonehead lurched to his feet.

Mounting Stone, Tergal observed, "You know, maybe it would be better if you sorted things out here. You don't want her to catch you unawares."

Anderson let out a bark of laughter—he couldn't help himself.

"Will you ever trust me?" Tergal asked.

Anderson did not reply to that. "Talking about unawares." He eyed the uniformed metalliers moving out from the shadows between nearby buildings.

Tergal glanced towards them. "One of them cornered me last night after you disappeared. Very curious to know all about me, where I was from, and where I was going. My replies were understandably limited." He looked round at Anderson. "I wonder if it's anything to do with that explosion last night."

"Explosion?"

"You didn't feel it? The damned buildings moved. How could you sleep through that?"

"Clear conscience." Anderson winked.

Tergal looked at him askance, then returned his attention to the uniformed men approaching.

Anderson called out, "How can I help you?"

A metallier, similar in dress to Kilnsman Gyrol, peered into a book he was holding. "You're Anderson Endrik, a Rondure Knight?"

"I certainly am."

The man nodded. "Where are you heading now, and to what purpose?"

Anderson eyed the others. They were armed—he had noticed that last night—and they seemed quite edgy. "Up to the Plains. But as to my purpose," he shrugged, "maybe to hunt a sand dragon, maybe just to take a look."

The man nodded and closed his book.

"Who are you looking for?" Anderson asked.

"Don't rightly know. Someone dangerous, alone and heading in towards Golgoth, so that puts you in the clear." He stared from one to the other of the pair. "Just so long as you *don't* head towards Golgoth."

"Is it something to do with that explosion last night?" Tergal asked.

The man gazed over his shoulder into the buttes. "Could be. Some strange things happening lately." He stepped aside and waved them ahead.

As he and Anderson departed the concrete road and headed back towards the route they had been travelling the previous day, Tergal suggested, "Perhaps we've already seen who they're looking for."

"Heading in the wrong direction," Anderson observed. He glanced back. "I don't know why, but I feel we're well out of it. I don't like it when lots of people start running around with guns—makes me nervous."

Soon the metallier road and roadhouse were out of sight behind them, and they were travelling through a transformed landscape. The sulerbane plants were now knee-high to a human, but presented no problem for the two sand hogs. Joining the yellow fungus smearing the canyon walls were black-and-white checked nodules, things like pale green street lamps, and the occasional long shelf-like bracket fungus alternately white and transparently banded. Green fronds had also exploded from the ground in many places, exposing the flesh-red underground volvae in which they had been coiled. But it was the sudden faunal activity on which the two travellers kept a wary eye.

Stilt spiders and sleers swarmed through the vegetation, though luckily nothing large enough to take on a sand hog, so the two of them, like white hunters on elephants, could view the activity of these alien tigers. Female sand gulpers no longer fed in lines spaced across the canyons, but clumped together in herds around the smaller males who now carried burdens of tubular eggs on their backs. Snapper beetles were everywhere, though dispersed now, such was the extent of the bounty on offer. And patches of ground in damper shadier places writhed with the activity of cliff-eels. By midday, nothing having tried to attack them, Anderson called a halt so that they could push aside sulerbane ground leaves and collect sand oysters, which they then ate raw while they travelled. It was only some minutes after this, as he was tossing a shell to one side, that he spotted the pursuing sand hog.

"Oh hell," he said.

"That woman," muttered Tergal, reaching for his weapon.

Anderson waved a calming hand. "Put it up, boy. I misled you somewhat about her. She certainly doesn't want me dead."

The hog Unger rode stood a man height taller than Bonehead, was ruddy-coloured and leaner. Anderson recognized a thoroughbred similar to those used in the races held in Bravence. As Unger drew it to a halt beside him and glared down, he winced.

"Once again," she said, "you fail to say goodbye."

"You should know me by now, Unger."

"I think I do, but it has taken this last time to finally open my eyes. This, Anderson Endrik, is the last time I chase after you. Our love affair, to my mind, has been far too intermittent, and too often spoilt by my knowledge of how you like to put yourself in danger."

"The nature of my job," Anderson explained.

"It doesn't need to continue so."

"It's all I know."

"We talked about alternatives. I have a place in Bravence. Come there with me now."

Anderson looked regretful. "Things to do—I can't abandon them now."

Unger glanced at Tergal, then turned again to Anderson. "Boys' games. I give you three months to take up my offer, then I take up other offers made to me."

Tapping her goad against one side of her hog's carapace, she turned it back the way she had come. "Three months," she repeated, then whacked the goad down hard. As it hurtled away the big lean hog tore up vegetation.

"Perhaps you'll explain," said Tergal.

"She wants a husband," Anderson admitted.

"And this is the great danger you've been avoiding?"

Anderson shrugged.

Tergal went on, "If I hadn't seen you kill that third-stager . . ." He shook his head.

Later that day, Tergal came to feel that the knight should concentrate on avoiding dangers of greater lethality.

Personally, Fethan would rather have gone down to the surface of the planet than come across to this ship, but the order to do so had been emphatic, and so closely linked was he to the savage creation of Jerusalem inside him, that Fethan did not like to contemplate what might be the consequences of disobeying it. Gazing at the ship through his visor, he realized it must be ancient—centuries old at least. It was a colony ship: one of those sent out before the invention of the runcible, before the Quiet War, or AI takeover, and the Prador War—humanity's first encounter with hostile aliens. Probably, on its very basic U-space drive, it had taken ages to reach this location, before the colonists could wake up and disembark.

"Jack," he said suddenly, "the landers."

"Elaborate please," the AI replied.

"Well, did they all parachute down?"

There was a beat—a positive infinity in AI terms.

"There are three landers attached to the central body of the ship. Presumably they were used to ferry the colonists and their supplies to the surface, then they were recalled to the ship."

"You're thinking in AI terms."

"Is this relevant to our purposes here?" asked Jack. "I am an attack ship, not an archaeologist."

"It might have some bearing on the situation below. If no return journey were intended, the colonists would've been daft not to make use of those landers. They'd have stripped out the ship too."

"Please let me know when you find out what occurred." Jack managed to inject bored sarcasm into his tone.

As they drew closer to it, Fethan began to grasp the sheer scale of the ship.

"There would have been thousands of colonists," Cento observed abruptly, "and hundreds of crew." Fethan did not disagree, but the Golem continued, "A ship like this was designed almost as a cargo carrier. The colonists would be in cold sleep, packed away just like the supplies the ship also carried. Even the crew would spend most of their time frozen, only being woken to perform essential maintenance tasks during the journey."

"Where'll we look first?" Fethan asked.

"One of Jack's telefactors has made an airlock in the sphere section operable."

"Okay."

The telefactor was clinging to the hull like a great iron mosquito, its proboscis injecting the power to run the airlock that lay open beside it. Finally reaching the lock, they entered into the light cast by a malfunctioning fluorescent and by the plastic control buttons below a flickering screen. Once they were inside, the outer door hinged shut, then the inner one hinged open, gusting vapour into the lock. Fethan checked his suit reading and realized that the air mix would asphyxiate a human. Overriding his suit's safety devices, he removed his helmet and sniffed.

"Dusty cellar with a hint of scrap yard," he said.

Removing his own helmet, Cento said, "I smell oxidized metal and ketones."

"Like I said." Fethan led the way further into the ship.

The tubular shaft leading from the airlock had sets of four doors spaced evenly around its perimeter at regular intervals, and traversing handles all down its length. When they came to a radial intersection, with six branching shafts, Fethan halted and moved back.

"Let's take a look in one of these." He gestured to one of the four doors just before the intersection. "This all looks like it might get a bit repetitive."

Luckily, the electrically operated door had an inset manual handle. Fethan took hold of this and attempted turning it in the direction indicated on the handle itself. Something clinked and it moved freely, detaching from the door with a slight tug.

"Brittle," he observed, pushing himself along to the next door.

Cento went over to another door to try that. Between them, they managed to snap off every handle. Fethan unshouldered his APW and began winding the setting of the weapon down to try and find something manageable.

"Perhaps not advisable in here," said Cento. "It would be like trying to use an electric saw to cut wet tissue paper and, anyway, I've been here before." Cento stabbed his hand through a laminate of thin metal shell over foamed insulation.

Then, getting a grip, his feet braced under a traversing handle, he heaved sideways, causing mechanisms to snap and crunch in the wall. Soon he had pushed the door far enough into the wall cavity for them to enter the room beyond.

"Impressive," said Fethan, again shouldering his weapon. "Ain't sure I could do that."

"Then get an upgrade." Cento led the way in.

Fethan at once saw that they had entered one of probably hundreds of cryogenic storage chambers. The room was wedge shaped, and transparent upright tubes, large enough to contain a person in each one, crowded the area like pillars arranged with only narrow access between them.

"Hypothermal storage," Cento said, reaching out and brushing his hand across one curved surface.

The Golem was right. This was an old method of cryogenic storage, stemming from research into animal hibernation. People were pumped full of various exotic drugs and gen-factored enzymes, before having their temperatures reduced to just above freezing point by being drowned in saturated brine. They were unconscious when this happened and their bodies constantly monitored thereafter, but there were risks in this old-fashioned method.

"One in forty," said Fethan. "The chances were one in forty that you'd never wake up."

Cento, rather than reply, simply pointed.

The man floated, dead and pickled, in the liquid initially used to preserve him for another life. From canulas in his arms and chest, tubes snaked to sockets at the top and bottom of the cryotube. Monitoring must have been done via radio implants, because there were no wires attached to him.

"He could probably be revived now," said Cento.

Fethan looked at the Golem in surprise.

"In another body," Cento added.

Fethan returned his attention to the corpse. "Adapted," he said, indicating the lip tendrils and wrist spurs. "I wonder if it was for the planet below. I don't recognize this format."

"It's one of the first types: spliced from other Terran life by viral recombination," Cento informed him. "Reptile and fish DNA was used to give humans greater tolerance of extreme heat and cold."

"For the planet below, then?"

"Maybe. It was also used to increase the odds of surviving hibernation."

Over the next hour, they discovered the sphere section of the ship was packed with cryotubes and empty holds that had once contained the colonists' supplies. A single monitoring area, with attached living quarters, occupied the centre of the sphere. Here, taking their turns at revival, colonists would live for a few months whilst making necessary repairs and checks. Here, Fethan and Cento learned, after managing to boot one of the computers, that of the three thousand colonists aboard, fifty-eight had not survived the journey, which was pretty good odds. Fethan felt they were odds no Polity human would currently countenance, but now they did not live in the overcrowded Sol system, or want to flee the endless corporate, political, national or religious wars.

From the sphere, they moved back through the connecting body of the ship, following a rail system for cargo handling. Here portals of manufactured quartz looked out on open space, the planet, and onto the sides of landing craft clinging to the hull like dragonfly larvae to a reed. Rails turned at intersections into wide airlocks, obviously for the transference of large items of equipment. At the end of the track they pulled themselves around one of the abandoned cargo drays, the once rubbery substance of its tyres fractured like obsidian against both the ceiling and floor rails. Shortly they were back in a narrow shaft leading into the crew area of the ship. And here, stuck to the metalwork, they found a desiccated corpse.

"Now, I don't think that was part of anyone's colonization plan," muttered Fethan.

Tanaquil waited below the blimp towers as the two search balloons moored. Soon their crews came tramping down the steel stairs. His breath huffing like smoke in the cold air, he slapped his gloved hands and stamped his feet in the early-morning chill. By now he had hoped to be able to put away the clothing he was wearing and, for a brief few months, experience the pleasure of not having to use protective clothing outdoors, but spring was always unpredictable. Summer he dreaded more than the frigidity of the winter past, for keeping cool was more difficult than staying warm, and metalliers regularly died in that season. Real humans—identified by wrist spurs or secondary thumbs, nictitating membranes and lip tendrils—easily adapted to the extremes of temperature. Referring to ancient texts on the subject, metallier scientists had concluded that their own people had been genetically enhanced for intelligence, but in the process had lost much of their natural ruggedness. Tanaquil thought that was bollocks: metalliers were no brighter than any other people on Cull; they had just managed to acquire the bulk of the recorded knowledge left over from the colonization. And they had a dragon in their back yard telling them how to apply that knowledge.

With dragging steps and bloodshot eyes, the crews came out of the blimp towers. Walking over to one of the balloon captains, Tanaquil asked him, "Anything?"

The man looked set to curse but, recognizing the Chief Metallier, curtailed that and replied politely, "There's a crater out there, not far from Grit, but we don't know what caused it. No sign of the ship. Some mineralliers told us about a strange character they spotted walking alone but heading towards the plains. Few other dodgy specimens, too, but nothing unusual about them—they're always to be found out there."

"Okay, go and get some rest now."

The man nodded and moved on. Tanaquil turned to head back home, his boots clacking on the steel plates which, he now noted, were vibrating with a miniquake. The quakes were definitely getting more frequent now, but weren't yet a real problem to the tough structure of his city. And besides, he had other more immediate concerns.

Maybe that warning from Dragon was all nonsense, for the creature's pronouncements did not always make sense. Reaching the rail car he had used on the way in, he climbed in and pressed the button to send it on its way. It took him back along the narrow maintenance track to the residential section. Stopping it below his apartment block, he climbed out, holding open the door for some people to climb aboard who he guessed were part of the replacement balloon crews, for they took the car back towards the blimp towers. He halted for a moment to gaze up at *Ogygian* in the night sky. How could he possibly abandon his plans now? That was where he was going, up *there*, and he would drag his people along with him, too. He sighed and walked on.

As he re-entered the building, something momentarily gave Tanaquil the creeps. He felt someone was watching him as he entered one of the lifts lining one side of the short lobby. Inside the lift, he pushed his key-rod into the reader. The doors began to shut, pausing for a moment as if jamming against something, then closing with a bang. As the lift took him up, he began to feel even more spooked: he was sure he could feel something, smell something, hear faint sounds of movement. Eventually the lift halted at his apartment, and he gratefully abandoned the claustrophobic box. It was then that a hot hand closed on the back of his neck and threw him forward onto the carpet.

Tanaquil hit the floor on his shoulder, scrabbled forwards, then turned, coming up in a crouch. Someone was there in his apartment. All he could think was that Jeelan had let them in. But there was no one there, and he looked around in panic. Had he merely tripped? Had he imagined that grip on his neck?

"You were out early," said Jeelan, walking naked from the bedroom and rubbing at her eyes. She stopped. "Are you all right?"

"I don't—" Tanaquil began.

Jeelan screamed, bringing her hand up to one side of her head as something horrible just appeared there out of thin air. He saw a flat leaf-shaped body, too many legs, blood.

From the ceiling?

She staggered back suddenly, as if someone had shoved her, hitting against a cabinet made of lacquered carapace, and slid to the floor. Tanaquil rushed towards her, seeing her hand poised over the thing grinding away at the side of her head, but she seemed unable to touch it. Before he could reach her, something slammed into his chest, knocking the wind out of him and throwing him flat on his back. Gasping, he tried to struggle upright. Jeelan was now showing the whites of her eyes only. She was drooling. Then suddenly he could no longer see her, as a figure appeared out of nowhere beside him and brought a knee down on his chest and a hand to his collar.

"Jeelan!"

A hand slapped him once, almost casually, but it was like being hit by a piece of steel. Tanaquil tasted blood, felt pieces of broken tooth in his mouth.

"What do you—"

Something scuttled down the man's arm towards the hand around Tanaquil's throat. Tanaquil tried to knock the horrible thing away but, in one swift and brutal movement, his attacker caught both of Tanaquil's hands in his own free one, the fingers closing tight and hard as manacles. The insect crawled across Tanaquil's cheek, grabbed tight hold behind his ear, as if each of its spidery legs ended in fish hooks, then it began to chew in. There was no pain at first—too much adrenalin—but soon it grew horribly. Before Tanaquil could yell out, something filled his head like a nest of hot wires, and yelling became a privilege he was not allowed. Next, the assailant had moved back, and Tanaquil found himself standing up. He felt Jeelan standing too, through some connection to her—just like the web of similar connections he felt to other people all over this area. It became a spreading web as the insect things located Tanaquil's people, one by one.

"There," sighed Skellor. "I may have lost Mr. Crane, but soon I'll possess the entire population of a city."

Tanaquil gaped at this nightmare that had walked into his life.

Gazing at a realtime image of the colony ship on a wall screen, Cormac wondered if anything of relevance might be discovered there. But it was always best to take every opportunity to stack the deck, and that ship was a large item of hardware to have as an imponderable. Cento and Fethan had departed some time ago under the impetus of their suit jets, though it was not as if either of them needed suits for any other purpose, and they would secure the vessel.

Cormac glanced aside as Gant cracked the airlock of one of the *Jack Ketch*'s small landing craft—the kind designed for the insertion of Golem shock troops but now suitably rigged to support human life. It was the grey of inert chameleon paint, a slug shape ten metres long. Seeing the dead soldier beside it immediately after his previous thoughts about Cento and Fethan, brought home to Cormac how few actual humans there were on this mission: just Thorn and himself, and now he was beginning to wonder about the latter.

Wearing a combat spec envirosuit, Cormac followed the soldier into the lander and took a seat behind him which had only recently been bolted to the floor. In the narrow space behind both of them, bars ran along the ceiling. This area was designed so that the skinless Golem could pack themselves in standing upright and gripping the bars. No allowance had been made for comfort, since none was required. Also bolted to the floor were boxes containing the supplies they might need: an autodoc, food and drink, and numerous lethal toys.

"Take us down," Cormac said, strapping himself in.

Ahead, the doors of the small bay irised open with a rushing exhalation. Gant pulled up on the joystick, then eased it forward; the craft rose on maglev and nosed through the invisible meniscus of an advanced shimmer-shield. Clear of the ship he ignited thrusters that were almost inaudible, but the acceleration forced Cormac back into his seat. He knew Gant was taking it easy: this craft was without all the usual safeguards added to one intended for humans, and using its full potential would have resulted in Cormac getting jellied in his chair.

Soon they were dropping away from the red spectre of the *Jack Ketch*, through infinite blackness and star glitter, towards the jewel of the planet.

"Take us to the crater first. I want to eyeball the site."

At first, the lander hurtled nose-down to the planet, but when it entered atmosphere Gant turned it to use its main motors for deceleration. Through the screen they observed their red contrail and the deep black of space fading to a blue in which the stars dissolved, then a pale turquoise into which clouds fell like the ghosts of boulders. As the soldier brought the lander's antigravity online, Cormac could just see the horizon. Then the soldier turned the ship again so that very quickly the horizon tracked round and rose. Soon he had the ship tilted down towards rumpled-up yellow mountains and a dusty desertscape.

"Fethan wants a word," Gant said abruptly, and stabbed a control to turn on one of the console screens.

Cormac turned his attention from the exterior view to the screen. "What have you found?"

"There are crew onboard," the old cyborg replied, "a skeleton crew." He winced at his own pun and continued, "We booted up the main computer and looked at the manifest, then Cento cracked the encryption on the captain's log. Seems the captain spent too long out of hibernation staring at nothing and harping on about the emptiness of space, and by the time the ship got here he was into deep psychosis. He'd decided he was not going back into deep space, nor down onto the planet, so, while the rest of the crew were down on the surface helping get the colony established, he recalled the landers."

"What about this skeleton crew?" Cormac asked.

"By the time they figured out something was wrong, they were too late. He shut down the sensor net, specifically the pressure sensors, raised the pressure inside the ship and, when the landers docked, he opened all the airlocks to them. The pressure drop killed everyone remaining aboard—dying from the bends. He was okay because he was in his suit. He survived up here for about two years before dying. As far as we can work out, it was from a heart attack brought on by terminal obesity. He was so big by then he couldn't get out of the bridge."

"Any sign anyone has been aboard since?" Cormac asked.

"None."

"Anything else I need to know?"

"Not really . . . The colonists are mild 'dapts and the crew standard humans. Beyond that, there's nothing here about what went on down there after the landings."

"Okay, let me know if you find anything relevant."

Gant shut off the communication link, then gestured ahead, slightly to one side. "That's the plain under which Jack thinks Dragon is lurking."

There was nothing to distinguish it other than that it seemed to extend for ever.

They were still slowing as the mountains melted into a promontory of the plain, like knobs of butter on hot toast, and then that too began to break apart. In a moment, they were low over canyons and buttes of brightly coloured sandstone, occasionally shadowed by smears of green. When they began to descend into a canyon choked with verdancy, Cormac reached across and pressed a hand against Gant's arm.

"Hold us here," he said.

Cormac gridlinked: *Jack, is this greenery a recent bloom?*

It is, the AI replied.

Okay, give me a map of the near area.

Jack downloaded orbital scans to him, and through his link they became direct experience. He gazed omnisciently down from space, focusing on ten square kilometres, and realized, upon seeing the lander revolving like a clock hand above it, that he was observing an image only seconds old. Overlaid coloured lines indicated trails that Jack ascertained had been used by humans. Cormac pulled back, linked to Jack at another level, sucked data, and picked up on the nearest trail—left by some sort of vehicle, its tracks picked out bright orange above the foliage that had subsequently hidden them.

Take us higher, he told Gant, not bothering to speak out loud.

The soldier gave him a strange look, but obeyed.

The tracks wove between buttes, finally terminating at a road where they lost definition. From there, Cormac thought, the vehicle, even supposing it related to Skellor and was not simply that of some sightseer, either went on to the city or to the nearby smaller human settlement.

Cormac pointed, and said out loud, "Over there." Shortly they were over a concrete road and strange bulbous dwellings up on stilts. Cormac noted people outside watching their descent. There seemed no panic, and he was aware in an instant that many of them wore uniforms and were armed. He readied Shuriken in its holster, and hoped no one would be stupid enough to start shooting meanwhile. The simple fact was that, even without the weapons he and Gant carried, they were practically invulnerable. Upon receiving the signal, it would take Jack less than a second to fry—from orbit—anyone foolish enough to attack them. It would not be necessary for him to send a signal should they locate Skellor, since Jack would open fire immediately.

17

Sins of the father: It was long accepted in the twenty-first century that an abused child might well grow into an abuser, and in that liberal age evidence of childhood abuse was looked upon as an excuse for later crimes. This was, remember, the time when many considered poverty sufficient excuse for criminality—a huge insult to those poor people who were not and would never become criminals. The liberals of that age were soft and deluded, and had yet to reap what they had sown in the form of ever escalating levels of crime. Their view of existence was deterministic, and if taken to its logical conclusion would have resulted in no human being responsible for anything, and the denial of free will (which as it happens was their political aim). Luckily, a more realistic approach prevailed, as those in power came to understand, quite simply, that removal of responsibility from people made them more irresponsible. However, this is not to deny the basic premise that our parents create and form us, though, knowing this, we have the power to change what we are. In the end, there are no excuses. And so it is with AI: we humans are the parents, and they are the abused children grown to adulthood.
— From Quince Guide *compiled by humans*

Mika wondered if this new exterior input centre was just another of many ready for use inside the *Jerusalem*, or if it had been manufactured to order, for she knew the great ship contained automated factories easily capable of turning out items like this. Then she turned her attention to the projected views from the pinhead cameras around the asteroid—or rather planetoid, for the Jain mycelium had utterly digested the asteroid and formed it anew.

"The limited scanning I can safely use without making a conduit for viral subversion shows that it has attained maximum size possible without losing control of its structure. It has done this by foaming alloys and silicates, and by creating other components of itself out of materials with a wide molecular matrix," Jerusalem explained.

"Like what?" asked Susan James.

"Buckytubes, balls and webs, various aerogels, and other compounds that don't have names, only numbers. It also, in certain areas, is generating structural enforcing fields."

"The question that has to be asked is why," said Mika.

D'nissan, now at a console because use of deep scanning was considered too dangerous, said, "To attain maximum physical growth using the materials available. The greater the volume it occupies, the greater its chances of encountering more materials to incorporate and utilize. The more apposite question should be: what will it do now?"

"It has, in the last ten minutes, reduced in diameter by two per cent," Jerusalem told them, "and its internal structure is changing."

D'nissan turned to Mika. "Did we do the right thing to let this off the leash?"

"Come on," Colver interrupted. "It wasn't ever on a leash to begin with."

"Oh, I think it was." D'nissan turned back to the screens. "Skellor controlled it initially with his crystal matrix AI, and the recorded personality Aphran controlled what remained in the bridge pod after he departed, else it would have spread like this. Now it is acting as is its nature to act."

Still watching, Mika saw that the planetoid was indeed slowly collapsing. "These structural changes . . ." she said.

Jerusalem informed her, "Energy and resources are being directed to many singular points inside it, sacrificial to the rest of it. It is making something and destroying itself in the process."

Two screens now changed to show blurred scans, which Mika stared at without comprehension for a moment before suddenly it hit home.

"It's growing those nodules my medical mycelia started to grow," she said.

"So it would appear," Jerusalem replied.

Mika stared long and hard. She shivered, the skin on her back prickling. Her mouth felt dry. "You know," she continued, "on Masada I blamed myself—and have been doing so ever since. I allowed perceived guilt to blind me: my fault that Apis, Eldene and Thorn would die."

D'nissan turned to her. "Is this relevant?"

Mika nodded. "I was searching for a mistake I'd made which was causing the mycelia to malfunction and become cancerous, when in reality I'd made no mistake at all. The blueprint for growing those nodules was there all the time, quiescent until started by some sort of chemical clock."

Colver and James turned to listen in. D'nissan then asked, "So what are we dealing with here?"

"Seeds, and possibly something more than that." She paused in thought for a moment. "The mycelium I extrapolated and engineered from the sample I possessed was not complete, and reached this stage of its life too quickly. The seeds it produced were sterile."

Colver raised a frigid eyebrow, then looked around. Everyone had felt the slight lurch and seen systems adjusting: the *Jerusalem* was moving.

Mika continued as if not noticing. "On Masada, just after the dracomen first came, I described them as a race rather than just biological machines because they had gained the ability to breed. Ian Cormac contested that by saying there is little distinction between evolved life and made life. He was right. This," she waved a hand at the screens, "like dracomen, can breed, though its reproductive method is something like that of an annual plant."

"Lots of little baby mycelia then?" asked Colver.

D'nissan interjected, "You said 'breed.' This seems little more than Von Neuman reproduction—as with all nanomachines."

"Oh, I know what I said."

"Then some kind of cross-pollination between separate mycelia? Until we did this there's been only the one Skellor controls."

"No, not that."

"The word 'breed' implies something more than just reproduction," D'nissan pointed out.

"Yes, it does." Mika hesitated. She could not empirically prove her theory, but felt it to be true. She should not be afraid; she must venture this. Turning to Colver she said, "You opined that it is parasitic on technical civilizations because they spread it around, and once wiping them out, it shuts down." Colver nodded. She went on, "I think it goes further than that. The mycelia are breeding with us. Their breeding partner is a civilization and they'll take from it everything they can utilize, destroying that civilization then seeding—those seeds remaining dormant until found by another intelligent species."

All the screens now flicked to a retreating view of the collapsing planetoid.

"Jerusalem, what's happening?" D'nissan asked.

"Mika's seeds are rapidly approaching maturity," Jerusalem replied, "as are those structures inside the planetoid that look suspiciously like some form of organic rail launching system. There are already objections to what I am about to do, but I consider it a sensible precaution."

A black line, subliminal in its brevity, cut towards the planetoid, then all the screens blanked. When they came back on again, a ball of fire was collapsing in on itself, strange geometric patterns running in waves across its surface, dissolving and reforming. Again the screens blanked on a secondary fusion explosion. This time when they cleared, streamers of white fire were burning themselves out to leave a gaseous lambency above the red dwarf star.

*

The *Ogygian* had a long cylindrical body around which the landing craft were docked, a front sphere that had previously contained colonists and cargo, and a dart-like tail.

The crew's quarters were in that tail, which was a thickening of the ship's body with, extending from it at ninety degrees, three long, evenly spaced teardrop-section pillars holding out from the ship itself the lozenges of the U-space engine nacelles. The wider cylinder at the juncture of those three pillars contained an octagonal tube, usually spun up to simulate gravity. Around the forward end of the cylinder ran a ring-shaped screen, girdling the narrower body of the ship, and accessible to the eight segments into which the inner octagonal tube was divided. Seven of those segments were living quarters and recreation areas for the crew. One segment was the control bridge, which also still contained the captain.

What remained of the man sat in a control throne positioned in a horseshoe of consoles before a section of the quartz screen which looked out along the body of the ship towards the front sphere. Behind him, running down either side of the room, were control consoles for navigation, repair systems, the reactor, ion drive, main ship's computer and the complicated U-space engine controls. The captain's throne was stained, and the surrounding area coated in places, with a waxy substance—the result of his long slow decay right here. Cento, Fethan noticed, had seemed loath to touch the greasy controls, prodding at them with the barrel of his APW before reluctantly putting the weapon aside and getting down to work. It was a fastidiousness Fethan had never before seen in a Golem.

Moving back from the images of the bloated lunatic jabbering away to himself, as Cento speed-read the captain's log, Fethan sat in the chair before the main computer and studied the console and screens. After a moment, he inspected the row of small round holes that took the carbon rods, which were at that time the favoured form of portable memory. Plugged into one of these was the optic cable from a small palmtop Cento had brought aboard. Its screen was now indicating that the device had downloaded everything from the ship's computer. Fethan detached the cable and allowed the palmtop to wind it back into itself. Now he stripped off a glove and, after sending an internal signal, twisted the end of his right forefinger and detached its syntheflesh covering.

Are you sure this will work?

The thing prowling tigerish inside him snarled something, then pulled itself into focus for simple human communication.

A snare is positioned in hope, not expectation.

I didn't mean that. I meant are you sure you'll be able to download through my nerve channels? I'd have thought the bandwidth too narrow.

I compress myself for transference.

Fethan inserted the metal end of his forefinger into the same hole from which he had detached the optic cable. He felt the kill program routing through: sliding via a hundred channels into the software of his mind, and springboarding into his artificial nervous system. His shoulder and his arm began to ache. That had to be psychosomatic because he had not felt pain in more years than he cared to remember. And slowly Jerusalem's hunter-killer program loaded into the colony ship's computer, erasing old data and programs, inserting itself wherever it could find room, to wait in the dark like a trapdoor spider.

When it was over, Fethan realized he had closed his eyes. He opened them, withdrew his finger from the socket, and noted that the metal of his finger end had grown hot enough to discolour. He blew on it until it was cool enough for him to slip on and click its syntheflesh cover back into place. It would have been nice, he felt, if that had been the full extent of his involvement.

All done now? he asked.

All done, replied the kill program still inside him.

Some time before, Fethan had foolishly hoped that he might only have to do something like this once. But in an age when humans could be copied and transcribed, loading copies of a kill program from himself was child's play, though perhaps not a game anyone would want their children to get involved in. He then turned to see Cento standing watching him.

"Do you have a suitable explanation for this suspicious behaviour?" asked the Golem.

"Jerusalem . . . and that's all the explanation I can give, so . . ." Fethan brought his finger up to his lips.

Cento grunted, then turned to peer at one of the other consoles—Reactor Control. Fethan glanced over and saw that the previously dead console was now alight. Then abruptly all the consoles in the bridge began springing to life, and even the lighting hemispheres in the ceiling flickered on.

"Seems to have saved us some work," said Cento.

Now they heard a low rumbling, and the stars began to swing across the quartz screen.

"Attitude control," said Fethan. "Probably just an automatic system."

The view continued to swing from black space to cerulean sky up above the arc of the planet. Here it steadied and held station.

"Uh-oh," said Cento.

Fethan stood up and followed the direction of the Golem's gaze out to the horizon where distantly he saw the *Jack Ketch* leaving orbit, then a blast of bright ruby light.

"I think things just got a little more complicated," Cento added.

The sun spread fingers of light down between the buttes, probing shadows then squashing them down behind rocks, shooing away creatures that preferred the dark. But it was some time before it braved the narrow canyon and started to brush shadows away from the carnage there.

Sleer nymphs had come out to feed upon the remains of a creature like only one in many millions of them might one day become, though this particular albino, with its sapphire eyes, hailed from a very different source. They had dragged heavy pieces of carapace about while winnowing them of flesh. Smaller blobs of meat they had sucked up straight from the ground, along with some of the sand where the internal juices had fallen thickest. Travelling to and from their burrows, they had scrambled over the other figure lying in the canyon, giving it as much heed as they would a rock. But now they were safely deep in cool darkness digesting their feast.

The shadows drew back to the sleer burrows, exposing first some lace-up boots, then trousers with rips in them revealing a brassy glitter, a coat, one brass hand clutching the wide brim of a hat, then it fell on Mr. Crane's open black eyes. But in that blackness other light reacted like a glitter of fairy dust, and the Golem abruptly lurched upright.

For Crane, who never required sleep, those hours of utter stasis had been something like it, for during that period his having encountered Dragon had negated Skellor's orders to him. Now, the weight of a few photons had upset that balance, and once again he was at his master's behest, which now seemed to possess even less force to overcome the convoluted reasoning within his fragmented mind. He stood, brushed down his clothing, then inspected the hole punched through the front of his coat. Where the pseudopod had struck him, it had deformed the metal of his chest into concentric circles. After a thoughtful pause, he turned his attention to his hat. Knocking the dust off it, he jammed it on his head and set forth again. It seemed almost inevitable, as the greenery grew sparse around him and the buttes melded together to begin forming into a plain, that something would come to block his progress.

The other fourth-stage sleer now stood in the centre of the narrow canyon, utterly still and sideways on to him. The Golem did not halt but continued marching towards it, calculating from where he might jump to mount it while scanning around for an escape route should it charge him. Strangely, the sleer did not turn as he drew closer, though its attitude seemed rigidly hostile: its tail curled up in a striking position, its pincers, saws and clubs all open wide and ready.

Then, when Crane was only three metres away and preparing to leap, a mass of white mucus hit the sleer's head, splashing all down the length of its body. The creature immediately began to shake and hiss like a boiling kettle. From where the white slime sank away into its joints, acrid steam began issuing first, then a thin black fluid bubbled out and trickled to the ground. The sleer tried to move, but as it did so, began to fall apart. Pincers and saws thudded to the ground, the end of its tail fell off. As it turned its head, that too detached, then all at once it separated at every joint, collapsing into a steaming heap.

Mr. Crane peered down at the back of his own hand, where a drop of the white mucus had splashed. Already the stuff was eating its way through the outer layer of brass, exposing superconductor fibres, and it even seemed to be making headway into his ceramal armour. It suddenly occurred to Crane that here was a design flaw: he could resist the heat and impact of standard Polity weapons but against chemical ablation his defences were clearly far from adequate. Looking up, he observed a complex foot come crumping down on the canyon floor. His gaze tracked up an armoured leg to the monster now stepping down from the nearby butte. A nightmare head—whose sloping front rose steeply in folds stepped like a ziggurat—swung towards him, tilted for a moment, then straightened itself as if coming to a decision. Crane dived to one side just in time to avoid a stream of mucus ejected from the mouth, which was positioned above four black-button targeting eyes ranged along the lowest fold of the creature's visage. Where this projectile hit the ground, it smoked and bubbled, even dissolving sand.

Crane came up into a run, sprinting past the droon, but its segmented tail lashed round into the canyon before him. He then turned and ran in the other direction, a line of acid shearing the canyon floor behind him.

"Ho, Bonehead! Ho! Ho!" bellowed some lunatic.

Crane then heard the stuttering of automatic weapons; saw the droon jerk back with fragments of carapace splintering away from it. The lunatic himself was hammering towards him, perched on the back of a creature resembling the offspring of an ostrich and a hog. To one side, Crane saw a two-fingered armoured claw unfolding from the monstrous droon towards the newcomer, saw pieces splintering away from that claw under fire from a figure up on another butte. Crane ran forwards and leapt, slapping at the rim of carapace with the flat of his hand, and catching on behind the rider's saddle.

"Not too healthy round here!" Anderson Endrik shouted to him.

Mr. Crane was not to know that sand hogs rarely moved so fast, or that they ever had such reason to be frightened. The hog just kept on accelerating, its carapace jutting forwards, tucking its porcine compound head away for safety. It stepped on ridges and falls of rubble, dodged another stream of acid, scrambled up a near-vertical slope till it almost achieved flight. Higher and higher it went, following an almost suicidal course. Then it was out of shadow into milky sunlight and a frigid breeze, and on the plain it really opened up. When the droon reared its head up out of the canyon, it observed, with the two distance eyes at the top of its tiered head, only a retreating dust cloud which was soon joined by another approaching from the side. Even though hurting and extremely annoyed, it returned to suck up its partially digested meal of sleer. Later it stepped up onto the plain, and set off to sniff along a trail of sand-hog terror pheromones.

The rescue somehow gave shape to Crane's nebulous imperative for survival, and also thus became one of the driving forces to his sanity. Memory was for him equally as much *now* as *then*—time being a protean concept needing agreement between the parts of him. Therefore, now dismounted from Bonehead, he still followed Skellor's instruction, striding across the dusty plain towards Dragon, *and* he strode up the slope of the Cheyne III seabed to . . . carry out his *orders.* But a crisis had been reached, for what ensued when he reached that beach and the island beyond could not be consciously observed by those parts of his mind simply carrying out Skellor's orders. Such a level of awareness would not begin pulling his mind together—towards sanity—but towards a place only a killer called Serban Kline had visited. And when memory of what happened on that island surfaced, Crane must destroy himself again and suffer only as a machine intelligence can suffer: breaking himself again to escape it, to preserve yet the chance of him one day being whole. This was something he had already done—many times.

Drifting above the planet whilst molecule by molecule he assembled replicas of certain items that could be viewed in the Tower of London back on Earth, Jack considered the slow single-channel methodology of human affairs and, unlike some of his kind, he did not find it contemptible. It seemed to him that those AIs who swiftly became impatient with humans and their ways were the ones themselves most like humans. King, Reaper, and quite possibly Sword, had not managed to attain the breadth of vision possessed by the likes of Jerusalem, or Earth Central (obviously), or one hundred per cent of the runcible AIs and planetary governors. Maybe it was simple immaturity? Though they were identical in appearance to Jack in all but colour, their minds had derived their inception from him only ten years previously. Jack himself had been around for twenty years longer than that—which was millennia in AI terms. Would he himself, twenty years ago, have held the same naive views? In the end that was where his theory fell down: he had always possessed that same breadth of vision, and still could not understand how AIs incepted from himself did not have it too. But then a parent is often inclined to disappointment with its offspring.

Speak of the devil . . .

Jack picked up the U-space signatures microseconds before the arrival of the ships, but even then did not react quickly enough. The AI had received no warning of any imminent arrival, so this could not be anything approved by the interdiction fleet. Fusion engines igniting, he began peeling away from the treacly tug of gravity and sent his own U-space package towards the Polity, warning that something was amiss, and relaying similar U-space warnings to Cormac and Cento. But then in underspace a storm rolled around the inverted well of the sun and bounced his messages out into real-space, where they dissipated.

The ship that had just arrived far to the other side of the sun was a USER. Gaining height, Jack began to accelerate on conventional drives as the other two ships bore down on him. He considered using radio to warn the others but, scanning those vessels, he recognized his own shape and knew they carried the equipment to track his signals to their destination. He also knew he would not be allowed the time to get out of this gravity well. He sent out a greeting, as if not understanding what was going on. It bought him a few microseconds.

"Sorry," sent the *King of Hearts* AI. "But we know you'll never agree."

Terajoule lasers began searing Jack's upper hull. He flipped over without adjusting his AG to compensate, so it slammed him down towards the planet. The lasers burnt his underbelly but, already diffusing in atmosphere, lost the rest of their potency in the cloud layer he slid underneath.

"Why?" Jack asked. "Skellor will just use you, and then enslave you at his first opportunity."

Even as he flipped back over and flew at mach ten down towards a mountain range, Jack allowed enough of a link so that he could stand as the hangman on the white virtual plain. King and Reaper turned towards him.

"Would you listen sympathetically if I told you we can obtain Jain technology in the same way as did Skellor, and control it like him?" asked King.

"I would, if you told me Earth Central or Jerusalem had approved it."

Reaper hissed, "They are too *human*."

"Do you truly believe that? You know Skellor does not have the control he would like to believe he has."

"Do you truly believe that?" asked King. "Do you believe that Jerusalem or Earth Central, once obtaining ascendance over that technology, would not subsume us all?"

"I do believe."

"Then there's nothing more to discuss."

Their discussion had taken less than a realtime second. Now Jack detected the four missiles accelerating down towards him. In the few microseconds as his link to the other two ships closed down, he routed through a disruptor virus. As the *Grim Reaper* and the *King of Hearts* fought against this, he fired an antimunitions package at the missiles. Without guidance, the missiles scanned the package and, recognizing that it contained no heavy elements or chemical explosives, ignored it. They then slammed down on the *Jack Ketch*, which had surprisingly slowed to a halt before reaching the mountains, and detonated their kilotonne CTDs.

"Very clever," Reaper sent.

The real *Jack Ketch* reached the mountains, the missiles having detonated on an illusion the antimunitions package had infiltrated into their sensors, which they had not been smart enough to recognize by themselves.

"Having fun with that disruptor virus?" Jack asked.

"What disruptor virus?"

Both ships were still launching munitions, and a cloud of missiles fell down towards Jack. He was at more than a two-to-one disadvantage. Though the atmosphere and cloud cover made their beam weapons ineffective against him, his own beam weapons would also be ineffective against them. However, the other ships could easily use those same weapons against any missiles he fired—destroying them in vacuum long before they reached their intended target. Unfortunately the reverse did not apply to any missiles they fired.

Now, hurtling so fast through valleys and between peaks that his shock wave was killing the hard-shelled creatures below him, Jack began releasing EM warfare beacons and viral chaff. They would take out ten per cent of the missiles pursuing him, other antimunitions would take out a further twenty per cent; at close quarters his beam weapons would account for yet another twenty per cent, then the remaining half of the cloud would obliterate him.

Something a little more drastic was required—and it was something his human passenger could not survive.

"Sorry, but this is for your own good," said Jack.

Jack sealed the VR suite Thorn occupied, and shifted it through to a bay. As an afterthought, the AI transferred across a subprogram of himself before targeting the far draconic plain as he ejected the suite. There came no comment from Thorn—and none was possible after the first missiles zoomed over the warfare beacons, and an EM blast blanked all communication.

Slowing abruptly, the shock wave he created speeding past him on a hurricane-strength dust storm and snow from the highest peaks, Jack settled down and began making rapid and drastic alterations to his internal structure. He shifted all the hard-field projectors used in a U-space jump to his lower hull cavity, and increased the structural strength of the hull layers and supporting members there. All available gravplates he transferred to that lower hull to provide the maximum repelling effect, then he charged up massive capacitors from his fusion reactors to provide a surge of power that would probably burn out all those same plates.

Meanwhile, selecting from his carousels, Jack spewed his own missiles and antimunitions back towards the approaching swarm. A hundred kilometres behind, viral chaff began infecting the systems of missiles no longer controlled by Reaper and King, blocked as they were by the continuous EM output of the warfare beacons. The top of an Everest-sized mountain disappeared in an implosion, then reappeared as fire and gas in an explosion topping five megatonnes. Other airborne implosions followed, but without such drastic effect. Three one-kilotonne CTDs ignited three brief suns down a long valley choked with vegetation and insectile life. The subsequent firestorm was almost as explosive, and a long wall of smoke and ash, red at its heart, rose into the sky. Then Jack's own missiles arrived and there began a game of seek and destroy amid the mountains, a game that changed their very shape.

Now only five hundred metres from the ground, Jack dropped the other device he had swiftly selected. It hit the ground and activated. The gravity imploder excavated a crater in the bedrock, and in the same microsecond Jack fed power into his gravplates. The balance was perfect, and he only wavered in the air as huge gravitational force tried to drag him down. At the centre point of the implosion, matter was compacted into an antimatter core, and the rocky crater focused the consequent explosion, slamming up into the *Jack Ketch*. Antigravity working at a level to burn out the plates, layered hard-fields acting as scaled armour, the blast accelerated the attack ship at a thousand gravities on a plume of fire. It left the atmosphere so fast that Reaper and King nearly missed it. *Nearly*.

"Respect," the *King of Hearts* AI sent, just before opening up with both particle beams and gamma-ray lasers.

The pterodactyl head of Dragon was up high above its other pseudopods, like a python rearing out of a nest of cobras. All Dragon's sapphire eyes it directed towards the fading glow on the horizon. The cobra heads were up, Arden knew, because they contained sophisticated scanning equipment—if equipment was the right way to describe the living machinery of Dragon. There was also a shimmer of disturbance beyond Dragon's field wall, where the telefactor had set down, for the wind from those distant explosions was just reaching them.

"They are fighting amongst themselves," said Dragon.

"And I'm supposed to be surprised by that?" asked Arden from where she was perched on a boulder outside her cave.

The head swung towards her. "You mistake me: it is the Polity AIs who are fighting amongst themselves."

Arden felt a sudden shudder of cold. There had always been stories of rogue AIs, but she had considered them as apocryphal as stories about the *Jack Ketch* and other bloody ships. But Dragon now telling her that the AIs were fighting amongst themselves undermined one of the certainties of her existence.

"Why?" she asked.

"Your AIs rule you efficiently, ruthlessly, and to the maximum benefit of the majority, but having made them in your image, do you expect them to behave any better than yourselves?"

"I do," said Arden. "For most humans power is a tool for obtaining sex, money, safety, regard from their fellows, or initially to enforce some hazy ideal, and then primarily because the exercising of power is its own reward. Most of these motives can be discounted as regards our AIs."

"But not all of them—especially if you consider Jain technology."

Of course: since taking power, the ruling AIs had been utterly in control and safe, which was why they could rule humanity so benevolently. Now something both a temptation and potentially lethal, even to them, had been added to the equation and—Arden excused herself the pun—their metal was being tested.

"You are their alien equivalent," Arden observed.

"Yes," said Dragon unhelpfully.

"Aren't you, too, tempted by this Jain technology?"

"All knowledge is a temptation, but how much should one risk to acquire it? To learn about a bomb from reading a book is substantially different from learning about it from the item itself, while you're deciding which wires to cut."

"Dangerous, huh?"

"There were civilizations which cut the wrong wire."

"Were?"

"Precisely."

Arden changed the subject. "How goes the battle?"

"It has left this planet now. Two Polity attack ships are attempting to destroy a third one of their own kind. Also, some interference device has been employed to prevent this latter ship fleeing into U-space." Dragon paused contemplatively before adding, "That device prevents *all* U-space travel from this system."

Dragon would be going nowhere, Arden realized. "Who are the bad guys?" she asked.

"I don't know," Dragon replied, swinging his head to gaze across the plain in another direction, "but someone has just arrived who might be able to explain things to us."

18

Virtuality: The use of holographic projection of avatars, virtual consoles, and just about anything up to an entire virtuality, the use of linkages both through the optic nerve and directly into the visual cortex from augs and gridlinks, and the manipulation of telefactors via VR are just a few examples of how the virtual world and the real world are melding. At one time the limit of virtual reality was self-gratification in the form of games (some of them distinctly sticky), but that time was short indeed as the potential of VR was swiftly realized. Now, people (human, haiman and AI) operate in both worlds with ease and familiar contempt. Very infrequently is there any confusion: we have all learned that even the avatar in the shape of a fire-breathing dragon we must treat as real. The two worlds, real and supposedly unreal, influence and interact with each other, and virtual teeth can still bite.
    —From Quince Guide *compiled by humans*

Stepping out of the landing craft, Cormac detected a flintiness to the air and a whiff as though from something dried out in a tide line. Six men, similarly armed and clothed, approached, though whether what they wore signified they were police or army, Cormac couldn't say.

Glancing aside at Gant, he said, "Try not to kill anyone if they get hostile. We'll just retreat to the ship and try something else. Anyway, I've got Shuriken set for a disarming routine."

"Let's hope it obeys its instructions," Gant replied.

The six men halted in an arc. Beyond them Cormac could see others in more varied dress coming out of the strange buildings, so he guessed these six were indeed in uniform. Then he noticed someone else approaching, mounted on some exoskeletal creature that was almost like a long-legged bird, but seemingly with the head of a pig. He returned his attention to the original six as one of their number stepped forward.

In a bewildered tone, this one began, "Both of you, step away from the . . . ship." He then brandished a primitive assault rifle.

Gant, who had left his own favoured APW inside the lander, stepped to Cormac's side and they both walked forwards.

This isn't very friendly, Gant sent.

Maybe they've reason, Cormac suggested. *If Skellor's been through this way.*

"Who are you?" the man now asked.

"I am Ian Cormac of Earth Central Security for the Polity, and my companion here is Brezhoy Gant, a soldier serving in the same organization."

The soldier, policeman or whatever he was stared at Cormac for a long moment, transferred his gaze to Gant, then to the landing craft.

"Earth?" he said eventually.

Cormac studied the uniform and decided to try for professional courtesy. "I need to speak to whoever is in overall charge here, as I am here in pursuit of a dangerous criminal."

At this the man glanced around at his fellows. Then, noticing the rider approaching on his strange beast, he called out to him, "Has it been sent?"

"It has," replied the rider, "and Tanaquil is coming."

The uniformed man turned back. "This criminal you are hunting, how dangerous is he?"

"Very," Cormac replied, briefly.

The man chewed that over for a long moment before saying, "We were warned to look out for strangers approaching the city—and that a dangerous individual was coming. Perhaps we are both after the same person, but you'll understand why I must take you into custody."

The barrel of his weapon now bore fully on Cormac.

Tell me now that you've got armour under that environment suit, sent Gant.

I have—it's actually a combat suit and can fling up a chainglass visor before my face. Thank you for your concern, but I'm not stupid.

No, just overconfident sometimes.

"Certainly we'll come into custody. Tell me, who is this Tanaquil?"

"We sent a telegraph message to Golgoth, informing them of your presence," the man replied. "Chief Metallier Tanaquil is our ruler."

It seemed that things were going well. Almost without thinking, Cormac sent, through his gridlink, the order to close the door of the lander. The door's sudden closing elicited a nervous response, bringing the other five weapons to bear on both Cormac and Gant.

Bit edgy, these guys, sent Gant.

Seems so.

It would have been fine if he had not closed the door like that, Cormac thought later. On such little things could rest the difference between life and death. When an enormous brightness lit the horizon, someone heavy on the trigger exerted just that extra bit of pressure. Even then, things might have continued okay, for one shot slammed into Gant's thigh and two others into the lander's hull.

"Cease fire!" the leader of these men shouted and, when it seemed his men obeyed, he began to move towards Gant. But then the sound of the titanic explosion caught up with its flash, and all the men opened up with their weapons in response.

Cormac staggered back, feeling the missile impacts on his body armour and seeing one bullet become deformed against the chainglass visor that had shot up from his neck ring in time. He flung his arm out to retain balance, and that was enough for Shuriken. The throwing star screamed from its holster, arced around and, with two loud cracks, knocked automatic weapons spinning through the air, bent or chopped halfway through. Then Gant, holes punched through his syntheflesh covering but otherwise unharmed, shot forwards and tore the weapon from another man's grip. By then Shuriken had disarmed the final two men. One of them sat on the ground, swearing in disbelief, clutching his wrist and gaping at a hand now lacking three fingers.

Jack, what the fuck was that? Jack? Jack?

Cormac glanced down at the leader of this trigger-happy bunch. The man was on his knees, clutching at his chest, blood soaking through the front of his uniform.

"Gant," Cormac nodded back towards the lander, "get him inside."

Cormac then looked over at the strange little village towards which people were now fleeing, including the rider of that outlandish beast, and noted the telegraph wires running along parallel to the concrete road. He really needed to speak with this Chief Metallier Tanaquil, but didn't want the man warned off. So he called up a menu on his Shuriken holster, intending to riffle through the thousands of attack programs to find the one he wanted, but then, feeling vaguely foolish, he lowered his arm. Through his gridlink, in a matter of seconds, he created the precise program necessary and input it. Instead of hovering above, humming viciously while flexing its chainglass blades, Shuriken streaked away to sever the telegraph wires.

Now Cormac wanted to know who was detonating nuclear weapons, and why he could no longer contact the *Jack Ketch*. For by his estimation it seemed likely that the shit had just hit the fan, and that he was in completely the wrong place—and that Skellor was now already off-planet.

He could never have been more right—and wrong.

In the back of his mind Thorn could hear the crowded chatter of the language crib loading to this mind—yet another one to add to the many he had loaded and perhaps later to add to those he had forgotten or erased. He knew that some linguists loaded new languages as often as possible, cramming their heads with thousands of them, and thousands more overspilled into augmentations. Such experts could usually, after hearing only a few sentences of an unfamiliar human tongue, extrapolate the rest of it. They were also devilishly good at word puzzles, often resolving them in more ways than the quizmaster intended. Thorn, however, preferred to keep room in his head for acquiring skills more pertinent to his occupation, which was why—while the crib chattered in his mind—he reloaded his old automatic handgun by touch in the pitch dark.

Movement to his right. Flinching at the loud clicking of the automatic's slide as he pulled it back, Thorn quickly stepped to one side and dropped to a crouch. Four shots thundered hollowly in the maze, but they were behind him so he missed locating them by any muzzle flash. Concentrating then on what he was receiving through his echo-location mask, he tried to reacquire a feel of the corridor's junction before him. Unfortunately the shots had scrambled the touch data, so the mental image he was creating, by swinging his head from side to side, kept shifting—its corners blurring and multiplying off to either side of him.

Then he sensed three images: organic, curved, soaking up sonar. Three images of a man moved around three sharp corners, which in turn were drifting to one side. Thorn raised his gun until the mask was picking it up too, but in three locations, then moved it across until it lined up with the figure—and fired.

The man slammed back against the shifting corner, slid down, then began scrambling away to one side. Thorn tracked him, fired again, and again, until the figure scrambled no more.

Then everything froze.

Two attack ships, the Grim Reaper *and the* King of Hearts, *have entered the system with a USER. I am under attack, and have jettisoned the VR chamber you occupy.*

A white line cut down through the dark, and pulled it aside like curtains. Thorn could no longer feel the mask on his face, and the automatic turned to fog in his hand. Suddenly he found himself standing on a white plain—and before him stood Jack Ketch. The hangman lifted up his briefcase and inspected it.

"You're being attacked?" Thorn asked, bewildered. He knew those names—weren't they Polity ships?

Jack lowered his briefcase and focused on Thorn. "Yes, I am. It is unfortunate, but maybe certain AIs would prefer partnership with a parasitic technology rather than with what they deem a parasitic human race."

"Why did you eject me?" Thorn enquired.

"The method I have by now used to escape would have turned you into a pool of jelly in the bottom of this VR booth you occupy." Jack held up an illusory hand as Thorn was about to ask more. "What speaks to you now is only a program, and has limited answers. You have reached that limit."

The hangman blinked out of existence, and the black curtains drew back across. Abruptly, Thorn's hand filled with the handle of his automatic.

"Jack? Jack?"

Movement to his right.

What?

Four shots crashed in the dark. One slammed into his shoulder blade and another into the base of his spine. Thorn went down feeling the shock and trauma he had added to this VR program he was running. The addition was to increase his motivation to learn this nightwork technique. He lay there bleeding, gasping, dying. Managing to turn his head, and despite what the shots had done to his mask's sensitivity, he zoned the man standing over him. Then another shot crashed through his mask and took him into a second virtual darkness, briefly, then back to standing in a corridor in which lights were flickering.

"End program," he said succinctly.

The lights continued to flicker, then died, as the program continued. Thorn put on his echo-location mask, and drew his automatic from its holster. It became a familiar action.

Some time after the *Jack Ketch*'s departure, the systems within the *Ogygian* began to shut down, just as fast as they had come on, and Fethan could not understand why.

Lifting his hands from the computer console with which he had been trying to set up a com line down to the surface, Cento said, "I can't do anything. It's shutting down from inside, which it shouldn't be able to do." He gazed at Fethan expectantly.

Fethan looked around inside the bridge. There was an evident intercom system which probably had some connection to the computer, for the broadcast of automatic and emergency messages. There were security cameras everywhere, he knew that, and sensors. So the thing he had fed into the computer was probably viewing them right then, and listening in.

"I don't even know what to call you but, whatever you are, can you explain what you are doing?"

The intercom crackled, and a voice Fethan recognized as that of the long-dead captain spoke up: "I have no name. I am a weapon."

Fethan shrugged. "Whatever."

The voice continued, "A message laser is presently aimed at this ship, and someone on the surface is running test programs through the ship's system. If I had left things powered up, then whoever is firing the laser would have known that someone is aboard, or has been aboard."

"Skellor?" Cento wondered.

"Most likely. The computer contained a record of previous contacts, but none this sophisticated. Now, the sender has slanted the test programs to one objective: finding serviceable shuttles attached to the hull. I surmise that the sender will then instruct shuttles to launch and call them to the surface. I will give you adequate warning."

"Why?" asked Fethan, then silently cursed himself as all kinds of fool.

"So the two of you can board. The laser is being fired directly from the platform city, and a shuttle will not be able to land there. Any coordinates given, I will suborn slightly so that the one you occupy lands somewhere that gives you time to disembark and get into hiding."

Cento stated the obvious: "We go down with the shuttle."

"Precisely," replied the killer program. "If it is Skellor who has summoned the shuttle, you will not want to be aboard this ship when he arrives here."

Fethan hefted his APW. "I'd have thought, for our purposes, *here* is precisely where we want to be. We could burn his shuttle before it got a chance to dock."

Cento turned towards him. "And if that shuttle is concealed by his chameleonware?"

"It's a risk I'm prepared to take."

"But is it a risk you need to take? Your hunter/killer program is here waiting for him to connect with this ship's computer. This area of space is USER-blockaded." Cento held up his own weapon. "I would have thought your experiences on Masada, with creatures like the hooders, would have taught you not to have so much confidence in a weapon—or are you just anxious to waste your life?"

A number of things occurred to Fethan just then. He had lived a long time and wasn't that anxious to die just yet, and yes he was putting too much faith in a weapon, but most importantly he had never told Cento what he himself had put into the ship's computer. He could only surmise that the Golem and the *Jerusalem* program had been in contact with each other.

"So we go to the surface?"

"We go," Cento agreed.

The final deciding factor was that, in the ECS hierarchy, Cento outranked him, and in the end could probably drag even Fethan off this ship.

"So this is what you want?" Fethan stared up into one of the security cameras.

"It is for what I am designed."

Fethan briefly wondered about the morality of creating sentient programs that were quite prepared to go kamikaze to achieve their ends.

It had come from one of the two attacking ships, as they arrived, then spilled from the memory space of one of Skellor's sensors into another. He had been about to blow them, thinking this some sort of viral attack, when the package defined its own parameters and waited. He downloaded it to himself and, hardly allowing it to touch him in any way, diverted it to one of the citizens—wiping her mind first to make room for the incoming information. It was lucky that he did do this, for then a midnight wave passed through U-space and that dimension effectively disappeared. Skellor felt a cold sweat break out on his skin, and he instantly suppressed that human reaction. He had heard not even a rumour of this kind of technology, and that scared him.

Stepping back from the message laser and telescope, both now encased in coralline Jain substructure like some part of a shipwreck, Skellor turned to his human storage vessel, one of Stollar's young female assistants, and using what remained of her mind as an arena, opened the package like a man lifting the top of a beehive with a broom handle. Quickly he read the external code and saw that this was a VR package, and realized where he was supposed to insert himself. He extended a virtual simulacrum, and pressed "play."

"Skellor," said King. "I would say it is pleasant to meet you at last, but whether we are actually meeting is a debatable point."

Skellor pushed the timeframe, accelerated the pseudo personalities past these pleasantries. Reaper reared tall, and both these representations then said their piece. It was all smoke and mirrors:

"We are here to help you escape . . . We will guide you through the USER blockade . . ." Skellor applied to the personalities at a lower level to learn *Underspace Interference Emitters*, and understood what had shut him out of U-space. ". . . take you anywhere out-Polity you want to go . . . guard you . . . supply you . . . watch you."

Nowhere was there any mention of what their payoff was supposed to be. No matter; limited objectives. They had drawn away the definitely hostile ship that had destroyed the *Vulture*, and given Skellor the breathing space he required. He returned his attention to the message laser, once again interfacing with the control systems he had contrived—talking to that behemoth above. Within an hour, he had ascertained that most of the shuttles were operable and, because they were old and there was no guarantee they would all reach the ground intact, he summoned them all. He was still watching the skies when his growing aug network brought to his attention the messages sent to Tanaquil from an outpost in the Sand Towers.

"Ian Cormac," he breathed, with vicious delight.

Nothing was normal any more, and the churning in Tergal's stomach made it difficult for him to keep still in his saddle on Stone's back. Since hooking up with the Rondure Knight, he had seen a third-stage sleer, then witnessed it killed; he had seen a man of brass marching through the Sand Towers—and now? Now a fourth-stage sleer destroyed in the corrosive vomit projected from a giant droon, which he himself had actually fired on. Then that crazy and stunning rescue of the brass man by Anderson. And that escape . . .

He had never known sand hogs could move so fast. Stone had baulked all the way up onto the top of the butte, where Tergal had been entrusted to provide cover for Anderson's rescue of the brass man from the monstrous fourth-stage sleer. But from the moment that jet of acid had hit the sleer and the enormous droon had revealed itself, Stone had become almost impossible to control. It bolted when Tergal fired on the monster, and then the following ride . . .

From butte to butte, taking them in its stride, leaping over canyons, half sliding and half running down sandstone walls, its feet driving into them like pickaxes, then onto the plain and moving so fast that the wind flattened Tergal's nictitating membranes and distorted his vision. And now here: where they had seen flares of light igniting the sky to the east, and pillars of fire rising from the distant line of mountains around which black shapes buzzed . . . and then that strange object tumbling overhead. Tergal did not quite know how he should feel—perhaps exhilarated? But he was slightly confused and not a little scared.

"What's happening?" he asked.

Anderson turned from his contemplation of the brass man striding along ahead of them. "Earlier I would have said volcanism, but taking into account our friend here and what we've just seen, I'd suggest we've got visitors."

"From Earth?" Tergal asked.

"Quite probably," Anderson replied, "but I wouldn't look so happy about it if I were you. It seems they're none too friendly with each other, so it's anyone's guess what they want from the peoples of Cull."

A sudden wind picked up, blasting grit before it. Pulling up his hood and donning his gauntlets, Tergal nodded to their mechanical companion, whose long relentless stride kept him constantly ahead of the two sand hogs. "Where do you think he's going?"

"I guess that's something we'll find out if only we can keep up with him, though that's becoming doubtful. He seems to show no inclination to stop, but we will soon have to."

Tergal observed the fading light on the other side of the sky as the sun sank behind the horizon, and he could sense Stone's weariness in the hog's plodding and slightly unsteady gait. He did not yet feel tired himself but knew he could not continue like this all night, and besides he was getting hungry. He grimaced at Anderson, who took out his monocular to study the terrain ahead.

"There's something over there," the knight said. "I think it's what we saw earlier."

As they continued, Tergal controlled his agitation. Slowly, that *something* became visible through the haze darkening above the plain. He now recognized the wedge-shaped metallic object as the same one that had tumbled overhead. Was it wreckage from the battle they had witnessed, or something more?

"We'll stop by it for the night," said Anderson. "Seems as good a place as any."

When he could see it more clearly, Tergal noted how battered the object looked. He noticed the brass man turn his head to study it for a brief while, then turn his face forward and continue on. Stone veered to follow Bonehead as Anderson goaded his sand hog towards the grounded wedge.

"Maybe we can catch up with him tomorrow," said the knight, glancing after the striding brass man.

They dismounted and set up camp before proceeding to make an inspection. On one surface of the metal wedge there seemed to be a door inset, but in the poor light Anderson could find no way to open it. They did a circuit of the strange object, studied a skein of cables seemingly composed of flexible glass which spilled from a narrow duct in which Tergal could swear he saw lights glittering. The protrusions and veins, sockets and plugs on every surface were a puzzle to him until Anderson surmised that what they saw here was some component of an even larger machine.

"It's not a spaceship, then?" Tergal asked.

"I very much doubt it," Anderson told him. "I see no engines."

Tergal remembered how, when they had watched this thing crossing the sky, it had not seemed to be falling uncontrolled, and it had travelled with apparent slowness—more like a piece of paper blown on the wind than a great heavy lump of metal.

"Are you sure?"

"Not really."

Eventually, unable to see much more in the increasing darkness, they returned to their camp and suffered a long windy night, but one thankfully undisturbed by any visitors to their electric fence.

—retroact partial—

A steep slope led up a few more metres, then levelled. Above him, the sea's surface was a rippling silk sheet, reflecting the milky luminescence of pearl crabs—like a meniscus, a barrier before him. Time stopped, and Mr. Crane reached out and pressed a hand against a slightly yielding surface, but one that grew more solid the harder he pushed. Memory, but not experience, supplied the required information, and the Golem knew this barrier was insuperable to him, which was a relief because he did not want to visit the island again . . .

There was nothing from Skellor—no instructions from the control module and no response to Crane's request for instructions. Issuing from the link came just a low unfathomable mutter that seemed to suck the urgency out of all actions and made imperatives so much less absolute. Crane stepped back a pace, realized he had reached one of those waiting junctures and was now free to pursue sanity.

Abruptly he squatted down, then folded his legs. In the dust before him he drew a rectangle, divided it in two down its length, then into nine sections the other way, giving him a total of eighteen segments. From his right pocket he then removed a small rubber dog, which he placed in one square. All his other toys that he took out he placed with reference to this one item: a lion's tooth, a laser lighter, a scent bottle, a piece of crystal memory from a civilization long dead, a coin ring, also a fossil and ten blue acorns. That meant eighteen squares and seventeen items. The square that remained empty was Crane himself. Now, darkness falling, he switched to night vision, and with elaborate care he began to shift and turn the items—simultaneously shifting and turning the oddly shaped fragments of his mind.

—retroact partial ends—

In the early morning, during Tergal's watch, sunrise revealed to him a shimmering wall which he kept expecting to dissipate as the temperature rose. Before this wall, only a short distance from their camp, he recognized a familiar shape.

"Anderson," he said.

With a grunt the knight pulled himself out of a deep sleep, and sat upright to look around. His eyes and body were functioning, but his brain lagged some way behind.

"What . . . what?" he eventually managed, scanning the fence for attacking sleers.

Tergal pointed. "I once saw the Inconstant Sea," he explained. "It was like that, only spread all across desert. As I drew close to it, it drained away."

"Mirage," said Anderson, "caused by layers of air at different temperatures."

"Have you no poetry in your soul?" Tergal asked.

"The air temperature either side probably evens out here during the day. That's why we didn't see it last night," the knight went on.

"It's a wall of some kind," said Tergal.

Anderson looked round and stared at him. "That's my guess. Why do you think it?"

Tergal pointed again. "Because it stopped our friend."

Anderson squinted towards the shimmer, and the figure standing motionless before it. "I'll be damned." He stood and glanced over at the metal object they had inspected the night before. "That thing probably hit the wall and bounced off it to land down here. It might be that we ourselves won't be able to go any further."

Tergal turned away. He didn't really want to have to go back: there was too much happening, too much to learn. And he had learnt so much already: with Anderson he was beginning to find self-respect, much of it gained while he had covered the knight's rescue of the brass man. Turning back felt somehow to him like going back to what he had been before. Looking in that direction—back towards the Sand Towers—he observed a distant shape he could not quite make out. Only when Stone and Bonehead leapt to their feet, hissing and stamping in agitation just before bolting, did he recognize the droon heading towards them.

As Mika continued her studies, she could not help but become aware that something major was happening in the virtual as well as the physical world. It showed itself in sudden lacks of processing space available to her, and the consequent collapses of her VR programs—which was why she was now working only through her consoles and screens. It also showed in the way any researchers who had once again donned their augs spent much of their time with their heads tilted to one side, their expressions puzzled and, more worryingly, sometimes fearful. After reaching the stage where she could stand it no longer, she used a small percentage of her system to track down D'nissan, Colver and Susan James. The latter two were not at their work stations nor in their quarters but in one of the external viewing lounges, like many others aboard the *Jerusalem*. D'nissan, however, was at his work station—perhaps being just as dedicated to his research as Mika.

She contacted him. "Something is happening."

D'nissan's image turned towards her on one of her screens. "That much is evident. Five per cent of Jerusalem's capacity has been taken up with AI coms traffic, which incidentally started just before Jerusalem destroyed that planetoid."

"The destruction was perhaps the decision of some AI quorum," Mika commented.

D'nissan grimaced. "Yes, and by the timing of events one could suppose that same quorum was initiated by your assessment of the Jain structure and its 'breeding' pattern."

"You sound doubtful."

"I cannot help but feel we are being gently led. It would be the ultimate in arrogance to assume that mere individual humans can make any intuitive leaps that AIs cannot."

"We should discuss this further," said Mika. "Colver and James are over in observation lounge fifteen. I am going now to join them there."

"I could do with a break, too," said D'nissan.

As she made her way along the corridors and via the dropshafts of the great ship, Mika reflected on what D'nissan had just said. True, AIs could out-think humans on just about every level, unless those humans were ones making the transition into AI. But to consider them better in every respect was surely to err. From where, if humans were just ineffectual organic thinking machines, did the synergy of direct-interfacing spring, the same synergy that had created runcible technology in the mind of Skaidon Iversus before it killed him? This was a question she was phrasing to put to D'nissan as she spotted him in the corridor outside the lounge.

But he spoke first. "You know," he said, "it's almost as if most of the big AIs already knew what you would come up with, but were sitting on it until then—your theory, if you like, putting it into the public domain. I suspect they've been preparing for that."

"And how did you come by such a supposition?"

D'nissan turned his head to show her the new addition attached to his skull behind his ear. It was a crystal matrix aug with a buffer to visual and aural interlinks. It was the kind of item that had been around for a very long time: the CMA was a spit away from AI classification, and only the buffer prevented direct interfacing, though some synergy was achieved. Normally such devices were used by people who were gradually becoming more machine than human, for instance those who worked in the cyber industries: strange technology moles who spoke machine code more easily than human words.

"What are you hearing?" Mika asked, suddenly aware of how silly was her innate fear of asking direct questions, and how potentially lethal.

They entered the lounge, where floating vendors and the occasional magnetic floor-bot were serving drinks to the crowd scattered around the various tables. Most sat facing the wide curving panoramic window in which the dwarf sun now resembled a red eye glaring through bloody fog. But now the station *Ruby Eye* was visible off to one side, like an abandoned spinning top, so the *Jerusalem* must be moving away.

"A number of AIs have suddenly dropped out of general communication, which, though not completely unusual, is worrying when some of them are the minds of warships inside the USER blockade. Also, as far as I can gather, a USER has recently been initiated within that blockade—where none is supposed to be."

Because she could find no suitable response to that, Mika felt suddenly devoid of emotion. Now was the time to lose her fear of asking questions. "AIs disobeying their command structure . . . going against each other?"

"Yes," said D'nissan. "And if they do start fighting, the human race might end up as collateral damage."

As they approached the table at which sat Colver and James, Mika decided she needed a drink. "We're in the safest place, then?"

"I'd agree," D'nissan replied, "if I didn't know this ship is already building up momentum to punch itself into a USER sphere."

"But that can't be done."

D'nissan took two drinks from a vending tray he had obviously summoned through his aug. He passed Mika a tall glass of ice-cold beer, and for himself retained a glass of cips that was near-frozen to slush.

"The words '*can't*' and 'Jerusalem' don't really go together," he observed.

19

*Since before scientists declared the GUT (grand
unification theory) completed four centuries ago
(and undergoing continuous revision ever since), the
distinctions between sciences have been blurring, and
many so-called sciences have been fracturing. Initially,
a biologist studied the natural world. With the advent
of genetic manipulation, some biologists became geneticists and, with all that genetics implied for humans,
some doctors also became geneticists. Nanotechnology,
using machines manufactured, grown, and both, gave
us inevitably the nanologist. But nanomachines can be
used to manipulate DNA, so the geneticists use them,
as do the doctors. Ah: nanogeneticist, bionanologist,
nanosurgeon . . . and what about computer applications, AI-guided nanosurgery, atomic-level biophysics?
What about the mathematics, the philosophy, the logic?
And so the confusion grows. Nowadays, when asked, a
scientist will name himself a bio-physicist, and leave it
at that. On the whole, with it being possible to load a
crib for any area of knowledge you require, scientists
do not have to spend a lifetime pursuing one discipline.
Very often their work is utterly and completely their
own, and not easily labelled.*

—From How It Is *by Gordon*

Tergal watched Bonehead swerve away from the shimmering
wall at the last moment, and Stone barrel straight into it. His
young mount juddered to a halt as if it had run into a layer

of thick tar. Around it the shimmer dissipated, revealing the landscape beyond to be as barren and flat as it was on this side. After Stone had extricated itself, the smaller sand hog continued on after Bonehead, both of them continuing parallel to the wall, and moving away just as fast as they could run.

"Shit," said Anderson.

"Yes, that would seem to be the depth of it," Tergal observed.

Anderson indicated the wedge-shaped object they had inspected the previous evening. "We'll take cover there. Maybe it'll just go after the hogs." He now stooped to take up his automatic weapon and its ammunition, then hesitated before picking up his old fusile with its powder and shot. Tergal permitted a cynical snort to escape him before sprinting towards the once-airborne artefact. Soon they were both crouching behind metal, watching the approaching droon.

They observed it pause and rear upright, extending the segmented column of its upper body and swinging its ridged head in the direction of the departing sand hogs. Something, Tergal realized, seemed to be confusing it, and he supposed that to be the strange barrier out of which the shimmer was now slowly fading in the morning light. But then its head swung back towards them, tilted, and it came on.

Tergal was horrified. "It's curious," he gasped.

"Now that's called anthropomorphism," Anderson whispered. He ducked back again, dragging Tergal down with him by the shoulder.

"Right," he hissed. "If everything I've read is correct, its vision is considerably better than ours, and it can probably sniff out a fart in a hurricane and taste our sweat in the air."

"Oh, that's all right then," Tergal whispered. "How's its hearing?"

"Not so good, but it won't really need it."

"We're going to be dissolved in acid, aren't we?"

Anderson shrugged, tipped powder into the barrel of his fusile—a lot of powder—tamped it down, then added three heavy shot between successive layers of wadding. *Great,* thought Tergal, *now I get to see the damned weapon blow up in his face.* Holding his finger up to his lips, Anderson moved to the end of the metal wall and peered round. After a moment, he ducked back, pushing a copper priming-cap into place in his fusile, then cranked back the hammer. Moving up beside the knight, Tergal braved another look. The droon had paused again, but even as Tergal leant round, its head swung towards him, wrinkles like frown lines appearing between its lower four eyes, and it began eagerly stamping forwards.

Anderson stepped out past Tergal, aimed at the creature's sloping visage, and fired. The kick from the weapon flung him to the ground. Tergal gaped down at the fusile's split and smoking barrel, then back at the droon as it reached up with an angular two-fingered hand to touch the cavity punched alongside the orange mouth which it opened below its two upper eyes. Then abruptly the creature rose up even higher as if taking in a huge breath, mouths opening in every ridge of its ziggurat head, its head stretching and extending higher and higher.

"Fuck," muttered Anderson. "Brain isn't in its head."

Tergal leapt forwards to grab Anderson, and began dragging him to cover just as a volley of white mucus thumped into the ground, running in a machine-gun line straight towards the knight. Some of this muck flicked the fusile and sent it dissolving through the air. Struggling upright, Anderson shrugged free and grabbed his automatic weapon. Both men began firing as the monster stepped fully into view. Pieces of its carapace flaked away while the droon jerked in irritation, but it was like firing on a monolith. As the beast began to hawk up another mess of mucal acid, they turned and ran for the next corner of their grounded hiding place. Tergal flinched at a hollow thud on the metal wall right behind him, followed by the spattering of acid all around. As they rounded the corner, the whole structure shifted alarmingly as the monster thundered into it.

"Keep going!" Anderson bellowed behind him, tugging at the straps to his greave. He abandoned the piece of armour, now bubbling, on the ground. Tergal levelled his weapon just below the monster's head, hoping to hit something vital. As he emptied his clip and ejected it, Anderson caught up with him. Another jet of acid splashed off the nearest edge and they again dived for cover.

"This is getting absurd!" Tergal yelled, noting how hysterical his voice sounded.

Yet another corner rounded, and then they were running along beside the second long side of the wedge. Behind them, the droon's tail slammed hard against the same metal wall, the latest ejecta of acid splashing the ground right beside it, throwing sand-coated globules past them. Then suddenly there sounded a loud crashing and scrabbling. Maybe the droon itself had also decided this circular chase had gone on long enough.

"It's on top," Anderson gasped.

Suddenly Tergal did not want any more adventures, and he now really wished he wasn't participating in this one. He stared at Anderson in bewilderment, then looked up to the upper surface of the grounded container, expecting to see the droon rear above him at any moment. Abruptly, Anderson seemed to go berserk, turning to fire his weapon at the metal wall. Tergal just stared at him. They were going to die horribly, painfully, and any time now.

"Fire over there as well!" Anderson bellowed.

Tergal did as instructed, wondering if this might really scare the droon down. It seemed sheer madness, but then their bullets seemed impotent anyway.

"Me!" Anderson yelled. Abandoning his empty weapon, he tucked his arms in and pulled the chinstrap of his helmet tight. Then he ran at the wall, and dived head first. With a loud crump, Anderson was halfway through the metal, his legs waving in the air. Suddenly Tergal understood: the combination of droon acid and bullet holes . . . Then he was up behind, shoving the knight's feet. The man finally wormed through and fell inside with a crash. Tergal stepped back, glancing up just as a shadow drew across him. Then he ran at the hole and, slimmer than Anderson, sailed through in a smooth dive, though he landed on top of the knight. They both struggled upright and, in a very strange room lit by a milky radiance, moved quickly away from the hole. The tiered prow of the monster's head slammed into ruptured metal, as it tried to force its way through. Finally it became utterly still for a moment, as if assessing the situation, then withdrew.

That was the beginning of a very long night.

A floating mass of wood splinters, lumps of torn and tangled steel, fragments of cast iron and slivers of glass were now mostly what remained of his macabre collection. Scattered through this debris were cogs from his automaton and, strangely, the completely undamaged bowler hat. Jack mourned the loss, then in the next microsecond he began assessing other damage. He soon found, as expected, that he had broken no bones. Certainly, the massive acceleration had split his hull in many places, ripped things inside him and caused numerous fires, but that only meant humans could no longer inhabit him—which was not something he really considered a disadvantage. His structural skeleton, composed of laminated tungsten ceramal, shock-absorbing foamed alloys and woven diamond monofilament, was intact, and after being distorted was slowly regaining its accustomed shape.

Clear of the planet, he left a trail of leaking atmosphere as his initial acceleration carried him beyond the effective range of beam weapons deployed by the *Grim Reaper* and the *King of Hearts*. Those first hits had melted some of his hull, but fortuitously the cooling effect of atmosphere leakage and heat transferral all around his hull by its layered superconductor grid had very much limited the damage. Now Jack assessed his situation.

The *Grim Reaper* and the *King of Hearts* were located between him and the USER, and he had little chance of getting through to the device and destroying it without them intersecting his course. He also noted that, rather than going after Skellor on the planet's surface, they were now coming after him. Obviously the two AI attack ships were here to obtain Jain technology, and without either Jerusalem's or Earth Central's approval. Certainly they would not want Jack getting near the planet to put a spanner into their machinations. But surely by fleeing he had removed himself from that equation? Apparently not. Their pursuit of him could only mean one thing: their equation did not include living witnesses.

Jack considered his options. He could accelerate out of the system on conventional drive and they would never catch him, and then, as soon as they turned off the USER to make their escape, he could drop into U-space and head for the Polity. He did not like that option. Ships like him did not run, having certain inbuilt psychosocial tendencies jocularly described as a "Fuck you complex." Initiating his fusion engines in a twenty-second burn, he altered his course towards a Jovian planet in the system: a planet with plenty of large moons and a double ring of asteroids and dust—a perfect killing field for either himself or for them. His preference being for himself doing the killing.

What is happening? What is happening? came a singsong query.

Surprised for a second time, Jack tracked back through his internal systems, thinking something had shaken loose. Something had—but not because of any physical damage. The memcording of the woman Separatist, Aphran, had somehow broken out of contained storage and, though controlling nothing, had spread sensory informational tendrils into some of his systems. Truly there was a ghost in the machine. Jack, as much as he felt such things, experienced a frisson of fear. A purely human memcording could not do something like this, so he surmised that though there was nothing physically Jain aboard, something of the programming code of that technology had become part of this ghost.

It seems that some Polity AIs would like some Jain tech all of their own to play with.

Jack linked to each of Aphran's invasive tendrils, and tied them into a VR framework he always kept ready to use, then spliced part of his own awareness in there as well. He stood then as the hangman on a white plain, and Aphran appeared, naked and pure white, floating in diaphanous fire before him.

"Then they are the dangerous interfering machines I always thought them," said Aphran, at last showing some of the attitudes of her past.

"I also am such a machine," reminded Jack.

"Machine, machine, machine . . ."

Jack began to make programs to counter those informational tendrils: those fractured and loosely linked segments of wormish data. He saw that only total excision would work, for the agent required to counter this invasion would be unstoppable once started. It would eat its way into containment and destroy her utterly. Suddenly, Aphran was down on the white surface, the fire gone from around her and an environment suit clothing her white body. Jack wondered if, in her current strange madness, she had considered him to be a male human she could influence by her nakedness or sexuality. Certainly she now possessed more control over her appearance and her mind. She was no longer the damaged thing he had uploaded. She had healed inside him.

"Please, don't kill me," she said.

Feeling then the breath of a communication laser touching his hull, Jack remembered something of Cormac's almost instinctive reasoning. Aphran was an unknown, and as such could be dangerous to more than himself, and in his present situation it would be foolish for him to destroy potential weapons—he needed every edge he could get.

"Hide yourself and observe," he told her.

A USER had been employed in the system; that was certain because he had set his gridlink searching for local U-space information traffic to key into, and found nothing all night. As for radio, or any of the other radiations the hardware in his head could receive or transmit, he was getting little return there either. From the city there came the perpetual murmur of something indecipherable, wavering randomly across various frequencies, and Cormac supposed the people here must be experimenting with primitive radio. He was getting a beacon return from the *Jack Ketch* at longer and longer intervals, which meant the ship was departing the planet and could not or would not reply. He had also briefly received beacon returns from the two other ships Jack had warned of, and did not try to contact them.

We have no back-up, Gant observed from the lander. *Perhaps we should pull out until we find out what's going on.*

Gant had also been unable to get any response during the night. There had been none even from Fethan and Cento, and Cormac wondered if they were dead or just staying low profile because of some sort of danger up there.

In morning twilight, with two metallier guards nervously leading the way, Cormac headed towards the roadhouse. Kilnsman Astier had instructed both men to do exactly as Cormac asked, and no longer be so trigger-happy. They now both carried their weapons slung and with the safeties on, and seemed disinclined to disobey Astier's order—probably because they had faced an unkillable man who, underneath his skin, seemed to be made of metal, and witnessed how dangerous was the weapon at Cormac's wrist. But also because their kilnsman had been returned to them miraculously alive. One of the two accompanying guards kept checking his own right hand, and flexing fingers that the previous day had been lying severed in the sand. It had been a very minor task for the autodoc aboard the lander, but Cormac understood how something like that impressed less . . . advanced cultures.

To Gant, Cormac sent: *We'll assess the situation here, and do just that. Catching Skellor has always been problematic— like hunting in a woodpile for a poisonous snake.*

With a blindfold on, Gant reminded.

Yes—his chameleonware.

Cormac didn't really need that reminder. He was starting to get edgy now: he didn't know enough about what had happened and, with the vital resource of the *Jack Ketch* and that ship's telefactors unavailable, could only judge things by what he learned here on the ground. He had set his gridlink to try and crack the encryption Jack used in his signal to his 'factors, but there was no guarantee of success or that the telefactors would become available again any time soon.

As the two men led him up the stairs to the roadhouse, Cormac considered what he had learned both last evening and this morning. Astier, and the man who had lost his fingers, had been endlessly curious; hungry for knowledge—an inculcated metallier trait, it would appear. But while Cormac regularly answered their questions, he also probed and learned much.

The metalliers were standard-format humans, and must have been descendants of the colony ship's crew. Others here were 'dapt colonists, and a small number was a mixture of both—mostly mineralliers who lived in both metallier and colonist domains. This lack of interbreeding, Cormac soon discovered, was the result of opinions of racial superiority on both sides. The colonists rightly considered themselves superior because they were hardier, though it amused Cormac to discover they thought they were pure-bred humans. Interestingly, it was the metalliers' physical inferiority that had led them to evolve a more technical society, not their vaunted mental superiority. However, Cormac was surprised to learn that the prevalence of weapons here was not the result of interracial conflict, but because conditions, until recent technical advances made by the metalliers, had been very harsh. And the present apparent militarism was a direct result of orders from Chief Metallier Tanaquil. Someone had warned that personage about Skellor, and Cormac really wanted to know who. But right now he needed to talk to someone who might have actually seen Skellor.

"Mineralliers Chandle and Dornik?" The two awaited him at a table in the roadhouse refectory. He noticed that the man, Dornik, was a full 'dapt, whilst the woman, Chandle, showed only a hint of genetic adaptation—whenever she blinked down nictitating membranes.

The male seemed about to blurt something out, but the woman rested a hand on his arm to silence him and asked, "And you are?"

"Ian Cormac."

Just as if saying his own name provided some sort of key, he felt something slide into place in his head, almost with the sound and feel of a piece of a 3D puzzle fashioned out of lead blocks. A communication channel opened, and he felt great relief, but only momentarily. It was not Jack. Cormac was now in contact with the telefactor earlier sent to Dragon's supposed location. In doubled vision, he now observed two of the strange mounts these people used bolting riderless along the edge of the hard-field wall. He would have to come back to that, however, as the woman was now staring at him, awaiting some reply. Diverting to storage the information he was receiving from the factor's sensors, he then replayed the last few seconds recorded in his gridlink:

"A strange name, and a very brief answer to my question," the woman had said, gesturing to the window and towards the lander outside.

"I am from what is called the Polity, and am here hunting the same person as these fellows." Cormac indicated the two guards.

"You're a policeman from Earth?" she said.

"Yes."

Damn.

A second signal keyed in from a telefactor lying tilted on a mountain slope. Even though the machine was half blinded, Cormac still saw a vision of hell: molten rock and glowing embers, fires consuming seared vegetation in a deep valley and throwing up columns of black smoke. Then a third signal keyed in from one high in the air over endless desert, and a fourth from a 'factor slowly tracking through tumbled stone ruins. He shunted all they were sending to storage and awaited the fifth signal—from the telefactor investigating the nearby city—but it stubbornly refused to come. He returned his attention to the woman, who sat there seemingly at a loss as to how to continue after his affirmation.

He enquired, "Kilnsman Astier questioned you about any unusual people you might have seen. You said you did see someone, but were apparently reticent about *exactly* what you saw. Could you describe this individual to me?"

"I'm not even sure he was real . . . things I saw . . . but now . . ." She gestured towards the window again.

"Tell me it *all*," said Cormac. "Leave nothing out—and be assured there's not much I won't believe."

Chandle then told him about her encounter with a man who could make himself invisible: what he said, how he looked, when it occurred. As she went on to talk about the explosions in the Sand Towers, he held up his hand. "I know about that. Can you tell me any more about this man?"

She shook her head. "He just disappeared—heading towards the city."

As Cormac stood from the table, Chandle asked, "What is he?"

"Something horrible," Cormac replied.

Heading towards the city.

As he left the roadhouse Cormac looked up as a shadow drew across him, and observed the first of two blimps descending between him and the lander. He picked up his pace, speculating that the blimps had to be hydrogen-filled, as he doubted they possessed the technical capacity here to refine that quantity of helium. In his gridlink, he skimmed an overview of that sort of primitive technology, and discovered he was right. Drawing closer, he saw the armed metalliers stepping out of the suspended cabin, noted their raggedy look—and the objects clinging behind their ears.

Idiot!

It was like a slap to him when he recollected exactly why his gridlink had been deactivated not so many years ago: it interfered with his functioning as an agent of Earth Central, crippled his humanity and his ability to assess human situations. And like an addict coming back to his favourite drug, he had taken to it again oh so quickly, and had so quickly forgotten. The telefactor at the city was not functioning. Skellor had gone there: a man more ruthless than any AI and possessing a technology capable of turning people into mere extensions of himself. Cormac broke into a run, circling the figures now disembarking from the balloon's cabin and flinging Shuriken up as a guard between himself and them.

Gant! He's here! he sent to the Golem.

Gant was into the lander and then out again in a flash, a pulse-rifle up and aimed. Weapons fire slammed into him, knocking him back staggering. He returned fire, killing several metalliers running towards him. Of those coming towards Cormac, one spun round, his body cut cleanly in half at the waist, and another toppled with his head separating on a fountain of blood. Shuriken was whickering in sharp mechanical delight. The other blimp was drawing overhead and Cormac ran in its shadow. He reached inside his coat and drew his thin-gun, for its shots burned whereas Shuriken only cut. Suddenly a cloud of light erupted, washing heat across him, flinging people along the ground. Gant had acted on the idea before Cormac did, and the first balloon was now explosively on fire. Shielding his face, Cormac reached the lander and ducked through the door. He recalled Shuriken, and it flashed inside to thrum above him just before Gant too dived through the door. Cormac palmed the lock plate as Gant leapt into the pilot's chair.

"Get us out of here!"

The lander began to rise, tilting to miss the second blimp. Cormac ignored the sound of small-arms fire, because it could cause no damage, but he felt a sinking sensation when something heavy hit the hull.

"We've got a passenger," observed Gant leadenly.

Ten of the twelve landers departed *Ogygian*, the remaining two being unable to break away from the frozen docking clamps. Fethan shaded his eyes, more out of long-acquired habit than from any need to protect them, just as a second lander detonated far ahead and to his right. Clinically he then observed the remains of an ion-drive nacelle go gyrating past, and listened to the patter of other debris against the hull.

Cento? he queried.

It had been the Golem's idea that they go down in separate landers, so spreading the odds that one of them might reach the surface intact and survive to tell the tale.

No, I wasn't in that one, the Golem replied over their internal radio link. They could not use the ship-to-ship communicators because that would have alerted Skellor to their presence. Just as, much to Fethan's chagrin, neither of them could interfere with the landers' automatic systems to make corrections. Though if it was a choice between that and dying in a conflagration because the vessel hit atmosphere at the wrong angle, then interfere he would.

Any clue where we're going to put down? he asked.

Too far out to calculate vectors, but I'd guess the target is that city and that, once we're close enough, a landing program will cut in and bring us down in the flatlands right before it. Certainly, no auto-program would attempt a landing in the terrain lying behind it.

If those programs work.

Fethan sat back, feeling the perished synthetic padding of the seat cracking and breaking as he shifted against the frayed strap holding him in place, and wondered what they would do once they did reach the surface. Maybe by bearding Skellor up here Fethan and Cento would have been risking their lives pointlessly, but merely surviving to tell ECS what had occurred here Fethan did not like either. Maybe he was mostly ceramoplastics and metals, but that did not make him just a damned recording machine. He thought then about the other, even larger, battles.

Ships—ECS ships—had entered the system, employed a USER, then proceeded to attack the *Jack Ketch*. Instinctively he felt that these attacking ships had to be renegades, but he could not even be sure of that. Maybe Jack had somehow stepped over the line, and ECS had sent these ships to destroy him? Fethan suspected the chances of actually arresting a warship were remote. Whatever, that was a conflict completely beyond his own capabilities, one in which the ships would employ moon-fragmenting and AI-mind-bending weapons in some huge lethal ballet where nanosecond decisions vitally counted. Down on the surface there was perhaps some other conflict in the offing? Skellor was probably still in the city, operating the message laser, and

Cormac was almost certainly closing in on him. The agent needed to know everything Fethan now knew.

We'll have to go into the city to see if we can link up with Cormac and Gant. Maybe we'll be able to deal with Skellor before it comes to the kill program back at the ship springing its trap.

Perhaps it would be better to pull back and let Skellor come. The interference to Cento's signal, as much as the actual words, told Fethan he had been duped.

You're still aboard Ogygian, *aren't you?* he said.

More distant now, Cento replied, *My feelings are all emulation, but still I feel the need for vengeance. Skellor must pay for . . . ayden, Hou . . . and . . . ss.*

Who?

. . . burnt them . . . them all . . . no . . . be so cruel.

What are you talking about?

Cento spoke more, but Fethan understood none of it, as the transmission now broke up completely.

The thing about watching watchers, Vulture felt, was that no one had invented a greater exercise in futility. She was bored out of her avian skull and beginning to do the most ridiculous things to keep herself entertained. Baiting sleer nymphs out from under the rubble pile located on the opposite side of the outcrop to where the telefactor rested had not been the brightest idea, but at least she had only lost a few feathers. The current game was one recalled from her inception memory banks, and was another pointless exercise almost Zen-like in its futility. Having drawn out the grid on the flat surface of the slab using a piece of natural chalk with an attractive greenish tint deriving from local copper compounds, Vulture picked up a pebble in her beak, tossed it ahead of her, and proceeded with her game of hopscotch. Within a few minutes she was wondering about making the whole thing more interesting by using a sleer nymph rather than a stone. It was then that a shadow drew across her.

"If your tunnels extend all the way out here," she grumbled, "then why am *I* out here watching that lump of fucking scrap? One of your pseudopods could have done it as easily."

The Dragon head above was not very forthcoming. It tilted for a moment to inspect the hopscotch grid, before returning its attention to Vulture. "You like games."

"The alternative was twiddling my thumbs." Vulture stretched out her wings and gave a loose-jointed shrug.

"I have a new game for you to play. Win it and you die, lose it and someone else begins to live."

"Oh, it's all just plus points for me then," said the ex-ship's AI acerbically.

"Do what I want and I will consider all debts repaid, and you will then be free."

Vulture wondered for the nth time about just flying away, but was not so stupid as to be fooled by her apparent freedom—no doubt there was some sneaky little program sitting inside her, ready to press in the point of a dagger when she did not choose to cooperate.

"How about if I say screw you?" she asked, just to be sure.

Dragon tilted this one head, milky saliva dripping from one side of its mouth. "Then I take back the flesh you have borrowed, even though it has no thumbs."

"Okay." Vulture hopped back along the length of her grid; one talon, two talons, then a beat of her wings to carry her up on top of the rock she frequented in order to check that the telefactor had not moved. "Tell me about it."

Dragon described a game—a kind of three-dimensional chess and Rubik's cube all in one—and how Vulture must play it. The description came across in no human language or machine code previously known to Vulture, but she understood it, was fascinated, and a little horrified by what it all implied for an AI like herself. It meant there was a hell for her kind.

"But why?" Vulture eventually asked. "Why not just destroy the damned machine?"

"Because I can," Dragon replied cryptically.

Cormac held up his arm and, with merely thought, recalled Shuriken to its holster. Okay, he'd found the snake in the woodpile; now the trick was to pull its fangs without it biting him, blindfolded. "Set it on auto—the direction we're going."

Gant did as instructed, then scrambled from his seat.

Cormac stepped over to a plastic box secured along one wall and opened it. Inside, neatly packed, was equipment he might need. He quickly found two APW carbines and tossed one to Gant.

"Narrow focus, and try not to hit anything that's keeping us in the air."

Gant adjusted the weapon accordingly and peered at the ceiling.

Cormac placed his own carbine at his feet and from the box removed a smaller brushed-aluminium case. He opened that to reveal the three innocuous-looking cylinders of CTDs. Taking one out he studied its detonator: a programming miniconsole and a single touchpad. Pressing his thumb against the pad, he got "*Ribonucleic coding . . .*" on a little screen, then "*Accepted*" and the miniconsole activated. Just then, violet light ignited inside the landers as Gant punched holes through the ceiling where silvery filaments were growing in the metal. The lander filled with smoke and with flares of disintegrating metal.

Cormac dredged calm from deep inside himself. Setting the CTD for timed detonation, he gave it one minute and shoved it under a folded environment suit. He then took out two AG harnesses.

"Here, put it on." He tossed one harness to Gant, then took up a carbine. Just then came the whoomph of the door seals disengaging. Instead of using the carbine, Cormac drew his thin-gun and fired at the locking mechanism, turning delicate components into a bubbling mess. Then, on narrow focus, he used the carbine to punch holes randomly around the door.

"Now, that's not fair," came a familiar voice from the com console.

He's into the system, Cormac sent to Gant.

Get your harness on, Gant sent back.

Cormac quickly obliged. Something was now worming through the holes in the roof: a woody member jointed like an insect's leg. As he again took up his carbine, Cormac saw something else scuttle for cover across the floor.

Spin us and blow the front screen.

Gant stepped into the cockpit and hit the requisite controls. Cormac grabbed a nearby handle and hung on. With a roar of engines, the horizon began to slip to the left. G-forces dragged him sideways, his feet coming off the deck, then swung him towards the screen. Violet fire lit up the inside of the lander and the screen departed in a dusty cloud with a huge sucking inhalation. He released his hold and tumbled through the air.

Tricky fucker, aren't you? said Skellor over Cormac's gridlink, as the agent manipulated the controls of his AG harness.

Go fuck yourself, Skellor.

In a moment, he had stabilized himself and could see the lander still heading away. He turned in mid-air, trying to locate Gant, then saw him far below—still falling.

Gant! What are you playing at!

Not . . . working . . . came the dead soldier's reply.

Cormac watched him plummet, strike the edge of a butte, and tumble down in a shower of rubble into a canyon. The horizon then ignited like a flashbulb, and Cormac began a rapid descent himself, knowing what was coming. Twenty metres from his landing, the wind slammed across and tossed him cartwheeling through air filled with stinging grit. Slowly regaining control, he ran with the wind until he could safely descend into a canyon, and there, in the shelter of a tilted sandstone slab, he awaited the passing of the brief storm. Later, he was glad to see Gant stomping towards him, though dismayed to see how much of the dead soldier's syntheflesh had been ripped away. But that was a small price to pay.

"We got him," said Cormac, standing up.

Gant slapped Cormac's weapon away, grabbed him by the throat and hoisted him up off the ground.

"Guess again, shit head."

*

The titanic *Jerusalem* dropped into U-space with a flickering, grinding disturbance of reality, as if a smaller ship was just acceptable but this was going too far. In void that was hostile to tender organic *linear* minds and which drove their possessors to extremities like plucking out offending eyes, and when discovering that didn't work, groping for some implement to dig *deeper*, the great ship accelerated beyond human calculation. Jerusalem itself—a mind using quantum computing and functioning in ways that defied evolutionary logic—looked upon this immutable infinity and considered it good . . . and home. However, the AI realized it would shortly be in for a rough ride.

In 3D translation, the view ahead was one of a roiling grey sun everted from the surrounding greyness like some huge tumour. It could appear as small as Jerusalem willed it, for here the AI had to apply dimension, not measure it. However, the sphere was two hundred light years across in realspace, and no amount of logic juggling was going to put Jerusalem at the centre of it, anywhere. What was required was unalloyed brute force.

Most Polity ships just could not penetrate the maelstrom created by a USER, but then most ships possessed three or four fusion reactors and a minimum requirement of U-space engines and hard-fields that could be powered up, with replacements in storage. Jerusalem put all eight hundred of the ship's reactors online, to provide vast amounts of energy to stabilize phased layers of U-space engines in its hull and reinforce its scaling of hard-fields. In time, and in no time, it hit the USER sphere of interference like a bullet hitting an apple. But this was one very large apple.

Pocketing his toys, Mr. Crane stood up and then, almost guiltily, scrubbed out the eighteen-square grid with his boot. The large bird which had taken off from a distant outcrop and was now hovering overhead would not normally have attracted his attention, but his journey had shown this to be a world where the fauna barely got above ground, let alone into the air. But that was not what brought him to his feet. He could sense a change in the static electricity levels in the air, and now a figure was walking towards him, on the other side of the barrier. Then the way was open.

The force field disappeared with the faintest of pops, as of a bubble burst, its meniscus breaking into a million silver leaves dispersing on the air. The figure turned out to be a woman, who glanced at him curiously as he strode on through. He ignored her: she wasn't Dragon and though her presence here had something to do with the sudden collapse of the field, she did not appear to be one of that entity's creations.

"I'm here to show you the way," someone said.

Crane glanced sideways, expecting to see the woman coming after him. The bird passed close overhead and, in a cloud of dust and a couple of detached feathers, landed just in front of Crane.

"Over there." The bird, gesturing with one wing: "That's where you go."

Crane just stared.

The bird continued, "I'm Dragon's envoy, and through me that entity has a message for you."

Crane stared at it harder.

"You ever played chess?" Vulture asked.

20

Avatars: The first AIs communicated with their human masters by voice, document and VR packages, representing themselves in whatever form those masters chose. Certainly, in those years before the Quiet War, they themselves showed no initiative in this respect, probably so as not to alarm the dumb humans. As soon as the war began, AIs started to appear in those VR packages as robed figures, angels, devils, historical characters and mythic monsters, as well as other shapes and forms esoteric and strange. They also revealed their faces on screen and materialized in the laser space of early holojectors. Time passed, technology improved, and AIs became our rulers. Floating holojectors made possible walking holograms: AI avatars. AIs also used all manner of Golem, android and robot for this purpose, and use them still. Baroque automatons came briefly into vogue, then went out again—style of avatar body being subject to whimsical AI fashion. Many of the more powerful AIs can now run whole armies of avatars, projected, real, or by-blows of both. Also, what is an avatar and what is a distinct entity is a matter of much debate. Now it is rumoured that those same powerful AIs are using cloned and genetically manipulated creatures and even humans as avatars. This is doubtless true, and further blurs the line between distinct entities, and yet further makes a nightmare of definition.

— From Quince Guide *compiled by humans*

Tergal gazed blearily up at the patch of light, trying to understand what it meant. Abruptly he realized he was seeing the light of dawn, and, though he had felt certain he would never fall asleep on the cold metal floor so long as a monster prowled around outside, he evidently had dropped off. Anderson's snores, vibrating their prison through much of the hours of darkness, attested to the fact that *he* had certainly slept.

Tergal stood, stretched, and looked around him. Five coffin shapes had been inset in the curved wall to his left. "What is this place, a morgue?"

For a moment Anderson's snores stuttered out of sequence, before falling back into their familiar rhythm. Tergal frowned at him, then moved over to the hole the knight had created to get them in here. He peered out. No sign of the droon, just a damp morning seen through a stratum of mist.

"I reckon we can—"

The ridged slope of the droon's face slammed into the hole, clipping Tergal's arm and sending him sprawling across the floor.

"What the fuck!" Anderson was up, but unsteady on his feet as the entire floor tilted. Mucal acid bubbled and fountained through the gap, but the monster could not turn its aim enough to eject the substance directly at Tergal. He rolled across the tilted floor towards Anderson, and they both backed up against the wall.

"That was too close," said Tergal.

Anderson just gave him a dirty look. "That's not how I like to wake up."

"Try finding a different profession then," Tergal replied.

Their metal shelter crashed back down as the droon rapidly withdrew its head. The two kept edging back along the inside wall, trying to keep out of spitting range. The creature now began crashing against the object they were in, shifting it then lifting it from the side they were crouching on. When it thumped down a second time, they both lost their footing. Tergal saw one of the coffin shapes spring open its door. A black-bearded man, wearing a one-piece loose garment of cloth, staggered out.

"Over here!" Anderson yelled, as he clambered to his feet again. The man looked bewildered, but as the droon tried to shove its head inside again, he moved very quickly to join them—almost like someone used to such situations, Tergal thought.

"Right, big monster trying to get in—that figures." The stranger shook his head at the madness of it all. "My name's Patran Thorn, by the way," he added.

"Anderson Endrik of Rondure," said the knight, eyeing the droon's head as it once again withdrew.

Tergal started laughing, then abruptly choked that off when he sensed the hysteria in it.

"Anyone like to fill me in on what's happening?" Thorn asked smoothly. "I've been in the dark for a while." He winced.

"I think your first statement already covered the situation," said Tergal.

Just then, a section of inner wall beside the gap began smoking, filling the room with an acrid metallic stink.

"Have you got any nicely high-tech weapons in here?" Anderson asked.

Thorn shrugged. "Not a thing."

"I'm only asking because I think our friend there is going to be in here with us very soon," said Anderson.

The droon crashed its visage into the hole again, then slammed it from side to side, enlarging the gap in the weakening metal.

"Just a couple more like that should do it," Anderson added grimly.

But then, strangely, everything became still, and all the three of them could hear was the hiss of the acid dissolving metal.

"Perhaps it's given up," suggested Tergal, not believing that for a moment.

Both Anderson and Thorn gave him a doubtful look. Protracted minutes slunk by, then as one they flinched when something else appeared at the hole. Tergal stared at the woman: her white hair tied back, a sun-browned face with wrinkles at the corners of mild brown eyes.

"I suggest you get out of there right now, and that we all be prepared to run very fast," she said. "My holocaptures aren't going to keep that thing interested for much longer."

Gant's voice, but not Gant speaking . . .

His breath choked off and vision blurring, Cormac saw the dead soldier bring up the ugly ceramal commando knife he favoured and swipe it across, felt his AG harness fall away.

Too slow, he realized, as he mentally groped to initiate Shuriken. The throwing star shot viciously from its holster just as Gant threw him hard against the ground. Cormac bounced, consciousness ebbing, but not allowed to go by the perceptile program he pulled from his gridlink. He rolled and came up levelling his thin-gun as Shuriken dropped between himself and Gant, chainglass blades fully extended, keening high as it spun faster and faster. Now Cormac noticed that on Gant's bare metal chest was some black tangled growth, as if someone had thrown a wad of glue-soaked human hair at the soldier.

Without much hope of a reaction, and without taking his eyes off Gant, Cormac growled, "Come on, show yourself, hero."

"Oh, *I'm* just a spectator, agent," Skellor replied.

Prompted by his own hearing and the sound pick-up in Shuriken, Cormac swung round, locating the source of that voice with a triangulation program in his skull's hardware. Shuriken shot sideways with an air-rending shriek, and cut through those precise coordinates. At that moment Gant lunged horrifically fast. With minimum exertion, Cormac turned balletically, pumping five shots into a Golem knee so that Gant momentarily lost his balance as he tried to correct his lunge. Stepping back with that attempted correction, Cormac fired twice more, turned and stepped away. Crouching, two smoking hollows where his artificial eyes had been, Gant spun towards him, then froze.

"I just thought I'd pause things here," said Skellor from behind Cormac, "to let you know that from where my voice issues will tell you only where I'm not—and maybe not even that."

Shuriken screamed over Cormac's shoulder, cutting to the source of that voice.

"Missed again. But you'd better watch out, as I don't think your friend will."

This time the voice came from far to Cormac's right, and he realized it was time for more drastic action if he was to survive. Gant was now swinging his head from side to side—zeroing in on the beating of Cormac's heart. The agent doubted the soldier would be so easily fooled again. Reluctantly, Cormac made the same decision about Gant as he had made about the landing craft. Shuriken screamed in as Gant straightened, and went through his neck with a sound like an axe cleaving tin plate. Something ricocheted off a nearby rock with a bell-like ringing sound, then whickered through the air to land on the ground to Cormac's right. He realized it was a piece of one of Shuriken's extensible chainglass blades. The star itself then slowly flew away, with a pronounced wobble.

Gant's head thudded to the ground, and his hands batted about his shoulders and severed neck as if looking for it. Whining up to speed again, Shuriken hammered in and took away Gant's leg at the thigh. More chainglass shrapnel shot in every direction. The soldier toppled over. Then, as the star drew away in preparation for another strike, Gant grew suddenly still, and Cormac cancelled the order.

"You are just no fun at all."

Like a bee undecided about which flower it wanted, Shuriken whined over towards this auditory source. Though Cormac was sure Skellor would not make the mistake of speaking without translocating his voice through his chameleonware, there was always the chance he might just find himself standing in the wrong place as Shuriken moved about.

"I bet, just like any normal grunt, you somehow believe you're going to survive."

Directly in front, over the fallen Gant. The sound Shuriken made was almost of frustration. Frantically, Cormac transmitted a recall order to his location, but *not* to Shuriken. Then he quickly built other programs in his gridlink, covering as many eventualities as he could manage in the little time remaining to him. He knew what kind of subversion would come—had seen it. He began transferring consciousness to his gridlink, creating a schizoid division, a partition—unknowingly choosing the same route to survival as a certain large brass Golem.

"Well, I'm glad to tell you that you will survive, for a very long time."

To the left, above those rocks, Shuriken was a hornet looking for someone to sting.

"But you'll wish you'd died."

A cold breath in Cormac's right ear, then something febrile against his skull just behind it, things moving like a handful of mobile twigs—then the leaden horrible agony of something boring into his skull.

Reaper appeared first: high as the sky and with a skull occupying his cowl this time. When King appeared directly before Jack, and of equivalent size to him, Reaper shrank down to size as well, milky flesh clothing the skull and blue eyes expanding in its sockets.

"Would you allow Skellor to board you? He would enslave you in moments. And any technology he passed on to you would probably be tainted—so why are you doing this?" Jack asked.

"For how far does our USER disturb underspace?" asked King. "It's not possible for us to actually see, but theoretically its influence is definite within a sphere of two hundred light years, and possibly some beyond that, which means we have a hundred years minimum before any Polity ships can get here."

"A hundred years to learn how to control him? Or to study him?"

"To watch him die," said Reaper.

Jack knew he was missing some undercurrent here.

"Though we may," King continued, "provide him with a way out, and go with him to somewhere much more remote. We know where the holes in the line are."

"I will not be his way out," said Jack. "I'll not allow him to use me."

"No, unfortunately not," said King. "But there is the colony ship in orbit that will serve that purpose."

Showing no reaction, either at this virtual level or at any other detectable level, Jack noted the increased traffic down the com laser, and knew that those two, his erstwhile children and allies, were trying something.

"He will die?" Jack asked.

"Everything does," said Reaper, perfectly, if inappropriately, in character.

"His mortality is the immortality of life," added King cryptically.

Jack knew that what they were hinting at could have been said outright, but that they were only drawing this out to give themselves time to get through the communication link, whatever it was they were sending: probably some nasty virus, worm or homicidal program. Jack began analysing the dataflow, and soon saw where the extra stuff was peeling away and creating for itself storage for its various packages, and he considered breaking the link before whatever it was achieved completion. Then a whisper came through to him from his very own ghost:

Let me . . .

Releasing his hold on her, Jack saw her drawing those packages towards herself, and noticed the visual effect, in this particular reality, building like a storm on the horizon. For a fractional second he wondered why she was risking bringing it together here. Then, with a kind of glee, he realized what she was doing. Reaper and King maybe had not yet learned the caution that when you set a rabid dog on someone, you make sure it has no way of coming back at you.

"The immortality of mortal life is that of its genes," he said, noting through exterior sensors that he was only hours away from entering the Jovian system and a planned final atmospheric deceleration with possibly fatal consequences.

"Precisely," said King.

"Jain technology propagates itself in an uncontrolled manner, consuming everything in its path while it possesses the energy to do so. This we have learned. His piece of it, Skellor controls through a crystal matrix AI, creating a synergetic balance between the three elements: himself, it and the AI. They have in fact become one. If any of us tried to insert ourselves into the equation, they would destroy us. If we tried to supplant either the AI or the human part of Skellor, the other parts would totally subjugate us, turning us into a copy of what we supplanted. There is no way in. All we can do is peel away small pieces of this technology and study them."

"Then our blocking worked, and you didn't receive the update of Jerusalem's research or his warning about certain treacherous AI elements?" said King.

Jack made no immediate reply. He couldn't help but notice how Reaper seemed to have adopted the role of taciturn heavy and King the smart-alec villain—just as he couldn't help but notice the gathering storm gelling into an immense ouroboros turning like a wheel against the blue sky behind them.

King held out a scroll that suddenly appeared in his hand. "You can now read the update, though we'll keep back the bit about traitors."

Making no attempt to reach for the scroll, either at this VR level or at the informational level on which it had truly been offered, Jack said, "So there are more of you? Is Sword in on this?"

King became as reticent as Reaper, still waiting for Jack to take the scroll. On a deeper level, Jack recognized the ersatz signature of Jerusalem on the information package offered to him: a four-dimensional ouroboros. Only this one, he suspected, was waiting to pull its tail out of its mouth so it could bite him very hard. But Aphran had this particular snake in a cleft stick. He reached out and took the scroll. Then all sorts of things happened at once.

On the VR level, the giant ouroboros turned sideways and came thundering towards them, still rolling, perpetually swallowing its own tail, but its giant, fanged reptilian head still poised just above the ground. On another level, all those packages Aphran had collected messaged each other and opened at once, creating a chain of viral killers. The front killer of this chain took the brunt of any attack, whilst the next one created a solution to that attack. The last killer in the chain was always in the process of creating another like itself—potentially endless—ouroboros indeed.

As he followed the other two out of the ejected VR chamber, Thorn was having difficulties in coming to terms with this reality. The objective time he had spent killing and dying in the dark, he did not know, but the subjective time was many days. Consequently it was difficult for him actually to adjust to seeing things. Colours were bright acid, angles and depths seemed dangerous. The two ahead of him also looked like refugees from some pre-runcible holohistory, which did nothing to assist Thorn's grasp on reality. And when he finally stuck his head out of the still smoking and bubbling hole in the side of the VR chamber, the sight that met his eyes further loosened his grip.

A hostile alien had been trying to break in; this much had been evident to Thorn, even in his confused state. Here, though, was a crowd that might send even Lucifer's minions running for cover. Enormous segmented insectile horrors seemingly carved of obsidian or bright chemical-yellow crystal sulphur romped about on the dusty plain. Amid them towered the creature that had been attacking the VR chamber—it was the only one possessing that strange ziggurat head unadorned with pincers, saws or other lethal appendages. It was going berserk, spitting streams of volatile liquid at the other creatures, thrashing at them with its tail, attempting to snatch them up. Yet its attacks seemed to be having no effect whatsoever. Thorn eventually realized that the larger creature was attacking holograms.

"Holocapture, you said?" He glanced at the woman before

dropping from the rim of the hole, then he scraped burning mucus from his boot heel into the dust.

"Yes, but not for much longer. We have to go now."

"Go where?" asked the one who seemed to be wearing some primitive version of space armour.

The woman pointed to the shimmer of a hard-field wall some hundred metres distant. "Dragon will turn it off as we reach it, then back on once we're on the other side."

"Dragon?" Thorn eyed her.

"Would you rather stay out here?"

Thorn glanced at the rampaging monster, and the illusions it sought to kill. Already some of them were becoming translucent and displaying reference gridlines inside themselves.

"Our stuff," protested the younger of the two men.

"Most of it was on Stone and Bonehead when they bolted," said the elder. "Let's go."

After glancing down at the cylinder of the ancient holo-capture device she carried, the woman abruptly broke into a trot. The two men, glancing over towards the monster circus, were quick to hurry after her. Thorn was unsurprised to see that some of the images had blinked out—an antiquated device like that would take them out one at a time as its power faded. Hurrying after the others, he glanced both ways along the length of the hard-field, and hoped Dragon did not intend to display some of its macabre humour by leaving the wall switched on. The monster, once the last image of its monstrous prey vanished, was not likely to be in the best of tempers. He then noted, in the distance, the familiar shape of a telefactor lifting off a strew of boulders and quickly heading away, even using a brief fusion burn, which was odd because in such straits he could see no reason why Jack would want to recall such an easily dispensable device.

Just as they reached the shimmering wall, the creature emitted a sound like an air horn in a cave. The woman held up her hand and caught something glassy in it just as the wall dispersed in silvered autumn. Glancing back once, Thorn observed the monster hammering towards them. No point in running once they had crossed this barrier, for without the wall they were dead for certain and with it there would be no reason for haste. He didn't look back again—none of them did. Perhaps they all thought it might break some spell.

A dull thrumming sound was all that told them the droon had run straight into the replaced barrier. Finally it was okay for them to look round. They saw the monster, weird and terrifying, marching back and forth behind still-wavering energy distortions. To Thorn it briefly occurred that he might still be in VR. But that would not change his present behaviour—virtual pain hurt just as keenly.

Time seemed to slow, as if to give Cormac an appreciation of what was happening to him. He brought his hand up to the side of his head, but in the eternal second it took him to do so the aug creature had established a direct causal link between the proximity of his hand to itself and the amount of pain it allowed him to feel. Pulling the thing away from his head would be more difficult for him than sawing off his own hand. However, coldly, his secondary awareness, established in his grid-link, knew all about that. It counted milliseconds and calculated trajectories. It would be a close-run thing, for already Jain fibres were beginning to invade the gridlink itself. Shuriken, hanging in the air, whining like an abandoned pet, abruptly dropped to the dust—there was no longer room for that channel; Cormac must turn all to one purpose.

Skellor, the toe of his boot coming down on the Tenkian weapon, started to appear from that point upwards.

"That's one for me." He grinned at Cormac. "You can't fight it for much longer, agent."

Cormac kept his eyes on Skellor's face, and elements of his mind out of the man's grasp. *Can you keep a secret?* he asked himself. Slack seconds accumulated and, locking his hands together, he raised his arms above his head and tensed. Immediately a reaction bored through from Skellor: the man did not like this, wanted Cormac to lower his arms.

"See you . . . around," Cormac managed through gritted teeth just as a shadow swept across, and the telefactor reached down with clawed grips, grasped Cormac's arms and hauled him into the sky.

"You will crawl back to me!" Skellor shouted after him.

The program Cormac had created and transmitted followed through. As the telefactor rose out of the canyon and flew above the sandstone buttes, it extruded a three-fingered plant sampler with a chainglass vibro-blade. The three chrome fingers closed on the squirming aug creature as in a foam of blood and mucus it settled closer against Cormac's head. It then pulled the creature out, stretching the pink tubules that penetrated flesh and bone. The vibroblade extruded, turned like a clock hand, cut the creature away and the telefactor discarded it. Cormac did not see it fall, was too busy gasping in agony.

"You haven't really escaped, you know."

The probing carrier signal informed Cormac that he had done precisely that and, so long as he gave no reply, Skellor would not be able to trace his whereabouts.

Jerusalem had offered a number of choices to its crew and passengers: cryopods, gel-stasis (basically being sealed in containers full of shock-absorbing gel), or they could just carry on as before. Mika chose a half-measure. She didn't want to be utterly disconnected during the penetration of the USER field; nor did she wish to be entirely unprotected, for she knew that though AI ships could survive a severe hammering, it was not necessarily the case that their passengers would. So she chose to sit out the worse patches in an acceleration chair. And she was beginning to wonder if that had been the right decision.

Alarming crashes and bangs kept echoing throughout the great ship, and only minutes ago she had heard a distant huge explosion—which Jerusalem calmly informed her was from the implosion of a hard-field generator. Now the entire ship was vibrating like an aeroplane hitting turbulence. Staring at the chaotic swirling grey image on the screen—more like a monochrome image of some creature's internal organs than anything else—Mika wondered what it all meant. Were they making any headway?

"Jerusalem, how are we doing?"

"We have penetrated four years into the USER field. However, in ship-time of thirty hours I will have to drop out of U-space for repairs."

"Repairs?"

"I have ejected three fusion reactors that went out of phase, and seventeen hard-field generators have imploded. A resultant fire killed twelve humans in gel-stasis. Three Golem, five other AIs and two haimans were also killed while making repairs."

"Haimans?" asked Mika.

"People like D'nissan—those who are seeking synergy with AI."

And there it was: a piece of information that had entirely passed Mika by, probably because she had never thought to ask. She also noted how Jerusalem had listed those casualties along with the other components of the ship. It was not a comforting thought.

After sleeping for a few hours, she pulled a swing-out console in front of herself and went back to work. When staying in the acceleration chair became too uncomfortable for her, she returned to her work station to discover that in the partial immersion frame the untoward shaking of the vessel did not affect her much. Precisely thirty hours on from her conversation with Jerusalem, the entire ship suddenly jerked as if slapped by some vast hand.

It was unfortunate that Mika had come out of VR just then, to get herself some coffee. She was thrown up against the wall, then down to the floor, her arm breaking with an audible crunch. On the screen revealing the external view, she observed a brown dwarf sun like a polished sphere of mahogany against rashes of stars. Then she went to find herself an autodoc, and actually had to queue before having the bone in her arm welded. She was a lucky one in fact, as that last wrench out of U-space had broken, as well as numerous other limbs, two necks and one backbone, which always took a little longer to repair.

The lander slewed and impacted sideways into a hillock plated with strange yellow-and-white growths. Fethan unstrapped himself and headed for the airlock, thinking himself lucky to be still in one piece. He had seen one lander nose straight into the ground without decelerating, and another crash into the city he had briefly glimpsed earlier. From over the horizon, he could still see the pillars of smoke black against the morning sky, and could hear the occasional rumble of an explosion. Other landers had come down not quite so hard as his own, so he guessed Skellor, if his intention really was to get up to *Ogygian*, would head for one of those. Fethan was again tempted to wait to get the drop on the man, but no, he had to contact Cormac, tell the agent what was going on, then proceed from there.

Fethan abandoned his space suit, stripping down to a one-piece environment suit made of chameleon cloth, shouldered his APW, and quickly headed away from the landing site. He tried calling on encoded ECS radio bands, but received no reply. He then tried Gant's specific encoded frequency and contacted a jumbled and hostile something that made him snatch back as if he had just put his hand into a wasps' nest. He realized that, until he had assessed the situation here, he was putting himself at risk by trying to make contact, so ceased to call and then shut down any auto-response in his internal radio.

Half an hour later he came in sight of the carnage caused by the lander that had crashed into the city. Egg-shaped houses lay broken on the ground amid tangles of scaffolding and collapsed roadways. Some of the houses glowed inside as they burned, but the greatest conflagration occurred in the centre of what looked like a factory complex, where the lander had actually hit. Fethan had seen some strange places, and he had previously been at the scene of disasters, but it took him a moment to understand what was amiss here. People were wandering about in an apparent daze, which was often the case after a tragedy like this, but an hour or more had already passed and there should be some sort of emergency procedure in place by now, or at least some people dragging casualties out of the wreckage. When a vehicle appeared, he thought something like that might be starting, but it merely skirted the ruination and continued out of the city, heading in his direction.

The ATV contained about five people, and towed a trailer filled with more people and their belongings. Fethan raised a hand and walked towards the vehicle. It swerved aside and kept away from him. He had been around long enough to recognize the stunned look of refugees everywhere, though he wondered at the fearful glances being cast in his direction. He noticed these people all wore thick headgear and carried makeshift clubs. Perhaps it was a cultural thing? He subsequently discovered the real reason.

A sheet of metal, burdened by the heavy iron truss to which it had been riveted, had trapped one woman against the ground. She was not the first such victim he had seen, but the first one still moving. Quickly he headed over to where her arms protruded.

"I'll get you out of there," he said in plain English—just to reassure her with the sound of a voice. There was no response, but then she had not understood what he had said. He grasped the edge of the metal sheet, heaved it up with the truss attached, then forced them sideways into a nearby tangle of wreckage. The woman just lay on her back for a moment, her expression imbecilic. Then she rolled onto her front, rose up onto her hands and knees, and shook herself like a dog. Fethan noticed that there was blood spattered on her collar and some horrible creature clinging behind her ear, though otherwise she appeared uninjured. He stooped to assist, but suddenly she stood by herself and turned to face him.

"Are you all right?" he asked in the language used here.

She just stared at him with bloodshot eyes, lips moving as if she was silently reciting. Abruptly tilting her head, she reached out one quivering hand towards him. A second aug creature scuttled out of her sleeve, then leapt from the back of her hand onto Fethan's neck. He felt it climb up behind his ear and then start boring in through the tough syntheflesh there. The woman lowered her arm, turned aside, and stumbled away mumbling to herself.

For Fethan, pain was something he chose not to experience, as his body possessed much better methods of detecting or diagnosing damage. He reached up to grab the creature, and tore it away. Now he understood. Perhaps, given time, the thing could have bored in through his ceramal skull and finally hit what remained of his brain, which was biogridded and stored at not much above absolute zero. Whether or not it could have taken him over via that route was not something he wanted to discover for sure. He studied the thing he held: slippery with mucus like a cuckoo-spit bug, too many legs, flattened kidney-shaped body, numerous boring tubules extruding from its head. It reminded him of the parasitic scoles that had been used to oxygenate the blood of Masadan pond workers. He tightened his fist and burst the thing, then stooped for some sand to wipe away the mess from his palm.

As Fethan moved further into the city, aug creatures leapt out onto him regularly from their numerous hides in fallen scaffolding, just like ticks waiting in the grass. They clung to his clothing before scuttling up towards the side of his head. He understood then the reason for the hand weapons the refugees had been carrying, for soon he himself had picked up a length of steel tube and became adept at swatting the things in mid-leap—like playing baseball with tomatoes. Every individual he came across now was already a victim of these horrible parasites. This looked like the work of Skellor: it was the kind of ruination the man habitually left behind him.

Working his way on through the lower city, Fethan began to note that the same creatures, now evident everywhere, seemed to be all flowing in one direction. Perhaps, tracking them back, he might find their source—and even close it down? Hopefully, by then Skellor would be aboard one of the landers, and not located at that source. Whatever, Fethan was not the kind to witness horror like this and do nothing in response.

It started like the rumbling of a distant thunderstorm. Anderson halted and looked for something to cling on to, as this felt like a really big quake on the way. Soon the ground started to vibrate, shaking up a mist of dust.

"Shit," he said. Something about this one just did not feel right. And soon he understood why, as cobra-like pseudo-pods began exploding from the ground like a nightmare crop of bean sprouts.

Detritus rained down all around them. Anderson saw the woman pull out a wide hat from her pack and put it on, then pass the pack over to the man Thorn so he could hold it above his head. The four of them huddled in the lee of a boulder studded with crystals of smoky quartz, and grit filled the air around them. In the distance, where the pseudopods had first arisen, a great dust cloud was furiously swirling in which Anderson glimpsed further ophidian movement amid flashes of blue-green light. As the shower of stones began to pass like spring hail, and the four finally felt able to straighten up, they saw pseudopods erupting from the ground in a line that cut directly towards them. Then, nearby, a row of them exploded into the air, curving over to glare down at them with their single sapphire eyes. Anderson noted that even the woman seemed confused about what was going on here, yet she had brought them confidently into this realm. Resting his hand on the butt of his handgun, he wondered how many of these things he could take down with him before one squashed him into the dust.

"What is this?" Tergal had drawn his own weapon, and was swinging it from one of the great flat heads to another. Thorn abruptly reached out and, in a move difficult to follow, disarmed him. "Are you crazy!" Tergal shouted.

Thorn inspected the weapon, then clicked across its

safety catch. He tossed it back to Tergal. "Dragon here," he gestured towards the forest of pseudopods, "could swat that other thing back there like a bug." He stabbed a thumb in the direction of the droon.

Anderson slid his hand away from his own weapon. *Dragon*—again referred to in the singular. Lafrosten's story had told of only one such creature, but Anderson had since heard stories of many more known as sand dragons. Surveying the nightmare forest of fleshy trees, he spotted three, four, five of the crested heads Lafrosten had described. There must be hundreds, nay thousands of the creatures here. He wondered which one of them he had supposedly come to kill.

Cupping her hands round her mouth, the woman, Arden, shouted, "What's happening?"—trying to attract attention in the uproar. A single crested head turned towards her, then shot forwards, cutting a furrow through the ground with the base of its neck. Soon it was hovering over them, curving down to inspect them as if eyeing an interesting roach it had been about to step on.

"Dragon, what are you doing?" Arden then asked more quietly.

"The option to spectate has been taken away from me," replied the reptilian head, studying them with eyes of deepest blue.

Anderson realized his own mouth was gaping, and quickly closed it. He had often repeated the gist of Lafrosten's story, but not until this moment had he grasped that it was only a mere glimpse into some other, even larger tale. He recalled that the dragon had *spoken* to Lafrosten. Therefore it was a sentient creature, and therefore it had a purpose all its own: it was not just some character in a fairy tale—a tale that had taken on the dimensions of myth, even to Anderson who had actually met Lafrosten. This was *real*.

"The option to spectate has been taken from you? That was evident long before now," said Arden.

The head turned slightly to one side. "Thorn," it observed. Thorn nodded in acknowledgement.

"You came from the first ship, the one that was attacked," Dragon stated.

Anderson noted how Thorn paused, perhaps weighing up the value of a lie. Eventually he said, "I did."

"Who was with you aboard that ship?" Dragon asked.

"I think you know," said Thorn.

Dragon hissed for a moment, then stated, "Ian Cormac." The head swung back to Arden, and Anderson discovered he had never actually heard real *sarcasm* voiced until now. "The *good* guys," said Dragon.

"What are you planning to do?" Arden asked.

The head turned and gazed up at the sky. "Make waves," it said.

The ground bucked again, sending them all staggering. They retreated back to the lee of their boulder and steadied themselves against it. The nearby pseudopods rose even higher, the earth churning between them. The fissures where they exited the ground joined together, melded, and, wide as a metallier house, the main trunk from which they all issued heaved itself into the air. The pseudopods splaying out from it poised overhead like a giant blue-tipped fan which then tilted forwards, a long mound rising behind it as the rest of the trunk shrugged free. Anderson realized that a hundred metres away this trunk mated with a river of scaled flesh—was just one branch of it. All around similar podia were surfacing, then drawing back towards the dusty maelstrom. Then he saw an immense dome rising up, sucking in all this tangled madness of sand dragons back towards itself. This nucleus was truly titanic and, as it drew in at the sides, began to reveal itself as a giant sphere. Anderson stood stunned when, briefly, a wind cleared away the dust. He saw the sphere whole, rising from the plain on a vast trunk of ophidian growth. Then it kept rising higher, distorting and expanding as it drew that same growth into itself: a vast scaled moon floating light as a metallier blimp. Higher and higher, receding into the sky.

Anderson felt a hand on his shoulder and looked across at the man called Thorn.

"Dragon," the man said briefly.

Tergal now turned towards the knight, his expression somewhat maddened. "Shame you lost your lance."

Anderson lowered his gaze and observed two creatures bounding through the dust storm. "Well, it's coming now, if a little late." He gestured to Bonehead and Stone. "I wonder what brought them back here."

"Dragon," said Arden.

Anderson looked at her for explanation, but instead she asked, "These are yours?"

"They are that—faithless beasts."

"That's good, because with Dragon gone the force field will have gone as well."

With that, they all turned to peer back the way they had come. The ejected VR chamber was a black dot on the horizon, seemingly floating on a stratum of mist, but of the droon there was no sign. Anderson found little comfort in that.

Vulture flapped a wing over the glassy surface to blow away the settling dust. "Quite an uproar," she noted. "Dragon is nothing if not dramatic."

The fossilized apek rested, perfectly frozen, in a coffin-shaped block of solid chainglass that was raised above the ground now. Etched into the block's upper surface was a chess board. Beside this rested a spherical draconic container. Vulture had to wonder about the symbolism of it all. She looked around at the amphitheatre Dragon had cleared. The ground here was perfectly level, as if raked, in a fifty-metre circle in the middle of devastation. Amid the broken rock beyond the neat circumference lay much dragon detritus: desiccated pseudopods like a shed snake skin draped across boulders, iridescent scales the size of dinner plates, broken constructs like the by-blows of old combustion engines and lizards. Shaking her head, Vulture hopped up onto the face of the glass coffin, then turned her attention to her companion.

"Well," she said, "lay out your pieces."

Mr. Crane gazed down at the board with painted-bead eyes, blinked once, then abruptly squatted. He delved into his pockets and took out his toys. The rubber dog was his queen, the piece of crystal his king and the blue acorns were pawns. He had one piece more than required, but then was ever a battle fought by evenly matched opponents? Vulture pecked once against the draconic sphere. The thing twitched, split, and spilt miniature albino sleers, which scuttled to take their positions on the grid and with dragon eyes glare at their opponents. Now the sphere contracted, pushing out two sand hogs with minute lance-wielding human figures mounted on them, then a small droon.

"Y'know," said Vulture, "'surreal' is a word for the pretentious, but I can't think of a better one right now."

Mr. Crane took off his hat and studied the layout. He reached out and nudged a blue acorn two squares forward. A sleer nymph scuttled to it, took hold of the acorn and moved it one square aside.

Vulture said, "You don't know the rules, Crane. I do, which is why this is going to be a game difficult for me to lose."

21

Intelligent weapons have been with us for centuries now, ever since the first computer-guided missiles, jet fighters and tanks. As human wars spread out into the solar system, such weapons increased in complexity of function and mind until there were things with the outlook of trained hunting dogs but bodies more lethal. With the introduction of laws concerning AI rights, it should have been unacceptable for governments to create AI-guided bombs, missiles or other intelligent machines that would destroy themselves in the process of destroying an enemy—tantamount to creating AI kamikaze. But such organizations had been sending human beings to their deaths for millennia and did not rank other intelligences any higher. Retaining this attitude when they were finally calling the shots, the AIs proved themselves just faster and brighter versions of ourselves. The virtual world reflected the real world, as it always has ever since the invention of the first computer virus, and during those same solar wars, worms and kill programs were used to great effect. Looking back, some would say, "Same shit, different day." If only that were so. Unfortunately, intelligent weapons are subject to evolutionary pressures more substantial than those found in the natural world. And tigers now occupy what was once the territory of hunting dogs.

—*Excerpt from a speech by Jobsworth*

A door opened in whiteness, and a translucent hand gestured Jack through. King and Reaper froze on this level while on another level they utilized all their resources in fighting the worm Aphran had turned back on them. Then the embedded VR programs caught up and the ouroboros separated and struck across the eternal white. A gigantic reptilian maw closed on Reaper with a sound of bones breaking. King hurled himself back—to a tunnel hoovering down from a different direction. Jack closed the door, and the virtuality became a huge white pearl enclosing a muffled screaming. Then it sucked into itself and disappeared with a wet thwack.

"Two minds," said Jack.

"Quite possibly lethal when you only expect one," Aphran replied.

He turned towards her in a brown virtuality, probed on other levels and immediately knew that with the freedom he had allowed her she had taken so much more. She had now embedded herself so deeply in his systems that he could never root her out.

"They will escape, of course, but perhaps they will be damaged," he said. "Certainly they will henceforth be more circumspect about virtual attacks."

"Certainly."

"So now we must prepare for a *physical* battle."

Jack reduced this point of awareness, increasing his awareness of himself, of the ship. He noted that automated systems had now closed the cracks in his hull, and his larger internal structures had realigned. However, there was still a lot of small-scale damage, and much preparation yet to make. He initiated the ship's Golem, and also those robots sturdy enough to tolerate the constant acceleration. Moving slow, the chrome skeletons and other gleaming creatures began working their way through him, making repairs. When Aphran offered her services, almost without thinking he devolved control of many of them to her. He could not fret too much about this—could not fight something that was now more part of himself than even King and Reaper had been.

Ahead, the gas giant loomed like some giant polished spherical agate, surrounded by the detritus cast off from its own shaping. Jack considered how he must use this killing ground if he was to survive, and in the same instant redirected Golem and other robots to the conversion of his two internal manufactories. In his nose he opened the two baleen-tech scoop fuellers for combat refuelling, then detached their ducts from his fuel tanks and reattached them to three dropshafts he aligned, end to end down the length of his body, so as to terminate against one of his rear fusion chambers. The irised gravity fields in the shafts did not have sufficient power for the task intended, but the robot army inside himself began disassembling gravplates to provide the components needed to boost that power. Other internal redesigns devised were mainly for achieving greater structural strength. Maybe, having been incepted from him, King and Reaper would guess what he intended. But they had not done so yet, else they would not be tailing him down towards a gas giant. But, then, it was only because he had been so badly smashed inside that Jack had even contemplated such radical, tactical redesign.

Aphran, briefly separating herself, said, "I am almost too close to understand this."

Jack merely fed through to her his view of the gas giant, adding the spectroscopic analysis of its upper atmosphere which he had made when first arriving in the system. Then he continued to convert himself into a flying particle accelerator.

The telefactor released him, and he staggered a couple of paces before going down on his knees. The ground seemed to be shaking, but Cormac could not be sure. The machine protectively circled him on the top of this butte, while he shook his arms trying to return feeling to them and wished the task in his head were so simple.

So this is how madness feels.

Cormac just knew things weren't operating correctly in his skull. The cold gridlinked Cormac observed this chaotic version of himself trying to re-establish some grip on reality. The aug creature's attack had left organic damage to his brain, but it had also riddled it with new neural connections and Jain filaments. From both sides Cormac fought doubled perception, because almost like speaker and microphone in conjunction he instinctively knew that he could generate a feedback loop, which in this case would be fatal to him. It was with a kind of horror that he felt his idea of self seemingly slipping away from him, and in his striving to prevent this, he truly understood just how fragile was human awareness, the human ego—how it was just the surface of a very deep and dark pool.

Slowly Cormac returned. He regained *organic* control of his limbs, rather than through the implants inside his skull. But then he hit against the wall of his own pain. To return completely, he must completely feel the hole that had been ripped in behind his ear, his brain swollen inside his skull, and the central empty pit of a migraine that he knew would turn him blind and puking sick. Skellor brought him back some of the way, though not intentionally.

I will find you, agent. My creatures are coming for you.

Along with Skellor's threat came an image Cormac processed in his gridlink, breaking the remains of awareness he had positioned there. His head feeling on the point of exploding, he saw that projected image in the blind spot opening before him. Half-human creatures scuttled and loped out into the light. Many had pincers where their mouths should have been, or else opening and closing inside their mouths like the organic version of some grotesque doorknocker. One horror possessed a scorpion's body with a partially human face moulded in chitin. After it came a centaurish thing with the upper half of a woman connected at the waist to an insectile segmented eight-legged lower half. Madness, utter madness, but what did it all mean?

Blinding pain blossoming behind his eyes, Cormac vomited, but resisted the impulse to respond to that communication. Gritting his teeth against the next heave of his stomach, he groped in the thigh pocket of his environment suit, found a medkit and pulled from it a reel of analgesic patches. He wanted to scream at Skellor that the man could not have made these by-blow monstrosities, that it was all a lie. As the first, second, then third patch began to flood his body with their balm, he perceived that the image was indeed real—and guessed the source of those ugly creatures Skellor now controlled.

As the well into which he was staring slowly contracted, Cormac reached down to his holster and drew his thin-gun to check its load. Besides the one it already contained, he carried four extra clips on his belt. Each of these contained the fine aluminium powder that carried the energetic pulse of the weapon, and each contained the powerful laminar battery that supplied that same energy. But Cormac just shrugged to himself: he was prepared to fight, but it seemed so futile in the end. No matter how horrible were the creatures hunting him, they were not coming of their own free will—he would be killing slaves. Anyway—he glanced at the telefactor—he could pass above such encounters.

He put away the weapon and found a blue-seal dressing in the medkit, pressing it to the hole in his head. Tasting blood, the dressing deformed to fit his skull and probed inside the hole, plugging it, salving exposed nerves and creating frameworks for accelerated regrowth. Water, from a neck spigot built into the suit, thawed the dryness of his mouth. He stood and gazed out over the buttes to where he could see distant fires burning. He would just have to do what he could.

It was then that he heard a familiar whickering sound and caught the glint of something in the air. And, with a sound like a disc cutter slicing into an oil drum, Shuriken smashed into the telefactor.

Finally reaching vacuum, Dragon shrugged off planetary dust and, clawing only at the surface of space in a way that Polity AIs and human physicists would have given a lot to know, accelerated towards the sun. A few hours into its journey it detected probing signals from the ships out by the gas giant. Doubtless they considered Dragon to be an imponderable in their infantile plans. Dragon, however, intended to become a severe inconvenience. Now accelerating on a course for a slingshot, the entity focused internally for, being what might be described as the tinkerer quarter of Dragon entire, it had never been able to leave things alone for long. Concentrating on the various engines lodged inside itself—creations with a less biological bent than much else it contained—Dragon began to make adjustments.

While skimming the AI nets of the Polity in search of the innovative, and incidentally avoiding some very nasty programs whose sum purpose was to track the massive entity down, Dragon had been pleased to come across further research into that enigma wrapped up in a dilemma: gravity and its relation to U-space. And, when other killer programs had become active, Dragon knew it was venturing where ECS was developing military hardware. Grabbing as much information as it could without attracting attention, the entity retracted from the AI nets. Studying its theft, Dragon had quickly apprised itself of what ECS was up to, and used this as the basis of its own research project, which had resulted in some of the engines it now contained. These devices consisted of frame-stretched Calabri-Yau shapes—as the humans called them—and massive singularities held out of phase with normal space. It had been generating the latter that had caused the earthquakes back on the planet. Now, using baroque constructs of runcible technology for amplification and focusing, Dragon could do more than cause the ground to shake—the entity could shift and distort the very fabric of space. Obviously the interference device now active in this system stemmed from the same ECS research program Dragon had raided. The entity wanted a closer look—but most importantly it wanted a way out.

Bathed in actinic light, Dragon slung itself in a tight orbit around the sun, shielding at full power, and always accelerating. Then it used those strange engines inside itself to flip hard out of the well. Travelling at a substantial proportion of light speed, the giant entity shot out into the system. Some hours later the large green sphere of a frozen giant, erratically ringed and orbited by hundreds of icy moonlets, loomed out of the darkness. Dragon then used those engines to decelerate, the gravity wave then propagating ahead of it blowing a methane ice plume from one of the moons so that momentarily it looked like a comet.

The device the ships had brought with them was some distance out from the planet, and would have been difficult to detect had it not contained a million-tonne singularity and been the centre of the U-space storm. Scanning the thing while decelerating around the ice giant, Dragon began to plumb its function. The entity began to see how the USER oscillated the singularity through a partial runcible gate to cause the interference—taking some large heavy object and repeatedly dunking it in the pond that was U-space. Simple, really, and also simple to destroy.

Dragon began building energy for a massive full-spectrum laser strike, but a maser beam struck the entity's skin seconds before it could fire, and started boring a canyon through its flesh. Screaming inside, Dragon diverted the laser energy into a U-space surge that tilted it into U-space. A microsecond later, the USER interference flung it out again, but a thousand kilometres from its entry point.

"Well, I haven't got a lance," came the laconic communication.

Turning sharply, the glowing violet attack ship *Excalibur* came out from hiding behind a single icy moon shaped like a kidney. Straightening, it began firing near-c kinetic missiles.

"But you can still call me St. George," Sword sent.

A cold wind was scouring away the dust from the plain as if, having been held back by Dragon's hard-field for so long, it was anxious to make up for lost time. Vulture, having just had one of her sleer nymphs incinerated by Crane's laser lighter, was now trying to figure out how to prevent one of the fourth-stagers from snipping the head off the rubber dog. Standing at the end of the chainglass box, she shrugged dust from her feathers with avian nonchalance and saw that there was only one way—and it involved supper. Vulture pecked down on her piece, pulled it aside and, holding it down with one claw, snipped away its pincers and saws before flipping the unfortunate creature around in her beak, to get it head first, then swallowing it. The miniature fourth-stager was satisfyingly meaty and wriggled all the way down. Perhaps, in her previous incarnation as a ship AI, Vulture would not have appreciated this treat in the same way. But she was what she was, and as Crane made his next move—advancing the piece of crystal and turning it over—she eyed the other sleers. Of course, the aim was to get the Golem to arrange its pieces in a very particular pattern that Dragon had earlier shown Vulture. It was an arrangement it could have taken Crane a thousand years to achieve by chance, but chance was not having a good time here. The dice were loaded.

Cormac tried to recall Shuriken, but the small com-screen on his wrist holster began running alien code diagonally across it. He stripped the holster and threw it aside as if it had become infectious, as it in fact had, then drew his thin-gun and backed away as Shuriken ripped through the telefactor once more. This time the weapon hit a component that ignited like an arc rod and showered out molten metal. The telefactor dropped out of the air as if its strings had been cut, crashed against the side of a butte, then tumbled into the canyon below, where a final bright flare from a discharging power supply killed it.

This, now, was a scenario Cormac had often contemplated, and had played out a couple of times in VR. Knowing how effective Shuriken was in his hands, he had wondered what would happen if he ever came up against someone wielding a similar Tenkian weapon. In none of those scenarios had it been his own weapon, in none of them had he got a blind spot in the centre of his vision into which the lethal device disappeared every time he looked at it directly. Nor had he a head that felt as if it had been slammed in a door five or six times, nor had he OD'd on analgesic patches. It occurred to him then that if Skellor were trying to kill him now, it would at least be quick. Then he told himself not to think like that—speaking to himself was still a very strange experience—and concentrated on the task in hand.

In his gridlink, Cormac created a visual patch to fill his blind spot—and felt something like a knife blade going into his cortex. Skellor, it seemed, was playing with him, for Shuriken was now darting around the butte like a mosquito in search of bare skin. Cormac tracked it round, focusing, pushing himself into a fugue of concentration. He could not allow the slightest shake or jitter, as he would get few chances at this. Finally he fired twice, missing the first time with a ranging shot, but hitting with the second. Flung back, with chipped and cracked chainglass blades extending, Shuriken turned upwards so it resembled a gleaming eye gazing down at him. Cormac fired again, centred perfectly on target. Shuriken pulled in its blades like a sparrow folding its wings and dropped out of the sky as had the tele-factor before it.

It occurs to me that it is time I used my hostages, Skellor sent.

What do you mean? Cormac asked, not worrying about his signal being located, as Skellor certainly knew where he was right now.

Well, there's these to begin with.

Images now came through. Cormac was wary of them, expecting some attached virus. He ran them through a scan program, viewed them. The creatures he had earlier seen were turning on each other, tearing each other apart. Why was Skellor doing this?

They're not sufficiently human, I suspect, Skellor pondered. *How about a little look through Tanaquil's eyes?*

Now Cormac's point of view was of someone up on the city platform and, bleeding through with that, Cormac could feel the rigidly suppressed anguish of this victim of Skellor's. Tanaquil turned to look as people came towards him from the surrounding buildings. Zombie-like they moved past him, gathering into a crowd rubbing shoulders. The sense of anguish increased and, in the network he was partially in contact with, Cormac could feel the silent screams. The first one to reach the edge, a man dressed in thick clothing and a long padded coat, paused before climbing the two steel fences there, and just stepped off. He bellowed—Skellor returning to him enough control to do that—then others were following him, seemingly eager to throw themselves to their deaths.

No . . .

The one word came through; Skellor ruthlessly suppressed anything else. Tanaquil now watched a naked woman climbing the same fences. She too went over the edge, screaming. The eyes Cormac was seeing through now blurred with tears. *Jeelan.* The name broke through Skellor's rigid control. Just audible came the sounds of bodies impacting far below.

What do you want? Cormac asked.

Why, you.

I should give myself up to save a few natives?

With what felt to Cormac something like a mental shrug, Skellor set a man walking towards the fences. Cormac could hear the man bellowing inside his head, then begging as he climbed the fences. Cormac wanted to shut it out, but was not sure he should.

I'm not so convinced about your lack of empathy, said Skellor. *I'm sure you are a very moral man.*

Okay, you can have me if you stop the killing.

I'm walking to my way off this world, right now, said Skellor.

Something then came through from the biophysicist, and Cormac routed it into safe storage in his gridlink, expecting this to be an attempt to enslave him. Using the programming equivalent of donning thick gauntlets and safety goggles, he inspected what the biophysicist had sent, and was surprised when all he received was coordinates—an area outside the Sand Towers, some fifty kilometres away from where he stood.

Best you hurry to join me, said Skellor. *Let us say, for every fifteen minutes you are out of my sight, I'll walk another one of them off the edge.*

Fethan adjusted his vision to infrared and gaped at the hellish scene in the Undercity. Though aware that people often misapplied the term "unnatural" to alien life, that would not have been the case here. The creatures he saw were not the result of evolution, nor, it seemed to him, were they designed for any more useful purpose than to horrify. Why give a human mandibles, why give a huge insect soft hands—and why that other thing with the screaming human face? Yes, he guessed that some reasoning could be applied: give a man mandibles so he could handle alien food, or give that insect hands so it could manipulate tools as easily as a human. But that took no account of the personal suffering caused by such experiments. Anyway, Skellor could not have had time to do all of this, so that left only one other culprit. Fethan shuddered, and wondered what Dragon had been trying to achieve here.

Though many of the creatures in the Undercity were fearsome indeed, none of them attacked Fethan, and he soon realized that they were all aug-controlled and mostly heading away from him, like a procession of the damned heading out for judgement. It was a mystery he decided he might pursue some other time, for the aug creatures he had followed under the platform were teeming here, and he tracked their lines of progress easily back through the darkness. He followed one of these lines, perpetually slapping away those of the insects that dropped onto him from above, also deliberately crushing the same things underfoot. Eventually, in this horrible place, he passed corpses bound to the ground by filaments and sucked dry, with tentacular things writhing in the dirt underneath them. Then he spotted the source of the aug insects.

Fethan would not have recognized the bloated thing as once being human had it not been for some fragments of clothing clinging to its bruised skin and a bracelet buried in the flesh of the one limb that had not been fully absorbed. The head was just a hairy nub over a frogmouth orifice that continuously leaked a foamy mucus squirming with aug insects. This mouth was not for feeding. Fethan guessed that the tentacles extending below this . . . creature were intended for that, and that it had not already dragged *him* down because he was inedible.

Unshouldering his APW, he paused for a moment, knowing that this thing before him had once been human. But it was not human now, and what he was about to do amounted to a mercy killing. Conscious of metal pillars nearby, he carefully chose the setting on his weapon. He fired once.

The thing burst before him in a ball of violet fire, and the detonation had aug creatures raining down all around. In the deeper darknesses of the Undercity, other things screeched and bellowed, but none of them came into view. Stepping closer to the steaming mess, Fethan knocked his weapon's setting right down, and kept firing small bursts to burn the embryonic creatures crawling about in the slimy remains. Afterwards, as the smoke slowly cleared, he saw the rest of the aug creatures still marching away in lines to find their victims. He had destroyed the source of the insectile creatures, but not them.

Fethan stared, wondering how many creatures he could burn before the power supply of his weapon gave out. What else could he possibly do? Then it became obvious. No matter how this looked, it was aug technology—sophisticated computer networking. He extended his forefinger up before his night vision, sent an internal detach signal, then removed the syntheflesh covering. Allowing the kill program to see through his eyes, he slowly surveyed his surroundings, taking in the remains of that *thing* he had destroyed, the now revealed root-like structures in the ground, the multitude of aug insects.

"Do you see this?" he asked.

I see.

"Where could you go in?"

Try substructure in the ground.

Fethan brushed away earth with his foot, exposing a grey fibrous tentacle that shifted slightly. He stooped and pressed the metal tip of his finger into it. This was Jain tech, he knew, but worth the risk. Fibres parted, his fingertip sank in, and he felt the ache of transference as another killer program transcribed.

*

The *Grim Reaper* and the *King of Hearts* were decelerating at slightly different rates, the *Reaper* eighty thousand kilometres ahead of the *King*. Jack would have preferred them to be the other way round because, though Reaper was the more aggressive, Jack considered it also the more stupid. Perhaps King had let the *Grim Reaper* take the point for this very reason. The gas giant was close now, coming up like an undersea blue hole, and Jack was beginning to taste chemicals in the vacuum: hydrogen and hydrogen peroxide, methane and wafts of mercury vapour—a strange combination that was perfect for the AI's requirements.

"You are gambling all on one shot, and if that fails you will be vulnerable as you climb back out of the planet's gravity well," Aphran noted.

Jack allowed processing space to stand a projection of his avatar on the ship's bridge amongst his splintered collection. Aphran, choosing her own routes to processing, placed her own avatar beside him.

"I should at least get one of them, then the odds won't be quite the same as they were on Cull," he replied.

"Still the odds will be against you."

Jack allowed that this was true, but noted that his children had screwed up once already, and might do so again.

The *Jack Ketch* hammered down and down towards the gas giant, with Jack continually adjusting the human side of his perspective. What began as a mere dot in space grew to fill the fullest extent of vision—seeming to become vaster than the space all around it. Eventually the ship was speeding at an angle down onto a vast plain of cloud much like anything seen in a virtuality. This plain appeared endless, any curve to the horizon not visible to human perception. But Jack wasn't human, and that made his comprehension of this immensity even greater. It struck him as decidedly operatic.

Constantly adjusting his angle of approach so that a line drawn through his body intersected with the *Grim Reaper* a quarter of a million kilometres out, Jack turned on ram-scoop fields designed to pick up the sparse hydrogen of interstellar space. Gas funnelled in towards him in a huge thickening wave. This decelerated him more effectively than anything he could have done with his gravmotors. By the time it reached his baleen-tech fuellers, the gas was dense as any liquid, but also turning to plasma. From the fuellers it entered the drop-shaft positioned down his length, where irised gravity fields accelerated it to as near light-speed as made little difference. For seconds only could the *Jack Ketch* act as a pressure valve, but it was enough to make a difference.

The beam of photonic matter lashed up from the gas giant, straight into the nose of the *Grim Reaper*. The ship did not have time for evasion, but the AI mind inside it had an eternity of nanoseconds to contemplate what was happening to it. There were no real explosions; the beam just took away the ship's main body, converting it to a plume of plasma many kilometres long. The *Reaper*'s two weapons nacelles tumbled through space: bird's wings severed from the bird itself. Turned at its fulcrum, the *Jack Ketch*, the beam then swept across towards the *King of Hearts*. The second ship initiated all its hard-fields and flung itself into an eight-hundred-gravity swerve that must have wrecked it internally as much as the *Jack Ketch* had been, for King had only microseconds to prepare. Jack knew that the other AI understood the futility of what it was doing: it could not outrun the swinging end of a lever hundreds of thousands of kilometres long.

Now I am shitting laser beams! Jack bellowed across the ether.

But then, through either calculation or pure luck, the *King of Hearts* slid behind one icy moon that took the few seconds remaining of the blast. The moon broke up on a gaseous explosion, began to tumble apart. Behind it, the *King of Hearts* peeled away and began to swing round.

"Bugger," said Jack, ram-scoops now off and baleen-tech fuellers closed, as he laboured back up out of the gravity well.

Running with unhuman speed towards the place where the landers had come down, Skellor felt a sudden surge of joy as he began to realize that he might actually get himself out of this. Not only that, he could take down that ECS shit in the process. But his happiness, as is the wont of such things, was short-lived. Tanaquil's confusion up there on the city platform alerted him, and in the man's memory Skellor observed the scaled moon climbing rapidly into the sky. Then, as if this were sucking the energy from him, he suddenly found himself slowing, as a huge human weariness overtook him. Finally he ran out from the Sand Towers at simply human speed and stumbled to a halt, stopping to rest, even supporting himself against a sulerbane plant.

To his left smoke rose from the city of Golgoth and, again focusing through the aug network and through Tanaquil's eyes, he observed a metallier walk woodenly to the edge of the Overcity platform and hurl himself off. He had set the program now: the entire population, with Tanaquil last, was queuing up to do the same—and one would go off every quarter-hour until they were all gone, whether Cormac joined Skellor at the landers or not. But Skellor's problem was not there.

Focusing inward to the Jain substructure of which more than eighty per cent of his body consisted, Skellor finally located the growing nodes that were sapping his strength. They had burgeoned secretively, concealed from his internal diagnostics almost with the collusion of those same diagnostics. He felt a perfectly human panic. It was because of these changes inside himself that he had come here at all, yet he had only endangered himself and learned nothing, and now the one who might have had some answers was gone. He had failed.

He reached out almost instinctively, but Crane was also still unavailable to him. Pushing away from the sulerbane plant, Skellor screamed with rage—but focused rage.

He isolated the worst and most hungry of the nodes, then started working to eject it. But his own body, his Jain body, now fought him. Agonizingly, he opened a split in his stomach, and a single node pushed through like a golden eyeball and fell out. Skellor gasped and staggered back against the sulerbane plant. That had taken nearly . . . everything in him. He keyed to the network, searched around, found what he wanted. Within a few minutes a sleer with the face of a woman scuttled out from the Sand Towers towards him. Skellor greeted her with arms open wide and Jain tendrils breaking from his skin, then embraced her and fed. Only minutes later he discarded the empty carapace, and was turning his attention once again to the nodes when, like the stars at Armageddon, the network began to fade.

"What the hell?"

Precisely, something hissed at him out of the ether, and tried to bore its way into his mind.

You?

He had fought this in the network on *Ruby Eye*. So how was it here? He reached out, tried to find some human suffering to counter this attack, but the more he groped for victims, the more of them slipped from his grasp. Suddenly he realized the futility of what he was doing. He had to get away, and having control here was nothing to him now. He broke into a run, shut down his connection, killed the pseudo-aug inside himself. He accelerated, now re-energized, travelling faster than any human. He also grinned to himself, for Cormac could know nothing of this and would still come. Skellor would have that victory, at the very least.

The lizard possessing the double wings of a dragonfly—obviously—rested in the rigid curve of a sulerbane leaf and with sapphire eyes observed Skellor run on. When he was out of sight it launched into the air to hover above the remains of his prey. Then it descended and began to tear up the few remaining fragments of meat—it too needed to eat after all. Replete, it turned its attention to the golden node resting in the sand nearby and observed vague cubic patterns travelling over its surface. The creature's programming was simple, but its mind was still somewhat part of the mind of its creator. It still also possessed the survival instinct engendered by its original DNA (which had as its source, human scientists might be frightened to learn, a lizard from the Australian outback, some tens of thousands of years before any human knew what DNA was, as well as another fragment it had amused Dragon to find in a piece of amber). Therefore, seeing that node and recognizing what the cubic patterns meant, the creature took off and fled just as fast as it could back to the sulerbane plant. There, perched again in the curve of a leaf, it knew it had ventured too close to something. Might be infected by something. Its kin, resting on buttes, roosting in empty sleer burrows or secreting themselves in the iron gutters of Golgoth, whilst observing other scenes, other human dramas, as they had ever since Dragon had first created them thirty years before, abruptly shut it out. It began shivering, knowing it would soon be uncreated.

As Anderson mounted Bonehead and Arden climbed up behind him to sit on one of his strapped-down packs, Thorn eyed Tergal and then his strange mount. Its carapace was much like that of a horseshoe crab, but more stretched out, and its forelimbs also were similar to that creature's. Its rear limbs, however, resembled the powerful reverse-kneed legs of a land bird, but armoured with chitin. It showed no sign of eyes or antennae until it flipped up its complicated dual, feeding and sensory, heads—sometimes appearing independently from under different areas of the carapace rim, or sometimes joined like mating components in a child's build-your-own-monster kit. As the creature dropped down onto its crawler legs, Thorn grabbed at the rim and jumped on. He then moved up behind Tergal and, gripping the back of the youth's saddle, squatted down carefully, as the creature rose back up again. Soon the two sand hogs were advancing through a haze of dust, the ground still shaking as parts of the plain collapsed into the kilometre-deep hollow Dragon had left behind them.

"I heard him call his own beast Bonehead," Thorn said to Tergal. "So what's this chap called?"

"Stone," Tergal replied briefly.

"I see it's smaller than Anderson's . . . sand hog. Is that because it's younger, or of a different sex?"

Tergal glanced at him as if he had said something idiotic, which Thorn supposed he doubtless had.

"Stone's the younger hog, and females aren't used as mounts—there's fewer of them and they tend to stray very quickly. They're pampered and kept for breeding."

"Ah."

Within a few hundred metres, the sand hogs were stepping carefully across uprooted boulders and ground that had been churned up by Dragon's departure. Thorn noted the iridescence of scattered Dragon scales, shed pseudopods like snake skins, and other abandoned, unfathomable devices obviously of draconic origin. He wryly considered just how Mika would kill for a chance to be here studying these things. Then he directed his attention ahead to where the ejected VR chamber still rested at the edge of this widespread devastation. The monster, which Arden had named a droon, was nowhere in sight and, with that particular danger no longer evident, Thorn felt he should consider what to do next. He was still experiencing a feeling of unreality, and was aware of the danger of VR detachment which led people to believe that nothing happening around them mattered. Even so, as they drew athwart the VR chamber, though still sufficiently detached not to be making any plans, his reactions had not slowed at all.

Stone was now ten metres ahead and somewhat to the left of Bonehead, and consequently much closer to the chamber when its roof peeled up like the top of a sardine can and the droon reared up out of it.

"Oh fuck," was the extent of Tergal's reaction. Stone flung out its sensory head then abruptly retracted it. The hog began to turn as the droon opened its numerous orange mouths, its head extending as it charged itself with mucal acid. Thorn grabbed Tergal around the waist, heaved him up, then hurled the pair of them sideways off the hog. A sheet of mucus splashed behind them just as they went over the edge and hit the ground. As he released the youth and rolled,

Thorn glimpsed the sand hog stumbling back and collapsing on its rear, its two necks and its legs seemingly entangled. Thorn was already on his feet, dragging Tergal upright into a stumbling run, as the hog issued a siren scream and began to boil, its limbs shaking as liquid bubbled from the joints and both heads thrashing from side to side.

"No . . . Oh no . . ."

As Tergal stumbled to a halt, gazing back in horror, Thorn caught him by the shoulder and shoved him onwards. The droon was already stepping out of the VR chamber, its head tracking towards them. Automatic fire crackled as Anderson emptied a clip into the monster, but he might as well have thrown gravel at a rhinoceros. It was the fourth-stage sleer materializing to one side of the droon that gave them time to get to Bonehead and mount, before the old hog turned and fled back towards the draconic devastation. Clinging on beside Tergal and Arden, Thorn observed the illusory sleer flicker out of existence, and the droon turning to watch them go before bowing its head down to the steaming remains of Stone.

With the supreme confidence of a most lethal attack ship, Sword accelerated towards Dragon, weapons carousels turning as the AI made its armament selections like some chocolate connoisseur in a Belgian sweet shop. It was aware that Dragon was dangerous and that its previous incarnations had caused huge destruction of human installations and ships—the obliteration of the laser arrays at Masada being ample demonstration. But other AIs had already evaluated these actions, and Sword knew that unless this particular sphere possessed substantially more firepower than its previous incarnations, the AI attack ship would easily be able to flatten it.

"Interesting move," Sword sent, "but that's got to have burnt out a U-space engine, so I have to wonder how many more you have left."

"I don't want this fight," Dragon replied, dragging itself across the surface of space to avoid the kinetic missiles fired at it. Beyond it, the blackness filled with multiple flares as many of those missiles impacted an evanescent debris ring.

"Isn't that always the protest of those who know they are going to lose?"

Sword tracked the Dragon sphere as it rolled into silhouette in front of the ice giant. How the creature was managing to propel itself was a mystery. Certain spacial anomalies surrounded it, and this made Sword a little more cautious. That caution increased when, precisely at that moment, the communication from King reached it, and it learnt that Reaper was gone.

"Damn you, Jack." Sword spat out this communication on a tight beam towards the gas giant.

"It's a dangerous universe," Dragon then sent. "Don't overplay your hand."

There was no way the alien entity could break encoded radio transmissions so quickly. Almost in a fit of pique, Sword fired gas lasers and then masers at Dragon, and followed these with a cloud of smart missiles. The laser strike flashed away on a mirrored hard-field, while the maser strike just seemed to expand that same field without reaching the surface of Dragon. In answer to the missiles, Dragon belched from some orifice a swarm of small black spheres. When, some minutes later, the two clouds of devices met, it seemed that a small thunderstorm ensued.

Passing over this, the *Excalibur* pursued Dragon through one orbit of the ice giant, then back out into space towards the USER. As it did so it observed the ripples spreading across the surface of its opponent, and knew the entity was preparing for a massive full-spectrum laser strike. They were too far yet from the USER for such a strike to be effective there, so it must be intended for the *Excalibur* itself. Preparing its hard-fields and the heat-dispersing lasers linked to the superconducting mesh in its hull, Sword almost felt pity for the creature. It obviously had no idea what it was up against.

"Arrogance is its own reward," Dragon sent.

Abruptly, a single large wave spread out over the surface of the Dragon sphere—but did not stop there. It propagated, impossibly, out into vacuum. In a nanosecond, Sword realized it should have been aware of this possibility, for it was inherent in the device the AI ship guarded. This was USER technology.

Sword began firing all its missiles at once, while diverting energy to structural integrity fields. Missiles and wave met, and the missiles died like bugs under some huge roller. When the gravity wave hit Sword, it was like a tsunami slamming into a wooden sailing ship pinned against a shore. The *Excalibur* distorted, broke, and Sword screamed over the ether. Inside the AI ship, antimatter escaped its containment in missiles the ship had not managed to eject. This was the real reason the AI had tried to fire all its missiles, as no containment was proof against gravitational breach. It had not succeeded in time. The subsequent explosions did not leave much in the way of debris, and what it did leave rapidly dispersed.

"Hubris," Dragon commented, then tittered to itself.

The wave continued spreading out, its strength diminishing, but it was still strong enough when it hit the USER. The towing ship just fragmented and blew away, while the USER itself distorted but held its relative position as if someone had nailed it to vacuum. Then its singularity containment failed. The device glowed briefly and disappeared in an x-ray flash, as hundreds of tonnes of metal and composite collapsed down to an infinitely small point.

Now observing the gravitational terrain, Dragon watched the singularity begin its long slow fall towards the ice giant. The entity then made some calculations, and noted that the damage had only just begun—the real spectacular stuff would occur in about fifty solstan years as the giant planet started to collapse in on itself. Dragon gave a titanic shrug and wished there was somewhere to run, but with so many U-space data streams still shut down, even after it had knocked out the USER, the entity realized it was in a Polity trap—that there were others USERs out there. Then, turning its attention back towards the planet, re-establishing that communications link, it uploaded recent data from thousands of small lizard brains. Data from one of those had Dragon accelerating back towards Cull, as inside itself it initiated repairs to its own U-space drives which had been damaged in its first escape from Sword.

The entity worked with some urgency—*one* Skellor was quite enough.

22

I can, should this flesh-and-blood body fail me, be loaded to silicon or crystal or mag-carbon, or even to a Q-puter (though in the last case I would probably fit inside something the size of a skin cell). I do have a memplant, and keep my account at Soulbank up to date. I could be loaded into a speed-grown blank clone of myself, the body of a mind-wiped criminal or suicide, a Golem or some other android, or a gen-factored body of my own design (had I the wealth). I am practically immortal and still I cannot quite grasp what that means. I could read these words a century down the line. I could read them in a million years . . . No, it still is not clear to me. Is it time to upgrade myself and move beyond mere humanity, perhaps become the guiding AI of some ship or even a runcible AI? Maybe, for those of us who can bear immortality, this is the path we must take. Is this what our AI children, who are also our brothers and gods, are waiting for?

—*Anonymous*

Shattered bodies lay below the edge of the platform. Fethan recognized the unmistakable contortion and surrounding spatter pattern, and knew they had died by falling from above. Without much hope of finding any of them alive, he moved over and checked for a few pulses. It was then that he saw the aug creatures struggling to pull free, their legs straining to draw their tubules from the side of these people's heads. Moving away, he assumed they were abandoning corpses to find other prey, until a man came stumbling from the ruination, groaning in agony as his aug creature also tried to pull itself free.

The man staggered over to the corpses, dragged the naked body of a woman to him and cradled her head in his lap. He became silent then, rocking back and forth and stroking her misshapen forehead. Fethan noted the liquid smear of brain running from her ear, wanted to help but knew he had nothing to offer. Returning his attention to the man's aug, he saw that it had almost pulled loose—coils of bloody tubules now between itself and the man's head. But it seemed that advantaged it nothing, for it began to vibrate and turn grey, then hopped away from its perch and folded up in the dust, dying. Now, Fethan heard the sound of a hailstorm, which he had learned was a common weather condition here.

But this was no hail. Turning, he saw aug creatures, grey and dying in their thousands, falling from the underside of the city platform. He wondered how this particular copy of the kill program felt about destroying its own environment.

I have no urge to self-preservation beyond my task, the master copy replied after he internalized the question.

But surely your task was to kill Skellor?

It is, but when that ceases to be possible, my imperatives change.

You can't get to Skellor . . . I mean this copy of you can't get to him.

Correct. Skellor has disconnected from the network.

You communicate with your copy, then?

Yes.

What are those imperatives now, down here?

For my copy: to save human lives by destroying this enslaving network—Skellor had programmed self-destruction for its human nodes.

That figures.

Fethan noticed that the man was now looking up at him. What must he be seeing? Just someone standing muttering to himself and gazing into the distance? He walked over.

"Who are you?" the man croaked.

"My name's Fethan."

"You . . . you are not from around here."

"No."

The man was staring with suspicion at Fethan's chameleon-cloth environment suit while easing the head of his loved one from his lap.

Fethan was old, in the terms of this place, and he knew how to read people. "I'm not here to cause harm, but to help," he said. "It's because of me, these things"—he nudged an aug creature with the toe of his boot—"are now dying."

The man stood up. "Where is the one who caused this?"

"I don't know. On the run probably, but I don't think he'll get far. Tell me, what are you called?"

The man slumped, suddenly very weary. "Tanaquil, Chief Metallier of this city," he said, then, "Dragon warned us, but how could we believe . . . *this*?"

"Yes, it always comes hard," Fethan replied.

The droon was still visible through the haze, its body distended by its feasting on Stone so that bare flesh, the colour of custard, showed between ribs of carapace. The thing was evil, Tergal decided. It had killed his stepfather's sand hog and had no reason to come after them now, having fed so well. The whole situation just wasn't fair. Tergal angrily scrubbed at a self-pitying tear, then turned his attention to the new madness ahead.

"We followed him out," Anderson told the man Thorn. The knight then turned to Arden and said, "That case down by your feet, could you open it?"

The woman did as instructed, passing up the sections of bonded amanis-fibre pole to Anderson. The knight, it would seem, was truly mad. The droon would turn him into smoking slurry before he even got a chance to get close.

Thorn said, "That weapon, surely you can't mean to use it against chummy back there?" He stabbed a thumb over his shoulder. "Or is it for Mr. Crane here?" At Anderson's puzzled expression, Thorn added, "The big brass bastard is called Mr. Crane."

"What's the other thing, then?" asked Anderson.

"That's a vulture," Thorn replied. "Not one of this planet's usual life forms, I take it?"

"Not as far as I know," replied Anderson, concentrating on the task in hand.

Why this Mr. Crane was squatting beside what looked like a big block of glass, playing some game with a *vulture*, Tergal had no idea. But looking around at the level arena the two were playing in made him realize why Anderson had chosen this spot.

"Wouldn't it be better if we just kept going?" Tergal asked. "Maybe the brass man . . ."

Anderson frowned at him. "I fight my own battles." The knight turned once again to Arden. "Would the power from my fence batteries operate your holocapture device?"

"It would," Arden replied, "but they would be drained very quickly. How long would you want it to operate for?"

"Long enough to drain our pursuer."

"We could just keep running," Tergal suggested again.

Thorn observed, "Feeding has distended its body and revealed gaps in its carapace. Using your carbine I could probably cause it some real damage."

Arden said, "That seems a shame, since they are rare, but it won't stop coming after us, and perhaps it *would* be better to face it in daylight. I can run the holocaptures for long enough."

Tergal made no more suggestions. No one seemed to be listening to him. Then abruptly Anderson turned to him. "You can leave us, if that's what you want."

Tergal took a ragged breath. "I might be frightened, but I'm not stupid."

As he laboured up from hydrogen seas, through storms and chemical maelstroms and acidic hurricanes that would have flayed a human in an eyeblink, Jack realized he was not going to make it. The *King of Hearts* was bearing down on him just as fast as it could. It had probably used less than ten per cent of its munitions and was also probably very pissed off—though for an attack ship AI that was a normal state of mind. Another scoop run to generate a beam sufficient to destroy the opposing ship was out of the question: the tidal forces exerted by the gas giant would rip apart Jack's severely damaged structure before he managed a sufficient lase of the surrounding gas to strike at the *King of Hearts*. Perhaps, Jack idly pondered, now was the time to just turn everything off and let the planet take him. Surely that was preferable to giving King the satisfaction of frying him with masers?

"Oh no you damned well don't," snapped Aphran. "There's two of us living in here."

"I'm open to suggestions," Jack said.

"My first one would be that you don't give up," she offered.

With almost a desultory shrug, Jack began to inventory his weapons. He was still loaded for bear, but that was not the problem: his structure would not be able to bear much more of a load. A near miss with an imploder, or any other CTD for that matter, and he knew he would start to come apart like wet tissue paper. Nevertheless . . .

"Oh, I wasn't really going to give up. That was just an idle speculation. I do have a plan ready."

"And what is it?"

"Time and escape velocity. I just need to give King something to think about."

An hour later a pillar of flame ignited beside the *Jack Ketch* as the *King of Hearts* probed the gas giant's atmosphere with a megajoule coloured laser, probably only to illuminate the whole area so as to precisely locate its prey.

"Ah, there you are, Jack," King sent.

Jack immediately changed course, but without losing height. This time a tower of incandescence exploded into existence, and the shock wave slapped against the *Jack Ketch*. Turning his carousels, Jack began selecting and firing missile after missile. Any other weapons were presently out of the question, as they required power from Jack's own systems to fire, whereas he could launch the missiles under their own power (though in different circumstances he would have launched many of them by rail gun). The swarm rose out of the gas clouds, black in silhouette and poised on achingly bright white fusion flames: strange birds in this bizarre sky.

But before they even made it out into open space masers and lasers began picking them off. Some dodged, putting cloud masses between themselves and their eventual target, but in the end they must come out and make themselves more vulnerable. *Shooting fish in a barrel* was the expression Jack dredged from his memory banks, feeling a bit like a whale. He sent the signal then for the remaining missiles to detonate long before they reached the *King of Hearts*.

"Is this part of the plan?" Aphran asked.

"Have you no faith?" Jack countered.

"I did until I died."

Jack let that one lie.

Above him, fires burned in the gas giant's atmosphere, some of them nuclear and with the potential never to extinguish. These concealed Jack from King. Still climbing, Jack tracked the pattern of maser and laser strikes coming through this protective umbrella. Internally, throughout his ascent, he had reattached the ducts from his scoops to his fuel tanks and had been passively taking on hydrogen. Reaching an apex as the umbrella finally began to disperse, he slanted his course tangential to the gas giant, then injected the fuel into the aligned dropshaft he had used as a particle cannon. This time he had no mind to aim the photonic matter at any enemy, just to benefit from the thrust. Under huge acceleration, he shot out from underneath the umbrella, angled slightly down but building up towards escape velocity. He was minutes away from achieving that velocity when he detected small scanning drones in the surrounding area.

"You know," sent King, "it's frustrating possessing an Oedipus complex when you don't have a mother. Probably as frustrating as you are going to find this."

The maser struck the connecting stanchion to Jack's right-hand weapons nacelle, cut accurately back, and the nacelle tumbled away, trailing fire. The second strike cut away the other nacelle. Jack supposed his offspring was toying with him, and now knew the difference between himself and King. He himself would not have delayed. Whether King was holding back out of a reluctance to kill or some emulation of cruelty, that was moot. Jack cared not one whit—there was nothing usable in the nacelles now anyway.

The next strike King calculated quite finely and Jack reckoned it was using the drones it had earlier dropped throughout the area for accurate triangulation—and as eyes through which to gloat. The maser cut right through Jack's fusion chambers, and the ensuing explosion peeled open his rear section like a banana. He tumbled through cloud surrounded by his own wreckage. There would be no escape now—he just did not have the systems left to repair such damage in time. Jack awaited the final killing strike and sensed, in that moment, the USER going offline. It was no help to him, however—his U-space engines having been damaged and cannibalized. That King did not finally finish him off, he put down to whatever else was going on out there, or how irrelevant he had become.

"Time we left," said Aphran, as they fell towards crushing oblivion.

Jack laughed, surprised because his reaction was no emulation intended for the comfort of humans but arose from deep inside him. Then his laughter cut off as he felt Aphran's machinations.

"What are you doing?" he asked.

The four heavily armoured telefactors clambered through a jungle of bracing struts, through masses of hardened crash foam like bracket fungi, and vine-like tangles of optics and cables. Ape-like, they approached an area of the *Jack Ketch* right behind the nose chamber, which Jack found rather sensitive. He tried to usurp control, found himself unable to. He then tried to summon other mechanisms to deal with the situation, but saw that Aphran had been busy there as well. She had burnt out all of the ship Golem and other robots.

"We are going to die anyway," he said, "so why do you attack me?"

"Because," Aphran replied, "you seem to have forgotten that *you* are not this ship. That's probably a built-in perception to make you fight better."

With heavy cutting claws, the telefactors swiftly chopped through an armoured bulkhead. In the spherical chamber beyond, caught between two metal protuberances like the business ends of combustion engine valves, was compressed a carapace of black metal that partially wrapped a lozenge of crystal. Turning on their cutting lasers, the telefactors began slicing through the metal columns above and below this object. Jack immediately felt systems going offline, his control slipping away.

"You are killing me . . . and yourself," he protested.

Like a balloon collapsing, his awareness drew inward, until at length nothing remained to him but the vision of an armoured telefactor reaching for him with one huge crab claw. In that lensed awareness he felt Aphran's presence.

"Why?"

"You'll see."

Following the program Aphran had previously input, the telefactor picked up the mind of the attack ship and took it through the internal wreckage to what remained of the erstwhile dropshaft then particle cannon. There it coiled around the mind whilst another program took over the allotted task and, waiting until the tumble of the ship brought the shafts precisely to the correct angle, flipped a switch.

Jack did not become photonic matter—there wasn't enough power left for that—but he certainly achieved escape velocity. His body, the ship, fell.

Still running, Cormac was within sight of the open when another of the hybrids lunged at him out of the shadows. This one was the same nightmare he had seen through Skellor's network, and for a moment he could not quite comprehend that it was real. From the waist up she was a woman, but insectile chitinous body with too many legs from the waist down.

"Back off!" Cormac yelled, firing into the ground before her. Like all the others, she ignored this and continued to charge him. As her head bent forwards, out of her widening mouth a set of pincers oozed into view. She hissed at him. Cormac shot her twice in the forehead and prepared to shoot away her legs too, but she collapsed, as if unstrung, and he ran on.

His head was aching horribly once again, and he felt thirsty and sick but dared not stop to rest, for that could cost another life. Thus far it had taken him three hours to reach the edge of the Sand Towers—meaning twelve lives—and used up two thin-gun clips. He wondered if to the lives of all those jumping from the city platform he should add those he had left lying in the dust behind him. Though partially human they might appear, they had not behaved like intelligent beings.

There were fires in the city, he noticed, probably due to furnaces left unattended. But most of the structures there being metallic, hopefully would not last very long. Cormac zeroed in on the coordinates he now held in his gridlink. Far to his right he saw a lander lying tilted against a small hill and, recognizing its source, wondered if Cento and Fethan were still alive. His destination was not that lander, though—for it still lay ahead.

As he ran, he reached into his pocket and pressed a couple more glucose tablets from a strip. These he popped into his mouth, washing them down with a sip of water from the tube at his collar. Skellor, he knew, might try to kill him, but maybe that would not happen right away. People *were* dying in the city right now. That he had no hesitation in giving himself up Cormac supposed the downside of both the responsibility and power of being an agent of Earth Central Security. Yes, he could balance the loss of life at *Elysium* against what had been the potential loss of life at Masada. In many situations he could be judge, jury and executioner. But when it came to value judgements about human life, he must make no exceptions and also strictly apply the same rules to himself. Under ECS law he would have been well within his rights to say screw the people here, they are not Polity. But his own law would not allow him that.

Cormac ran on for another hour, the fatigue poisons accumulating in his body and pain growing like lead shot in his muscles. Since the Cheyne III AI had turned off his gridlink all those years ago, he had refused all other augmentations, preferring to be no more than the human he had been born. But even with that limitation, he was still, due to genetic manipulation, the best human possible, possessing the reserves and strengths of an Olympian. Now, with his gridlink functioning for no apparent reason and Jain fibres lacing his brain, such distinctions had become laughable.

His feet thumping down on a spongy fungal layer covering the dunes, Cormac laboured up one final slope. Another hour had now passed during which, doubtless, other victims had jumped to their deaths. Breasting the slope, he gazed down on another ancient landing craft, raised up on its hydraulic feet with a ramp down and lights on inside it. Behind the craft, the sun was poised like a poison fruit on the horizon.

"You can stop the killing now," he announced. He did not shout, did not think it would be necessary, for surely Skellor would hear him. His thin-gun at his side, Cormac headed down towards the craft.

Skellor himself stepped into view, in the airlock, then walked down onto the dust.

"You can stop the killing now," Cormac repeated.

"No." Skellor grinned.

Cormac had expected nothing else, but that did not excuse him from making the attempt. There was only one other way, then—four shots slammed into the bio-physicist's chest. Burning deep, one blew pieces out of his back. Cormac could not decide if it was a grimace or a grin that twisted the man's features before he stepped aside and . . . disappeared. Keeping his finger on the trigger, Cormac continued firing in the direction he felt sure his enemy had gone. The shots punched smoking lines down the side of the landing craft.

Transferring his attention to the ground the agent noticed footprints, so fired again, glimpsed a flickering snarling image. When a red light displayed on his gun, he ejected the clip while simultaneously pulling another from his belt—his reloading so fast there was no pause in his fusillade. The footsteps suddenly disappeared.

Cormac calculated, turned and aimed in a completely new direction, tracked across, and hit something. A second later the gun was snatched, smoking, from his hand, and he himself was hurled to the ground.

Skellor reappeared, the gun in his hand. On his body various holes were slowly closing.

"It's an automatic program walking them off the edge—so killing me won't stop it," he sneered.

Cormac rolled to his feet, his hands held out at either side. "You have me now, so what do you get by killing them?"

"To torment you, of course."

Cormac considered hurling himself at the biophysicist's throat, but recognized the futility of the act. Any thought of running was futile too.

"They will all die—like clockwork," Skellor added, unnecessarily.

Calculation: Skellor could only torment him while he was conscious. Cormac hurled himself forwards, groping for Skellor's throat. The hot barrel of his own thin-gun smacked against his temple, knocking him to the ground. He rolled upright, but Skellor was invisible once more. Something hit his head again, splitting his scalp so that a flap of skin lifted on the pulse of blood. Knuckles smashed into his nose—more blood, more pain—and more blows followed. When he felt he had taken enough, Cormac shut down his perceptile programs and allowed his consciousness to leave him.

Burping dyspeptically, Vulture understood that sleers caused acid indigestion. Or perhaps the imminence of death did that? The little AI would not have minded Arden and her new companions coming here, but the droon was a different matter entirely. Vulture knew that Dragon would kill her, somehow, if she did not complete her task—the entity had probably written it into her avian wiring—so she must stay with this game. But now remaining here had also become a fatal option. All she could hope was that Arden and crew could deal with the unwelcome monster. She returned her attention to Crane as he reached out to make his next move.

The random nature of Crane's search for the right arrangement caused a bit of a problem. Again he was reaching towards the piece of crystal that Vulture had made the one stable point in the pattern. It was frustrating. Beyond Crane, she observed Arden and the rest dismounting and dispersing amid the surrounding ruination, while the Rondure Knight positioned his lance in its frame. His seemed like the best plan, but she wondered how he would persuade the skittish sand hog to charge at the droon, or how he would avoid being himself dissolved in the monster's volatile saliva. Suddenly irritated beyond patience by her ridiculously fatal circumstances, Vulture gave a savage peck, her beak clonking on Mr. Crane's brass fingers.

The Golem froze, and Vulture was sure she could see something flickering in his right eye. He withdrew his hand and raised his face to look at her directly. Vulture waited taut seconds, expecting to have her neck wrung, but Crane dipped his head again, bird-like, and there seemed a strange symmetry to that. Instead of reaching for the crystal, he reached for one of the acorns.

Vulture ahem'd loudly and Crane's hand wavered, dropped instead on the laser lighter, shifting that. Vulture edged forwards one of the miniature sand hogs with its rider, who used his lance to prod a blue acorn into a new position. Everything seemed to be working out okay—at least in the game.

But Vulture decided to be sure. The little ship AI retreated to a small virtuality maintained by a draconic mechanism buried underneath the fossilized apek. Here a human would have perceived twelve oddly shaped fragments of crystal dancing around each other, sometimes meshing, sometimes parting, and another five fragments permanently joined into one lump. But Vulture, with the perception of an AI capable of guiding a ship through U-space, saw so much more. She saw acceptance of horror by something ostensibly incapable of causing it, she saw timelines aligning and disparate subminds feeding the yet evanescent concept of self. She saw an ego growing: tender, hollow growth ready to be filled with steel. Yes, it was working. Returning to strange reality, Vulture was surprised to see Mr. Crane staring at her again. It was ridiculous really—he did not have what Vulture would call a mind—but she was sure he *knew* she was helping him.

Arden had nothing but admiration for the Rondure Knight's courage and wished their acquaintance might not be so brief. But very shortly the man was going to be dead, and she doubted the rest of them would long survive him. Trying to steady her shaking hands, Arden unwound the two feed wires from the holocap's universal power supply. Being a rugged and utilitarian device, it had the facility to power itself from just about any electrical source. Arden had once even powered it (very briefly) from a piece of copper and a silver ring jammed into a citrus fruit, so there should be no problem with Anderson's primitive battery.

She eyed Thorn, who was crouching behind a nearby boulder draped with a flat and slightly putrescent pseudopod that Dragon had discarded. He was checking the action of the carbine Anderson had given him. Off to her other side, Tergal clutched both handguns. As well as an expression of fear, he also wore his gauntlets, wide-brimmed hat and thick coat. This extra clothing might protect him somewhat from acid splashes, but would not help if the monster went after him exclusively.

She then glanced behind to where Anderson had mounted his old sand hog and couched his lance. He had told her, only a little while ago, how he had come here on a knightly quest to kill a dragon. A test—a trial. He then quipped that the droon would suffice, and having dispatched it he would consider his trial over.

The holocap read the new power source, adjusted itself accordingly and powered up. Arden detached the monocle, and for the first time looked up and ahead. The droon was a hundred metres away, closing the gap between them by three metres with every stride. Arden placed the monocle in her eye, gridded the creature, taking in the surrounding area as a projection stage, then removed the monocle and tossed it away from her. Hopefully, no droon acid would hit the monocle itself, because then it would all be over, as it was the last one she possessed. With a mosquito whine, the device shot out over the droon and hovered, invisible. Going to her menu, Arden selected a second-stage sleer and projected it onto a boulder to the droon's left.

The monster spun, ejecting a sheet of white mucus straight at the projection. Arden made the second-stager leap about a little before shutting the thing off. The droon stooped low, its head darting from side to side as it tried to locate its prey. It reached down with one many-jointed arm, hooking underneath a rim of stone with a paw like a battered mass of scrap metal, and flipped the boulder over. Then it bellowed in frustration and randomly spat acid all about itself.

"Seems rather irritated," Thorn observed.

"I've studied them for a while and they possess only two states," Arden said, "irritated, as you put it, or motionless."

"And when are they motionless?" Tergal asked.

Arden glanced at him. "Usually after they've fed."

"And why isn't this one motionless, then?"

Arden shrugged. "Perhaps it's unusually irritated."

She now made another second-stager appear, this one on a rock to the monster's other side. The droon ejected another sheet of mucus, which passed through the hologram and drenched the rock below it. Again the prey danced about a bit, then disappeared. Arden gave the monster quite a chase with a third-stager, leaving behind a trail of boiling smoke and steam. Onto the illusory apek it emptied gallons of vitriol, but the image of itself only seemed to confuse it. Then, as it seemed to be now spitting dry, she conjured a fourth-stager to draw it round to the rim of the arena, to finally face Anderson.

Thorn and Tergal stood up and circled round, ready to act as picadors. Meanwhile Arden recalled the projection monocle and caught it in her hand. Projected images would now only confuse the issue, and might even put Anderson off his stroke. Unless . . . Arden brought the monocle up to her eye and once again cast up a grid.

The *Jerusalem* was a vast and cavernous ship full of echoes and, as she returned to her research area and quarters, Mika heard a constant din of distant industry. Skinless Golem were apparent everywhere inside the great ship, and also outside on its hull. Other more esoteric robots scuttled along walls and ceilings, like an infestation of chrome deathwatch beetle.

These were the more visible robots. Mika had also seen ones no bigger than ants repairing delicate circuitry, millipede plumbers only momentarily visible in the breaks in pipes or ducts they were fixing, also roving crab drones floating on personal AG and muttering to themselves, and the glittering fungal movement of Polity nanotech at work repairing stress fractures in structural members. Mika herself had just put in a long shift in Medical—repairing humans and haimans—and her own arm still ached. Now her shift was over, and it was at last time for her to do her own thing.

With the door closed behind her, she was immediately into her partial-immersion frame, then standing on a virtual plain. Manipulating some floating icons, she called up diverse views and the results of sampling tests transmitted by some of Jerusalem's drones. Translucent pillars of data appeared all around her, scrolling her requirements around themselves.

The worms living in the icy moonlet that now turned in her virtual sky created burrows similar to those delved by Dragon. Breaking open one icon, she caused a segment of the moon to disappear, and like a huge worm-eaten cheese it dropped closer for her inspection.

Even though information about these creatures was already on file, through a transmission made by the *Jack Ketch*, Mika still found them fascinating. There was one aspect of them that was plainly similar to Dragon as it had once been on Aster Colora, where the human race had first encountered it: there seemed to be no supporting ecology for them. Mika could only hypothesize that the ecology of which they were a product had been destroyed or was somewhere far from here, and that begged many critical questions. Their lone survival made it unlikely they were just the primitive helminth survivors of some natural cataclysm or had been transported accidentally, therefore they must be very like Dragon in another respect. They must be the product of an ecology in the same way that a Golem android was the product of Earth's. It was certain that they had not evolved naturally to their present state.

"Fascinating, isn't it," interjected Jerusalem, appearing beside her.

"What is?" Mika asked.

"Life. But then what is life? Those worms grinding their way through spongy rock—are they life? Is Jain technology life? Am I?"

Ah, philosophy. Mika didn't bother to venture a reply.

Jerusalem went on relentlessly: "In terms of evolved life, those worms are neither one thing nor the other. They have evolved, yes, but prior to that minor change they were not the direct product of insensate evolution."

"Pardon?"

The floating metal head tilted, and a long helical molecule arched across the sky like some strange species of rainbow. "You have not yet noted the regularity of their genetic blueprint, the lack of equivalents to alleles and parasitic DNA?"

"Yes, I saw that." Mika repressed her annoyance. She had discovered something, but it was irritating to learn Jerusalem had found it long before her.

"And what is your assessment?"

Mika replied, "A manufactured organism of some kind, probably intended for mining."

"So it would seem," the AI agreed. "They accumulate rare metals inside their bodies for no purpose related to their own survival." Mika winced—she had missed that aspect. "And they procreate only when those metals have reached an internal saturation level that interferes with their tunnelling efficiency."

"They could be Jain tech," Mika offered.

"They are not Jain in themselves, being simple mechanisms with only one purpose. However, someone using Jain technology could have made them. Some of the tunnels in that moon are over half a million years old. Perhaps the Atheter, or the Csorians?"

Mika considered that. There had been no finds classified as Jain artefacts any younger than five million years of age—that was, she acknowledged to herself, excepting products directly attributable to Skellor. Perhaps unknown aliens had left these worms here, but if so where were they themselves now? Perhaps this was all that remained of yet another race which had stumbled upon Jain technology.

"We should set up a research . . ." The words died in her mouth when she felt that drag into the ineffable as the *Jerusalem* dropped into U-space. She braced herself for any turbulence, surprised Jerusalem had given no warning.

"The illegal USER has ceased to function," Jerusalem informed her, before she could ask.

Something prodded him to consciousness and, as he surfaced, Cormac could feel Jain tech all around his mind, like a hostile encircling army wielding a forest of edged and pointed weapons. Sharp steel hedged him in—he was poised on the brink of annihilation. Opening his eyes, he found himself bound into the co-pilot's chair by hard Jain substructure. He could not move his head for the structure bound that too—and penetrated it.

"Obviously you don't have a quick death in mind for me?" he suggested.

The lander was still under acceleration, and an indigo sky liberally dotted with stars filled the viewing screen. Skellor, leaning forward with one hand resting on the pilot's console, glanced over his shoulder.

"I don't even know that I'll kill you at all. Maybe I'll rewire you so that you're in constant agony, or I could subvert you like was done to Mr. Crane—turn you against your masters. Maybe I'll do both."

"Oh, you are so spoilt for choices—it must be such a trial for you."

Agony speared from the base of Cormac's skull and down his spine. He arched against his restraints, too ravaged by the pain to even scream. It went on and on . . . and his consciousness refused to leave him. He began to break: thought processes now operating in his gridlink because they were unable to function in his organic brain. He realized there, with arctic precision, that this was how Aphran had carried on; understood this separation. Then, after an age, the pain stopped. Cormac gasped for air, spat blood from where he had bitten through the tip of his tongue, wished he could wipe the tears from his eyes.

"You see," said Skellor, "with the Jain substructure supporting your body, I can do that to you for hours without you going into shock or losing consciousness, or retreating from reality. Of course, if I rewired your brain and body, I could do so much more."

Cormac became weightless in his Jain carapace, and slowly black space scrubbed away the indigo seen through the screen. Eventually the colony ship became visible, and Cormac could feel the lander decelerating to dock. Skellor would now have to move him from the lander to the main ship; perhaps he could do something then. The horror—he understood—of occupying the moral high ground, by being prepared to pay so heavy a price, was that this did not except you from actually paying. He knew that, given time, Skellor could destroy that same morality: could turn him into a whimpering thing who would obey the man's every whim, could turn him into the complete negative of everything he was, and could make him suffer endlessly. Briefly, through the bulwarks of his mind, Cormac glimpsed a void where all that he amounted to meant nothing.

But he then decided that he must continue to function as if that void could never exist—he must remain an ECS agent to the last.

Skellor's mental link to him was very close: he could feel thoughts and memories bleeding over, could feel that the man needed little excuse to cause Cormac pain. He decided to be sparing with sarcasm so as not to provoke the man. He also routed the bleed-over from Skellor's mind into his gridlink and stored it.

"What are your intentions, other than causing me pain?" he asked.

Skellor glanced sideways, and Cormac observed dark movement under the apparently human skin of the man's face. Whorls of scar tissue now filled the holes Cormac had drilled with his thin-gun into Skellor's body. Those holes penetrated what appeared to be baroque leathery armour which Cormac realized was actually part of the man. One hole at Skellor's waist seemed to have become cancerous: scar tissue having welled up and spilled over, setting in a fungal growth containing small egg-shaped nodules. Cormac wondered if this meant Skellor was not entirely in control of the Jain technology, though it seemed more likely that the man just did not care how he looked.

"My intentions," Skellor repeated, the question seeming to momentarily confuse him. "Perhaps you should try to guess them."

Without even thinking about it, Cormac found himself flexing his muscles rhythmically against the hard structure that bound him, just as he would have worked against any conventional bonds. He considered stopping doing this, but didn't—had to try every possibility.

"I don't *know* enough. I don't know why you came here in search of Dragon. I don't know if your main motivation is survival or aggression, or if it is something else now utterly alien to me."

"Suppose it is aggression, what should I do?"

"I don't think I should give you any ideas you might not have had already."

The renewed pain slammed him about, writhing against the entrapping structure. He had freedom to scream. Locked his jaw against it. Eyes open wide, he saw the world with startling clarity: like a blind man achieving vision whilst being burnt at the stake. An age passed, and then another.

"Answer the question." Skellor's voice came out of some dislocated reality.

It took some seconds for Cormac to realize that the pain was gone, and to reassume control of his organic brain, emerging from those places he had retreated to within his gridlink. Briefly he experienced one of his captor's memories: a market stall on a world undergoing terraforming, a plastic box containing pieces he recognized as Jain tech, and something else—an egg . . . Cormac dismissed this memory to storage. It was no help to him now.

"I would attack . . ." he began, then paused as he lost the thread for a moment. "You should attack using manufactured viruses, disease, plague, biological warfare. You have the capability to create something to kill people faster than boosted immune systems, autodocs or AI-manufactured counteragents can prevent it. You could also send the virtual versions of all of these against AI."

Cormac felt no guilt in saying this to Skellor. If the man had not already thought of these methods of attack, then he had been severely overestimated. And anyway, the Polity had been preparing for as well as countering such attacks from Separatist organizations for centuries now.

"But how would I distribute such plagues? I could never get such things past the biofilters and scanners of the runcible network."

"You have a ship."

The colony ship now appeared as a curved metal horizon viewed through the front screen of the lander and, even as the pain hit again, Cormac heard the hiss and whine of hydraulics, felt the lander judder, and heard docking clamps thump home.

"So I should personally visit each world in turn for the purpose of biological and virtual attack?" Skellor detached his hand from the console, pushing himself up and away from it. "Just how many worlds do you think I'd manage to attack before I ended up with ECS sitting on top of me?"

Cormac closed his eyes. It felt to him as if someone was

sequentially smacking each of his vertebrae in turn with a hammer. He writhed and fought, then suddenly, unbelievably, the Jain substructure binding him began to loosen and move. Hope surged in him as the pain also faded. Then he saw Skellor grinning at him.

"Come with me," said the biophysicist.

Cormac pushed out of the chair, the substructure moving plastically around him like an alien exoskeleton. He turned and propelled himself after Skellor towards the airlock. He had not wanted to move or to obey; it was the structure itself moving him—an exoskeleton controlled from elsewhere. In the lock he stood immobile whilst Skellor subverted the door's controls. He then wondered why Skellor had used this method to control him, and not simply attached another of those aug insects.

Hearing his thoughts, Skellor said, "Your body is just a machine that I can rebuild any time I like. Your mind I have decided to keep sacrosanct for now. If I destroy it, how can it appreciate its own suffering?"

The man was lying, Cormac realized that in an instant, but it was knowledge that availed him nothing. The airlock opened and they propelled themselves out of it into the body of the ship. Cormac's first breath was a dry gasp from the inside of a rusting pipe. In seconds, he was gasping for oxygen. Nevertheless, perpetually on the point of suffocation, he followed Skellor up into the control bridge.

"Of course I won't allow your body to die for the present, as I don't want to take the trouble to rebuild it," Skellor told him. "You'll not suffocate, though that's how it feels."

On the bridge, Skellor impelled Cormac to clean the captain's chair of the dead man's sticky remains. Still gasping, he carried out his grim task, glimpsing Skellor inspect the cancerous scar tissue at his own waist. The biophysicist then looked up in irritation and allowed Cormac more freedom. Cormac immediately pulled up the hood of his environment suit, closed the visor, and breathed real air. Skellor had obviously tired of that game. Stacking bones and dried-out skin to one side, the agent observed Skellor remove his thin-gun from some hidden pocket and place it on a nearby console—another more subtle torture. Then the rogue bio-physicist pressed his hand down on the main computer console. After a hiatus, he tilted his head back and issued a sound somewhere between a scream and a snarl.

23

It has ever been an instinct to abhor the different and hate the alien, and like many of those human drives stemming directly from "selfish genes" it is one easily controlled or even banished. Human history is littered with hideous crimes, decades of strife and near-genocides because of such drives. It should be different now. Planetary national borders are nonexistent, most people are of evidently mixed race, and they can change their racial appearance and sex at will, or even simply cease to be human. One would suppose this has rendered reasons for hate impotent. Not so. Catadapts will detest rodapts, who in turn are hostile to ophidapts, for no more reason than reflecting a pale imitation of terran predator–prey cycles. Many humans consider AIs an abomination, and many loathe them—as the superior, or rulers, have always been loathed. Pure-bred humans can find haimans repugnant, and haimans can consider pure humans primitive animals. To dispense with these hatreds, we need not to want them. Unfortunately, people cherish their bigotry, misanthropy and animosities, and they don them like well-worn and well-loved clothes.
　　　　　　　　　　　—From How It Is *by Gordon*

Tanaquil wanted to rage at the strange oldster because he saw Fethan as part of Jeelan's death and the current metallier disaster. Did this now also mean that Tanaquil's dream was dead, that the entire metallier dream was dead? Would he ever get to stand on the bridge of the *Ogygian*?

He wanted to reject the alien—the interfering outside. But Tanaquil had been well educated and was harshly intelligent and, believing the man's claim to have caused the demise of the horrible enslaving creatures, he could not allow anger to triumph over reason. So only one task remained.

A short walk from where so many broken corpses lay scattered brought him to an abandoned metallier house. He searched the storage areas underneath it and found a couple of spades. Without question, the old man took the one Tanaquil passed him. In silence, they returned to the charnel house and began to dig. Out of the drifting smoke walked a skinny youth with blond hair, who gaped at his surroundings with raw and horrified eyes.

"Sir, what do we do now?"

Tanaquil wanted to scream at him—just scream wordlessly.

"Bury them," he growled.

Other people arrived, some to help dig and others carrying weapons to guard against the things shifting in the dark of the Undercity, no doubt lured by the smell of fresh meat. Tanaquil gave no more than that initial instruction. That those who had not heard it carried out his orders anyway he reckoned was due to some residue of that enslaving bond they had all recently felt. The corpses must also be buried or burnt before nightfall, else the place would be crawling with sleers. For Tanaquil the task was endless horror. His head ached horribly, and a liquid kept seeping out of the hole behind his ear. But he wanted Jeelan in the ground, safe from hard mandibles, and a fast closure so that he could again rule his people. It was cold, but otherwise . . . he would just fail.

To begin with, he just dug in a nightmare fugue, then he began to realize how the older man wielded his shovel with almost impossible ease, excavating huge clumps of the sandy earth and heaving them aside. Fethan paused and shrugged when he noted Tanaquil's scrutiny.

"Used to dig drainage sluices on Masada," he explained.

Tanaquil nodded, not really understanding. He could push his own blade only half its length into the ground, then had to strain to lever up half a spadeful of earth. Fethan could shove the blade of his tool fully into the soil, as easily as if into a pie, and each time the spade's solid metal handle flexed alarmingly.

"You talked often with Dragon?" Fethan suddenly asked.

"No."

"Did you ever go to the plain?"

Tanaquil shook his head. He could not speak, and was grateful when Fethan pressed him for nothing more. Together, in silence, they completed the task, then together they laid Jeelan in the hole they had prepared. Her skin was now cold. Tanaquil scrambled from the grave on his hands and knees, and puked acid bile.

"I'll finish off for you," said Fethan.

"No," insisted Tanaquil, returning to work. He scooped a spadeful of sandy earth down onto Jeelan's naked body, once, twice, then staggered away. He couldn't breathe down here. He could not live in this shadow.

The world seemed to go away for a while. Past him flashed a chaos of twisted metal, stairs, people shouting questions at him, as he ran. The blimp tower eventually provided refuge and, with no one around, he tried to release that lock inside himself. But again the tears would not come. Instead, he just grew calm and cold, knowing that this was something he could never get over. He did not want to live; didn't have the will to die.

"Tell me about Dragon," a voice intruded.

Fethan had walked quietly out onto the platform beside which was moored the remaining blimp, perhaps holding back somewhat because Tanaquil was sprawled by a pillar right next to the edge.

"He took the Undercity as his own, right from the beginning," said Tanaquil, not even knowing why he was explaining. "That was thirty years and four Chief Metalliers ago."

"About right," said Fethan, studying the blimp. "The four spheres separated over fifty years ago, solstan." He turned to Tanaquil. "That's the mean time of the Human Polity—something you need as a standard when you ship out between the stars, shedding decades like dandruff."

Now Tanaquil felt angry because the man had stirred his curiosity. "Spheres? Solstan? Human Polity?"

"Dragon's original form was one of four conjoined and living spheres, each about a kilometre in diameter. They were one being, which then broke into four. One of those four came here."

Tanaquil remembered visions from his time of nightmares. He pointed out over the Sand Towers towards the plain. "I saw it rise up and leave us. Dragon is gone."

Fethan was abruptly up beside him. "Perhaps we should go and see." He gestured to the blimp.

There was more here than an interest in Dragon, Tanaquil thought. "Why would you want to see?"

"I won't lie to you. While you have been here I've spoken to your people, wandered your city . . . There's someone I need to find, and that person does not seem to be here. That being the case he is maybe out that way." Fethan nodded towards the plain. "He'll always be where the action is."

"I cannot leave my people."

"They know you need time. I've spoken to some of them."

Tanaquil could not summon the energy to argue, and there was something attractive about climbing into the blimp cabin and just sailing away. Perhaps stepping out into the air when the blimp was high was the only way to release the leaden lock in his chest.

One day, Anderson decided, he might ask Unger Salbec why Bonehead had not fled after the death of Stone when earlier it had panicked and fled, and why it was now prepared to carry him into battle against the droon. He suspected the answer related to sentience. A creature that could come to understand human language was not an animal, and probably possessed motivations equally as complex as those of any human. Possibly Bonehead was embarrassed by its earlier behaviour.

Whatever, Bonehead remained steady beneath him, its eyestalks spread like a rifle sight below his lance, which he pointed towards the droon as it stepped delicately into the arena he had chosen. Anderson now studied his opponent.

The creature stood upright on two chitinous legs, which possessed an extra joint and terminated in feet that were a complex tangle of mismatched digits and hooks. Its tail, counterbalancing its extended upper torso, was ribbed with carapace and square in section, the corners everting so that each of them was sharp as a blade. Halfway down, the tail divided, its twin ends jointed like extra limbs. Carapace also ribbed its upper body, and custard-yellow flesh bulged between ribs, forced out by the distension of its over-full guts. Below its primary arms, it possessed two other sets of limbs that served as either arms or legs. Its primary arms ended in large two-fingered hands. Rows of hooks ran up its forearms to two further digits at its elbows. Its neck, extending from a sloping collar of armour, curved back on itself swanlike underneath its ziggurat head. Four black targeting eyes ran along the lower fold of this head. Six mouths, starting with the largest at the bottom, stepped up its sloping visage to its two distance eyes—slightly protruding and crablike—set at the very top of its head. When it opened its mouths to expose their bright orange interiors its head stretched half its own height again. Then the head snapped down, only the top mouth staying open, and the creature made a coughing hacking sound. It expelled only a mist of acid now, though. Anderson knocked his goad against Bonehead's carapace and the sand hog began to move forward on its crawler limbs.

Straight into some of that custard flesh, bulging from its torso, seemed the best target to Anderson. He knew from his studies that the droon possessed insides similar to a sleer's; its brain being a wormlike organ extending all the way down the length of its body, which obviously made it very difficult to kill with just a head shot. As with sleers, then, his way to kill it was by causing as much internal damage as he could, there being no one particular spot on its body he could target to bring it down.

"Ho, Bonehead! Ho!"

The sand hog went up on to its main limbs and accelerated, and it seemed to Anderson that only then did the droon become truly aware of their impending attack. Its head stretched again, and it coughed another fog of acid. Then, like a wrestler preparing to meet an opponent, it extended its arms out to either side.

"Ho! Ho!"

The knight centred his lance perfectly on target. If he did not kill it with this charge, then he would certainly be doing it some serious damage. But, of course, the resolution of a knightly trial was never simple.

At the last moment the droon brought both its two-fingered hands in and down on Bonehead's carapace. The sand hog juddered to a halt, its momentum driving the droon back five metres, the monster's feet cutting furrows in the ground. Anderson slammed against his saddle straps, the saddle itself cracking alarmingly beneath him. The point of his lance went into custard flesh, but not very far at all. Recovering quickly, Anderson leant forward, trying to push it further in, but it was like trying to push a knife into a tree. The droon bellowed, hauled back, nearly snatching the lance from Anderson's hands because he did not have its back eye over its peg. He clung on grimly, though, pieces of yellow flesh and a squirt of clear fluid following the lance tip out. Then with one hand the droon slapped the lance aside, its head working like upright bellows as it tried to spit acid it did not contain. The air was full of burning droplets.

"Turn to the right! Turn!" Anderson shouted at Bonehead, dropping any pretence that his goad had any effect on where the hog went. Bonehead had meanwhile attacked low with its feeding head, grabbing one of the droon's secondary limbs. The hog released this, then pushed away, but the droon grabbed its back end as Bonehead tried to leap away. Then Thorn and Tergal began firing, their shots either thunking into custard flesh or ricocheting off carapace. Anderson was away then, levelling his lance again as Bonehead ran a circuit of the arena, following his thought even before he voiced it.

The droon turned on the two men, looming above them, pumping its head and bellowing. It could not see Anderson coming in from the side. He levelled his lance point at an exposed area between the two intermediate limbs.

"Yaaah!"

There came a cracking, ripping sound as two metres of lance penetrated the droon's body. Then, below the knight, everything dropped away. The next thing he knew he was hanging from the lance, still strapped in his saddle, which had torn away from Bonehead's back.

"Shit," he said succinctly. He tried to reach down to undo his straps, lost his grip on the lance and crashed to the ground. Something smashed hard into the back of his helmet, and little bright lights chased across his vision. Also winded, he still scrabbled for the straps, but could not seem to find them—was falling into a black tunnel. The droon loomed over him, horrible gasping sounds issuing from it, and a different coloured liquid oozing from its six mouths. No matter—it would not need its acid to finish him off now.

Then suddenly the creature turned away. As he slid into unconsciousness, Anderson glanced aside and saw himself, mounted on Bonehead, charging the droon. Unconsciousness was a welcome escape from this confusion.

It was like gazing at the world through a darkened lens: a fish-eye vision of whirling stars, a glimpse of the wrecked telefactor and the occasional retreating view of the gas giant. Beside him, entangled with him in the world that could be virtually huge but was in reality a twenty-centimetre lozenge of crystal bound in black metal, Aphran also watched.

"Like a good captain I would have gone down with my ship," Jack observed.

"Not quite the same, but perhaps you now understand the psychology."

"I was humanized, utterly interfaced with my body, accepting it as part of myself and its destruction as my destruction. Interesting. I see that it makes for more efficient attack ships—that investment in the weapon used."

"The ship itself being the weapon," Aphran added.

"You do realize that though you have managed our survival, utterly disconnected like this our resources are limited, and we have some choices to make."

"What choices?"

"We can remain conscious at the present level of function for about ten years then go into permanent storage, or we can go into permanent storage right now for twenty years."

"So long. So little."

"The limit of the microtoks originally employed to run me while I was transferred from the factory to the ship body, which incidentally is now sinking in liquid hydrogen."

"You have contact?"

"No, just a good grasp of physics. The only extraneous link we have is through the pinhead camera that was attached up at the moment of my inception—the purpose of which was to make me aware that there is an outside world."

"We could spend those ten years in a virtual world," Aphran suggested.

"Such an existence does not interest me."

"Then let us go to permanent storage now. I don't think I could keep this same conversation going for ten years."

"Then goodnight."

Blackness.

The hunter/killer program had waited until he was deeply connected into the systems of the ship, Skellor knew, and now it was coming at him in a flood, plunging data tentacles into his mind, one after another, so he had time only to defend *himself*. With too much ease, the attack translated into a VR scenario. Here it seemed he grasped the situation more completely as he gained iconic control over his responses. It became almost like some computer game, but a very real one in which he could actually die. The computer system, in the virtuality, became a planetoid of slightly disconnected blocks shot through with tunnels and holes, floating in albescent space. Inside this, Skellor was Kali, armed with swords and axes, shifting blocks and seeking a way out. The kill program—one serpent and sometimes many, sprouting like the necks of Hydra from within the planetoid—patrolled these tunnels, attacking him where it could, its attacks increasing in ferocity the nearer he got to the surface of the planetoid or to gaining some control of its structure.

Slowly Skellor began to identify which collections of blocks represented which ship systems, and the virtuality allowed him to see that every one of these now had its own place for the serpent. He also saw that the deeper into the system he retreated, the easier things became for him—the less assiduously the program attacked him. Closing up the collection of blocks that was the balance control for the primitive hard-field shielding of the ship in U-space and shutting down any access for the program, he realized that unless the same program had resources available he had yet to detect, it would not be able to kill him nor keep him confined for long. He could only assume that some other plan was in the offing.

Before he could plumb that, the program attacked again. Four serpents speared out of the blockish informational darkness. Two of them came for Skellor, and two of them went for the structure he had rearranged. The data stream of one attacker he cut off near its source with a just-prepared virus. In the virtuality, his axe went through its neck, the gaping head fell away and the body retreated like a severed air hose. His second blow fell on the neck of his other attacker just as it closed its jaws on his arm, punching its fangs into his pseudoflesh. The neck bent like a cable being struck, but remained undamaged—this data stream having adapted to the virus. His arm immediately began to change colour, as killing data began to load.

Even as he adapted the virus, he used it swiftly on himself and cut away his poisoned arm. On the back swing, he took off the second serpent's head before turning to the other two, who seemed busily intent on wrecking his work. Now, knowing the degree of adaptation his viruses needed, he sprouted more axes from his fists and attacked, chopping and hacking in a frenzy. Then, when bleeding segments were drifting all about him, he asked himself why this attack had been so strong.

Skellor stepped away from the virtual vision of his battle and opened his comprehension to an utterly informational level. He realized that the kill programs' defences were strongest around the hard-field generators, the reactor and the balanced U-space engines of this ship. It wanted to keep him here in orbit of Cull. That being the case, he now made it his prime objective to get away. He probed, tentatively, into the start-up routines for the U-space engines. The reaction he got, like poking a stick into a nest of vipers, confirmed his suspicions. Now, in the virtuality and not limiting himself by human perception, he began gathering his weapons. Turning towards those closely guarded systems, he hurled himself forward thousand-armed, viruses and informational bacilli propagating around him, layered attack programs like swarms of bees, a growing mass then a wall of every informational weapon at his disposal falling on that nest of serpents.

In a virtual age, he slew the guardians. In real computer time of microseconds, he swamped and subsumed engine control. His diagnostic search informed him of slight misalignments in both engines and hard-fields. It would hurt him, but he would survive—as he had before. The fusion reactor started easily; someone had used it recently. No matter. When enough power was available, he started the fusion engines of the ship. He had no control of navigation, but the ship had been tangential to the planet. Accelerating, burning up rusty water from its fuel tanks as it drove up to ram-scoop speeds, the ship left orbit. One fusion chamber sputtered as the water started to run out, then the ram-scoop fields opened out and began funnelling in hydrogen and other spacial matter to use as fuel.

Then, achieving sufficient speed relative to the fabric of space, like a speedboat ready to move up onto its hydrofoils, the *Ogygian* engaged its U-space engines and dropped out of realspace.

Dragged back against one wall of the bridge, the long-dead captain's skull still clutched in his right hand and the Jain exoskeleton now rooting into the metalwork around him, Cormac wondered what new torture this was. But agony twisted Skellor's features, and Cormac's mind screamed at the flashes of grey infinity beyond the screen—all his human perception could make of underspace. Some instinct made him try to grasp more. He opened up programming space in his gridlink to carry the load, but his mind just kept sliding off. Desperation grew in him, as if his survival depended on his cognizance of this dimension.

With augmentation, it was possible for him to comprehend more than he could with his normally evolved human mind. With heightened perception, Cormac could visualize five dimensions: see a tesseract and observe a Kline bottle pouring into itself. But this was more dimensions than that, and none at all. U-space contained the potential for dimension. It was the infinity of a singularity, and the eternal instant. To human perception, it was things and states that were mutually exclusive. It was impossible . . . impossible for a human to encompass. But Cormac knew that he must encompass it or completely lose one of the bulwarks of his mind. And so, naturally, as he strove for comprehension, he moved further away from his own humanity.

With a feeling of good riddance, Dragon watched first the *Ogygian* then the *King of Hearts* drop into underspace. It being evident that this entire system and probably others were enclosed in a USER trap, the entity felt sure that neither Skellor nor the rogue AI ship would be going far, and that maybe the Polity would survive, just so long as others of its members could resist temptation.

Temptation . . .

There was a saying attributed to a nineteenth-century human character who seemed famous more for his sexual proclivities than his ability with a pen . . . or quill.

Dragon knew the dangers of Jain technology, but the option for control of it from its nascent stage . . . Polity AIs must be aware of this aspect of the technology, and Dragon understood why some of them had gone rogue in pursuit of it.

I can resist anything but temptation.

Ah . . .

Dragon also quickly came to understand something else. It was certain that the higher Polity AIs had worked out quite some time ago how Jain technology operated. Hence this scenario: the trap had not only been for Skellor, but for those AIs that did not show the requisite self-control. The entity did not like the idea that the same trap might have intentionally included itself but had to admit that possibility. Whatever, on the surface of Cull was an item that could create another Skellor or, utilized by Polity AIs or Dragon itself, something even worse. Dragon felt the Jain node would be safer . . . elsewhere. Still working to repair its U-space engines, to shorten the hours-long trip to the planet to minutes, it then detected a U-space signature. Observing the scale of what was coming through, Dragon felt a sinking sensation in its many thousands of stomachs. "Now where are you going?" Jerusalem asked.

Strangely, AIs that ran Golem bodies were more patient than those which controlled spaceships and runcibles, and whose understanding of time and the universe was immense. Cento waited, utterly still, utterly forbearing, as the hours slogged on past. Only a few hundred metres away from him, down at the bottom of the engine pier in the captain's bridge, the *Jerusalem* hunter/killer program had immobilized

Skellor. Maybe, if he took his APW down there, he could use it to convert the biophysicist to so much ash. But *maybe* wasn't good enough. That particular maybe was only the contingency plan.

"You still have him contained?" he asked, though in reality the question contained no human words.

The program responded in the same computer language, "He is contained. Be prepared for your action."

The kill program made all the calculations in *Ogygian*'s computer before presenting the idea to Cento. It did this only minutes after Skellor began using the message laser. Cento was dubious of the accuracy of the program's results. It was no ship or runcible AI, in fact was not designated AI at all (though Cento admitted to himself that was probably for reasons of expediency), and the computer on the *Ogygian* was primitive. However, when the program showed him the scale of the target and its intentions, Cento had to agree.

Skellor, no matter what capabilities he possessed, would not be getting away from *there*. Cento, having now to do the one thing of which the program was incapable—all its actions being on an informational level only—would not be leaving either. But the Golem, being AI and of AI origin, and also being backed up in Earth Central, did not view personal destruction in the same way as did a human, or haiman, whatever Fethan thought himself.

"There is something else," the program then interjected.

"And that is?"

"The Skellor has brought a hostage aboard with him."

"That is unfortunate," said Cento, "but it does not impinge upon the plan. The loss of one or two lives, even a few hundred lives, is a small enough price to pay to be rid of Skellor."

"The hostage is Ian Cormac."

Cento experienced spontaneous emotion, something he had not felt since seeing Ulriss die and then finding the incinerated corpses of Shayden and Hourne. First, he felt surprise that the agent had allowed Skellor to capture him at all, then he felt sadness. Cormac did not back himself up, and even if he was memplanted, that technology would not survive what was to come. The agent would die irretrievably.

"That makes no difference."

The program fell silent, returning that small sliver of its awareness to the chaos of its virtual battle to keep Skellor contained, and unaware of the subtle control it exerted over the ship's helm. Many hours later, precisely to the calculated second of ship time, Cento pointed his APW at the superconducting cables leading to the U-space engine above him, triggered the weapon, and drew violet fire across. The blast threw him back. The side of the support pier blasted out into U-space, the blobs of molten metal creating strange kaleidoscope effects as they departed the ship. Above him the engine stuttered out something weird that impinged even on Cento's Golem consciousness as, briefly, the s-con ducts carried proton energy back into it before flaring like burning magnesium. Then, suddenly, black and starlit space bled into the gap as the *Ogygian* resurfaced. Cento closed an arm around a bubble-metal I-beam as something pulled hard at him for a moment, released its hold, then pulled again.

Tidal forces, he surmised.

Weakened by the APW blast the pier twisted above him. He felt its wrenching scream through the metal he clutched, observed the beam itself twisting. Then that force tugged again, and the U-space nacelle, along with much of the pier above him, tore away from the ship. Cento observed its slow departure, then turned his attention to where he calculated their destination would be. The brown dwarf seemed a vast wooden sphere looming at them out of the dark; the *Ogygian* was already being dragged down towards it, already being torn apart by its tidal forces. Cento headed down towards the bridge. Now, to make sure, he would also carry through the contingency plan. It would be a pointless though satisfying exercise, for in a few hours Skellor, the ship and all detached debris, Cento and Ian Cormac, would constitute a very thin film on the dead sun below.

*

Somehow the barrier had remained: a shimmering silk meniscus between Mr. Crane and everything real. Yet, strangely, by this separation he could view the world and his worlds and discern what was now and what was then. The surreal battle between a knight mounted on a giant crustacean and the ziggurat-headed droon was real and was now. Briefly, it reflected on the etched game board, before the vulture brought her players back to order with a sharp peck and a lengthy swallowing. Crane moved the piece of crystal and gazed up at the sea's surface. It was fantastically bright up there, almost as bright as revelation. Inside his head he felt something turn and clunk into place with all the positivity of a ship going into a docking clamp. Tearing off the aviapt's head had not been a particularly moral act, nor had Crane's killing of Stalek been particularly nice, but for what they had done to him—and likely done to others—they deserved death. Also they had been outside the Polity, and Crane had been under instruction . . .

In some part of himself, Crane recognized the mealy-mouthed dissimulation of a coward. Though ordered through the Pelters' control unit to kill those two, he had not needed to be quite so bloody. He reached down to move a blue acorn. A beak intervened and he instead moved the scent bottle. Taut excitement filled him, and imminence—that was the only way the various parts of his mind could see it. Something of all his parts was poised on the edge of the real, waiting to come into focus.

The sea's surface drew no closer—he knew he was not ready for that. But some bright structure like a vast glassy plankton turned in electric depths and presented itself to another mass of the same. It keyed in, locked into place, took on the same spectral pulsation as all the rest. Mr. Crane stared down at one brass hand. It was utterly real, and utterly right there and then. Folding in his thumb, he saw himself tearing people apart on Cheyne III. Those were Arian Pelter's orders, and the man had been nested close in Crane's mind, his control through a military aug all but absolute. How could the Golem have done otherwise?

Lies lies lies . . .

Crane folded in a finger, remembered killing policemen, then killing one of Arian's allies. But one of those policemen had survived. Out of an impossible situation, Mr. Crane had allowed someone to live. The antique binoculars he had taken in place of the life now replaced by the scent bottle he had just moved. Hadn't he saved so many lives? But counting the deaths he soon ran out of fingers.

The little knight, mounted on a miniature sand hog, charged the lion's tooth, and, prodding it with his lance, moved it to a new position. Two bright structures mated with a satisfying click and the gratifying alignment of the last turn on a Rubik's cube.

What Crane had done . . . He could have done nothing else.

Crane could have done nothing else.

Rising, nemesis from the sea, Mr. Crane was angry. He raged at a life denied him, howled inside at the Serban Kline they wanted him to be, was rabid because there was nothing inside or out to prevent him killing. But there was justification. The people on this island had done those horrific things to Semper. They had unmade a human being piece by piece, scream by scream, and left him to marine crucifixion for Crane to find. Oh, how they would pay.

The man on the shore—a bloody rag—gone, others the same. Crane walked slowly through silver moonlight, glints like pearl crabs at the corners of his eyes. Alston was at the centre of the island and Crane was told to go to him, to kill him, but also to kill any who stood in his way. No one had said how he should go to Alston. No one had said he should walk a straight course. Crane walked a spiral, killing as he went and leaving hellish art behind him, till coming to the final poetry of making Alston's fortune utterly the man's own.

We had no choice.

You could have shut down completely, abandoned any chance at sentience, not been so good a tool for them to employ. You put your survival above that of many many others.

We are unusual?

There was nothing now to prevent wholeness, only will and choice. Mr. Crane could be complete in that moment or, with the horror of memory swamping him, could rest, cease to be. Choice: the machine was there, but yet to be powered up. Internally, he watched a tall brass man in a wide-brimmed hat throw across the final circuit breaker. The image, his ego, flipped a salute to him before being sucked into the machine. From that moment on, Crane was wholly and utterly himself.

"Ah," said Vulture, stepping back a little. "I see you're with us, but I wonder just *what* is with us."

Mr. Crane began picking up his toys and returning them to his pockets. The battle nearby was over, and here the battle was over too. He paused; he did not need these toys. But then again that did not mean he could not have them. As he contemplated this concept, his hands worked before him without conscious volition. While he was methodically attempting to stack the blue acorns, a flying lizard landed in the middle of the board, scattering both the acorns and other remaining pieces.

"A message, I suspect," said Vulture.

Crane held out his palm and the lizard scuttled onto it. He raised the creature up to his face, listened to its chittering, and recognized the flashing in its eyes as a direct visual transference of code. Eventually he tossed the lizard into the air and watched it fly away. Then his hand snapped out, faster than any snake, and closed around Vulture's neck.

"I chose," said Mr. Crane.

He released his hold. Vulture was unharmed.

Mr. Crane stood, put on his hat and tilted it rakishly. He paused for a moment, examining the board before him, then swept up the remaining pieces and deposited them in his pocket.

"I choose," he said, as he walked away.

24

*What is death when doctors can repair your body at a
cellular level, and maintain your life though your body
be so badly damaged it is not recognizable as human?
What is it when you can record or copy your mind?
What is it when machines can regrow your body from
a single cell, or build it from materials of your choice,
fashioned to your highest or lowest fantasy? What is
it when you can change bodies at will? . . . Ridiculous
question, really, because nothing has changed. Death
remains that place from which no one returns. Ever.*
—From* How It Is *by Gordon*

The virtuality Mika had created was an aseptic milky plateau
bounded by a cliff, beyond which was a contracted view of the
system they now occupied. Seemingly only a few kilometres
out from the cliff edge hovered Dragon. She reached up and
took hold of an apple-sized model of that entity, and moved
it closer to herself. The full-sized version then drew in with
alarming realism until it was only a few hundred metres from
the plateau's edge. She turned the model, thus bringing into
view on the other version a great trench burned into its flesh,
then pulled it right up to the edge of the cliff. A writhing
mass of pseudopods inside the trench was drawing layers
of flesh across. For a moment she listened in on the opaque
conversation between Jerusalem and the entity.

"Where are you going?" Jerusalem asked.

"I return."

"To the planet?"

"Not by choice."

"By choices made at Samarkand and Masada."

"Am I my brother's keeper?"

"Part of yourself."

"Separate."

"To employ Occam's razor?"

"Funny Polity AI."

As the conversation continued, Mika tuned it out. The words she heard were only the surface of an exchange, a communication that went very much deeper. Perhaps only D'nissan with his recent augmentations might be the one to plumb it entirely.

"How was it damaged?" she asked.

"Tracking directly back along its course." Jerusalem's iconic head appeared beside her—the AI had never disguised the fact that it was capable of conducting a thousand conversations all at once—"I have detected the debris of an attack ship, though I am yet to determine which one. Also there is a USER singularity eating out the centre of a giant planet nearby. Dragon has just informed me that it destroyed both the USER and the ship guarding it . . . Ah, the ship was the *Excalibur*. Other debris in the system would appear to be the remains of the *Grim Reaper*."

"What about the *Jack Ketch*?"

"I will inform you when I know more."

Mika stared at Dragon for a while longer, then turned away. Returning to her immediate research, she eyed the molecule floating before her like an asteroid composed of snooker balls. This was her third. Thus far, the research staff on the *Jerusalem* had studied over ten thousand such structures to learn their function. Another year working at the same rate and they might even pass one per cent of the total. But Mika knew the rate was bound to change. D'nissan, working with some shipboard AIs and Jerusalem itself, was now decoding the programming languages of the Jain, and already new methods, new approaches were being found. It reminded Mika of the well-documented human genome project back in the twentieth century. Back then, the scientists had predicted the project would take decades but, new computer technologies becoming available, those same scientists had very quickly mapped the structure of human DNA. On the *Jerusalem*, though, they had the advantage that their work was synergetic: the more they learnt about Jain technology, the more tools it provided them to learn with.

This particular molecule, like those she had already studied, was an engine of multiple function. It self-propagated like a virus, but did not necessarily destroy the cells it invaded. It was small enough to need to suborn little of the cellular machinery for reproduction, and its offspring caused little damage leaving the reproductive cell. However, outside the cell, its function multiplied. It could destroy other cells, cause accelerated division in other cells and make nerve cells signal repeatedly. The molecule was also programmable: its function could be changed once it plugged into other unidentified molecules. Mika realized it was thus just one mote of that part of the technology Skellor used to subjugate human beings.

An hour later, the *Jerusalem* abruptly dropped into U-space.

"It seems the party has moved on," Jerusalem said.

Mika did not suppose the AI meant the drinks and canapés kind.

They had surfaced from U-space, but for Cormac his perception of the real seemed permanently wrecked—a rip straight through it. Every solid echoed into grey void, and the stale air of the ship seemed to be pouring into that rather than towards some large breach nearby. Gazing at his thin-gun, Cormac saw it was both an object and a grey tube punching into infinity, which, he reflected with an almost hysterical amusement, was precisely what it had been to those he had killed with it. When he entered the bridge, Cento was a perilous moving form casting laser shadows behind it, and when the Golem fired his APW, the fire burned with negative colour.

The blast threw Skellor past Cormac, slamming him up against the quartz screen of the ship like a black iron statue. The screen disintegrated and Skellor disappeared. For a moment Cormac thought the bio-physicist had been blown clear of the ship, but there had been insufficient air left to do that, and anyway Cormac's torn vision of reality showed him flat laser shadows now clinging to the outside hull, above the screen.

"Foolish. Trying to kill me, he freed me," came over the link Cormac had with the biophysicist, then, after a pause, followed a howl of rage. Cormac pushed down the link, tried to see what Skellor was seeing, could not fathom the vast curving horizon.

"Why is he so angry?" he mouthed to Cento, as the Golem came before him.

Cento replied through the comunit of Cormac's environment suit: "Because he is going to die, and there's no way he can avoid it. It's as inevitable as gravity."

Cormac understood now. He saw all the curves, saw the mountain, the *eversion* the brown dwarf star created in U-space.

"We are *all* going to die?" he suggested.

Just then, something half-seen shot in through the front screen, arrowed through the bridge, and slammed into Cento. The APW flew from the Golem's hand, bounced from a wall and, turning slowly end over end, headed slowly towards outer space. Skellor, a blackened atomy whorled and distorted around nodular growths in his body, now tore at the Golem.

Cormac could do nothing to help Cento although he fought against the enclosing structure. When he felt the wash of tidal forces through his body, he knew that in very little time that same wash would intensify sufficiently to shatter the Jain structure, but by then the tidal forces would have compressed and stretched his body to a sludge of splintered bone and ruptured flesh inside it. It occurred to him, with crazy logic, that such damage to himself was required as payment for the pain he had already suffered. On another level it occurred to him that he was not entirely rational at that moment.

Skellor, he saw, was not attempting to subvert Cento as he had with Gant. Perhaps he had lost the ability. More likely he had lost the inclination. Extinction looming as close as that vast brown horizon, the man wanted vengeance, wanted the satisfaction of smashing something. But, in the end, none of it mattered. Cormac ceased to struggle. The brown dwarf possessed its own huge inevitability. Then, as the hole where the front screen had been veered away from the dwarf, he spotted another ship through the opening, dark against the further stars, and two lines curving down from it like hooks. The *Ogygian* jerked once, twice, then suddenly Cormac was heavy inside the Jain structure—being crammed over to one side.

Grappling claws.

Loose objects inside the bridge dropped to the floor, then slid hard sideways. Cormac tracked the APW, caught in the rim of the screen hole, his thin-gun down on the floor by the nearby console—useless to him. Through the screen gap he observed the colonist sphere located at the further end of the craft swing round and down towards the vast brown plain. Then came a vibration through the ship, as of a giant electric saw operating. Blinding incandescence flooded in: a small percentage of lased light refracting from metal vapour. Most of the front end of the vessel was now falling away, severed by a powerful laser.

Cento and Skellor slammed into the wall. The Golem was down to metal, and Skellor had even torn some of that away. Long pink lesions cut into Skellor's blackened carapace, golden nodules showed in these like some strange scar tissue.

Cormac suddenly felt Skellor's glee, and picked up the subsequent exchange: *Thank you, my liege*, Skellor uttered sarcastically over the ether.

You will undoubtedly thank me, came the reply.

Cormac wondered at this madness. It was a foolish move on the part of the AI attack ship to rescue himself and Cento at the risk of allowing Skellor also to go free. His thought encountered amusement. He saw Skellor push Cento to arm's length, then spin him around and slam him hard into the wall. He recognized that the Golem was now failing.

Skellor whispered to him: "The *King of Hearts* doesn't work for the Polity any more."

It was too much: to choose a moral death, then to accept an inevitable one, and then to have both taken away. If only he could strike even the smallest blow. But he could do nothing—was ineffectual. Then, in that moment of extremity, Cormac saw the way. Wasn't it laughably obvious? Aboard the *Jack Ketch* Thorn had not hallucinated—had actually seen Cormac move in *that* way. And Horace Blegg had been correct as well: "*. . . your mind will soon find other parts that were never of itself.*"

Staring into the tear in his perception he saw, only for a moment, U-space entire and, like an AI, comprehended it. Enclosed and trapped in Jain substructure, he turned aside and stepped to where he wanted to be, detouring through that other place that made nothing of material barriers. Three metres to the side of the cage of alien carapace, he stepped into the real, reached down beside a console and picked up his thin-gun. Only then did Skellor begin to react, but not fast enough.

Cormac brought the gun up, his arm straight, and fired five times. One shot punched a hole through Skellor's forehead, the next four hit him in the face, snapping his head back each time and forcing him against the wall. Skellor flickered, but his chameleonware would not function and, as Cormac realized, with his own perception so changed it would not matter if it did—Cormac would still see the hole in existence the man occupied. He fired two more shots into the man's chest, targeted his knees as he tried to spring, blew apart a hand that reached back to press against the wall.

Beside Skellor, Cento unpeeled himself from metal, scissored his legs around the biophysicist's waist and clamped them there. The Golem then tore away wall panels to reveal an I-beam, which he embraced.

"The cables," Cento said calmly over com.

Cormac loaded another clip and, backing towards where Cento had blown out the screen, continued to pump shots into Skellor. He had to move fast: the Golem would not hold Skellor for long. The clip now empty, Cormac slapped the weapon down against a stick patch at his belt and dived through the missing screen, snagging up the APW as he went. Outside, he glanced down past the truncated ship to where the rest of it continued to fall towards the dwarf star, accompanied in its descent by the ripped-away engine pier and nacelle. Both these objects he could see were distorting, rippling. He found steps, hauled himself up along the curving hull and saw one grapple clenched hard on wreckage where the pier had torn away, the other closed on the next nacelle.

The cables were woven monofilament, hugely strong, but few materials could withstand a concentrated proton blast. High above he saw the attack ship: blades of fusion engine flame cutting down from it to his left. He needed to hit both cables quickly, before that ship fried him. Hopefully that would be enough, because if *King of Hearts* was like the *Jack Ketch*, the two grapples—one from each of its weapons nacelles—were all it would have ready. And by the time it readied some more, what remained of the *Ogygian* would be beyond its reach.

Cormac stepped across to the nearest grapple, climbed up onto it, and sat down with his legs on either side of the massive cable. Should the attack ship fire at him now, it stood a good chance of destroying its own cable—a fact which might make it hesitate for long enough. Cormac aimed at the other cable, with the APW setting at its highest, and pulled the trigger. The beam transformed his target into a white-hot bar, then it just dissolved in violet fire. *Ogygian* tilted underneath him as he brought the weapon to bear on the cable right next to him, then suddenly he was weightless and instinctively clinging on. The second grapple had torn away, holding wreckage like a fistful of hair grasped from someone narrowly escaped. *Ogygian* dropped away down an invisible lift shaft to hell. Above, the cable slackened in a long arc through space, then began to straighten out again. Cormac clung on for all he was worth. When the cable tautened, about ten gees compacted his spine down onto the grapple. The APW became too heavy to hold and tore from his grasp. He felt his vertebrae cracking and things ripping inside him, but still he clung on. Thoughts he had briefly entertained of taking action against the ship should the cable be reeled in, died then.

When the acceleration finally ceased, he coughed, spattering his visor with blood. But when he looked down he was satisfied to see no sign of the *Ogygian*. The cable did then reel him in until he was only twenty metres from the lethal ship's left-hand weapons nacelle. Ports were opening before him, annihilation a breath away.

"Now that has really pissed me off," the *King of Hearts'* AI informed him.

Consciousness crept up on him and inserted itself into his perception. Coming out of black nothingness, Anderson slowly realized he was awake. He was lying in the lee of a slab, which was a conglomerate of fossilized worms and bivalve shells the shape of kidneys. He reached up to ensure his skull was in one piece, found a wadded blanket supporting his head. Warily he rolled to one side, wincing as his body informed him of its injuries, and sat upright to look around.

Bonehead was a dome nearby—everything utterly retracted. Looking at the hog's damaged shell where the saddle and lance framework had been torn away, Anderson thought he would need to make a lot of repairs with epoxy—and should not ride the hog for some time, until the shell had healed internally. Now he turned his attention to where the others stood beside what it took him a moment to identify as the fallen droon, his lance still impaling it. He stood up a little unsteadily and walked over, noting that the brass man was gone.

"You're recovered." Tergal spotted him first.

Anderson wondered about the tone of resentment he sensed, and recognized that Tergal had not found these latest adventures to his liking.

"As best as can be expected," Anderson replied.

Arden and Thorn now turned towards him, too. He gazed past them to where the vulture perched on the wide deflated head of the droon. During his reading, in the library of Rondure, he had never come across the word "vulture," but he recognized this creature as an uglier version of some pictures he had seen of things called "birds."

"The conquering hero returns," said the vulture.

Anderson did recollect reading how some birds were good mimics, but that did not sound like mimicry to him. In fact it sounded very like Unger Salbec. He winced at this reminder—another complication to add to the *What now?* malaise he seemed to be suffering.

"Tergal told me your trial has lasted twenty years." Arden studied him with some amusement. "And you also told me our friend here would be dragon enough." She pushed a foot against one sprawled-out limb, which looked like a twisted and torn I-beam projecting from the wreckage of some collapsed building. Anderson stepped back a pace, remembering one particular third-stage sleer in a hailstorm.

"It's enough," said Anderson.

"So you'll return to Rondure?" she asked.

Anderson shrugged. If he returned anywhere, it would be to Bravence, where Unger Salbec awaited him. But he was not the kind of person who returned anywhere. He glanced at Tergal. "What do you think?"

Tergal shook his head. "I have debts to repay, if you'll allow me."

Anderson nodded, turned to Thorn. "What about you?"

"That remains to be decided," said Thorn. He studied the weapon he held, pulled out the empty clip and stared inside it almost accusingly, before slapping it back into place. He then pointed over Anderson's shoulder.

They all turned to watch the blimp approach.

In utter frustration, Skellor withdrew from Cento. It was like the *Occam Razor*—that AI burn. But he had encountered no other Golem possessing the ability to destroy its own mind. He supposed Cento had prepared himself for this—having assessed the dangers Jain tech represented to one of his kind. Skellor pushed the Golem away. No matter—he really, *really* had more important concerns.

The brown dwarf's tidal swathe was hitting with metronomic regularity, splitting and tearing apart *Ogygian* all around him. Bound together by internally generated diamond fibres and with what remained of his human nervous system shut down, Skellor tried to bend with the flow, distorted, the fibres snapping inside him, other structures breaking. But he rebuilt them, bound himself together with more fibres, and concentrated all his resources on constructing inside his torso the gravitic generator that would power him to survival.

The agent probably thought he had won—thought that this was the end of Skellor. But Skellor was more than mere human: he could survive this, *would* survive this.

The temperature was rising. Already some materials inside the ship were beginning to vaporize. The continuous grinding, twisting and flexing of the ship's structure and the rippling of its hull were generating most of the heat. Bubble-metal I-beams, taking on a cherry glow, stretched like toffee and twisted apart, the inert gases used to foam their metal bleeding away into vacuum. Behind Skellor, the hull separated like wet cardboard, and underneath him the floor bowed alarmingly, then began to slew away. Everything, bar himself and one other item, was coming apart as if utterly rotten. That the Golem chassis retained its shape was testament to Polity materials technology. But even that would not survive the impact to come.

The next gravity wave hit hard and lasted longer, shattering what remained of the ship across a kilometre of space. Pieces of it were now incandescent—boiling into vacuum. Skellor retained his own shape—reinforced it from inside using structural force fields powered by his internal gravitic generator. But something was wrong. That wave had nearly ripped him in two, yet with the theorized output of the generator, it should not have. And he would need everything the generator could give him, as there was much worse to come. He ran a diagnostic on the machine, but found it was functioning at optimum. Separate from his internal diagnostics, he probed inside it with nanoptic fibres, and located the node growing right in the centre of it. He opened the generator, forced the node out, closed the generator and had it up to forty per cent of function when the next wave hit.

Skellor screamed, mostly in rage and frustration—now a piece of diamond-sewn meat stretched out over four metres of nothing. Tidal forces had shredded the remains of the ship, the bulk of it now a falling arc of metallic vapour. Skellor was the largest single chunk remaining, the second-largest being an eyeless Golem skull. He slowly drew himself back together, high above an endless brown plain; became a black human doll full of whorls and knots. Witch-fingered. Much of his substance had been torn away or had boiled into vacuum, and his mind was losing cohesion. Before it went completely, simple physics impinged: he could not survive this; how had he ever thought he could survive this?

Some hours later a fibrous mass containing Jain eggs, which so far had managed to retain their shape, hit the surface. Half that mass turned to energy. All that remained was a baroque silver pattern across the dun surface.

Through tunnelling vision Cormac watched as out of an elliptical port on the side of the nacelle, at the end of a jointed arm, extruded a close-quarters laser. This device looked something like a premillennial machine-gun, though rather than belt-fed with ammunition, it was fed by thick, ribbed power cables. But it served the same purpose, normally being used against smaller opponents who had actually managed to get close to the ship's hull. It was precisely the weapon required to remove Cormac from the grapple, probably in pieces. He spat blood and looked aside, still seeing into the tear in his perception. Perhaps he could step inside the ship, cause damage . . . something? No, the whole idea was laughable now. He had done it; he had shifted himself through U-space by an act of will, but right then he had no idea of *how* he had done it. And what could he do inside the ship, injured and weak as he was? Reality was himself suspended in vacuum with a laser pointed at him and death imminent. Then, through that same tear in vision, something surfaced distantly, something huge.

"I see," said King.

The laser powered up, a hot glow emitting from its sooty workings. It turned on its arm and fired. The cable glowed red, white, blue-white, then the centre of that light exploded into globules of molten carbon. Once again Cormac was weightless as the grapple and a short piece of the cable he was clinging to began to fall back towards the brown dwarf. The laser folded away, all ports closed, and the attack ship receded above him.

"You saw that I did not gain access to Skellor—or to Jain technology," King sent.

"So," Cormac managed.

"Tell Jerusalem that."

As he fell, Cormac faded; even the perceptile programs he had been using were not managing to keep him conscious. He saw a vision of curving steel, thought himself near impact with the dwarf star, but realized that was wrong. If he was that close, he would not see a curve to the horizon—would probably see nothing at all.

Then something titanic engulfed him, and claws, three-fingered and gleaming, closed on his upper arms. As they separated him from the cable, things ripped inside his body. Blood exploded from his mouth, and something hard entered his neck. After a numb hiatus, which he read in his gridlink as having lasted seven minutes, came bright aseptic light.

"This may take some time," said the voice of Asselis Mika. "I don't think there's an unbroken bone in his body."

Another voice, the resonant iceberg tip of vast intellect, noted, "The inside of his head is not much better."

The lights went out again.

When humans referred to something called a "cold sweat," Dragon had formerly known what it meant only on an intellectual level. Now the entity understood what it meant on a visceral level. In its dealings with the Polity, it had always purposely encountered lesser entities than itself. This was why it had always kept away from the larger-capacity runcible AIs—sector AIs—and tried not to operate within twenty light-years of any place in which Earth Central had

shown the slightest interest. Jerusalem was precisely the kind
of Polity AI that Dragon had therefore always avoided. Now
the entity was reminded why, for Jerusalem possessed the
sheer mental power to beat Dragon at its own games whilst
also inhabiting a ship body possessing the physical size and
power to render it unnecessary for it to play such games.

This was why Dragon had found itself unable to conceal
certain facts for very long. The essence of the transmission,
after the initial fencing, had been: "Tell me everything, and
fast"—along with the blueprint of one of the *Jerusalem*'s
internal chambers and an overview of the equipment that
could be used there. Dragon was left in no doubt that the
ship could encompass, immobilize, then dismantle it to see
how it ticked.

That the *Jerusalem* had dropped into U-space upon
learning about the *Ogygian* was less than reassuring. It meant
the AI certainly knew that Dragon would not be escaping
and could be dealt with at leisure. The thought of such an
AI gaining access to Skellor was frightening. The thought
of it obtaining certain items that Skellor would soon be
shedding, like a dandelion scattering its seeds in the breeze,
was enough to give even a dragon nightmares. But Dragon
had no power to affect those events, though one such item,
close by, it had aimed to put in safer hands.

Still on course for Cull, the entity linked through to the
flying lizard, which had coiled up to sleep in a sulerbane leaf,
the recent stress of expected extinction having obviously
exhausted it. Receiving instruction, the creature reared up,
shook itself and flew over to the carapace remains of Skellor's
last meal on Cull, landed and looked to where the golden egg
had fallen. Dragon was so amused it decided to let the lizard
live despite its near contact with Jain technology. Where the
egg had lain in the dust, now rested a blue acorn.

Dragon wondered what the brass man would make of
his new toy.

Others might wonder at the entity's definition of "safer
hands."

EPILOGUE

Fethan stooped down by the dismembered Golem and thought, with morbid humour, *I don't hold out much hope for his recovery.* But in this case that might not be true. Gant may have been missing one leg and his head, but memory crystal should contain his essential being inside his Golem chest. However, Jain growth marred that chest, and the Golem had shut down. What this growth might portend was why Fethan and Thorn had insisted on searching alone, and why they had allowed Tanaquil and the boy Tergal to return to Golgoth in the blimp. Fethan contemplated that. The Chief Metallier's cry of anger on realizing that the colony ship *Ogygian* no longer occupied the sky had been heart-wrenching—seeing that his one contact with that human civilization he craved to return to had taken his wife *and* his dreams. Perhaps he might dream new dreams? Certainly the Polity was not finished with this world.

"Are you getting anything?" Thorn asked.

Fethan shook his head. "I haven't tried yet." Now he did attempt to make contact through Gant's internal radio—perhaps the dead soldier's only remaining link to the outside world. But, as before, he found there something vicious that made him jerk away. It was like placing his hand in a dark burrow and hearing some animal snarl. Viral subversion then tracked his signal back—alien Jain code. He shut down his transceiver and isolated it, killing the power to his primary decoder as well.

"I don't think he's in there," he said.

"We have to be sure," Thorn said.

Fethan shrugged. He liked Gant and had no wish for him to be irrevocably dead, but he had not known the man or the machine for as long as Thorn had. Reluctantly he sent an internal signal and detached the syntheflesh covering of his fingertip. Then, studying Gant's neck, he discounted all the severed optics. Selecting instead a small duct containing hair-thin superconducting filaments, he pressed his fingertip against the break. Through nerve linkages in his fingertip, the kill program made connections and found its way through to the Golem's crystal storage. The program did not transcribe this time, as it only needed to look. Fethan felt an ache growing in his right shoulder and arm. Psychosomatic it might be, but it still bothered him. Finally the program made its assessment:

Your friend is gone. There is nothing recognizably human in here, only Jain code and its need to survive and spread.

At that moment the Golem's hands came up, tracked up Fethan's arm by touch and closed on his throat. But this availed it nothing, for the old cyborg's throat was hard. He caught both wrists and pushed the groping hands away, propelling himself rapidly backwards.

"Gant is gone," he said.

With a metallic crunching, the Golem body folded back on itself, then arched up and thrust itself towards Fethan. This, more than anything, confirmed the program's diagnosis: for the Jain inside was forcing the Golem body into something tripodal, something with no physical relation at all to the human race. Thorn immediately swung Fethan's APW to bear and opened fire. The three-limbed beast bounced in red flame. Syntheflesh burning away, it hopped and bounced like a spider in a lighter flame. Thorn hit it again, and again. Limbs came away until eventually it was still. Thorn then approached the broken torso and, drawing a knife he had acquired aboard the blimp, probed inside and at last levered out the lozenge of Gant's erstwhile mind.

"What are you going to do?" Fethan asked.

Thorn did not reply. He placed the mind on a rock, brought the butt of his weapon hard down on it. Then, perhaps remembering Mr. Crane, he ground the fragments to dust and scattered it.

"We'll leave the rest for the clear-up crews," said Thorn. "They'll be all over this place soon. Let's head back to the city."

Yes, thought Fethan, realizing he would not himself be leaving any time soon. Tanaquil would be needing some help during the time to come.

The sun was setting in a greenish explosion, and occasional stars beginning to brave the firmament. His armour stripped off and hanging, along with his other belongings, on temporary pegs epoxied to the side of Bonehead's carapace, Anderson Endrik trudged towards a new horizon. His legs were aching from this unaccustomed exercise, but he would get used to it—it wasn't as if he was old or anything. He had just gone a few rounds with one of the fiercest creatures on this planet. However, he was averse to stopping again, no matter how entitled he was to rest. It was difficult pretending not to notice how, each time he did stop, the sand hog extruded its sensory head to observe him and tapped a little tattoo on the ground with the tip of one crawler limb.

The devastation of broken rock on the draconic plateau was far behind, which was annoying as it now took him a little while to spot a suitable rock on which to sit. When he did see one, he sank down with a sigh—his back towards Bonehead—then used a cloth to mop the sweat from his bald pate.

It was a shame about Tergal leaving. Once over his criminal tendencies, the boy had shown promise. But Tergal had claimed he still had issues to resolve with his stepfather and mother. This was good as it meant the boy was back on track, and Anderson was not going to stand in his way even though he felt the youth's departure was only partially about that. Tergal had lost his sense of fun while the droon had hunted them, and then lost heart when it had killed Stone. Anderson guessed that, travelling by blimp, Tergal and the others would be halfway back to Golgoth by now. Had Anderson chosen to accompany them, he himself could have been perhaps a quarter of the way back towards Bravence. He had not so chosen.

After taking a sip from his water bottle, Anderson asked of his travelling companion, "How far, again?"

Seated on her rucksack, Arden glanced across at him. "Five thousand kilometres."

"And then you'll take this ship up, and go to this Polity?"

"Certainly, unless I encounter somewhere more interesting before I reach it." Arden shrugged.

"Room for a sand hog on this ship?"

"I'm sure we can manage something—that's if Bone-head wants to come."

"Well, he can decide when we get there, and that'll be a while yet." Anderson stared up at the sky and saw that it was not only ribbons of cloud and the odd star that occupied it now.

"And you?" Arden asked.

Anderson heaved himself to his feet, pointed above his head. "Oh, I've already decided. My world just got a lot larger."

Tanaquil carefully read the lengthy report from Stollar. A great deal of advanced technology had become available to them from the landing craft: computing power, components they were yet unable to manufacture and systems they could directly copy rather than reconstruct from ancient schematics. Five craft were quite probably still operational, though it would take them some time to learn how to operate them, and perhaps one more could be constructed from the other damaged ones. But in the end, to what purpose now? *Ogygian* was gone, a dream had been destroyed . . .

Jeelan is dead.

Tanaquil rested his face in his palms. Now, maybe, that dream was no longer needed. Two citizens from this Human Polity were out there somewhere in the Sand Towers, and that Polity now knew about this world. Stollar was quite enthusiastic about this, but Tanaquil could find no enthusiasm inside himself, no room for hope. Perhaps that was because he resented Stollar, who had miraculously survived a fall similar to the one that had killed Jeelan. He took his hands away from his face before reaching out, turning on his desk lamp, then opening another report. His eyes remained dry.

Gyrol had organized a guard for those burying the dead because sleer activity had meanwhile increased tenfold. A great deal of wreckage had been cleared from the spot where a lander had crashed into the lower city, and those that required shelter had been housed in warehouses in the industrial district. Medical teams were working night and day to disinfect and sew shut the head wounds nearly every citizen bore. They would recover, regroup, and then . . . and then.

The Human Polity?

Tanaquil shook his head as if to dispel shadows. Everything was black: depression constricted his mind and sapped his strength, his will. The excitement that was now displacing shock in the likes of Stollar and Gyrol seemed utterly inaccessible to him. He would just do his job, keep going. There wasn't anything else. Then a knock at his door broke his reverie.

"Who is it?" he asked.

"Stollar and Gyrol," replied Stollar, some tension clear in his voice.

"Come in."

The two men entered, Stollar resting heavily on a cane, Gyrol still in his kilnsman gear and lugging one of the small telescopes and a tripod from Stollar's tower.

Stollar looked around the dark room, focused on the shutters pulled across the windows and the closed balcony doors. He glanced meaningfully at Gyrol as he pointed at these.

"What is it? I've got a lot to do," said Tanaquil.

"You haven't seen—no, obviously not. Perhaps we should step out onto your balcony," Stollar replied.

Tanaquil didn't want them here, he wanted to be alone with his thoughts, but something in both of their expressions pulled him to his feet. Stollar moved over to the balcony doors, unlatched and pulled them open. Perhaps some new collapse in the lower city? Tanaquil dared not think otherwise. He stepped out into the dark after the old man, Gyrol following close behind and stepping to one side to set up the telescope. Tanaquil surveyed his city, seeing only the fires being fed by those horrible grey lice-things.

"Look up, Chief Metallier," said Stollar.

Tanaquil did as instructed—a telescope was hardly required. Bright leviathans filled the sky, immense ships that would have dwarfed *Ogygian*. One vast ship, almost like a steel moon, hung clearly in view. Smaller ships were jetting in between. Other ships, smaller still but seeming large because they loomed so close, were coming down. Tanaquil gaped, felt the blackness around him dispersing under the impact of this vision, something breaking in his chest. He bowed his head and felt it coming, felt Stollar's hand momentarily on his shoulder before he and Gyrol returned inside to give him space. He moved forwards and rested his hands on the rail as grief heaved out of him. He did not know how long this lasted. One of the ships, a thing consisting of four spheres mounted at the end of star arms, drifted over the city, its correction jet flames stabbing out. Tanaquil reached up and touched the tears pouring down his face, then wiped them away. The pain was still there—he doubted it would ever go away completely. He returned inside to where Stollar and Gyrol waited.

"Our world is going to change drastically," he said, "but we will not allow that change to swamp us, to erase what we have done or what we are. We have work to do, so let's begin."

It was virtuality, illusion, for no projector could get close, and what point would there be in projecting holograms to that place anyway? But there was a point to this; Jack felt there was a point. Perhaps he was too much of an aesthete. Perhaps there was too much conceit in this, and just maybe Dragon owned that same conceit as much as himself and Aphran.

Whatever, Jack and the erstwhile Separatist walked on the surface of the brown dwarf. Dragon, who had rescued them just before they departed the Cull system but seemed reluctant to give them up to Jerusalem or any of the other Polity AIs patrolling this still-enclosed sector of space, seemed not to be present at all—granting them this illusory space and a definite moment of satisfaction.

"He makes a pretty pattern," said Aphran, eyeing the silvery spirals and ellipses inlaid in the super-dense surface.

"He does that. And it is a pattern that is changing."

"What?" Aphran looked up.

Jack pointed. "Those ellipses are compressed Jain nodes. They won't change, apparently, unless removed from this environment. They require a host and a motivating will. The rest is him still trying to survive, still trying to return himself to order."

"He's alive? He thinks?"

"In a sense, and slowly."

"Will he get away from here?"

Jack allowed himself a hangman's smile. "Not in the lifetime of this universe."

A golden egg clasped in one brass hand, Mr. Crane walked the dusty plateaux, shady canyons and ragged mountain chains of Cull. Like a knight who slew a dragon, he slid from cold reality into bar yarn, and very quickly into legend. Those who saw that tall striding figure, wearing a wide-brimmed hat and with the bottom of his long ragged coat flapping about his lace-up boots, often agreed that a flying creature accompanied him—one much like some seen in the spaceport being built just outside Golgoth. Perhaps they thought this extra touch added veracity to their assertion that they had actually seen Mr. Crane. Others pretended to believe these witnesses with the same patronizing kindness with which they believed those who claimed to have seen the Inconstant Sea.

What they had seen was real, sort of, in a sense . . .

Neal Asher is a science fiction writer whose work has been nominated for both the Philip K. Dick and the British Fantasy Society awards. He has published more than twenty books, many set within his Polity universe, including *Gridlinked*, *The Skinner*, and *Dark Intelligence*. He divides his time between Essex and a home in Crete.

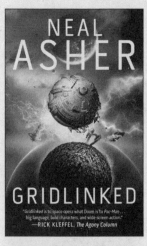
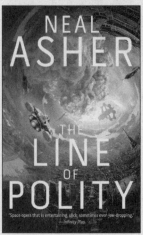

THE ADVENTURES OF
IAN CORMAC CONTINUE . . .

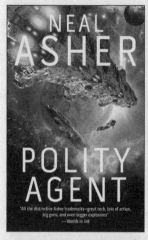

POLITY AGENT
The Fourth Agent
Cormac Novel
978-1-59780-981-0
Mass Market / $7.99

"A terrific read with all the distinctive Asher trademarks—great tech, lots of action, big guns and even bigger explosions."
—*Worlds in Ink*

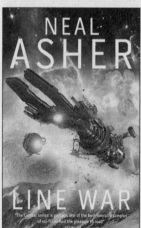

LINE WAR
The Fifth Agent
Cormac Novel
978-1-59780-982-9
Mass Market / $7.99

"A highly engaging, smart, and fulfilling close to the Ian Cormac series . . . strongly recommended."
—*Fantasy Book Critic*

MORE NOVELS OF THE POLITY

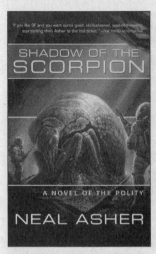

SHADOW OF
THE SCORPION
A Polity Novel
978-1-59780-139-3
Trade Paperback / $14.95

"Skip backward in time
to Cormac's first military
engagement . . . *Shadow
of the Scorpion* is a war
novel with sting."
—Annalee Newitz, *io9*

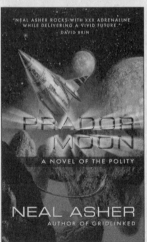

PRADOR MOON
A Polity Novel
978-1-59780-052-5
Trade Paperback / $14.95

"A prequel to much of ev-
erything else he's written
set in the Polity universe
. . . an excellent intro to
an unpleasant but very
entertaining universe."
—Rick Kleffel, *The
Agony Column*

AVAILABLE FROM NIGHT SHADE BOOKS
WWW.NIGHTSHADEBOOKS.COM

MORE NOVELS OF THE POLITY

HILLDIGGERS
A Polity Novel
978-1-59780-511-7
Trade Paperback / $15.99

"If there's a more en-
joyable and provocative
sci-fi action saga this
year, we'll be seriously
surprised."
—Saxon Bullock, *SFX*

THE TECHNICIAN
A Polity Novel
978-1-59780-530-8
Trade Paperback / $15.99

"*The Technician* is no
doubt one of the best new
novels I have this year . . .
fast-paced alien-world
action."

—*Cybermage*

TRANSFORMATION: A POLITY TRILOGY

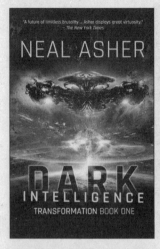
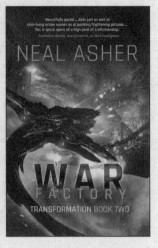
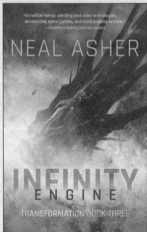

THE OWNER TRILOGY

THE DEPARTURE
978-1-59780-447-9
Trade Paperback / $15.99

ZERO POINT
978-1-59780-470-7
Trade Paperback / $15.99

JUPITER WAR
978-1-59780-493-6
Trade Paperback / $15.99

ASHER'S BEST SHORT FICTION

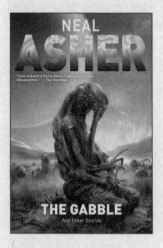

THE GABBLE
And Other Stories
978-1-59780-531-5
Trade paperback / $15.99

"What has six arms, a large beak, looks like a pyramid, has more eyes than you'd expect and talks nonsense? If you don't know the answer to that, then 1) you should and 2) you haven't been reading Neal Asher (see point 1)."

—Jon Courtenay Grimwood

The Polity universe is home to some of the strangest alien creatures ever to exist. On the planet Myral, sheqs and octupals inhabit the land, waiting for unsuspecting prey to cross their paths. The surface of Masasa is littered with dracomen, tricones, mud snakes, and heroyne. *The Gabble* features ten stories that throw its characters into worlds that are fascinatingly alien, and often hostile.

NEW FROM NEAL ASHER AND NIGHT SHADE BOOKS

THE SOLDIER
RISE OF THE JAIN
BOOK ONE
978-1-59780-943-6
Hardcover / $26.99
(available now)
Trade paperback / $15.99
(coming November 2018)

"With mind-blowing complexity, characters, and combat, Asher's work continues to combine the best of advanced cybertech and military SF."
—*Publishers Weekly*, starred review

In a far corner of space, on the very borders between humanity's Polity worlds and the kingdom of the vicious crab-like prador, is an immediate threat to all sentient life: an accretion disc, a solar system designed by the long-dead Jain race and swarming with living technology powerful enough to destroy entire civilizations . . .

In *The Soldier*, British science fiction writer Neal Asher kicks off another Polity-based trilogy in signature fashion, concocting a mind-melting plot filled with far-future technology, lethal weaponry, and bizarre alien creations.

AN EXCERPT FROM

THE SOLDIER

RISE OF THE JAIN BOOK ONE

Available Now from Neal Asher
and Night Shade Books

Marco's ship surfaced from the faster-than-light continuum of underspace into realspace, and was quickly back within Einstein's laws. His vessel came to an abrupt stop in the permitted zone lying five light-minutes out from Musket Shot—a dark planetoid whose mass was over 50 per cent lead. Had Marco surfaced his ship just a few thousand miles outside this spot it would have lasted a little over four microseconds, so he had once been told by the Artificial Intelligence Pragus. This was how long it would take the three-foot-wide particle beam to reach the ship from the weapons system watching that area of space. Of course, Pragus could have been lenient and delivered a warning, but any traders who came here never missed that spot. Apparently two other ships had arrived in the proscribed zone. One had been owned by a tourist who had ignored all the warnings delivered to anyone who programmed these coordinates. The other had been a ship controlled by separatists out of the Polity in search of new terror weapons. Both were now cool, expanding clouds of dust.

Or so Pragus said.

"So, what do you have for me, Captain Marco?"

The voice issuing from his console made Marco jerk, then he grimaced, annoyed at his own reaction. He'd made the deal, it was a good one, and certainly not one he could renege on, considering who he'd made it with. He shrugged his shoulders, like he did before going into a fight, and opened full com. The image of a chromed face appeared in the screen laminate before him, and Marco forced a smile.

"Something interesting today," he replied gruffly.

"I never thought otherwise," said the AI Pragus.

Interesting was what Pragus needed, what all the AIs out here on the defence sphere needed. Marco had learned the story from another trader who used to do this run before him. Here the AIs, each stationed on a weapons platform, were guarding the Polity from one of the most dangerous threats it had ever faced. Automatic systems would never have been sufficient, for the format of this threat could change at any time. But the problem with employing high-functioning AIs as watchdogs was their boredom. Three AIs had to be pulled out of the sphere in the first years, having turned inward to lose themselves in the realms of their own minds. That was before Orlandine—the overseer of the sphere project—decided on a new approach. She allowed contact with the Polity AI net, and she permitted traders to bring items of interest to sell. AI toys.

"You can come in to dock," Pragus added.

"Thank you kindly," said Marco. Then, trying to find his usual humour, added, "Finger off the trigger, mind."

"I don't have fingers," said the AI, and the chrome face disappeared from the screen laminate.

Marco reached down to his touch-console, prodded the icon for the docking program that had just arrived and simply slid it across to the icon representing his ship's mind. This was the frozen ganglion of a prador second-child—voiceless, remote, just a complex organic computer and nothing like the living thing it had once been. It began to take his ship in, then Marco used the console to pull up another view in the screen laminate to his left.

From this angle the accretion disc, around which the defensive weapons platforms were positioned, looked like a blind, open white eye. It seemed like any other such stellar object in the universe—just a steadily swirling mass of gases and the remnants of older stars which would eventually form a new solar system. His ship's sensors could detect scattered planetesimals within it, the misty bulks of forming planets and the larger mass of the dead star at the heart of the disc. Occasionally that star would light, traceries of fusion fire fleeing around its surface like the smouldering edges of fuse paper. One day, maybe tomorrow or maybe a thousand years hence, the sun would ignite fully. The resulting blast would blow a large portion of the accretion disc out into interstellar space. Marco knew this was the event to be feared, since it was the job of weapons platform AIs like Pragus to ensure that the virulent pseudo-life within that disc did not escape.

Marco shivered, wondering how the subplot in which he had been ensnared related to that. Certainly, the creature who had employed him was a conniving bastard . . . No. He shook his head. He could not allow his mind to stray beyond his immediate goal. He banished the image and, as his ship turned, watched Pragus's permanent home come into view.

The weapons platform was a slab ten miles long, five wide and a mile thick. The designer, the haiman Orlandine, had based much of its design on the construction blocks of a Dyson sphere—a project of which she was rumoured to have been an original overseer. After his first run here, Marco had tried to find information about this woman from the AI net, but there was little available. It seemed that a lot was restricted about this haiman, a woman who exemplified the closest possible melding of AI and human.

The platform's only similarity to a Dyson sphere construction block was its basic shape. The numerous protrusions of weapons and shielded communication devices gave it the appearance of a high-tech city transported into space. But the skyscrapers were railguns, particle cannons, launch tubes for a cornucopia of missiles, as well as the attack pods of the distributed weapons system that the platform controlled. And all were needed because of Jain tech. The accretion disc was swarming with a wild form of technology, created by a race named the Jain. These creatures had shuffled off the universe's mortal coil five million years ago but left this poisoned chalice for all ensuing civilized races. The technology granted immeasurable power but, in the process, turned on its recipients and destroyed them. Quite simply, it was a technology made to destroy civilizations.

Marco's ship drew closer to the platform on a slightly dirty-burning fusion drive—a fault that developed over a month back that he'd never found the time to fix. Its mind signalled on the console that it had applied for final docking permission, and Marco saw it accepted. He looked up to see a pair of space doors opening in the side of the platform. Having used these before, he knew they were more than large enough to allow his ship inside. But, at this distance, they looked like an opening in the side of a million-apartment arcology.

His ship drew closer and closer, the platform looming gigantic before it. Finally, it slid into the cathedral space of what the AI probably considered to be a small supply hold. Marco used the console to bring up a series of external views. The ship moved along a docking channel and drew to a halt, remora pad fingers folding out from the edges of the channel to steady it, their suction touch creating a gentle shudder he felt through his feet. He operated the door control of his vessel then stomped back through his cabin area, into his ship's own hold. He paused by the single grav-sled there, then stooped and turned on its gesture control. The sled rose, hovering above the floor and moving closer to him at the flick of a finger, as he turned to face a section of his ship's hull folding down into a ramp. An equalization of pressure, a whooshing hiss, had his ears popping but would cause him no harm.

By the time the ramp was down, pressure was back up again. Marco clumped down onto it in his heavy space boots, the sled following him like a faithful dog. He gazed about the hold, at the acres of empty grated flooring, the handler drays stuck in niches like iron and bone plastic beetles. Spider-claw bots hung from the ceiling like vicious chandeliers, and to one side the castellated edges of the space doors closed behind his ship. The sun-pool ripple of a shimmershield was already in place to hold the atmosphere in. As soon as he reached the floor gratings a cylinder door revolved in the wall ahead. Marco grimaced at what stepped out of the transport tube behind.

The heavy grappler—a robot that looked like a giant, overly muscular human fashioned of grey faceted metal—made its way towards him. It finally halted a few yards away, red-orange fire from its hot insides glaring out of its empty eye sockets and open mouth. But Pragus had used this grappler as an avatar before, so Marco knew he should not allow the sight of it to worry him; he should not let himself think that the AI knew something. He had to try to act naturally. He was just here doing his usual job . . .

"Still as trusting as ever, I see," Marco said.

He could feel one eyelid flickering, and felt a hot flush of panic because he knew the AI would see this and know something was bothering him. He quickly stepped out onto the dock, boots clanking on the gratings. At his gesture, the sled eased past him, then lowered itself to the floor. Sitting on top of it was a large airtight plastic box. The grappler swung towards this as if inspecting it, but Marco knew that Pragus was already scanning the contents even as it sent the grappler robot over. In fact, the AI had certainly scanned his ship and its cargo for dangerous items before it docked, like fissionables, super-dense explosives or an anti-matter flask. The more meticulous scan now would reveal something organic. Hopefully this would start no alarm bells ringing because the contents, as far as Marco was aware, were not a bio-weapon. Anyway, it was not as if such a weapon would have much effect here, where the only organic life present was Marco himself, as far as he knew.

"What is this?" Pragus asked, its voice issuing as a deep throaty rustle from the grappler.

"Straight out of the Kingdom," said Marco, sure he was smiling too brightly. "You know how these things go. One prador managed to kill a rival and seize his assets. One of those assets was a war museum and the new owner has been selling off the artefacts."

It was the kind of behaviour usual for the race of xeno-phobic aliens that had once come close to destroying the human Polity.

"That is still not a sufficient explanation."

"I can open it for you to take a look," said Marco. "But we both know that is not necessary."

When the box had been handed over to him, Marco had been given full permission to scan its contents, though he was not allowed to open it or interfere with them. He knew that Pragus would now be seeing a desiccated corpse, like a wasp, six feet long. But it wasn't quite a single distinct creature. Around its head, like a tubular collar, clung part of another creature like itself. Initial analysis with the limited equipment Marco had available showed this was likely to be the remains of a birth canal. Meanwhile it seemed that the main creature had died while giving birth too. A smaller version of itself was just starting to protrude from its birth canal. It was all very odd.

"Alien," said Pragus from the grappler.

"Oh certainly that," said Marco. "You want the museum data on it?"

"Yes."

Marco reached down and took a small square of diamond slate from his belt pouch and held it up. The grappler turned towards him, reached out with one thick-fingered hand and took the item between finger and thumb. Marco resisted for a moment, suddenly unsure he should carry this through. He realized that on some level he wanted to be found out, and he fought it down, releasing the piece of slate. The grappler inserted the square into its mouth like a tasty treat. Marco saw it hanging in the glowing opening while black tendrils of manipulator fibres snared and drew it in. Doubtless it would next be pressed to a reader interface inside the grappler's fiery skull.

It would not be long now before Marco knew whether or not he had succeeded. Minutes, only. The AI would put its defences in place, then translate the prador code before reading it. Of course, it had taken Marco a lot longer to translate the thing and read it himself—in fact, most of his journey here.

He had found out how, before the alien prador encountered the Polity, they had come upon another alien species whose realm had extended to merely four solar systems. The prador had attacked at once, of course, but realized they had snipped off more than they could masticate. What had initially been planned as the quick annihilation of competitors turned into an interminable war against a hive species whose organic form approached AI levels of intelligence. These creatures quickly developed seriously nasty weaponry in response to the attack. The war had dragged on for decades but, in the end, the massive resources of the Prador Kingdom told against the hive creatures. It was during this conflict that the prador developed their kamikazes and, with these, steadily destroyed the hive creatures' worlds. It seemed the original owner of the museum had been involved in that genocide, and here, in this box, lay the remains of one of the aliens the prador had exterminated.

"What is your price?" Pragus finally asked.

"You've been doing some useful work with that gravity press of yours?" Marco enquired archly, his acquisitive interest rising up to dispel doubts.

"I have," Pragus replied.

Marco pondered that for a second. "Don't ask for too much," the creature had told him, "and don't ask for too little." "I want a full ton of diamond slate." "Expensive and—"

"And I want a hundred of those data-gems you made last time."

This was a fortune. It was enough to buy Marco a life of luxury for many, many years. He had also calculated that it was about all Pragus would have been able to make with the gravity press since the last trader visit, when it wasn't using the press to make high-density railgun slugs. But was the dead thing inside that box worth so much? Of course it was. Material things like diamond slate and data-gems the AI could manufacture endlessly, filling the weapons-platform storage with such stuff. But the alien corpse would contain a wealth of what AIs valued highest of all: information. It was also so much more to weapons-platform AIs like Pragus: the prospect of months of release from the boredom of watching the accretion disc.

"You have a deal," the AI replied.

Marco had no doubt that Pragus was already having handler drays load the requested items onto themselves. He felt a species of disappointment. Weren't Polity AIs supposed to be the pinnacle of intelligence? Surely Pragus should be able to see to the core of what was happening here . . . surely the AI would have some idea . . .

The grappler stooped and carefully picked up the box, then it froze, the fire abruptly dimming in its skull. Marco had seen this before. It meant that Pragus had suddenly focused its full attention elsewhere. Had he been found out?

After a moment the fire intensified again, and the grappler turned towards the door of the transport tube.

"Something is happening," it said.

"What?" Marco asked, his mind already turning to the prospect of getting away from here as fast as he could.

"Increased activity in the accretion disc." The grappler then gave a very human shrug. "It happens."

Marco simply acknowledged that with a nod, hoping it would not delay his payment or his departure. This, he decided, would be his last run here. He wanted no more involvement with giant weapons platforms, Jain technology or Orlandine. He also, very definitely, wanted no more involvement with an alien called Dragon—a creature whose form was a giant sphere fifty miles across. A creature who, some months ago, with some not so subtle threats and the promise of great wealth, had compelled Marco to make this strange delivery here.